Shirley Jackson award-winner Kaaron Warren published her first short story in 1993 and has had fiction in print every year since. She was recently given the Peter McNamara Lifetime Achievement Award and was Guest of Honour at World Fantasy 2018, Stokercon 2019 and Geysercon 2019. Kaaron was a Fellow at the Museum for Australian Democracy, where she researched prime ministers, artists and serial killers. She's judged the World Fantasy Awards and the Shirley Jackson Awards.

She has published five multi-award winning novels (*Slights, Walking the Tree, Mistification, The Grief Hole* and *Tide of Stone)* and seven short story collections, including the multi-award winning *Through Splintered Walls*. She has won the ACT Writers and Publishers Award four times and twice been awarded the Canberra Critics Circle Award for Fiction. Her most recent novella, *Into Bones Like Oil* (Meerkat Press), was shortlisted for a Shirley Jackson Award and the Bram Stoker Award, winning the Aurealis Award.

T0118911

Kaaron Warren Titles
Published By
IFWG Publishing Australia

The Grief Hole
The Gate Theory (short fiction collection)
Slights
Mistification (released 2021)
Walking the Trees (released 2021)
Morace's Story (released 2021)
Tool Tales (with Ellen Datlow) (released 2021)

Slights

by
Kaaron Warren

Slights

All Rights Reserved

ISBN-13: 978-1-925956-75-7

Copyright ©2021 Kaaron Warren

First published 2009

V1.1

Written with assistance from the Australian Capital Territory government through its Cultural Council.

Printed in Palatino Linotype.

IFWG Publishing International
Melbourne

www.ifwgpublishing.com

Still for Graham, because I said I would and you believed me.

I envy Stalin. I wish I had the power to rewrite history and my part in it. I would change so much.

I would die only once, and I would not kill my mother. And my father would leave me a message; he would speak a meaningful sentence before going to work to be shot.

That would be my story, if I could change history.

At Eighteen

What should have happened was this:
We got a taxi home.

This is what did happen:

We went out for lunch to spend Mum's lottery win—she won just enough for a slap up meal. Food rich and creamy, chicken breast with camembert, salad with blue cheese dressing, a bottle of sweet wine, champagne, port.

We laughed and joked; talked loudly. Mum was in a good mood, not a nagging one. The waiter pretended we were sisters, and that made her giggle.

We just habbled on. We had no idea this was our last meal together.

"What do you think of my haircut?" I asked her.

"I wouldn't go back to that hairdresser, if I were you, Stephanie," Mum said. She had a fleck of parsley on her lip and when she talked it wobbled.

"I know. Stupid bitch. I said I wanted a change and she does this to me."

I had splurged and asked the hairdresser to give me a new style. She wanted to cut inches off, saying, "Once you pass eighteen, you have to be more careful."

I said, "Fine." How old did she think I was?

She snip snipped. Dark, wet entrails of my hair fell onto her thighs, criss-crossed the diamonds of her fishnet stockings. I couldn't take my eyes off her. The hairdresser said, "You know, you've got the sort of face which would suit a good red colour.

You need a bit of a lift at the moment. Everything looks a bit flat. And maybe we should have a go at your eyebrows."

She was a very slim girl. Her hair was black, cut like a metal helmet. She wore a tight silver T-shirt, a thick corduroy skirt, the fishnet stockings. She sat in a rolling chair, travelling around my body like I was an island, *snip snip*. She spoke incessantly, complained of slight after slight.

She sighed. "Anyway, I'm sure you're not interested." I looked up from her thigh and she wasn't happy with me. She dried my hair without speaking, then held the mirror up for me to see.

I said nothing.

"Are you happy with that?" she said.

"You are kidding me," I said.

It shocked her. I suppose you're meant to lie. I paid her even though she made me look like a fucking bimbo. All this from a woman who told me, confidentially, that she thought reading novels wasn't smart because it's all just made up.

"What *do* you read?" I asked her.

"Oh, I love my magazines," she said. "I can read them over and over, there's always something different."

Mum laughed and called me a fibber.

"Oh, Stephanie. You're just trying to take attention away from your hair," she said.

"This is how the girl talks. I swear." I took a sip of wine and grimaced. Mum always chose sweet stuff. "We might as well drink lemonade," I said.

"Well, your hair is fine, really. You're just not used to looking pretty."

"Thanks a lot. I'll book you in, if you like."

That's what we talked about.

I joshed Mum about, paying her attention, making jokes about the waiter, who had terrible acne, and telling stories about other diners in the restaurant.

She said, "You sound just like your Dad. He used to whisper into my ear, telling the most outrageous tales. Should have heard what he told me about my father."

"What?" I didn't like to talk about my maternal grandfather, Joshua. He died when I was five, and I have a feeling he used to touch me; sometimes I get a glimpse of his face in my memory. It's shiny, a sucked lollipop, and very close to me. He was a grouch most of the time, generous and soft when you were alone with him.

"Come on, Mum, what did Dad say?" I passed her the plate of chocolates the waiter had laid on our table. They were dark, rich, and we planned to eat every one.

"He said that your granddad Joshua had affairs with everyone willing in town. Everyone." She covered her mouth. We didn't often talk about things like that.

"What, the men too?" I said, and she coughed in horror.

"You're a storyteller, just like your Dad was," she said. I knew that was true; Dad was a detective long before he joined the police force. I wondered if Dad's stories were ridiculous, or if they were true.

I dropped the keys on the way to the car. I've never been good with alcohol; a couple of glasses, still under the limit, and I'm screaming. Mum was giggling and muttering away, feeling no pain.

Feeling no pain.

I suddenly grew tired of it; being with her, pretending to be friends, enjoying her company. I drove quickly, wanting to drop her at home and go somewhere alone, somewhere I didn't feel like a fake. I should have called her a taxi and sent her home; that way, she would have been resentful, but alive.

"The car smells nice," she said.

"New leather in a can," I said. One of the best smells. I drove quickly. I thought I saw a child in the road and I swerved, my wheels spun and I lost it. I remember very clearly, though I said I didn't. I said I had no recollection; my head ached trying to remember.

But I remember my mother's arm coming across to protect me, hold me in my seat as if I were a child. My arms went over my face and head but I still cracked my skull.

I remember looking at her; she looked at me. She was terrified of death; more terrified of my death.

"Careful," she said, then we hit the wall.

This wall was only there to keep the sound of the highway from reaching the wealthy residents in the suburbs behind it. If the wall wasn't there, my mother may not have died. The papers loved it.

"Wall of Death—the quiet life versus the long life," all that.

I told people, especially Peter, that she died straight away, without a word. I told no one about where I'd been, that I'd smashed my skull and found myself in a cold, dark room full of people, faces familiar but beyond my tongue; I couldn't voice their names. The board I lay on was ridged with razors, sharp lines of pain down my back.

The faces came into focus. Some I knew; people I knew were there. Their eyes watered. They weren't blinking; that was it. They stared like zombies. I could smell them. They were so close now I could see the blood *bang bang* in their veins.

I touched my wrist to feel my pulse. *Bang bang.*

Bang bang.

"Peter?" I said.

He was there. He stepped forward when I saw him. His hands rested by his side; he carried a potato peeler. I laughed. They all shrunk back. These were weak creatures, scared of the light and the sound of my voice.

"Where's Mum?" I said, to keep them away.

They shuffled forward and I recognised some of them. The lady from the lolly shop at the end of the road, her fat arms spilling out of her tight, flowery sleeves.

"I'll have a red traffic light," I said. She grabbed my tongue but I slipped it out. Her fingers tasted of piss and dirt.

A middle-aged man with spiky blond hair, his eyes bulging and red, began to pile books onto my chest. One, another, then another. A handsome boy with dark brown eyes and one tiny scar on his chin held me down by the shoulders. Another book and another, I couldn't breathe, the weight crushed my chest.

A little girl with greasy hair breathed into my mouth.

"You need to get off the anchovies," I said. She bared her teeth at me.

And all these strangers surrounded me; people with car keys, shopping bags, bus tickets. All surrounding, leaning in to sniff me.

Kids I remembered from school clung to Peter like he was their father. I knew their names, could remember their weaknesses: Darren, Cry Bobby, Belinda Green, Neil. I tried to say milk fight but milk was in my mouth, sour milk, and I couldn't turn to spit it out. I dribbled some out of the corner of my mouth but the rest sat there, waiting for my epiglottis to give in and allow the swallow to continue.

I felt a nibble at my ear; now I could turn my head. My neighbour, Gary, a gross sleazebag who thought he ran the street, thought he could manipulate me. I spat milk into his face; he grinned, let it drip to the floor.

I sat up, causing a ripple through the room. There was the waiter from the restaurant Mum and I had eaten in, his face full of acne. The food he had served me was still in my belly.

"Acker Face," I said. Miaow. He wrinkled his nose, lifted his arms, pushed the sharpened tines of a fork into the meat of my thigh. I could feel the idea of pain but not pain itself. A thin clear liquid ran from the holes, like the cooked blood of a well done chicken.

Behind him were more strangers; from the restaurant? Had they been there, seen my mother's last meal?

I wanted to ask them about her face. Was she happy? Was this the best time of her life? Could things only get worse?

It was lucky then that she died.

Someone tied knots in my hair, tugged at it. The skinny hairdresser. "I paid you," I said. She pulled harder, ripping out clumps of my hair out by the roots and tossing them to the floor. She wasn't listening.

None of them listened.

Another kid from school, a shitty little bore, Ian, Ian Pope, was there and some young kid in cricket whites, "You're out," I said, and he swung his bat flat onto my nose.

I heard a crunch and felt blood cover my chin.

This was no sun-dappled heaven. These people did not love me. The driver of the other car—was he dead too? Did we all die? But there was no other car. A wall. A box which looked like a child. Another car. Opposite direction. Stopped to help.

Caught in the wrong place at the wrong time. I shouldn't be here. I should be at home.

I shouldn't be here. This is not where I belong, stinking weakness waiting for something, pain. I moved my limbs, opened my mouth to scream, leave me, leave me. They seemed to exist for me.

Somebody saved my life. Rescued me from the dark room.

I missed my mother's funeral. Peter and I were now orphans. He took charge of everything, "I made the arrangements," he said. The image in my mind was of Mum's body, people moving her rag-doll limbs until she sat as they wished her to sit.

In hospital, the smell of jasmine saved me. The nurses brought it in when they realised it made me smile. I lay with jasmine under my nose, I sucked it in, because my nostrils were full of shit and mothballs and the woman in the next bed began to choke and moan. I sat up to comfort her, but I could not sit up. I could not move. Then I felt myself lift, my body turned over, and I looked at the two of us. She was writhing, dying, and there was nothing I could do. I realised then that I had died too, and I closed my eyes and waited to be taken to the cold room. It's time to go back, I thought.

They're waiting.

This second death, so soon after the first, surprised the nurses, I think. They did not expect me to go into arrest once I was in the safety of the hospital. Once they had brought me back from the dead at the scene of the crime. Scene of the accident.

It surprised them in the dark room, too. But I was not there for long this time.

Someone came along and saved me.

"Stephanie? Stephanie? Are you with us?" The stink of shit and mothballs was gone. It was the hospital, antiseptic, starch, medicine and blood. I returned from the room and there were people surrounding me, but they were medicos doing their job, watching tensely for me not to die so they wouldn't be blamed.

"Mum?" I said. I knew the answer. One of them sat by my bed and took my hand. There was kindness in the touch, and pity, but no respect.

"Your mother died instantly. She didn't suffer," the nurse said. I knew that wasn't true. I remembered her screaming. I didn't want to say that. The scream was on me and I didn't want anyone to know about it.

Peter said, "God, you gave us a fright."

"He's been shuddering like the Nazis were goose-stepping on his grave," my nurse said. I quite took to her. She could shock a room full of patients without blinking.

"I've been somewhere terrible," I whispered to Peter, but he didn't want to hear it. To distract me, he told me about Mum's funeral. His eyes were suitably red and swollen. He looked cold, almost blue.

"I reckon all the would-be Dads were there,"

Peter said, making me glad I'd missed it. "Remember that one with the red hair we called Bozo? He got really fat. And there was that one we quite liked, who got pissed on Crème de Menthe so his breath was minty. And remember that total dickhead, the shoe-shop guy?"

"The one you really liked?"

"I didn't like him. He was a dickhead." Peter frowned.

"You liked him."

"Well, anyway, he was there. They all asked about you. None of them knew what happened.

There were some cops there, writing notes, making everyone feel guilty, even if they hadn't done anything."

That was supposed to make me feel guilty, I suppose. I said, "So what did the shoe-guy have to say?"

"He asked me how my feet were. That's the first thing he said, how are those feet of yours? Sounds like he went a bit downhill after Mum kicked him out. He got a job in the shoe department of some big shop, but he said they sold mainly vinyl shoes, and people tried them on without socks. He said it was disgusting."

"He was pretty disgusting, don't forget."

"He's married now, to a woman with tiny little angel's feet. He said to me, 'Not as lovely as your Mum's.'"

I shrugged. I'd received Dad's big plates o' meat.

"He told you all this in how many minutes?"

"Oh, I gave him a lift home. He got there by public transport, can you believe it? A train, two buses and a long walk."

"I'm sure he had the right shoes for it."

"Oh, ha ha. He lives in a flat with his wife and kid. Ugly kid. The wife doesn't speak English very well but he likes that. They don't talk; everything's non-verbal. He said it made him very happy."

"Yeah, and makes it harder for her to get away. So the kid was ugly?"

"Yeah, bit of a slug. You know. Just sat around not talking. I smiled at it and it blinked like I was insane."

"Poor old shoe man. Were there lots of shoes in his house? Did he have a shoe tree?"

"They take their shoes off at the front door and leave them there. I didn't do it but they didn't say anything."

Peter hated to take his shoes off. There is no deception to be had in socks or bare feet.

"He asked me to stay for tea and I said, 'I've got family to get to.' He said, 'Oh, Little Stevie. Little Stevie.' It was like his wife recognised your name.

She came over, rested her hands on his shoulders.

He started crying, Steve, I swear. Tears ran down his face and he's going honk honk. I said, 'Oh, well, must be off,' like I was there on a social visit.

'Thanks for coming,' he says, snot running down his face. It was pretty disgusting."

"Who else was at the funeral?"

Peter looked away. "I wasn't going to tell you about her."

"Who?"

He coughed. "The garden lady. Do you remember her? Eve?" It was astonishing he would imagine I could forget her, when he was the one who threw me to her in the first place. Peter never warned me about Eve. I'll ask him why one day. I'll ask him how he could have led me into that woman's clutches. Was he so terrified he was happy for me to go in his place? That didn't work well; she had us both, then.

I followed Peter home from school one day when I was ten, hoping to catch him at something disgusting. Doing detective work to find out why he was always so late.

He collected stones, ate some Twisties. I picked up the packet he discarded. When Mum was cooking the casserole, I asked her to put the Twistie packet on a tray and put it into the oven for a few minutes. It shrank beautifully. I told her I wanted to make a collection and the kids at school would give me their empty packets. That was okay, Mum said. So long as I wasn't eating the rubbish myself.

Every time I followed Peter after that he had a packet of something. He'd stop when he rounded the corner from school, shuffle through his school bag and pull out his treasure. I collected and shrank them all, then presented them to him in a pile.

"I know plenty," I told him. I told Mum I was training to be in the softball team so had to practise after school. Ages later, Mum said, "Whatever happened to the softball thing? You were so keen for a while there. Didn't you get in the team?"

"Yeah, they picked me," I said. This was a good answer.

"I'll come and watch you practise one time."

I knew where I was on those missing afternoons, and I didn't want her finding out. "Nah, don't worry, Mum. It's pretty boring if you're not playing."

Peter went to the same house every afternoon, a neat one, not like ours. Nice flowers in lines and the lawn all green and even. As I got older, I heard gossip about the woman who lived there, though I never added our stories, Peter's and mine.

In high school, the boys talked about mowing her lawn; she had a different boy every week, made them strip their shirts off and work in the garden till they glowed with sweat. Then she summoned them inside, where she gave them an envelope full of money and a glass of beer, regardless of their age. Before they were allowed to enter and drink their beer, they had to clean the tools; rake, spade, shovel, mower, and stack them in the garage. I heard of rebellion just once; a boy who said, "That wasn't part of the deal." She said, "And we must stick to deals," paid him his money, sent him away, never hired him again. Peter and I put the things away and took a bubble bath afterwards.

Eve the garden lady was in control of her boys; had them terrified. Most were strangely coy about the activities which followed the beer drinking. I think perhaps nothing at all happened, that perhaps she talked to them, or asked them questions, perhaps embarrassed them with her interest. I think perhaps the more boys who visited her without saying what happened, the more boys were too frightened to admit nothing went on. I imagined whispered conversations between two boys, one sleeping over, restless on the floor, one comfortable in a known bed.

You know when you went to mow the lawn?"

"Yeah."

"Did you ever tell anyone what happened?"

"Nah. Did you?"

"Nah. I didn't know what to say."

"Me neither."

"Because I didn't know what happened to the others."

"Me neither. So what *did* happen to you?"

"I dunno. What happened to you?"

"Nothing, really."

"Me neither."

That's what should have happened. I don't know what did happen to those boys. I know the woman's garden was very neat for many years. She became a joke as we all got older, as she became elderly rather than middle-aged.

I think perhaps she mostly liked children.

I followed Peter to her house three times.

He was crying the third time he came out of her house. He managed to control himself before he got to our street. He stopped on the corner and seemed to be stroking out the wrinkles in his clothes.

I teased him at dinner. Teased and teased until he began to cry again. He wouldn't look at us and he hardly ate a thing.

"Ate too many Twisties," I said. "Ate another mother's tea. Don't you like Mum's tea any more?

Don't you love Mum?" I swung my feet till my school shoes kicked the underside of the table.

Every second word I kicked and plates and glasses rattled.

"Tell her to stop it," said Peter.

"Tell the lady? Tell the lady to stop what? Stop doing bad smells?"

Mum giggled. She loved crude jokes; now she could laugh at them without Dad stopping her with a grown-up's look.

Then I blew raspberries at Peter till he was so angry he stopped crying.

Mum had been laughing; she always thought I was funny. She said, "Oh, Peter. Do you think your father would have cried at the table like that?"

"I never cry," I said.

"Yes, Stevie's my little strong girl," she said. She smiled fondly at me, her eyes crinkling in a way Peter never got to see. She had to work for my love; Peter's she got just for being alive.

After dinner, I followed him to his room and jumped on his bed.

"Peter's got a girlfriend, Peter's got a girlfriend."

"Shut up."

"Is she a nice lady?"

"None of your business."

"Tell me or else I'll tell Mum you go to a lady's house."

Peter said, "I'll take you to meet her if you like. She's very nice."

With those words, he offered me up for sacrifice.

One day I'll ask him why he did that. He should have protected me no matter what.

On my first visit to Eve, she was very nice. Peter left me alone; snuck away. She stared into my eyes, looking for something.

She gave me lemonade to drink. We sat down on her pretty bed and she held my hands.

"You're much sweeter than your brother," she said. She tore open a brown paper bag; lollies spilled out.

"Your brother eats many of these. I'm surprised he can eat his dinner."

"Sometimes he doesn't. He eats too many Twisties."

She laughed. "Too many Twisties. Peter's a good boy, though. Very kind. He makes me very happy. Does he make you happy?"

I shook my head.

"He does lovely things to me. He rubs powder into my feet. My husband doesn't like to do that. And he washes my hair in the bath. And I wash his hair, too. Sometimes he arrives here a little grubby from school. You look like you might be a bit dirty, too."

I couldn't smile; I had a face full of lollies.

Peter and I never discussed the things which happened to us at Eve's house.

We had to dance around in these special clothes and she took home movies of us. The clothes she dressed us in were too small. We looked like we had doll's clothes on. Her children had died when they were younger than us.

She told us to wave at Daddy but our Daddy was dead.

"Daddy's coming in now. You children better go and play." But all there was was Lisa Sargeant's brother, who was much older and very handsome with that perfectly flawing scar on his chin, but still only a kid. As we left, he stared after us, and I think I've been on the inside of a look like that. I wanna go with you. Don't leave me here alone. We left him there to be the Daddy.

I tried never to arrive dirty at Eve's place, because I didn't want a bath, but the time they drained the creek nearby was the chance of a lifetime.

Every kid who had any control over parents was there. Kids said there was gold at the bottom of the creek, bodies, dead kids, treasures for all.

There was a car, a push bike, three headless dolls and a bunch of wallets. We scrabbled on the creek bed, searching for clues, until the people chased us off. Then I went to Eve's and had a bath, but it was worth it.

We always had to leave when Eve's real husband Harry came home. We had to be out that damn door and gone before his car hit the driveway.

Once I pretended to leave but hid in the alcove near the front door, behind the plants. It was very, very dark there. When you first walked in from sunlight, you were blind. It was that dark. You had to stand a moment, only just inside, and wait for sight to return. She'd say to you, "Come on, don't dilly dally letting the flies fly in," and made you feel like you were scared.

I hid there and didn't move, wanting to know what happened to the house when I wasn't there.

Was she a robot who stopped moving? I also wanted to see what the husband was like. I wanted to know whose brother he was. *Bang bang* front door, *clunk* of something.

Noises.

It was hard to identify what was going on.

I'm told my great-grandfather was wonderful at picking sounds. He had perfect hearing. It was his party trick; people would try stranger and stranger sounds and he always got them.

I'm good with faces. Not as good with sounds. So it took me a while, crouched there behind the shiny ferns, smelling dirt and old furniture polish, to realise the thumping and the shouting meant he was beating her up.

I wished Peter was there to hear it. I wished I could run upstairs and watch it. I crawled out to hear better.

"You mad bitch. I told you to stop bringing kids here. I'll have you locked up, you mad woman. You've gotta stop it."

Did he know about all those teenagers carefully mowing the front lawn?

"I'll call the kids' parents if you do it again. I mean it. Leave the poor little mites alone."

She cried, but she liked to cry. She cried when she made me suckle at her breast.

After that, I wasn't scared of Harry.

Eve never tired of my daily visits. She loved to listen to me natter, so I thought up stories on the walk to her place. If I couldn't think of a good story, I told her about a TV show I'd watched, playing all the parts, being descriptive.

"Who needs a TV with you around?" she said, but she must have been very bored.

"Yes. I remember her," I said. Peter nodded, as if it was a happy memory we shared. It's hard to connect to that powerlessness. When you're a child, you do as the adults say, unless you're willing to be punished.

"I didn't talk to her," Peter said. I knew that small rebellion won him a lot. "You're lucky you missed it," he said.

Lucky I missed my mother's funeral. If that's my luck, I'm in trouble.

In hospital, the smell of jasmine cheered me. There were flowers from people I'd forgotten or hadn't seen in years. My school teacher Alice Blackburn sent flowers to me in hospital, not to my Mum's dead body. It was frangipani and jasmine from her own garden. The card said, "To remind you of the wonders of life."

Somehow I knew her card meant the opposite of what it said. We once had a discussion in class, about what a dead body might smell like, because we were reading a series of hard-nosed detective novels, all full of bodies and gore, and wondering about the imagery. She thought dead bodies smelt of frangipani and jasmine.

The card said, "Call me."

The police spoke to a lot of people after Mum died, and I had to prove a hundred times that it really was an accident, and one not caused by my imaginary deep-seated hatred of my mother.

"I didn't hate my mother, I loved my mother."

"And you didn't deliberately become intoxicated in order to lose your judgement, thus causing the accident?"

"I wasn't intoxicated. I wasn't even a bit pissy. I only had a couple of drinks."

"The head waiter at the restaurant where you had your lunch claims you were loud and over-excited."

"And you find that at odds with my natural character?" I said. Even sitting up in a hospital bed I wasn't scared of them. The cop smiled. I thought he liked me and hoped he'd offer me a lift home when I was well. On the way I'd tell him about Dad and his career, remind him who I was.

Peter said I was lucky to be Dad's daughter; I got off without a charge. He said if my father hadn't been a cop who died on the job, it would have been manslaughter. He reckoned I was lucky just to lose my licence.

I think it was because the cop who interviewed me liked me.

And Mum was a cop's wife, wasn't she? Why didn't they swear to avenge her, if that's why I got off?

The cops felt sorry for me; they tracked down so many people who said they didn't know me well enough to talk of my feelings for Mum. The cop running it, grey hair, wrinkles, held my hands and stroked me with his thumbs, said, "Isn't there someone who knows you?"

"Peter," I said. "My brother has to know."

"We've asked him. He gave us pages about how he felt, nothing about you. What about someone who looks up to you, who might see you as a role model?"

The only person who'd ever looked up to me was Tim, little Tim who was allowed to be bad when I babysat. And his brother Lee pretended not to care but he did. I'd say he worshipped the air I exhaled.

"There's a couple of kids I used to babysit. The Walshes."

Laurie, the young cop, gave me his card and said I should call him if anything came up. I tried to imagine he wanted to see me, that we could drive to a beach cabin which had been in his family for years and listen to the surf. I didn't call him though.

Peter put me off, saying how all the cops would know what we did because cops told each other everything.

My nurse let me walk around looking at the sick people. She didn't know what I was doing and didn't much care. It was the dying I wanted to see.

Those in their rooms waiting for one more breath before the last.

It seemed astonishing that I had been so close to death. All I could see were the faces of the people in that cold room. Two weeks I spent in hospital, then I sat up in bed and said, "I want to go home."

Didn't the papers love that, too?

As I was recovering, the cut on my head scabbed and was so itchy I couldn't resist picking and scratching it. It made the scar worse, but it was good to be marked with something. People were sympathetic; they asked me how close I'd come to death. It was like pregnancy; everyone thought my body belonged to them. When the scar was no longer bright red, people stopped asking. They didn't like to. People won't let me tell the story; they think it will upset me. But it's like when you see a cripple, or an amputee, or a sufferer of elephantiasis. It's far better to have a good stare and smile at them than to look away as if there was nothing to see. Everyone knows there is a story to tell, but they won't ask me the questions. Where were you going? Why was your mother with you? Why did you drive so fast? Was she in pain? Were you in pain? Does it still hurt? Do you feel guilty? What was it like to almost die?

There's an answer to every one of those questions.

I put on a pair of gumboots which had sat by the back door since Dad died. We never cleared them away.

I planned to dig up the yard; plant a sea of night blooming jasmine, surround myself again with that saviour scent. I had no idea what I was looking at, weed, vegetable, treasure. Some parts were green, some brown, and there were sprays of bright colour: purple, yellow, red.

Somewhere out there was a shed which no one had been near in nine years.

I headed in that direction. The whole area smelt composty and things rustled and slithered at my feet. I was amongst nature and it felt unnatural. I stamped fronds and flowers underfoot, bent to pick up interesting items.

I found a sock lost long ago from the Hills Hoist near the back door and a plastic, long-hated doll.

The shed had become a rusty mess. The door had never had a lock. Even though Dad was a cop, he wasn't bothered about security in our home. It was like he thought that his occupation was enough of a deterrent; that somehow thieves would KNOW who lived there and leave us alone.

The grass had grown up through the hinges and between the door and its frame. I used my bare hands to tug away the weeds from the door and pull it free. Inside smelt of petrol and metal. In the bright sunlight I saw the lawn mower, and Dad's rusty old tools.

I scythed away the grass first, then mowed it, not with Dad's old mower, which wouldn't start, but with one borrowed from the man next door, who watched me over the fence and waited in his front yard for it when I had finished.

And so my weekend went. After my hands were scratched and raw, I finally thought to go and buy some gloves. I bought books on gardening, too; about how to turn the soil, that sort of thing, if your soil is good, how to grow your turf. I didn't intend to grow any food. Easier to buy it. I just wanted to see the lawn neat, green. I wanted to be able to sit on it. People wouldn't think I was a weirdo if my garden was neat. I wanted jasmine to scent the house.

I read in one of the gardening books that manure was very good for soil, so I had a shitload delivered.

I'd hardly made a dent in the backyard, but I wanted this stuff to spur me on. It sat there, slowly spreading over the nature strip, the footpath, and spilling onto the road. I quite liked it as a piece of modern sculpture, an ever-changing study symbolising the unknown world. Then I went out and spent an age in the hardware shop. There was even a cafe, so I stopped and had coffee and "a piece of our own spicy, healthy carrot cake". As I walked around the corner to my street, the smell hit me. It really did stink; I had been used to it, but the trip away had cleared my nostrils. No wonder the street people, Rat Traps, I call them, kept meeting in clusters outside their houses. I never did bring that manure in; every now and then I'd have another load dumped on top. When I got back from shopping one Saturday, someone had shovelled all the shit from my nature strip to my front door, a huge mound.

I just used the back door.

In the dirt I found a coin holder, a plastic bracelet, a cat collar and a chipped crystal, with the remains of a piece of string.

The counsellor they made me see told me I needed goals. "Things to work towards, to avoid that sense of purposelessness."

I hadn't had a sense of purposelessness before that.

"I want to dig up my backyard and plant jasmine," I told her. "That's my goal."

She had this habit of nodding her head but at the same time pressing her lips together. "That's a good physical goal," she said, "but how about we come up with something a little more spiritual."

Honestly, the woman was an idiot. Though she did tell me to sort through Mum's things, and I found out a lot of stuff I had forgotten. Piles of papers I'd never been allowed to look at. Mum would have burnt them, if she'd had warning of her death.

One paper had yellowed a little, making it harder to read. I realised what I had, though. Dad's last words, scribbled down by Dougie Page, his partner.

I stared at the scribble for minutes, knowing it should mean something because it gave me a feeling in the pit of my stomach. It was the feeling I got when I thought about Dad and no other time; thinking about Mum didn't produce it.

"Tell her to promise [pause] never to move away from the house. Tell her to make the kids promise. I love her. Tell Pete to look after his Mum and sister. Tell Stevie she'll make a great detective."

I remembered the pride I felt, hearing those words.

When I was six, Dad took us into the station for a visit. Peter got all the attention as Dad showed us around. They called him young man and asked him when he'd get his badge. He was allowed to hold the guns and look at some horrible photos which made him sick. They wouldn't have made me sick.

I would have loved a look.

The policemen gave me lollies and said how cute I was. Finally one asked what I wanted to be when I grew up.

"A mother?" they guessed, "or a movie star?"

"A detective," I said. They all laughed.

"You'll have to be a cop first," one man said, thinking even that was impossible. They all laughed, especially Peter. He sat up on someone's desk, with someone's cop hat and someone's cop badge on.

It didn't matter to me what they said. My Dad said, "Steve can be anything she sets her heart on.

Because I say so." That was all I needed.

Wanting to be a detective—that was because I wanted to be like Dad, not through any inherited instinct. I wasn't born wanting it. I would have been good, though. You need a criminal mind to be a good cop.

Every time Peter rang up I was digging in the garden. He wanted me to stop; he said Dad would have wanted me to stop. He said I was obsessed and should have a break.

"You need to get out of the house," he said, as if the house was a disease. He begged me to come stay for a week. The time was specified. There was no chance I was to stay for longer than that. I couldn't anyway; no one would collect my mail.

And I didn't want to go. Here I felt in control, in command. I sprinkled some grass seeds on the manure out the front to see if they'd sprout. My garden was all I needed.

I found so many things when digging in the backyard. The pile grew by the back door, then I rinsed each item in the laundry sink. I found an old, squashed bottle top, a broken piece of an LP record, a fabric poppy and a little metal Dogs of War lunch box, one of those airtight boxes which buckle when kids sit on them. Inside were the remnants of a sandwich and an ancient box of raisins. People would pay money for these things, if I could wipe the rot off. I remembered a boy at school who'd had a lunch box like this. Little Pauly, who liked me, wanted to be me. It was a simple kiss, but I didn't know what to call it. I sat on my Dad's lap and whispered in his ear. "Pauly touched me in a funny way."

Dad squeezed me until I cried out. "Don't cry, baby. No one will ever hurt you."

It was the school holidays and I thought nothing more of Pauly. A week into the holidays, though, his face began to appear on the TV between the cartoons and in the paper, which Dad didn't let us see, but we saw it everywhere anyway.

"There's Pauly!" I said. I couldn't wait to get back to school to see my famous friend. My Dad had to work very hard for the next few days, because Pauly was missing. He had gone for a ride on his bike, all prepared with his Dogs of War lunch box and he was never seen again. I soon forgot Pauly and his kiss.

I dug and I found a whistle, a small bell, a foam ball and a compass.

My licence was taken from me. I had a difficult interview with my employer about keeping my job open.

He said, "You may be popular with the customers, but we need clean drivers here. You can't run a courier company with dodgy drivers. Even if you work the phones till you get your licence back, it's on your record."

"I'm not a dodgy driver." I was the most cheerful of all the drivers, a joke with every parcel delivered.

I loved the job.

It wasn't hard to be cheerful. People are desperate for a smile; they like you to be nice to them.

Some of the regular clients gave me gifts. Books, perfume, stuff they probably got for nothing. They never asked me out or tried anything, though they pushed their kidding as far as it would go.

So I lost my job and my mode of transport in one.

And my mum, of course. I lost her too. My car was towed to my place rather than the tip. I couldn't stand the thought of it being discarded.

About six months after Mum's funeral, Laurie, the young cop who'd interviewed me in hospital, came a-knocking. "Nothing came up, I take it?" He was in casual clothes, I had seen him for a few hours half a year ago, yet he expected me to recognise him. Well, I've got an eye for faces.

"Hello, Laurie. Not much," I said.

"I wondered if you'd like to go see a movie or something," he said. "Just if you weren't doing anything."

I saw, in a sudden flash, the two of us having a drink after the movie. Him saying shit about it, me not being able to think of a word. And what movie would we see, anyway? I knew he wouldn't like my kind of movie. And what would I say if he wanted me back at his place? I wouldn't know where the toilet was, how the fridge worked, how warm the heater made the place.

"Why don't you come in and we'll talk about it?"

He smiled.

"Are you off duty then? Do you want a beer?" I said.

"Sure."

It turned out he had a flatmate, so we always went to my place. I had things there just in case, so I could say, "I've got some brandy at my place, why don't we go there?" Or it was chocolate cake, or a DVD, something I could entice him with. I could say I'd left my contraception at home, but he used condoms anyway and wouldn't understand my caution. Knowing him, he might say, "Don't worry, we'll just hold each other," and that would be irritating. It was the usual trouble, though. Why do things have to change? He started wanting more of me, friendship, confession, emotion, and I didn't want a best friend. I didn't know how to tell him, so I just said he was a dud root. I didn't think I'd ever need him as a cop so I didn't care. He took it well, anyway.

"I thought we had something," he said.

"Maybe we could have," I said, to give him something to dream about, "but I just feel repelled by the shape of your penis. Not even hypnosis could help me get over that."

He kept in contact. Called me when he met women, said, "They don't think I'm funny looking."

I did call him once, professionally. My neighbours, the Rat Traps, complained about the noise I was making. It was only music. So I threw a rock through their window. Only it was the wrong neighbours, so they complained too. The police arrived; I called Laurie.

"I didn't know what to do," I said.

"I'll be right there." And he was. He talked to the other cops and it was fine. I thanked him by smiling at him and telling him how much I missed him, how sometimes I wondered what could have been.

He never asked me about the boys I'd babysat, and I didn't mention the steps Lee and I had taken.

They didn't need to know about the sexual fumblings we played at. They shouldn't think he was in my power. He had been, though. Right from the first time, when I was sixteen. The father, Mr Walsh, always picked me up and drove me home.

He was a talkative, ugly man with spiky blond hair far too young for him, who would ask me about school and not notice if I didn't answer. Gab gab gab, not even flattering me by trying to impress me.

I was just a set of ears. If he'd read a good book I'd hear half of it on the way there, half on the way back. Even mystery books—he'd tell me the whole thing. I finally shut him up when he was reading *And Then There Were None*, the Agatha Christie one.

"I'm only half-way through but by golly it's good. Can't believe I never read it as a youngster, maybe it was a little risqué. I don't know. Anyway..." Blah blah blah he said she said.

When we reached their house I told him who did it. He almost cried. He left the motor running, sat in the car waiting for his wife to emerge. She never shut up, either, always talking back instructions to people who didn't listen. They were going to a party. "Just a duty thing, we'll be home in a couple of hours," but these two never were. I could imagine it: "We really must go, oh, is that new?" "Yes, isn't it marvellous? Such a bargain, too, and there's only twenty thousand of them in the world."

Whatever it was would keep the women talking, so he'd get another drink and find another victim. They loved it. I'd seen them in action at my place, poor Mum trapped and almost tearful at the assault.

Their son Tim was eight then and at the TV and he didn't look up the first time I showed. Lee was sitting on the couch, watching his brother watch TV.

"Hi, Lee," I said. He looked at me. I smiled.

He said, "You didn't make the joke."

"What, hi lee contagious or something?"

"Everyone makes the joke," he said. He smiled at me. He pulled a cigarette packet out of his pocket and began to toss it up and down, spinning it higher and higher.

Tim changed the channel. It was close to adult viewing hours and I let him watch anything. He liked documentaries, and movies. We saw one about a Civil War and he wanted to know where the men were taking the woman.

"How come she doesn't get to die?" he said.

I said, "They'll probably rape her and then kill her."

"Oh," he said, as if that was a perfectly reasonable thing. Who knew what he had seen? There are family events no one ever discusses.

We certainly had enough in our family.

I said, "Anything to eat?"

"I'll have a look," Lee said. I followed him to the kitchen.

"There's heaps if you know how to cook," he said. I realised how perfect his skin was, how red his cheeks. He looked so young, but he had a man's voice.

"I don't cook," I said. I opened the fridge and stared in. It was a horrible fridge, full of veggies, milk, meat, cheese. I would never be old enough to think that all meant food.

"Have they got any money?" I said. Tim was with us now, using an instinct I had to admire.

Lee shrugged. "They hide it from me."

Tim said. "There's grocery change in the linen press and Dad's change in his drawer. He's got a magazine there, too."

I laughed. "Your future girlfriends," I said. Tim reddened.

"I haven't looked," he said.

"Of course you haven't." I didn't intend to tease him but I couldn't resist. "So do you like the boozies or the furry bits?" I said.

Lee laughed like a pistol. "Ya wanna fuck one?" he said. There was more cruelty in his voice than in mine. I was just having fun. He began threading the needle, in and out, one forefinger through the circle of his thumb and other forefinger. He made an ugly, sucking noise.

"Oh, yes, that's just what it's like," I said. I hoped he knew I meant it wasn't, that I knew he had never had sex and had no idea what it was like.

He stopped and stared at me. He seemed to realise that I wasn't a babysitter, I was an older woman.

"Wanna smoke?" he said. Tim sucked in his breath, shocked. "You're not allowed," he said.

"Go collect the money and we'll get some pizza," I said. He went to disturb the sanctity of his parent's bedroom. Lee and I went outside. We sat on the swings.

"You'll have to teach me how to do the draw-back," I said. He gave me one of his strong cigarettes. I had not even had a puff before; this seemed like the perfect time to learn. He was trying to be cool but he was in awe; he wouldn't laugh at me.

"You'll cough the first time," he said, a kindness which made me forgive him cruelties in the future.

"Close your lips around it all the way."

"Like a dick?" I said. He didn't know.

"Now just kinda breathe in, but only through your mouth. You haveta pretend it's air."

Tim came and watched us smoke. He sat cross-legged on the grass, fascinated at this glimpse of the adult world. I took to smoking as easily as I did driving. We got pizza and more cigarettes, we watched a true murder mystery on TV.

I babysat those boys for a good two years.

It all changed after Mum died. The Walshes forbade me visiting once their precious boys had been interviewed by the police. I had placed their children in the path of the law, and that was not suitable. Lee called me; he loved it. He was big time; he'd been questioned by the cops.

"Ya shoulda heard me. I raved about you and your Mum. I kept hoping I was saying the right things. I mean, you never even mentioned your Mum. I told them you always raved about her, said how much you loved her. I told them all these little stories I said you used to tell us; about outings, little adventures or something. And Tim told them you showed him hundreds of pictures of her. That was good wasn't it?"

I was a little stunned. I knew they'd done me a favour; the cops would give up the idea that maybe it wasn't an accident after all. But it shocked me they would think it was necessary. Did they have discussions and decide I needed saving? What had they seen which made them think I was capable of killing my mother? I missed the babysitting, but we kept in touch. I liked being with those two. They thought I was something special; always did. That was worth plenty.

At Nineteen

I was still a child at nineteen. Up until the day my mother died she looked after me. Shopping was the worst without her. I never even watched her do it, never went with her. Now I didn't have my car, or my licence. How could they take my licence away?

And tell me I was supposed to be grateful for it? I could never find the right change for the bus and I hated sharing transport. To quote Prince Charles, "*People* do that." And I could never figure out the protocol of the aisles in the supermarket. There's a certain end to start at, a certain direction you're supposed to go, or else people glare.

I wondered how Mum had done it every week; she was not a clever woman, yet somehow she returned home with bread and tins, ham, spices, fresh chicken, eggs. She only shopped in the supermarket, and she always said, "If you learn nothing else from me but this, it's okay. Supermarkets have high turnover of fresh food. They can afford to buy the best. You can't get that from those grubby little shops." Her joy increased as supermarkets grew.

She'd come home with bags of jars and new vegetables, three different cuts of beef, herbs to crush, cheeses, "Would you look at this?" I never found it very interesting.

Which is probably the thing. If I was interested in the details of food, buying, cooking, perhaps shopping wouldn't be such hell. I just like to eat the food. On the days when there was not much food left, before she did a big shop, she'd make golden syrup dumplings. I never have golden syrup, or flour. I can't remember to buy them.

I miss her golden syrup dumplings. She did them just right.

Shopping really was a bore, and so irritating I pulled half my hair out. There seemed to be some sort of politeness I wasn't interested in. You were supposed to shuffle quietly behind the people in front; but that's just time wasting. On one visit, the man in front was so slow I trod on his heel and he stepped half out of his shoe. When I finally made it to the check out, an old woman was there before me, and she fumbled in her bag, fumble fumble, so I stepped in front, saved myself probably twenty minutes. I left the right money on the counter and walked away. Perhaps the check-out chick sighed at me; perhaps not. If I used a credit card people sighed and huffed, so I used a credit card. I can't help but feel angry at my mother whenever I have to shop. I'm too busy to fend for myself. I've got too many important things to do to shop amongst the nobodies and keep my place clean. Carpets are meant to be dirty; that's what they're made for.

Filthy feet, rolling about. Not to eat off.

My activities caused some interest in the street. Mrs Di Matteo stuck her nose about, watching me dig, looking for clues that I was crazy, until I called her an old bag. She was not impressed; I don't think she's much more than forty.

We had never kept up with them all. We had no swimming pool. These appeared like dominos falling once the people at number two put theirs in.

I could never understand why they didn't just all swim in one or two pools, then realised it was because they didn't actually swim.

The kids in the street were really scared of me and my house after Mum died. I was often discussed in the papers as the girl who killed her mother, as if it was deliberate. When I went to the corner shop I saw mothers draw their children closer. I wanted to say, "I have no interest in your boring, brainless children." I think I muttered it once or twice, because people said, "Pardon?"

Hearing their voices shocked me; once I dropped a jar of golden syrup on the floor and walked away. The shitty looks people gave me. That was as close as I ever got to making golden syrup dumplings.

And I was never very popular, but after Mum died adults in the street were scared of me, too.

They began to treat me like they would a stinking killer dog. The man across the road, Gary, was very aware of my existence. He liked the idea of me being lonely. Gary, such a friendly name, such a mean man. He was huge in a bean bag way, his flesh as bumpy as one and a very yellow tan. No one would take him seriously.

He said, "Would you like to borrow my pen? It's pink and I keep it in my trousers."

No one even offered me token invitations. I began to feel like an outcast. I didn't mind it. I never liked any of them anyway. They thought

I was strange. I had a big pile of shit on my front doorstep that'd been there almost a year. I had lived with these people for most of my life and they had had no effect on me. There was anger about me now, and the kids came and stared up the path, trying to catch a glimpse of the girl who killed her mother. The newsagent banned me, but more because I read the magazines without buying them than because my mother was dead.

They all seemed to forget I was only eighteen when it happened. I didn't feel grown up. I felt like a daughter still, but my mother was gone.

The people in the street wanted me to clean the shit off my front step. They left notes in my letter-box or shoved under my door. Early on they sounded like this: "Dear Stephanie, would you mind doing something about your front lawn? It's only that the rest of the street is so neat. Perhaps you'd like some help from one of the men."

Peter used to do the gardening about every two months, when he lived at home, because he's as lazy as I am. Then he moved out, then Mum died, and no one does it. It isn't something I notice.

Gary across the street offered to do it, but I didn't need that kind of obligation. His wife was very nice, good looking, according to the men's talk I heard over the fence whenever there was a barbecue going on. But he came over and pretended he had important things to tell me, when all he wanted to do was to see me in my home clothes. He pressed me up against the fridge and told me he'd paint the house, too, if I wanted him too.

I said I didn't. I said, "Tell your friends to stop sending me notes," because I'd got one under my door saying "CLEAN UP THE FUCKEN MESS, PIG."

He said, "It was never like this when your father was here. You're nothing like him."

I threw a glass of beer at him, and he grinned.

"Like 'em passionate," he said. But he left me alone after that.

I felt adrift, even in my own home. All I wanted to do was dig up the backyard. The backyard was mine, now, to do with as I would.

It was large, an area twenty metres square.

Somewhere at the back was a see-saw; I can remember playing on it for a short while. I found it so boring, just up, down, up, down, nothing to look at but Peter's silly face.

He loved going up, didn't like going down.

"Going up you might be able to fly, you can lift your arms and might be a bird. Going down you land with a bump or squash your legs, and then you have to push up again." I watched his face, swapping joy for anticipation and as I was only three, I copied him.

I dug and dug and I found eight marbles and a small plastic bucket resting next to an indentation in the ground.

I remembered the leaving of the bucket. It was Christmas Day. Peter was riding up and down the driveway on his new bike, too scared to take it out onto the footpath. He learned to ride months before, on a secondhand bike a cousin had given him.

We always got stuff from Auntie Ruth's kids. Luckily this one was from cousin Diana—she always looked after her things, like Peter did.

The old bike should be mine, now, but the formal ceremony had not yet been held. That required Peter to say the words, "You can have my old bike, Stevie." Until then it wasn't mine, and my parents wouldn't take it from him.

The new bike was far more enticing, but I had at last tired of standing in the garage begging Peter for a turn each time he came near me. He made the most of it; had me fetching and carrying, never actually saying, "Get me a glass of cordial and I'll give you a go," but why else would he demand such a thing?

"Gimme a go, Peter," over and over, and he just pedalled up and down the driveway, thriving in my attention. He took his hands off the handlebars once, but the bike wobbled so he quickly put them back.

When I realised he wasn't going to give me a turn I started daring him to do things.

"Go out on the street. Take your feet off the pedals. Drive fast over that rock. Lift the front wheels up." He did none of them, just pedalled up and down the driveway.

It was such a great bike. The old bike was a girl's bike, with no bar across the front, and Peter was always getting teased about it. This one was a boy's bike, with gears and a bell which wasn't rusty. His feet didn't touch the ground when he sat on the seat. Maybe he didn't want me to ride it because he didn't want the kids in the street seeing a girl on it.

Or he was just being mean. Or he knew I'd ride it on the footpath and down the street, over rocks, probably scratch it.

I watched him all Christmas afternoon. Mum came out to entice me with my own gifts, "Come and play with your felt set," or whatever I got that year. But I was patient. I got up early on Boxing Day, thinking if I was first there I'd have to get a turn.

Peter surely must have been bored with the game. Up and down, up and down, because if he stopped one of them might say, "Why don't you give your sister a turn on the bike, if you're not using it?"

Finally I realised he was never going to relent and went and got my new bucket and spade.

"That'll be good for the beach," Dad had said when I opened it. The beach wasn't far from where we lived but still an expedition.

"What sort of things can you do with a bucket and spade?" Dad said. He liked to make us think.

"Dig in the sand, what else?"

"Collect water and shells and creatures," I said.

"Make sandcastles and move the sand away."

"Anything else, Peter?"

"Dig in the sand?" Peter said. I remember it so well because I loved it when Peter acted stupidly.

We had good Christmases when Dad was alive.

He never worked on Christmas Eve, but stayed home and cooked the dinner. He always made fried rice, very delicious, and heaps of it.

I pulled on my new bathing suit, got a towel out of the cupboard, took some cake from the tin and wrapped it in grease-proof paper. I collected my bucket.

"I'm going to the beach," I said. Mum and Dad were lying down, even though it was morning.

"We'll go to the beach later," Dad said.

"Only pretend," I said, and marched downstairs.

The backyard was a jungle even then. Dad had tired of working in it. He was never too keen anyway. He'd never provided a good crop of veggies, and must have hated mowing the lawn, because it always made him grouchy, as grouchy as he got. I loved the smell of him, though, that mixture of cut grass and sweat. I wanted hugs but he was too grouchy for hugs.

With the sound of Peter in the background, riding up, down, up down, I settled myself where I couldn't see the house and began to dig. In my mind I designed a trench so that when it rained, all the rain which flooded in our back door would lead up to the centre of the yard and into a hole.

I dug the hole first; quite deep it was. Then I began to dig out my trench. I got lost. I thought I was heading to the house but I was at a 90 degree angle from there. I realised this when I ran into my Dad's legs.

"What are you doing?" he said.

"Digging a trench to the door." I didn't stop.

"But you're nearly at the garage."

I stood up and surveyed my position

"Oh, well, I'll have two trenches," I said, and took a step towards the hole.

He clutched my shoulders with such strength I dropped my bucket and spade.

"You don't dig up the yard," he said. He picked me up, dumped me in the garage, freed Peter's old bike from the clutter it rested amongst.

"Peter said you could have his bike," he said, one of those adult lies I was happy to hear. Mum stood with her hands on her hips, watching him.

"Alex." That was all she said, but we both knew Dad was in trouble.

I was feeling tough and angry and I wanted to show off my new bike so I went next door to scare Melissa. She was older than me but terrified of storms, dogs, the dark, her dad, school and all. She was playing dollies, with little tea cups and fancy dresses.

She had a little dolly grooming set, with brush, comb and mirror. She loved the mirror most of all, because it was real glass. She thought it was magical.

"Let me brush Margie's hair," I said. She rarely had anyone to play dollies with, partly because she was so bossy.

"You have to comb first, then brush, then let her see if she likes it."

I combed and brushed under Melissa's careful eye. I picked up the dear little mirror, placed it between my teeth and crunched. It served me right; I cut my tongue and lip and had to go to the dentist to get the bits of glass out of my teeth.

But it was worth it. She was always terrified of me from then on, and would do anything I asked.

She never seemed to grow up. She was always little, even when she went away and got married.

She never said no when asked for a loan, and she always invited me to parties she had. I always declined. She wasn't my speed.

I should have sorted through all Mum's things, but didn't feel like throwing anything out. Uncle Dom called to offer help sorting. When Dad died, we thought we'd see more of Dom, but Dad's cop mates kept him away. Peter and I didn't know why; loyalty to Dad, was my guess. They didn't want his own brother moving in on Mum. It was a shame, cos Mum could've done with some help. And we could've done with some presents.

"Hey, Steve. You've done a lot of work back here," Dom said. He looked a lot older than last time I saw him. A bad haircut and really ugly shirt didn't help.

"It's my obsession," I said. I didn't want to speak to him. He'd ask about Mum, questions I didn't want to think about. There was nothing he could do for me. He should've been around earlier.

"I'm not feeling well, Uncle Dom. You might have to come back another time." I shut the door half in his face.

"You're just like your father, Stephanie. I can see him in you clear as day."

"Thank you," I said. I shut the door on him. Go away, you old fuck. I thought. You stupid, ugly, useless old fuck. Go away.

"I'll just leave this for you," he called, and slid something under the door. It was an envelope full of money.

Nice of him.

I enjoyed my empty house, but it was hard to pay the bills, and it was too big for me. So I advertised in the classifieds, and I found Mark, who was lovely at first, and another guy, Jason, who was too demanding right from the start. He had great clothes, though. I borrowed his green t-shirt and said I lost it. I couldn't wear it until he moved out, but it was worth it. They couldn't cook golden syrup dumplings, the liars.

Mark was okay for a while, as long as he kept to his own room. He was curious, wanted to know about the house, the room he slept in, details. It bored me very quickly, but he cooked well, did the shopping. One night I was feeling ratty, rebellious; I'd been fitting into the square, a frustrating way to live. Jason was interstate, with a lover, somewhere.

Mark cooked dinner and insisted we eat at the table, talk to each other, look at each other in the candlelight.

It was seductive, having such attention. Not that I starve for it, but it was nice to be listened to.

So we had sex. It was pretty disgusting; he was very eager, his mouth was too soft, he was so skinny his bones poked at me. After it was over I said, "That won't be happening again," and I sent him slithering into his own room.

I ignored him so completely after that I wasn't surprised when he announced he was moving out.

He must have been practising the words for days.

They came out stilted, a bad actor in a filthy soapy.

Love, love, blah blah.

It gave me the giggles, yet he was so serious.

He didn't like my twitching mouth. He said, "I thought that night was special."

"Oh, but it was," I said. "It was so special I don't think we should repeat it. We may ruin what we had."

I loved it. He didn't cry, but he didn't look at me, either.

Then he turned nasty. He said, "Someone as covered with scars as you shouldn't be picky."

"What could my scars possibly have to do with it?

"It just says what sort of person you are."

I stood in front of the mirror, trying to feel his revulsion. True, I was scarred, a white slash across my forehead from the accident which killed my mother, the scar over my right eye, scars on my arms, my shoulders. Scars on my knees and thighs.

Scar tissue thick on my fingers. The back of my neck. The top of my ear. And the neat, stitchy scar across my stomach, from when I lost my appendix.

My scars were real.

Oh, the pain, the pain. I burnt the sheets we slept in. Jason left soon after, so I got to wear his green t-shirt.

◆————————◆

Even though I couldn't drive my car, not for five years, I had guys come and look at it until, almost a year after the accident, someone finally said, "It'll take a lot of work, but I think we can do it." This bloke, Ray, didn't shake his head once. He was inspired by the challenge; he quit his job and came to work for me. I said I couldn't afford to pay him full-time mechanic's wages, so I wasn't sure if it was a good idea.

"Tell ya what, pay me what you can, shout me a few meals, a few beers, and let me crash on your couch. Then we'll be square." I'd gotten used to the house being empty again, after Jason and Mark moved out, but Ray quite liked the squalor of my place and ended up doing most of the cooking. He taught me the pleasures of beer drinking and drove me places. He really helped keep me sane, helped me cope with not having a car. I'd lost my freedom.

He had a fiancée to whom he was devoted. I'd fart if she was in the room and not apologise. I always said no if she offered me anything. They were saving money to buy a house, so she was living at home. He was, too, when he wasn't crashing at my place. I built up a sense for when they were about to have sex and I often walked in singing.

My car was a thing of beauty when he'd finished.

I'd been there every minute I could, and I knew where the bits went.

From what he taught me, I could fix my own car next time.

We drove it down the coast; I made the fiancée sit in the back seat.

"Oh, she's beautiful, beautiful," Ray said. I was speechless; my car was running again.

He took photos of my car, as a reference, and I wrote him one as well. From calling his repair shop to speak to him, I knew that he had been fired the day before he came to see my car because they discovered he was wanted by the police.

"He must have known we'd been out to look at your vehicle and thought he'd take a look himself.

We didn't want to turn him in, but we told him he had to find something else," they told me. I never said anything. His name or picture never appeared in the paper, so I can only hope the respite he enjoyed at my place, a stranger's place where no one would think of looking, helped him.

I couldn't understand the risk he'd taken letting his fiancée know where he was. What if they'd followed her? Seems cops aren't as dedicated as they were in my Dad's time.

Things came together for a while, then, with my car working. I couldn't drive it, but I could sit in it and rev it up. I had my house to myself, no one to judge me or tell me what to do.

Then Peter and his repulsive girlfriend Maria decided it was time for a memorial.

"Mum's been dead for a year, Steve, and you didn't get to go to the funeral. A lot of people are asking me about it," Peter said.

"No one's asking me." I polished my car. There were no dents left in it. No indication.

"It's a good idea," Peter said. "Maria thought everyone could come back here afterwards."

I looked at him. He hated coming to the house, hardly ever stepped in the door. Even being in the garage made him uncomfortable.

"I've got nothing to wear," I said. Peter laughed.

He gets my jokes; I guess that's one reason to keep a brother around.

"You'll have to find a dress. Jeans and singlet would look bad," he said.

They planned it all, and I pulled out a dress of Mum's to wear. Seemed like a waste to buy a new one. It was a pink thing, with red flowers, and I looked appalling. But that was the point, really. I didn't want to look good.

Peter collected me. He said, "Maria's going to meet us at the church. She's doing the flowers. So, it's okay for everyone to come back here afterwards?" He thought he was confirming that I had everything ready.

I had never thrown a party before.

I had never really been to a party either. I never knew enough kids when I was younger, and Peter always liked to go out for his birthdays; the movies, bowling, a picnic somewhere.

Peter always had a lot of friends as a kid. Kids liked him; he liked the same things they did, like a sheep, a mirror. I liked my own things. I didn't know his friends very well. He rarely brought them home.

They were so dull I had to kick and punch them when I saw them in a group one day at school.

They said piss off. They didn't chase me. I'm dobbing, I said. They laughed.

Peter waited for me after school that day, walked home with me. I thought I taught him a lesson but he only pitied me. He also dobbed.

"You're so like your father," Mum said. "I can see you following in his footsteps."

Much later, I realised she didn't mean that as a compliment.

I received little sympathy from her when I told her about my day at school. It had been a bad one; Peter's friends told me to piss off, and my lunch was stolen by the new kid, some guy who thought he'd make himself big.

Mum couldn't care less. She said, "Make a sandwich if you're hungry." I don't know what she would have said if I told her he tried to pull my pants down, too. I was so shocked I could only run away, lock myself in the girls' toilets. I could hear him outside, calling for me, telling people I was taking my pants off to get ready for him.

The new kid had all these tricks which were supposed to make him look cool. He lifted up his desk lid and felt around without looking for what he needed. Then he casually brought it out like it just fell into his hands.

I waited a week. I didn't plan anything, I just waited. I saved my orange juice bottle, washed and sitting in my desk. I didn't want to break it too soon; I didn't want to cut myself. I waited until I got into the classroom first, then I smashed the bottle and put the bits in his desk. There were large bits sticking up, small bits hidden.

I told Mum how well my trick had worked, how the blood filled his desk and he had to be sent home, and she just went about fixing dinner.

I left school before the eighteenth birthdays started happening and lost contact with them all.

Peter took me to a party once but we got there very late and everything was a mess. I had no idea I was supposed to have my house perfect, for people to stare into every corner. I didn't clean up a single room; not even the kitchen.

There were only a few clean plates. I was only nineteen; I was enjoying not having to clean up.

My bedroom had dirty clothes everywhere and a smell which wasn't sweat; it was something similar.

I was used to it, found it a comfort, but I discovered you weren't meant to smell like that when you were a grown up.

If I had thought about it, I never would have imagined guests thumping upstairs for a look; I had no idea how curious people could be.

Peter was good at the memorial service. Maria was kind to both of us, and she must have spent hours not to look glamorous. People gave her barely a glance; they grasped Peter by the hand, hugged, they said good things to him. They avoided me. No one knew what to say; I think people find it harder to deal with another's guilt than another's grief. My forehead scar has never faded completely, and serves to frighten people as my earlier scar did when I started school.

When we got back to the house ahead of the guests, Maria was appalled.

"Stephanie! Do you call this tidying up?"

I laughed "I didn't tidy," I said. I boiled some water for coffee as she huffed about the kitchen, piling, wiping, cleverly hiding the mess. I sat with my coffee and watched.

"Didn't you make me a coffee?" she said.

"You really shouldn't ask questions you know the answer to. It makes me feel sarcastic."

She opened the fridge. "Where's the food?" I had plenty of stuff in there and couldn't figure out what she meant. I had left-over things, a tin of beetroot in a bowl, some Chinese, some Thai. There was some bolognaise I made myself which was pretty bad but tasted okay on toast.

Maria left the kitchen and I heard her and Peter muttering. I followed; he was tidying the lounge room, using her technique of piling things into drawers and shoving them into cupboards. He was moving more quickly than I'd ever seen him move, clutching up armfuls of my things: bras, books, shoes, undies, magazines.

"I can't believe you, Steve. They'll be here any minute. Where are the drinks, at least?"

I opened Dad's liquor cabinet. It was something we'd never touched;

Mum used to take the glasses and bottles out every now and then and dust the shelves, but everything went back where it came from. She never took to alcohol, preferring something sweet and tasty, lemonade or juice.

The times I drink are always troublesome.

"There's heaps here," I said. There was vodka, scotch, rum, brandy. And tonnes of wine under the house. Dad used to have visitors sometimes, when we were all asleep. I loved the comfort of male voices, a low hum which would wake me, not because it was loud, but because it was continuous.

I never saw Dad bring home new bottles, but the old ones never seemed to empty, either.

These were the bottles I indicated.

"You're fuckin' joking, Steve." Peter swearing was pathetic; he did it so rarely he actually pronounced the "g". Maria stomped about, sweating, red, freaking out. I couldn't figure out what the big deal was.

I'd seen a party. Everything was a mess and the bottles were half-empty. It seemed easy to me.

Maria said, "We'll just have to keep them in here and the kitchen. Oh, God, what's the toilet like?"

I shrugged. "It's okay. The walls are pale purple and the tiles are white, but I don't mind it." She stared at me. I wondered if she was thinking, "Thank God we live across town."

She said, "I mean, how filthy is it?"

"Well, I usually do my shits down here, but it should be okay. I've been constipated lately."

Peter said, "What's the yard like? Maybe we can put them out there."

"It's looking good. I've got jasmine in one corner. Won't be long before I do the next batch." I liked to dig for hours on end, sleep, eat, buy my needs from Mrs Beattie at the corner shop. I really enjoyed entering that place. It was dark, cool, small, the goodies all lined up like a marching band. I loved picking things up and putting them down, just out of place, until Mrs Beattie said, "Can I help you?" as if I hadn't worked there for three years, from the tender age of fifteen. Her arms were fatter than ever, and she hadn't bought a new dress in years, so you could see a tight line of strain pressing into her flesh.

The thing she hated most was the way I bought lollies. I had half the kids doing it too; they had a fine instinct for what irritated an adult.

"I'll have a red traffic light. And a green traffic light. And another red traffic light. And a yellow traffic light. And a green traffic light," until my bag was full. I don't even like lollies; I gave them to all the sugar-starved children.

While I worked in the backyard, I didn't have to think about the bad stuff, like Mum, or not being able to drive, or losing my courier job, or everyone hating me. I thought about the yard and how I would fix it. I kept finding things which reminded me of Dad; I thought of him a lot. I don't know why; it was stuff I'd never seen before; so many things, so many. All of them things precious to men. There was not a woman's thing amongst them. Nothing to remind me of Mum.

People started to pile into my house. "I'm so sorry," they said fifty times each. "Your mother and your father, too."

I wanted to be outside, digging.

People muttered about the house, picking up our things. "Such a terrible loss, when the father died,"

I heard them say. "I remember the little girl could barely walk, she was so devastated."

It's very hard for me to make sense of the day Dad died. I was nine and considered myself grown up. I was in Year Four and finally doing real work; Art was now a subject with a name and we only did it once a week. There were three whole years of babies below me, kids I could bully. There were only two years ahead of me, and half of those kids were scared of me. I was a clever one in class and that made me feel older still.

I always got home before Peter. He liked to dawdle home, kicking stones, looking at boring boy things. I couldn't stand it. I wanted to be home as soon as I could, wanted the school part of the day finished with. I wanted to get home and investigate what Mum had done all day, look at the clues and tell her what I thought.

If there was washing on the line, that was easy.

Or if dinner was bubbling. Her other activities were more difficult. A faint scent of perfume in the air and an empty pantyhose packet meant lunch with her friends. Parcels on the bed meant lunch with Dad. Parcels on the bed and something nice to eat in the cupboard meant shopping.

This is what should have happened:

My Dad took me to the zoo. Not Peter; just me. He told me that I was the one who has to look after Mum and Peter. I am strong, and clever, and I will inherit everything. I promised I would look after them. I said, "But why, Dad? You're not going to die."

He hugged me, stroked my hair. "We all have to die," he said. And two days later, after a fight with my mother (because she so loved to feel guilty, I'll give her this part of the fantasy), after telling Peter off for acting like a baby, after winking at me, he left for work, to chase a criminal who wanted to kill the innocent, chase and catch and kill him. But the criminal had a partner, as they do, and the partner shot Dad in the back. Dad was paralysed, he lay in the gutter. He knew he couldn't live like that; he was not strong enough to live with any affliction. So he willed himself to die, knowing that I had everything under control, that his family would be safe.

Or this may have happened:

He is taken to hospital, where he begs me to turn off the machines keeping him alive. This I do.

This is what did happen:

I slept in, lied to Mum, said I was sick, sank back into sleep knowing I would not have to do sports that day.

There I lay, not wanting to move, because every crack and crease in the bed fitted me perfectly. Peter came in and stared at my face, waiting for me to smile.

"She's not sick," he told Mum.

"Leave her alone. Boys don't always know when girls are sick."

That was fascinating to me. I hadn't realised until then what magic I held. Men didn't understand, didn't want to understand, but liked to pretend they knew all.

Dad was still asleep. He was a good, solid sleeper, hard to wake once he slipped away. This was lucky for Peter and me. We didn't have to sneak about on his mornings in; the house wasn't run on his sleep patterns. He often worked night shift, because he felt people were more real then, less protected by routine. He liked to talk to people then, while during the day his tongue was still.

Mum and I spent the morning together, and when Dad got up he jumped straight in the shower.

I thought that was odd. Usually he'd come and say hello first, see how we were going. And he'd already had a shower in the night.

Mum said, "We might leave your father to it," and she bundled me up and we went shopping.

I called out "Bye, Dad," but he didn't hear.

When we got home after picking up Peter, Dad had left for work.

Mum hated Dad's job. Peter and I loved it; loved his uniform, his baton. He never brought his gun home. We both wanted to be policemen. Peter wanted to be like Dad, a uniform guy, out amongst it. I wanted to be a detective, catch the real crooks using my brain.

This is also what happened:

Dad's boss put his arm around her, and she began to cry.

"It was very quick," he said. "He is a hero. His action saved the lives of four other police officers."

"What?" said my mum. We all looked at her. "What are you talking about?"

"Alex is dead, Heather. I'm sorry. I thought you must have guessed. It was a surprise attack. No one could have seen it coming. These officers were with him at the time."

One stepped forward. "I just wanted to say, ma'am, that your husband saved my life. I intend to make him proud. I'm Doug. Doug Page."

"Did he say anything? What did he say?" Mum demanded. She was on her feet. She looked angry.

He flipped open his notebook. "He did say some things before he died, ma'am. I thought you'd like to hear." He read his own bad handwriting. I could see his pad over his shoulder as he knelt at Mum's feet. It was worse than my writing. He read, "Tell her to promise [pause] never to move away from the house. Tell her to make the kids promise. I love her. Tell Pete to look after his Mum and sister. Tell Stevie she'll make a great detective."

"I'm Stevie!" I said. "That's me!"

Doug Page looked at Mum to see if she was listening. She was pale and her mouth was open; she scared me. I began to cough. I couldn't breathe properly.

Peter hid in the pot cupboard. I could see him staring out like a mouse.

"Do some little poo poos," I said. "Do some raisin poo poos." He ignored me.

Doug Page coughed. "I'm sorry, ma'am. But he really was insistent I tell you these things. He didn't want it in the report. It's personal."

"Oh, God," Mum said.

"It's OK," said the senior officer. "We'll just lose the pages. If he didn't want the world to hear it, that's what it will be."

"Can I keep that?" Mum said.

"Well, ma'am, I might just have to write it out again." Doug Page held his pad out to show her his writing.

"No, look, I can read that. That's perfectly clear. You are a messy writer, though, aren't you?" He blushed. Mum smiled, and he tore the pages off to pass over. She folded them and tucked them into her sleeve.

Peter came out of the cupboard and held her hand. Her face had colour again. I stopped coughing.

"You have a lovely family, Mrs Searle. I'm more sorry than I know how to say that this has happened," Dad's boss said.

He kissed her cheek then there was silence. No one had explained to me yet what had happened.

"Where's Daddy?" I said. The officers quickly picked up their hats and made their farewells. No one wanted the job of explanation.

"Peter, call Auntie Ruth," said Mum. "Get her to come over." And I didn't see Mum for a lot of school days after that. She was in her room; Auntie Ruth fed us, mothered us, all three. She had a family of her own but didn't like them. She liked us better. She called me a little monkey, because I clung to her like a baby ape.

Dad's funeral, I'm told, was very nice. I wasn't allowed to go. Mum said I'd fidget and get bored.

I'm glad it happened when I was young. I think funerals must become more terrible as you get older.

People become more terrified of death when they've known each other longer. "It was twenty years," they can say.

My father was twenty-nine when he died. I was nine. Peter was eleven. Mum was twenty-eight.

Mum began baking for people so we had money from that. And there was some cop's fund which kept us going, and the grandparents, and Dad's granddad had given us the house. Mum made our lunch every day and we always had clean school uniforms.

And all of the men who thought they'd be our father paid for things, brought presents. "No obligation," they often said. I have never felt a sense of obligation to anyone.

All those dads disappeared when she died.

Years after Dad died, one night during a commercial break, I asked Mum if she'd known that Dad was dead as soon as those cops walked in the door.

Because it struck me later, when I thought about one thing leading to another, that she was pale and horrified and crying before the cops told us the news. And almost relieved afterwards.

"Did you know, Mum?"

"What do you know?" she said, sharp and nasty.

"I didn't know anything. I was only nine."

"But what do you know now?"

"Nothing. But I'm not talking about that. I'm talking about when Dad died. Did you know he was dead before they told us?"

"Of course not. How could I have known that?"

The commercials finished, and so did the conversation…

My house was full of dour-faced people. I didn't like them there, touching my things, leaving their finger-prints in my dust. I stood one step behind Peter, ignored.

Peter reached back without averting his gaze from the man giving condolences and pulled me to his side. He put one hand on my shoulder and offered the other to the man to shake.

It was the only time I ever felt his strength as an older brother and I believed he loved me.

It made me sad that Peter was being so kind. It reminded me of Dad's death, when Mum, Peter and I closed in on ourselves, forming a shell, because we were so damaged by being public property after his public death.

We were nice to each other then. I can remember that clearly. Peter was in his element, being kind and helpful, squeaking out advice about how to deal with things. The weird thing is, people listened. Crap which made me snort in disgust had the rest of them agape.

The people in my house cheered up. They drank Dad's wine and vodka, picked things up and looked at them. They forgot I was there.

Mr Krowska from next door spent a while upstairs, doing what I don't know. I counted all the cash I kept stashed about the place, and there was none missing, and my jewellery was untouched, but there was a dent in the middle of the duvet in the spare room, the one which used to be Peter's.

The weirdo had a snooze. He came downstairs, grabbed his wife, and left without saying goodbye.

That night there was a towel strung across their bedroom window. I couldn't see a thing. That was a shame. I liked laying in Peter's old bed to watch the Krowskas fight or make up. It was a nice bed-time story.

I asked some of the neighbours about who owned the house before us. "Who used to live here?" I kept asking. But nobody knew.

Someone had lined up all the cards we'd received. There were dozens. Even some of my teachers had sent cards. But they don't show up, do they? Cook my dinner, do my shopping? So what's the point?

It was my first memorial, so I didn't know what people did. Melissa was there, from next door.

"Haven't you moved?" I said.

She nodded. "I came back for this," she said. She stood there, shaking like a rabbit. I think she wanted to hug me, make me feel better.

I just wanted them all out of my house.

I lost interest in the people in my home, so, with the night lit by a huge moon, I went and sat amongst my work in the backyard. My Dad had loved the backyard at night; I had often seen him out there digging.

Maria came up and whispered, "You better get back inside. All of this is for you, you know. Because you missed the funeral. Don't you think you should be there?"

"No," I said. But I went inside and let Auntie Jessie tell me stories about my parents' lives. This was one of my favourites:

They made a good family, Alex and Heather Searle and Mike and Ruth Walker. They were a set, and great friends before the kids came along. Dinner at all sorts of mad places, like the Russian restaurant where you drank vodka straight from the bottle. They joined a bowling club where the other patrons stared and envied them their youth. And Ruth would laugh and touch Alex's thigh, tell Heather in the toilets there was nothing to worry about, when the very words were meant to create worry. Heather had never envied her older sister, not for her beauty, her wit, her liveliness.

Heather had always possessed the knowledge that she needn't be the best. It was a comfort.

For Heather's sake, Alex was patient with Ruth's antics, though he found the gossip, the laughter, more irritating that he could express, and he pitied her husband Mike, though by all accounts they enjoyed a full and adventurous sex life.

On one occasion Ruth paid Alex a visit at work.

"I want to report a crime," she told the desk sergeant, "but I'm too nervous to deal with anyone but my brother-in-law." She didn't look nervous.

Her lipstick was red and perfect, her eyes unblinking. Her hair was in place. She wore a skirt suit in a masculine cut, and she leaned one elbow on the desk as if preparing to give orders.

"Your sister-in-law's here to report a crime," the desk sergeant said into the phone.

"He knows about it," Ruth whispered, leaning in.

"She says you know about it." There was a pause, then the desk sergeant hung up.

"He'll be with you in a minute. Just take a seat."

Ruth did so, crossing her legs to display them to him. She smiled; he smiled back, glad of the excuse.

Alex had said to him, "Tell her she should have fucked the taxi driver on the way over."

Ruth did not drive; would not drive. She considered it menial, and preferred other people to do it for her.

"So, what crime are we talking about, here?"

Alex said. He didn't offer her a cup of tea.

"Well, it hasn't actually happened yet, but I'm terrified. It's Mike." she paused, wanting Alex to nod, throw himself at the mercy of her passion.

"Mike?" he said.

"I think he's trying to kill me."

Alex took a sip of tea, rose from his chair, walked around the desk and leant so close he could see the pulse in her throat.

Around him, all was silent. An attractive woman in the squad room drew attention.

"Right," Alex said. "And your proof is?"

"It's just a feeling. He's jealous. I don't think he loves me anymore."

"I'm sure his feelings for you haven't changed,"

Alex said. "I'm sure he loves you as much now as he did the day you were married." He wondered how far he could go, how deluded she was. Mike had never loved her.

"Perhaps if you could talk to him," Ruth said. She leaned forward She had a handkerchief and dabbed at her eyes, as if wiping away tears. There were no tears there.

"Or better yet, come over when he's not there and make me feel better."

Alex could hear his colleagues sucking air.

"Heather and I could do that," he said. "Certainly.

Now can one of my fellow workers provide you with a lift home?"

Her eyes flickered over the eager parade.

"No, thank you," she said. "I can manage. As for you, you'll be sorry when I'm found dead."

"I don't think so. I doubt that," he said.

He never told Heather how Ruth liked to corner him. She had bared her breasts once, making them an offering she imagined he would fall upon.

"Cover yourself, Ruth," he said. He didn't like the way Ruth tried to undermine Heather's confidence, or the way she wanted their kids to like her best.

She had a family of her own. Alex thought her time would be better spent home with her own children and he told her so. She was insulted;

told Heather he had banished her from the home. Heather told Alex she would not have her own sister banished from her own home, and he drew her to him and squeezed her till she laughed.

"I didn't banish her. But we have our own family now. You are the children's mother. It's you they love."

Ruth didn't visit for a while. She said she had to work in her garden.

There were people in my kitchen. They no longer talked about Mum and Dad; they were gossiping, arguing, flirting.

We have this great ceiling in the kitchen; sometimes Peter and I used to lie on the floor and gaze up at the pipe work, traced it with our eyes, find letters and stories in the curves and bends. We dreamt about swinging on them. Peter waited until I did it once, when Dad was at work and Mum was talking to the neighbour over the fence. Then we both did it whenever they weren't home.

The people were still at my house at midnight. Is that what people do at other people's houses?

Maria had drunk so much wine her teeth were stained red, but she still put on her pose of being mature and in control.

Lee came through the door. He'd been at the pub; he'd told me he wasn't going to show up.

Their mum wouldn't let Tim come, even though he wanted to. Lee and I shared a good friendship. Neither of us expected or demanded anything. We weren't disappointed with rejection or overjoyed with acceptance; we just carried on. I like things that way. I like to be able to do things if they need doing, and not have people beholden to me. I hate it when people think they owe you something. Lee and I liked to go out to pubs, to sit quietly and drink. We never felt we had to talk to each other.

We had been going out for a couple of years, since his 16th birthday, when it was legal and we didn't have to worry about being caught.

Lee took one look at the scene in my house and said, "Let's go down the pub." Brilliant suggestion.

I didn't say a word to Peter, snuck out the back door. No one noticed.

The pub was full, rowdy, almost too much. At least no one knew me. No one would tell me how sorry they were. I watched Lee's face slacken and redden, watched the people around darken or lighten, depending on who they were. I liked using drunkenness as an excuse, too; you could get away with anything. Knocking people so their drinks spilled everywhere, stepping on people's toes.

I was coming back from the toilets and there was this tall, blonde man standing alone at the bar. I fell against him, he grabbed me. I reached up and kissed him. A big, sweet bourbon kiss.

Lee saw it, but he wasn't confident enough to come over and make a claim. That wasn't my aim; I didn't want him jealous. All I wanted was the feel of this big man.

He was there alone; that was the two sentences of conversation we had.

"Are you alone?" I said.

"Are you?" he said. I nodded. He took my hand and we left. My house, people gone. He was gone in an hour, maybe two.

The next morning I went out and uncovered more treasures. I found a damaged glass cufflink, a pair of half-rotted Spiderman underpants, a bath plug and a tiny silver spoon. I was inside washing the things in the laundry sink when I got a phone call from a local department store. Tim had been caught shoplifting, and he told them I was his sister. I guessed he didn't want his parents there to ream him out so I went along with it. I caught the bus to the store, put up a good case; the police hadn't been called, so I knew we were dealing with a bit of a softie. I said how good Tim usually was, for an eleven year-old, how Dad had lost his job and we were struggling. I said it was Mum's birthday soon and Tim was probably stealing for that.

"She has odd taste in music, then," said the manager. He fanned out some rough stuff.

"Oh, Tim," I said. "You shouldn't pinch stuff for me." We gave each other a big hug. I tried to fake crying but couldn't; in retrospect that was probably a good thing. Less is more, they say.

I offered to pay for the CDs but the manager wouldn't hear of it. "I hope your Dad gets back on his feet soon," he said, and that saddened me, because my Dad was dead and would never be at work.

We went home on two buses. Tim said, "Where's the lecture?" but I had no idea what he was talking about. "Oh, yeah, that's really something I'm into,"

I said. I grinned at him. "Listen, don't worry about it. It's just another event in the rich vat of life." It made me feel quite sad, though, talking about Mum's birthday and knowing she'd never have another. I was in the mood for a celebration. For her birthday one year Peter and I put on a special show.

"The Elopement of Mum and Dad." We only did it once. Mum got too upset.

We both put on as many of our clothes as we could, and waddled down the stairs. We all laughed so much we didn't get started for about half an hour, and Peter and I kept cracking up, having to stop the show.

Mum stopped laughing and didn't start again. We didn't realise till the end how upset she was. I actually didn't realise at all; I was totally excited by my acting.

I danced around the room, throwing gear off, trying to cover every object in the room with an item of clothing.

"Stop it, Stevie," Peter said. He had his arms around Mum.

"Why?"

"Mum's upset."

"No, she's not, she loves it, don't you Mum?" and I went to dance in the backyard.

At Twenty

I don't know if I had the shortest career a checkout chick ever had, but I must have come close. Three weeks and two days into it, I knocked a mountain of spaghetti cans flying for the third time. I had already smashed the plate-glass near the information booth when a trolley went out of my control, and when marching proudly out in my uniform I had fallen over and cut my lip, splashing blood all up aisle seven.

The manager was very controlled. Her assistant hissed at me, "You fucking clumsy idiot fucking loser." But Mrs Gibbs said, "Stephanie, I'm afraid we feel that someone as accident-prone as you is not quite suitable to this kind of work."

"I don't do it on purpose. You can't discriminate against someone because accidents follow them around. My Dad always calls me accident-inclined,"

I said. Mrs Gibbs smiled. "I like that. Your Dad must be a lovely man."

"Oh, yes, he is," I said. He was. When I think about it now, I'm not so sure he was being kindly.

Accident-inclined, I'm inclined to do it, I do it on purpose. I'd been saying it for years, proud of it, proof of how much my Dad loved me. But what was he saying? I did it on purpose, to get attention or something? That I'm a victim of Munchausen's?

I didn't discuss that with my counsellor. She's got no more room to list the syndromes she's matching to me.

Mrs Gibbs said, "To be honest, Stephanie, I don't think you are suited for other reasons." I wasn't going to jump in and guess what reasons she had in mind. She went slightly red in the face as the silence continued.

"Well, for example, there was that woman you accosted."

I told Mrs Gibbs how ridiculous that was. The bloody woman hit me in the back of the ankles with her trolley to get my attention, then she says,

"Young lady, I have been looking for three hours for the tinned asparagus. Is it asking too much that it be placed in a less than hidden position?"

"I tell you what's asking too much," I told the woman. "You expecting me to believe you've been here three hours, but you've got a wet raincoat on, and it only started raining thirty minutes ago. I know that for a fact. It was sunny before that, that's why we're understaffed, people always stay home on the good days. And I'm guessing, from the look of your cheap shoes, that you're looking for the no-name asparagus that we got in from Asia. Because the good stuff, the local stuff, is out for all to see. We don't have the cheap stuff anymore. There were reports of tetanus."

"I beg your pardon," she said. Her shoulders were pulled back and her neck swayed.

"Will that be all, Mrs Adder?" I said. I giggled about that one all the way home.

Mrs Gibbs said, "Unfortunately, she was some sort of something high up in the public service, and she kicked up a bit of a fuss."

"If she's that high up, why's she such a tight arse? Her arse is so tight she needs a straw to shit through."

Mrs Gibbs found me funny. She liked the fact I was rude and cheeky; she got too many crawlers.

She spluttered. "God, you're awful, Steve," she said. I smiled and shook her hand.

"It's a fair cop. I'll go quiet," I said. One of those stupid lines you pick up in your life. I had an immediate fantasy; Mrs Gibbs asked me out for lunch, a farewell lunch, and when I got there the whole staff had turned up. Crying because I was leaving, giving me personal little presents, each with a private story I'd think of every time I looked at them.

That's what should have happened. This is what did happen; I got changed into my street clothes, walked out. Said, "Bye, Luke," to one of the guys.

He said, "Yeah, see ya, mate," and I was gone.

I didn't want to find another job. I hated the process; dressing up, getting your hair just right, wearing pantyhose, all the pretence which makes them love you.

I could have left, then. Moved overseas, gone to another state. But there were the bones. I was trapped.

I went home after getting the sack and started to dig in my backyard. I thought, "More jasmine. I'll dig further up the back, plant more jasmine."

I found the bones on the fourth day of digging. I dug up my backyard with the intention of planting a sea of jasmine but found bones, instead, and relics. Remnants, reminders, mementoes and rubbish. I hadn't planned to dig so deep.

I was out there early in the day, feeling the sun move across my body, sweating, breathing that dust smell, and I didn't have any music blaring to destroy my concentration. My train of thought. The yard proved a goldmine of memories. I piled all the things by the back door, until it began to look like a child's stall at a make-believe market. I found chicken bones bitten white and some slightly larger; then I found bones too big for us to have tossed there as meat detritus. I found bones in a shoebox with "MUFFY" written on it. Snails had eaten most of the letters. She never did dig her way out of the cave, where Mum told me she'd gone. I left her in the shoe box and buried her again. I had my own special service. I loved that cat. I tried to say the right things but I'd never heard them said before.

Somehow I'd missed all the family funerals.

I kept digging, and I began to pile the bones by the tree in the middle of the yard. It didn't occur to me to stop. For three more days I dug and discovered bones. Two hundred and twenty-three that week.

There were more the next week.

There are clumps of old jasmine left still, a legacy from my grandparents, and I remember it as a smell from childhood; I can close my eyes when it is in bloom and still picture the backyard clearly. I can close my eyes at the end of the street, stumble along blindly, and still know where to turn into my place.

The rest of the street had carefully groomed roses.

I can smell jasmine everywhere, even in the smell factory that's the kitchen.

While my bedroom was often warmer, being right over the kitchen, it often filled with secondhand cooking smells. Something happens to the smell of food when it travels away from the source; it becomes sickening, rancid. When you're in a fish and chip shop the smell is wonderful, hot fat, vine-gar, sea smell of the fish. Three steps away and you wonder why anyone would eat there.

It made me feel sick, early in the morning, or late at night, when Dad would cook up some fatty feast.

I'd have to breathe through my pillow and that didn't work, so I'd poke my head out the window and suck in the jasmine in the backyard, if it was in bloom.

When I'm on my own in the place I can be surprised by smells. I cook cheese on toast downstairs and by the time I go to bed, hours later, my room smells like curdled milk and a house burnt down.

And the jasmine saves me again.

I was digging down deep to find things, it was dark, but always the jasmine led me back to the surface with a scent trail.

I found a piece of coal carved into a panther and a scissor blade. I could smell the shit pile when the wind blew right, but it was the smell of home.

Peter called to ask me to the movies, but the movie was crap so we walked out. We tried to get into another movie, get our money back. The woman behind the desk said, "The show is sold out."

"What show?" I said.

The woman had not left her seat. She preferred to keep her seat. Her eyes were squinting because her hair was pulled into such a tight bun. "The show now playing. You won't be able to see it."

She seemed pleased by this; as if I had offended her and she wanted me to be punished.

It was astonishing how much she hated me.

Peter had been quieter than usual, and I'm not the type to fill in the gaps, so neither of us spoke.

We went and had a beer, then Peter said, "So what happened at the supermarket?"

I rolled my eyes and punched him. "Is that what's been bothering you? My job? It was crap, I hated it, they sacked me. That's what happened."

He pinched my cheek. "I'm not having a go, Steve. It's just that I've got this new idea, and I'm wondering if you could help me set it up."

Turns out he wanted to use his skills at telling people what to do and start running self-motivational courses. Though how they can be called 'self' motivational, when you're paying someone else to motivate you, is beyond me. I would be helping with the boring stuff—mail outs, listing names, all the stuff Maria couldn't be arsed to do.

She used her pregnancy as an excuse, as she'd use motherhood as an excuse once the baby arrived.

It sounded okay, and better than working in an office.

"It sounds okay," I said.

I found a curtain ring and a bead I recognised from Grampa Searle's well-used abacus.

My Grampa Searle was always a quiet one. He never lost his love for figures and sat like an addict adding up anything.

"Did you know that if you bought every sale item on this page you'd be up for $4,281.85?" he said.

There was no response; there rarely was to his announcements. He tried to make me and Peter add and subtract.

"Start with 400. Add 80. Subtract this. Multiply by that."

We stared at him, and my Dad said, "Leave them alone, Dad. They're not interested. Steve's not even at school yet." Grampa Searle always went quiet when his son spoke. My mum was impressed by it at first, thinking it showed respect. She thought the dad looked up to the son. I always liked Grampa Searle when he wasn't testing me with maths. He gave me private winks, like we shared a secret which didn't need to be discussed. He was the most gentle man I ever knew. For my fifth birthday he gave me an abacus of my own.

My fifth birthday was the greatest. The Grannies were there, with presents, and Peter swore at Dad in the morning—he said damn, but he said it rudely, tried to make Dad look silly. He got in so much trouble. Then he was quiet for the rest of the day. I laughed at him. He said, "You'll get a belting one day, then see how you like it," but Dad didn't give beltings.

He didn't tan your hide.

I wore my favourite trousers. Mum had presented me with my first dress, a cornflower blue thing with yellow lace. I hid it in my pillowcase and they couldn't find it, so I got to wear my trousers.

And a jumper one of the Grannies knitted for Peter; he hated it. The pattern on the front was supposed to be a teddy bear asleep in bed; Peter screamed, said, "He's dead, he's dead." He knew more about death than me. He had been at the funeral in the backyard of our little cat, Muffy, who had gone to live in a cave, I was told. I knew she was gone; I couldn't understand where to. I watched from my bedroom as Dad dug the hole and then put the cat in. Peter said some words. After Peter stopped talking they all came inside and we had ice cream with chocolate sprinkles. The whole Muffy episode made death mysterious, fascinating, some magical thing.

I always expected little Muffy the cat to appear once she'd dug her way out of the dirt. We never got another cat, or animal of any kind. Once I lived alone I thought about going to a pet shop and bringing a new cat home, but was concerned the creature wouldn't like me.

I forgot about Muffy until I saw a white cat on Play School. It must have been a few months later.

Around my birthday.

"When's Muffy coming out of the cave?" I said to Mum.

"Who?" She had forgotten the cat ever existed. I think she had that ability; things, people, vanished when they died. She wiped them from her memory so she didn't have to suffer. This helped me to understand all the fathers Mum bought home. The boyfriends, uncles. She wasn't being disloyal to Dad; she had simply forgotten him. She could have as many lovers as she wanted

I wanted to tell Peter but he was busy and didn't deserve to hear.

Peter gave me the jumper. I loved the teddy on it; he never woke up to yell and always stayed the same. And even at five I knew this would happen;

"Peter! Isn't that the jumper I knitted you? Didn't you like it?" said Granny Walker. It was a great jumper.

We had bowls and bowls of potato chips, nothing else at my fifth birthday party, though I think the adults ate sandwiches in the kitchen where I couldn't see.

Auntie Jessie was there; we told jokes on the front step. She wouldn't come out to see my roads in the backyard; she would never go into the backyard. All the kids in the street were there, although I hated them. The little weak girl from next door, Melissa, and a little girl with red hair and pink ribbons who I only remember because she hit me for taking the last cake.

I had four more birthdays like that, and then Dad was killed. Birthdays weren't the same, after that.

On my eleventh birthday Eve gave me jewellery for the first time, and I found a new jumper folded by the swings. It was a black jumper, a colour much sought-after but often forbidden.

"Black is nice, though," I said to my mother. "The fairies left it as a birthday present."

"You had your birthday presents," Mum said, but I hadn't. All I had was my first present from Eve.

Mum lost track of time after Dad died. She didn't remember things.

"Anyway, it isn't a school colour," she said. She wore the softest colours, pale pink, mauve, baby blue. She thought it made her look younger. And after a year in mourning she would never wear black again.

I wore my new black jumper to bed, to school, at home. It became encrusted, stiff with filth, but I would not let Mum wash it. Then, a month or so after I found the jumper, I tired of it. The boy who had left it in the park had already been punished for his loss, and did not want the ruined gift back. I didn't want it anymore. I was done with it. I left it where I had found it. It became a football, and a soak for blood, and a pirate flag. It stayed in the playground for two years, part of the playground equipment, unrecognised and left alone by adults.

After my Dad died, Grampa Searle changed. He was lighter, and he'd lost his fear. Dad used to tease him, make taunts about his quiet life. His boring life. Mum would get mad, because her dad was dead, but my dad had never concealed his disinterest in Grampa's life. When my Dad died, Grampa became silly, he laughed a lot, talked and joked and everybody else loved him too.

I had the fantasy that we were not popular in the suburb we lived in, which is why the families refused to come to our birthday parties. The other children in the street avoided us. Peter and I played together most often at school, and would fight anybody who wanted the exercise. That's what should have happened.

This is what did happen:

I played alone, elaborate fantasies, while Peter excelled at football. He had friends all over the place. We weren't friends. We rarely spoke, had nothing to say to each other. Peter, Mum and I sat at the table for every meal, but when we learned to read we brought books to the table and Mum allowed it, bringing her own magazine or book. Never the newspaper—she didn't want to know the news. My dad was the news bringer. He read it to her, analysed it, told her the opinion she should hold. With him gone she did not feel she had the filter necessary for the news. After he died, she never read it again. Peter and I did not bring newspapers into the home; newspapers were not read.

It was months later Mum asked where the black jumper was.

"I gave it to a poor kid," I told her.

She nodded. "That's good. We don't like black around the house," she said. She cut large pieces of the meat pie she had spent the day cooking, and watched us pick out the mushrooms and eat the rest. I heard her say to Auntie Ruth, "I doubt if they've ever tasted mushrooms, but they saw their father always quietly leave the mushrooms aside."

My dad never criticised her food. When she gave him mushrooms, and she did it every few weeks, he never asked why she persisted in giving him the fungus he despised.

"They used to grow in the hole we called a bathroom," he told her. "More than once, when Dad wasn't working and we had no food, we ate those mushrooms. I really don't want to see them again."

But she couldn't help it. Maybe it was a small power she had over him, because the struggle for power was definite if subtle. Now we put our mushrooms aside. "Eat your mushrooms," Mum said.

"Mushrooms grow in the shower," I said. I realise now Dad was probably lying about eating mushrooms out of the shower. Mum loved them.

Dad commented often on Mum's cooking, making sure Peter and I were aware of how lucky we were, when delicious dishes arrived on the table.

Mealtimes were always pleasant, because we enjoyed food. We loved good food; I continue to enjoy bad food as well. Dad told us terrible stories about his mother's cooking; how she made fried sandwiches using rancid lard, how her jelly never set, how her casseroles were soups and her soups stews.

When the family went to visit Granny Searle, sometimes we got the giggles just thinking about it.

Dad loved it the most, and that always made me happy. Dad trained me to ask, "Excuse me, Granny, what's for lunch?" and my tiny child's voice being so rude cracked them up every time.

Granny Searle knew what the joke was, and she provided lots of shop-bought goodies; pies and sweets, bread, all things nice. We liked going to Granny Searle's the best, because everything she had was bought. She didn't even make her own custard or scones.

She sang to us, sat us on her knee and sang her beautiful songs. We sat there, rich with shop food, and our Granny gave us shivers of pleasure with her songs. Our Mum tapped her foot, danced sometimes, smiled. Our Dad sat across the room and stared, fingers steepled. Every song he said, "That's enough, Mum," but it never was.

Peter and I never gave ourselves to it completely.

She was old and she smelt funny. We watched our Dad. We fought on Granny's knee. "You're too big to sit there anyway," our Dad said, and we waited until it was time to go home. I sometimes wondered who did the belting in that house; Granny and Grampa Searle both seemed so weak. Granny had a flat hard hand, though, and her eyes could go mean and scary if she wasn't happy.

Sometimes Mum, Peter and I would stay with one of the Grannies for a holiday. Dad didn't come with us, and we didn't stay away for long. A weekend, usually, so we didn't miss a minute of school.

Not that it made any difference; Peter would get As and I would get

Cs no matter how many hours we spent at school. I liked to pack my own suitcase.

Once Peter gave me the bear jumper, the granny knit, I packed that.

Mum said, "Good thinking, it can get chilly on the beach," when she saw my jumper. She didn't know I only had Dad's spare uniform in my little case. Peter immediately ran upstairs to get a granny-knit, of which he had hundreds and I had only one.

"Stevie ruins clothes so," Granny Searle said once, as if that explained why they never knitted for me.

One thing no one ever explained to me was why Dad didn't come with us. Shift work wasn't the reason; he didn't work when we were away. I knew because of the clothes in the dirty clothes basket.

No uniforms. Sometimes a going-out suit, or muddy, sloppy clothes, sometimes just pyjamas.

Mum and Dad always seemed happy to see each other after a short holiday.

We liked Grampa Searle, hated Grandpa Walker until he died when I was five, and Peter and I could never love the Grannies very much. They were too old. Their skin was loose and scary. They wore ugly clothes. They smiled with false teeth. I didn't mind the things they gave us, but I didn't care for them much. There must have been a time when they were younger, not so ugly, but we could not imagine it.

Peter did cruel mimicries of them, which Dad found hilarious but Mum didn't like.

"If it wasn't for them you wouldn't be here," Mum said.

"Yeah, we'd probably be rich," Peter said. He used to be naughty. Then he wasn't. I don't know what happened. One day I'll ask him.

As if.

I'd sit on Granny Searle's old knees, hearing her sing, but watching Dad, because there'd come a moment when he'd scratch his index finger on his knee. I'd leap off Granny, run across the room, throw myself at his chest. He'd hold me like a rope, all wound up, and I'd breathe in the smell of his throat.

"The usual path to destruction," he always said, because I always knocked over the high table, or stood on the cat, or something. That was the word he used; to. I remember it clearly. I wonder now. Why didn't he say path *of* destruction? Why path to? Oh, God, didn't I have a choice in anything?

Our two Grannies had been friends before our parents ever met; they got Mum and Dad together.

There was no jealousy between them; no competition. And when

Dad died, and Granny Searle grieved, Granny Walker was such a comfort the two could comfort Mum. To them we must have seemed shocked but unaware of the real implications of our father not being around.

They took over a lot of parenting roles. They even went to parent/teacher night so Mum wouldn't have to face it. Before, Dad did me and Mum did Peter. Dad never told me what the teachers said. He winked at me, "Good girl," and piggy-backed me around the house. Mum hated her children being assessed by strangers.

"How do they know what sort of boy Peter is?" she said one time to Dad. "They see him as a student and nothing more. They don't see him the way we do."

"What did they say?" Dad said. He stroked her hair to calm and comfort. He loved to touch her, stroke her. She was so very lucky. I didn't have hair like hers or else he would have stroked me too.

"She said he lacked courage," Mum said. She pulled Peter to her, squeezed him. "We know that's not true, don't we, Peter?" He nodded, but wasn't sure.

"He's weak," I said. "I can beat him up any time."

"Of course you can. You're the toughie of the family. You'll have to keep an eye out for Peter, protect him sometimes," Dad said. He was teasing me. I loved it. I threw my chest out, stamped around the room. "Who goes there?" I shouted.

"Who goes there?" I didn't know the meaning of the question; I had heard it shouted somewhere and liked the sound of it. I kicked an imaginary opponent.

"Stay away from my weak brother," I shouted.

Dad laughed and clapped. Mum laughed too, but she said, "Mustn't tease your brother."

The year Dad died, the Grannies were proud to head off to the school to talk about us. We stayed home with Mum and ate chocolate mousse for dinner. "This is the life," Mum said. Some people use clichés, nothing statements, when they want to be reassured, when they know something is wrong but they won't admit it. "It's nice, just us three," she said.

"I love it, just us three," Peter said. He sat with her on the couch. I can still summon the anger I felt, and the shock. They had forgotten.

"I wish Dad was here and you were both dead," I said. "I wish you were buried and dead."

"Stephanie!" Mum said. She was white. She always thought she was the favourite.

I had made a tactical error; I didn't need to be a grown up to see that. I had aligned myself with a dead parent. It seemed hysteria and guilt would help.

"I like Dad the best because you like Peter the best," I shouted, and ran up to my room. My last glimpse was of them looking like Siamese twins on the couch.

Mum came after me minutes later. She climbed into bed with me and squeezed me. She said a hundred times, "I love you, Stevie." But I knew she didn't mean it.

The Grannies came home while I was asleep, so Peter had the pleasure of giving me the news in the morning.

"You're in so much trouble, Stevie,"

"Am not."

"Am too. Granny Searle said the teacher said you were terrible. My teacher said I was clever and likeable."

"That's cos you give her all your lunch money."

"As if. Anyway, your teacher said there were concerns."

Neither of us were sure what concerns were.

They sounded like something neither of us wanted.

It was very quiet at breakfast. Usually the Grannies don't shut up. I heard how quiet it was and I decided to play in the park till school time.

Mum came and found me. We sat in the car while they talked about me. Mum said, "What do they know? How could they possibly know what my daughter is like?"

"But why didn't Alex say anything? Year after year. What was he thinking?" said Granny Walker.

"Perhaps he thought he was protecting her," said Mum. "From their nonsense."

"Who?" I said.

"Don't worry, darling. It'll be all right," Mum said. I hadn't thought there was anything wrong. I was strapped tightly in my seat, the belt cutting my circulation off. I wriggled and kicked Granny Searle's chair.

"Sit still, Stevie," Granny Walker said. She sat between Peter and me in the back seat. She slapped my leg; she loved to slap. I thrust my hands down the back of the seat, hoping to find a distraction.

"Money!" I said. I found five cents.

"Soldier!" I said. A plastic man with a big stick. It was what I needed.

"That's mine," Peter said.

"Mine now," and we fought across Granny Walker until we arrived at school. They never told me what the teacher said.

The Grannies were around a lot for the first couple of years after Dad died. I hated it; there were too many people telling me what to do. And they didn't like me, anyway. Peter was the one getting all the attention.

But we got all sorts of different food and there were three people to plead with, all softies, not strict like Dad. The Grannies helped Mum clean, they drove us to school, they told stories. I wanted them to leave. They smelt like baby powder, mothballs, shit.

One weekend it was just us and the Grannies.

Mum went away with one of the New Dads. Mum wouldn't take me, though I screamed. I cut up her best dress. I collected dog poo and put it in her shoes. But she left me behind with the Grannies.

They started by feeding me a lot, like you do with a vicious cat to slow it down. I ate so much I threw up; watching them mop the puddle made me feel better. We sat in the kitchen and I listened to them talk. That was an old butcher's block, with a sunken middle where they chopped, chopped, wearing the wood away with chopping and scrubbing. As a child, I imagined any dirt caught in the many deep scores was the blood of long-devoured creatures. I scraped it out with my knife and threatened to wipe it on Peter's arm. Chased him around the house and no one told me not to run with knives until Granny Walker came stomping down the stairs, and she was livid.

"You little savage," she called me. This was three days into their visit; I had vomited into her suitcase after finding her store of chocolate mints there, devouring the lot, then leaping about on her bed, because she'd brought her thick woollen throw and it felt delightful between clenched toes, and against your cheek.

I refused to eat the stew she cooked, giving Peter the excuse not to eat it either but I took all the blame. Granny Searle didn't eat it either; she spent so long calming things down it went cold. She said she'd heat it up later but she never did. It could even be still in the fridge. She brought me some potato soup, at midnight, and she explained about politeness and little white lies.

Granny Searle hugged me irrationally, squeezed me till I couldn't breathe. "I love you, Steve, and so does your mother." Peter came in and tried to tug Granny's arm away.

"Peter doesn't love me," I said. I stuck my tongue out at him. Granny pressed my face into her small, soft belly and I couldn't breathe. I tried to tell her; thumped my fists against her backside. She thought I was struggling against her love and she squeezed me all the harder.

Later I told Mum that Granny Searle had tried to strangle me.

"Peter loves you in a special boy's way," Granny Searle said. Years later, when I realised sex was not the glue which bound Peter and

Maria together, I called him a Special Boy.

"Peter's a real Special Boy, isn't he, Maria?"

"He is rather special, yes."

"And he loves you in that Special Boy's way."

"I guess so."

Peter called me a little savage sometimes, but I liked it. The Grannies talked about the new dad all weekend.

"So soon after Alex's death," Granny Walker said.

"Some women need release. It's like they've been let out of prison."

"But he was your son."

"I know. But he was her husband."

"I know." Peter and I shrugged. All we knew was that she had left us with two weak old ladies who only noticed what was right before their eyes. We stayed up half the night watching horror movies—my first ones, I'd say. We ate rubbish. We swore, words we'd only heard before. The Grannies lost their temper when we played stair races after the movie had finished, but their shouting didn't scare us.

The next day Granny Searle said, "We've got a few things to do today, so you just sit in the back seat and look at your books." They forgot how clever I was at noticing. That I was going to be a detective. I noticed these things.

They were so close, they even seemed to breathe together I thought married people held hands, and mothers and daughters. Not grannies. I told Peter and we watched them. They held hands a lot.

"Why are you holding hands? Girls don't do that," Peter said.

"We don't hold hands," Granny Searle said, a foolish lie, because now we knew it was supposed to be a secret.

They slept in Mum's room; I knew she hated that. Her room was private. When she came home I told her all my observations. She didn't mention it to the Grannies, not in my hearing or in Peter's, anyway, but we hardly saw the smelly old bags again. Not at our place, anyway.

I don't think either of them trusted me after that.

Maria insisted Peter keep my employment with them professional, so I had to go through an interview process. The other candidates were so desperate; I saw one guy waiting to go in with a side part. Who'd hire him? He didn't have a chance. So I got the job, of course. I think Maria was secretly hoping I'd fuck up and she'd have an excuse not to hire me. I ended up doing a lot more than Peter imagined I would. I helped him develop the shows (Maria called them lessons, but they were shows).

I knew his little tricks as well as he did. He liked to cook as he talked.

"Using your hands is so positive," he says. "Creating life, movement, energy. Whether you are silent or talk the roof off, sparks will fly."

I liked going off to buy my lunch every day; there were so many choices. I didn't get how you were supposed to be so grateful for people doing their jobs, though. In one sandwich shop, this guy with a straggly ponytail always left something out, cos I never said thank you.

I explored the city, finding my way. I hate to feel lost. I thought I had it made. I worked in an office, like a professional, I received a pay cheque, I lived alone but had enjoyed a live-in lover. I thought life was normal.

One part of the city I loved, because everybody else said it was the arsehole of the place. There were only two restaurants and one was condemned by everyone who ate there. There was one sorry bar, a place which no longer tried to seduce patrons. There had been an enthusiastic manager years ago who had theme nights, foreign beer, meals. It made no difference, and he was a painful man. He liked to talk to you, ask you about your weekend, and no one was happy with that. I stopped in there to have a beer quite often.

It was the perfect place to meet with Dougie Page.

To give me an idea where the bones might have come from in my backyard, I called the man dad had died to save. The man who'd been in our lives for a while after dad died. Who looked like becoming a new dad for a while. I called him to do the dirty work, to track down the antecedents of the property.

He walked into the pub, straight up to me and said, "Stevie, you look great. How's your Mum?"

He was very clean in a good suit, but his face was twisted wryly; he didn't take anything seriously.

I told him what I needed; he said it would be a simple matter to trace ownership. He didn't ask why I wanted to know, and I didn't take him home to show him my neat pile of bones.

We talked for a while, then he said, "You need to be sure about this. Sure you want to keep digging.

Most people would rather not know the truth."

He'd floored me, talking about digging. It took me a minute or two to realise he wasn't talking specifically about my backyard. He meant the past; what's gone.

"I want to know. I'm not afraid of it. I wish people had told me when I was younger."

He laughed. "Younger? How old are you now?"

"Twenty." I said.

He said, "I like your voice. It's very restful. I feel like you know something about the world." I realise now he was probably laughing at me; he would report my pathetic attempts at wisdom to his friends, who waited at another place, a restaurant I would not be invited to.

I said, "Maybe I do. I think I've had a near-death experience, but it was nothing like people say."

We shook hands. He left me there, in the bar, and I bought whisky and thought about what Dougie Page had seen in me. I had two more beers, drank them slowly, breathing in the smoke from a man's pipe. It was unusual to smell such a thing, and I watched him in the mirror. He smoked the pipe like he was reading a book; with that same intent.

There were only three other people in the bar, all alone, and they didn't complain about the pipe. It began to irritate me that he was allowed to smoke; it was such an intrusive thing. All of us were watching him; we were hypnotised by his action.

The barman smiled at me every time I looked at him. I don't know what he expected; I wasn't a certain sort of person just because I was in the bar alone. I wasn't what he thought I was.

I said, "Surely it's illegal for that man to stink up your place."

He looked at the pipe-smoker then smiled at me.

"He's not hurting anyone."

"He's hurting me." I blinked at him. "It makes my beer taste funny."

He walked to the man's table, watched by all. He leaned over, wiped the table, cleared the empty glasses away.

"Sorry, mate," he said. "You're going to have to put that out."

I don't know much about pipe-smoking but I know they're hard to keep alight. Auntie Jessie gave me an outdated *Guinness Book of World Records*, full of achievements, scribbles in the margins in faded grey lead, complex swirls I couldn't read. It said in there that the world record for keeping a pipe alight was less than two hours. This man had been smoking for an hour or so. He sighed as he tapped his pipe out and looked sharply at me. His eyebrows were a yellowed grey, as if his infernal smoking had dyed those overhanging arches.

I collected my things and left the bar.

It was cold. There would be a mist later on, and frost in the morning. I walked up the centre of the road, because it was deserted. Everyone was at home.

I didn't tell Dougie Page everything. I didn't say: I have to make the most of life now, because I know what's coming later. All that shit about the afterlife, those people who wait for you in the light, it's shit. What's waiting is a bunch of people who want revenge. That's what everyone sees. I have never seen the golden path, the sun-dappled air, the faces of people who love me. Anyone who says they do must be lying. There is no journey; I awaken in the place I am going, like a kidnap victim blindfolded until the prison is reached, so the escape route is lost. I am in the centre of a cold, damp room; I can feel mildew sinking into my lungs, though I can never remember breathing.

I've been there three times. Once, when the car crashed. Not long after, I was there briefly when my heart arrested in hospital.

And at seven, I nearly died. That's when I went to the room for the first time.

Even at seven I knew what the smell of death was, because of what Peter did when I was five.

I was already, at five, considered very tough at school, mostly because of the scar over my right eye from a terrible fight Peter and I had. It seems hard to believe, that a girl of three and a boy of five could have such a war.

I had been given a felt picture set by our kindly, childless Uncle Dom.

He gave us plenty of presents. I also had a wonderful happy face clock, which Mum kept high up in the kitchen because it had too many sharp edges.

That's why Dom gave me a soft felt set this time. Peter got a squishy car which didn't do anything except squish.

Dom was Dad's brother.

The felt set is long gone, though I found strands of it buried in the backyard.

He was our favourite uncle, and we were not supposed to see him.

I was playing with my felt picture set, seeing how many pieces of felt I could fit flat on the base. It was difficult work, because if I put a star in the wrong place, a triangle may not fit across the page. I believed that every piece should fit. Regardless of the number of times I am proven wrong, I continue to desire the pieces to fit.

It was minutes, at least, that I worked. I was left with too much blue space; nasty cracks, shapes, expanses which I wanted to cover. I remember clearly the disappointment I felt on seeing that blue space.

I raised my head from the board, preparing to shout for my mother. She would come and fix things, as we all imagine our mothers will do when we are very young.

Peter stood in the doorway.

I found out later he had been staring at me for minutes, standing in the doorway waiting for my attention to shift to him.

He gave me such a look my mouth was stopped.

He threw my happy face clock at me; it cut my skin but did not break. This was considered a miracle in some circles. The pain I felt, the stitches, the hospital, the fear, did not seem miraculous to me.

I could be proud of the scar, though. It made me scary for my first day at school. I had very short hair and my first teacher, Mrs Langdon, thought I was a boy and called me Steve. I made the most of it. Acted the bully, went to the boy's toilets, weed standing up. Glenn Guest had a good look once, and said, "You haven't got a willy," so I pissed on his feet.

My brother ruined his reputation by trying to boss me. It was my third week of school. That was a memorable week; I was finally allowed to have my own clay. I was the last child in class to receive mine, because you had to pass a test, and I had no memory for these things. You had to recite where you lived, your telephone number, and "I must not talk to strangers."

"What's a stranger?" Lisa Sargeant asked. She was the kid in class who asked questions. She was nudged throughout the day to ask when playtime was, could we do work outside today. I did not keep track of any of my school companions, because they meant so little to me, but I think if she had become a journalist I would have heard.

"A stranger is someone you don't know, don't love, aren't married to," the teacher said. I pinched Lisa Sargeant. "Ask her if she's married. Go on."

"Are you married?" Lisa said. The class tittered.

"Are you?" said the teacher. The whole class laughed at the idea of any of them being married.

When Greg Something went to a wedding a few weeks later, he took up the whole show-and-tell to describe the event.

"And my sister was called the bride and everyone thought I was so little and they smiled at me and said you were a late present and I said we gave our presents at home. I gave a card with shells on it.

They said No we meant oh it doesn't matter. And Robin-call-me-Rob was called the groom he had to wear a suit and a SCARF around his tummy."

Greg had brought wedding cake for us to look at and pass around. He didn't care what happened to it. He hated fruit cake. The pigs in class plucked candied fruit out and sucked on it. Whoever passed the cake to Lisa Sargeant said, "Here y'are, bride," and that remained her name throughout childhood.

The teacher told us a stranger was someone whose name you didn't know. I never forgot this.

As a child I asked people their names when they offered me lifts. Later in life I always introduced myself, and enjoyed seeing faces open up as if I was a friend now.

That's what should have happened.

When Peter came to find me in the playground, not long after I had told the teacher where I lived and received my clay, I was very happy. I had clay to mould and play with, I had streaks on my clothes and face.

I was eating my play lunch (a very nice homemade lemon biscuit. I can still conjure its fresh taste, feel the crumbs on my tongue) with clay fingers. Peter came from behind and knocked my biscuit away.

"Filthy girl," he said, "eating with dirty hands."

Luckily no one heard him call me a girl. I was not ready to be one just yet.

He dragged me to the taps, where he forced my hands, then my face under. As I spluttered, I heard voices, and knew half the school was watching.

I didn't know what death was. I was so well protected from grief. Our ginger cat Muffy had gone to visit its mother in a cave in our backyard and not returned, guinea pigs stiffly rested in their cages, fish were drinking from the top of the tank.

So when I coughed and spluttered, I felt no fear.

I didn't know I could die. I didn't know such a thing existed. There was a weird smell though. Not the playground or the school room. Not quite the toilets.

I was uncomfortable, and I couldn't breathe. I saw blackness, and stars. I still had my carton of milk.

Most kids didn't drink it; the crates of milk were left in the sun for an hour before distribution, so they were warm and smelled faintly of sick. If I didn't drink the milk I saved it in my desk. The day the teacher found it all there I got in trouble because she thought I had stolen the milk. She said, "We better share your loot around."

The milk smelt terrible when everyone opened the cartons.

I was famous throughout school for that one.

Brenda Green was sick in the hallway and they had to get the sawdust out and everyone had to go a different way to class. That's what she became famous for; we called her Brenda Green Face.

Cry Bobby cried because he wanted to drink his milk, and Neil got milk all over him as well. Belinda got a headache and had to go home.

I raised my arm over my shoulder and crushed my milk carton against Peter's head.

He let me go. The children laughed at him, beaten by a kid in kindergarten. His eyes were squeezed tight; I think there was milk in the corners.

"Aw, Steve," he said. He sounded weak, like he was not the boss any more. So I pushed him into the scary bush, where the spitfires sat and waited for victims.

Peter's best friend, a boy shorter than me, came to his aid and was splashed with the milk and pushed in the bush as well.

"Oh, Steve," he said.

"Oh, Darren," I said. By the end of the day they both stunk of milk.

Darren was one of those kids who never took their jumpers off. Why was that? He wasn't a particularly dirty child; even then I knew there was a difference between arriving dirty and getting dirty.

Your mum didn't clean right if you were dirty to begin with.

He would kick a ball around with the other kids, they'd slough off jumpers, undo shirts. He just kept running, redder and redder. He always reminded me of milk; he was pale and skinny. He looked like milk in a short glass; like Dad's favourite glass.

When Darren got hot he looked like strawberry milk.

Darren got in trouble at home that night—Peter told me. He got it for getting his jumper dirty. No big deal. Just wear your spare.

"I would if I had one, stupid," Darren said when I made my suggestion.

"Ooh, stir," I said, my arms miming the stirring of an enormous pot.

Peter dobbed when we got home, and got in trouble for not looking after me. "She started it," Peter said.

"I thought you were going to look after your little sister."

"She won't let me," he said, and that's always been the truth. I don't want his lectures, his hospitality, though a bit of his money wouldn't hurt. "I was trying to get her to wash her hands and stuff.

That's all."

They called Peter the Milky Bar Kid after that, even though none of us could afford chocolate. We knew the ad, though.

So I recognised the sensation of dying, without understanding it, two years later. I barely remember anything about being seven years old; I mostly remember just being eight one day, not seven any more, and people saying, "You're a grown-up now."

This I remember; I couldn't breath, I was in pain, but still I wasn't scared. I still wasn't up on death.

All I knew about my illness was what the adults had told me; consequently my memory of it is adult.

When I felt pain in my side, I ignored it. I told no one. I invented chants to keep my mind off it and waited for it to go away.

Then I was in agony and I couldn't hide it. Mrs Sammett moved slowly, unused to emergencies.

She assumed I was playing around. The other kids told me later she nudged me with her toe as I lay writhing on the floor.

"Get up, Steve," she said. The other kids said I drooled and wet my pants. They said I shit my pants and showed everyone what I had under there. The stories got more and more extreme until I said, "I remember exactly what happened."

I didn't, though; it was frustrating. The other kids never knew that, and they looked so guilty I wondered what they had done to my prone body.

No one would ever tell me. The teacher nearly confessed once, when she said, "I'm sorry for my part in it." The fact that I had seen most of them in a strange room when I was in hospital made me feel stronger than them. Mrs Sammett never believed a word I said. She tuned out. My favourite song was "What a fat we have in Jesus," or any other where I could say fat. Because she was fat.

Talcum powder got stuck in her folds. I got the feeling the class was mad at me for making them feel guilty.

This was the first of my special experiences. I didn't recognise it as such, then. I wasn't even aware I had almost died. My mother told me I had been asleep, that I had visited a lovely place. The place I visited wasn't lovely, though. It scared me; it remains the only thing I am scared of.

I was taken to hospital with a burst appendix, and I almost died. I did die for a while.

I heard clicking and smelt mothballs and these people leaned over me and I was only seven and I screamed.

I knew the room was very strange, because it was cold, and not well-lit. I was uncomfortable, something I still associate with death. I cannot bear discomfort. I never wear tight, revealing clothes or confining underwear. My hair is cut short so it doesn't itch or become heavy. I have one large, perfect armchair in my home. I pay for central heating because I do not like to be cold, and I do not store my clothes. If I am not going to wear them for a while, I throw them out.

I have no recollection of the fuss getting to the hospital, mother's tears, father's commanding voice, brother's white silence. These things I imagine easily.

When I woke up I was in the room.

I was naked and uncomfortable and cold. Peter was there and he stared at me. I tried to cover my parts but found my limbs sluggish and unwilling to follow orders.

The room smelt a bit like Granny's cupboards. It was mothballs; poison. They look like Kool Mints, a forbidden delight, a similarity my mother identified before I could taste the difference.

"This is poison. It kills moths and silverfish, so imagine what it can do to you. Even smelling it is dangerous, so you mustn't hide in Granny's cupboards."

And here I was, surrounded by the smell. I tried not to breathe, but felt my lungs filling. I began to choke; I did not want to be poisoned.

I heard a clicking noise and saw movement. Peter was not the only one in the room; there was a crowd of them moving to surround my bed.

Mum and Dad weren't there, or any of my friends except Lisa Sargeant. Some of the other kids from school were there, though. Cry Bobby and Belinda Green and Neil and that Darren.

There were little girls there; Melissa, that terrified, weak next door neighbour, and some red-haired girl with pink ribbons and a nurse with a very big nose. I recognised her uniform; I had been comforted by her sort before. I reached my arm out; stroke stroke. The hairs on it rose like there was a slight breeze but the air was so still I couldn't breathe.

"Get off," I said, but my mouth moved slowly, a dull roar, geroff, I said, like a cat learning to talk.

They let me sit up. All these faces. I saw my own face, but it was cracked, there were forty of me, all reflected in a huge, broken mirror, a doll's mirror grown up.

Glenn Guest was there, and Mrs Sammett, and the whole class, I was back at school in a play, where everyone had to be mean to me to teach me a lesson, but there was no toilet because they all pooed their pants, poo poo and I laughed but vomit came out.

"Little Savage," I heard, and Granny Searle was there, her hand on my cousin Nate's shoulder.

"Granny," I said, but she wasn't loving me. She scared me as she stepped closer, clicking, stepping, and there was something wrong with their mouths and I forced my limbs to work, curled into a ball to escape them.

The movement made me warmer. Then someone was stroking my hair and I screamed again but it was my mother and I was in a hospital room. It was warm and smelled clean, and, although people surrounded my bed I knew them all and they had normal mouths. When Granny Searle came I screamed and my voice wasn't a cat's. She had scared me the most in the room. Her eyes. Her hands, so cold. She held me down and her hands were warm, dry, familiar.

"Why did you poo your pants, Granny?" I said, and all my visitors laughed.

Peter told me I had nearly died of my appendix.

He said it with pure delight, and he told everyone at school. He thought it would make them hate me, but it turned me into a hero. Everyone wanted to know what it was like.

Peter denied all knowledge of the other room and I began to believe I had dreamt it. I asked Lisa Sargeant, too, and she scratched her arm and said no. I didn't ask anyone else. I decided I must have dreamt it.

I knew about dreams. They summoned Mum if they were bad and made you feel nice if they were good.

I stayed home from school for quite a while.

Mum was exhausted. "You'll have to look after us all, Alex," she said to my Dad.

I was allowed to sleep during the day since my appendix. I used up my days off, though. Mum was much stricter after that. I had one or two; the last one I remember was the day Dad died.

Mum came and got me up after Peter left for school one day.

"Come on, sleepy head. Lots to do." The day with Mum was nice. She was bright and lively, wanting to prove what a good life she had, I think.

She sat on my bed when I didn't leap up. She touched my forehead and smiled.

"Not too sick to help me with some baking?"

"Not really." She pulled back my covers.

"Mum! I can get myself up."

"Well, don't be long. These things are a matter of split-second timing."

We made biscuits, three different sorts out of one dough. I enjoyed it, because we sang and she told me stories about her and Dad. She made golden syrup dumplings.

Mum always made me pay in company when she let me stay home from school. Dad envied Mum this quiet time with us. He never got to do nothing with us. It was always something.

Mum liked to do girl things with me and I hated every minute of it. Cooking I still hate, though I'll do it in order to eat. That much makes sense.

Sewing, knitting, all that, cleaning, anything where you have to potter about achieving nothing you couldn't buy in the shops, or something you'll have to do again anyway. Peter's the one who's a good cook. His stove is set in grey marble in the centre of his small cream marble kitchen, and he stands there like a magician, performing even if there's no one to watch. I still spy on him to find out those sorts of things; people are so different when they're alone.

He creates stir fry without stirring, tosses the lot like a pancake. He makes soufflés, mousses with little surprises to make his guests gasp, soups with just one ingredient. He spends hours in the kitchen, and I must say the food is good. That's his gift from Mum.

Mum and I spent a pottering day. To tease me, she drove past the school every time we went out or came home, and laughed to see me tucked down in my seat.

We started making lunch, chicken drumsticks, it was, because it always was when I was home. Dad appeared in the doorway, looking perfect; hair in place, no cuts from shaving, his uniform crisp. I got off my stool and ran to him, because I loved the smell of his clean uniform. I hugged him, buried my nose in his tight belly. He stroked my hair.

"What's she doing home?"

"She's still sick." Mum didn't tell him I had wet the bed again. Dad thought I should be over that by age seven, though he wet the bed till eight, Granny Searle said.

"Sport today, is it?" he said to me. I wasn't big on playing sport. I preferred to be umpire. You didn't have to run as much and you got to be the boss.

I was never a popular choice as umpire. Too strict. One kid didn't talk to me for three years after I called him out at cricket. "It was off my pad," he told everyone who'd listen.

Dad ate his lunch, listening to Mum and I talk. I talked all I could, because he didn't often hear much from me. He didn't know my marks at school, who my friends were. He didn't know I was already a detective.

I knew, for instance, that he had gotten home two hours later than usual this morning after his shift; that there was blood on the uniform he had been wearing, and that he smelt like rum. These clues told me the story that he had been with a dead body yesterday, one of the bad, mean ones nobody wants to touch, and that he went drinking afterwards to forget. I knew that someone had given him a nice leather belt, one which he wore that day and then never again. One regret in my life is that I never told him. I was so scared of being a show-off I never told him my guess. It wouldn't have made him live longer, but he would have known I was a smart detective, not a little girl blobbing biscuit dough onto the tray. I think it was at that moment I decided I couldn't cook. I wouldn't cook. I wouldn't learn.

"I think he found a body last night," I told Mum.

"And he went to the pub afterwards."

"Is *that* it? I hope so," she said. At seven, I didn't know what she meant. Years later, I realised she thought Dad was having an affair. Dad left at three o'clock; he always did. Mum kissed him goodbye, then we went to pick up Peter from school, and for a treat we all went and had an ice cream by the river. It was often relaxed in the afternoons and evenings, just the three of us.

Grandpa Walker died a few months after I had my appendix out, but they wouldn't let me go, even though I was more grown up after being in hospital and nearly dying. I had a babysitter for three days and saw nothing. Peter came back with terrible stories of them putting Gramps in the ground and covering him up. He came to stay once a year, at Easter, and only then. He liked things ordered; liked his life planned. On the morning of his return to his own house, his bags would be sitting in the hallway at dawn. He always booked a morning bus, so Dad had to drive into town horribly tired after his shift, then drive home alone. Grandpa Walker never let Mum go, "You've seen more than enough of me," and she didn't ever stand up to him.

And then he died when I was seven.

I shudder now to think of how young Nadine, the babysitter was. Fourteen; it seemed so grown up to me at the time. She was very pretty, and knew about makeup already. She had a big bag full of it.

I still considered myself to be a boy. I was tough and felt no pain; the other kids tested me with pinches, tweaks and pins.

Nadine wanted me to be a girl. She trawled through my cupboards to find dresses and pretty lacy tops, and dressed me up, put all sorts of makeup on my face. Brown foundation, blue mascara, blue eyeliner, pink blusher, blue eyeshadow. I looked like a doll.

Nadine called her boyfriend Rick. He was quite old and smelled like Dad did when he came home from work. He wore a black T-shirt, jeans, he smoked cigarettes and let me taste what it was like.

He tickled her a lot and whispered in her ear. She kept saying, "No, no, not like that." He laughed.

I can see it very clearly, still. I sat on the floor and watched them, fascinated by the touching, the talking, the smell of them. She had her legs curled under her and he stroked her thigh, hid his hand under her skirt. She liked that. I liked watching it.

Her face was happy and so was his. He knew I was watching; he kept glancing over at me as he kissed her. He showed me his tongue. He took off his T-shirt and dropped it to the floor. I moved slowly, not wanting to disturb them, take their attention. I grasped his T-shirt and pulled it to me. It was warm, damp in places, and I tucked it into the diamond space formed by my entwined legs.

He kicked his shoes off with each foot, unbuttoned her blouse, hid his hands in there as well.

She didn't say no; she liked this. He rolled the shirt off her shoulders. She had some pimples on her chest and hardly any bosom. She wore a mauve bra. (A first bra, I discovered later. I got a training bra too, eventually, which I didn't like to wear. It cut into my shoulders and sat in pleats on my chest. The pleats made it clear I was not yet ready for a bra. The boys didn't even try to flick my bra strap until some girl in my PE class told them about my pale green number. Then they laughed. Called the Ironing Board.) But I didn't know what a bra was then. I didn't know about nipples or breasts, how they could change, harden, darken, as Nadine's did once her bra was off. I slipped my hand under my singlet and felt my nipples. They were soft, but I touched and touched and they formed little peaks I could roll between my fingers.

"No need to hurry" she said. "We've got three days." Those words sounded exciting.

I learnt a lot those three days. If I was quiet, she never knew I was there, but he always did. I still think of his face, have foolish fantasies of him landing on my doorstep. This is what should happen:

"Remember me?" He is only a few years older in my dream.

"Yes," I say. I invite him into the house I share with a friend.

"My housemate is away for three days," I say, and again we are both happy to hear those words.

Nadine was very sick after drinking Southern Comfort when they were at my place. He laughed at her and so did I. Neither of us would clean it up.

We let it dry on the walls and the floor, for her to scrape when she felt better.

He talked to me while she was asleep. We sat up at the kitchen table. He had a beer or two. I had green lemonade, glass after glass of it, and I didn't want to sleep.

He told me some wonderful things while Nadine was asleep.

He sat with his bare chest and hardly looked at me. I know he was just talking, that he loved to talk, but he was the first adult to tell me anything.

He told me about love, how some people fall in love over nothing, whereas others were careful, saved up the love.

I think he told me things he didn't say to anybody else. He told me to be one of the careful ones, because the only people who can really hurt you are the ones you love.

"Like her," he said. He didn't even point. I knew who he meant. "Just cos I fucked her she thinks it's love." Fucked was a good word. I thought it meant the whole lot, the kissing, holding of hands, the lot.

I got poor Pauly in trouble, later, when he kissed me after school.

"He fucked me," I told my mother proudly. I told my father too.

Nadine liked being fucked, mostly, but then she'd cry for no reason. She was kneeling on hands and knees and he was fucking her in the poo hole. She cried and cried.

"I said I wouldn't like it," she said.

"I like it," he said. They did it again later and she cried again.

He told me how to get into pubs, how to know what sort of person people were, how to get a seat, a drink, the last of anything. He told me how sexy a tattoo was and how guys liked girls who made a bit of noise. Not ones who cried. He went out to get junk food once. It was hamburgers and chips and it was the first junk food I'd eaten. It was so delicious, so salty it made me thirsty, and he bought me red lemonade. We didn't check if Nadine wanted any.

My mother called on the second evening. She was very sad, softly spoken, and didn't listen to me.

I said, "Is it OK if my friend drinks Daddy's whisky?" and she said, "Yes, of course, poor little thing, Grandpa's gone, isn't he. Won't be back."

She began to cry. My Dad took the phone from her and spoke kindly to me.

Dad said they would be home in the afternoon, and that we would go out for hamburgers. Peter, too, had been introduced to the wonders of fast food.

I gave the whisky to Rick. He had been getting bored. He was sick of her being sick, and I was only a little kid. He told me dirty jokes I didn't understand but never forgot, like the one about the prostitute who got more money from her customers because when she had their dicks in her mouth (surely not? Why would either party wish that? I did not ask him to explain) she said, or mumbled, if you do the joke properly,

"Gimme fifty bucks or I'll bite your cock off."

The men would give her the $50. Until one guy, who said, "You give me $50 or I'll piss down your throat."

"And that's where I got this," said Rick. He showed me a $50 note. I was very impressed. My collection was $4.50 in 20 and 10 cent pieces. I planned to buy a bike as soon as I could.

When I was old enough to understand the joke, when I was an adult, I discovered that there were some women who would have said, "Give me $1000 and I'll drink it."

"Have you ever played Dare, Steve?" Rick said.

"No," I said. I knew the older kids played it and were punished if they were caught. It was something fairly naughty, and the younger children never heard the details, so we couldn't copy. I had asked Peter once, but he knew nothing. I knew more than him.

"Dare is where I tell you to do something, and you have to do it, and then you tell me to do something and I have to do it. Some losers play Truth or Dare, where you have to tell the truth about something, but I could never see the point. I mean, how are they going to know if you're telling the truth? It's too easy," Rick told me.

He was the first adult who didn't tell me lying was a terrible thing. I realised, years later, to my advantage, that adults give you a lot of guilt about lying because they can only tell if you're doing it if you are guilty and shifty. Adults are better at lying because they have less guilt; a perfect liar is one who feels no guilt at all.

"Okay," I said. "You go first."

He laughed. "Game, aren't you?"

He drank some more whisky and I drank some more red lemonade.

Then he said, "You like watching us, don't you?" He shrugged his shoulder to indicate Nadine upstairs.

"It's different," I said.

"You could say that." He thought, looked at me.

"She feels really nice inside, soft and wet. I dare you to stick your finger inside her."

I was relieved. That was nothing; easy. I had been expecting to climb the roof, say something rude to Mrs Beattie the mean shopkeeper, or take my clothes off.

We walked the stairs slowly, making noisy giggles and he fell over once. His breath was whisky like Dad's, so I felt safe.

She was lying on my bed. There was still vomit everywhere. My room stank. She had a pink jumper on, and a wrap-around skirt. She had her legs tucked up and the skirt tucked all around, like she was in a cocoon.

"I dare you," he said.

I avoided the vomit on the floor and carefully tugged the skirt out from between her legs and the bed.

Bit by bit I revealed her flesh.

"Go on," he said. He was right behind me. I wasn't sure exactly what to do. I had watched carefully, but it was hard to see where he put his fingers.

She wasn't wearing underpants. All hers had been thrown out, unwearable, and mine were too small for her. Rick said he'd go out and buy more but he never did.

She had a bit of hair, down there, otherwise she looked just like me.

She was loose and floppy. He helped me turn her on to her back and he moved her legs so they were apart and her knees were bent to the ceiling.

"Go on," he said.

I kneeled on the bed beside her and got two fingers ready. I touched them to the hair and felt the split. I ran my fingers along the split until they came to the hole. It was hot there, and sticky. I didn't like it.

"Go on," he said.

I pushed my fingers inside, and it felt like a warm, muddy hole. I pulled my fingers out then put them in again. She groaned, opened her eyes, saw me.

"Stevie?" she said.

He put his hands on my shoulders and moved me away.

"One for the road, eh?" he said. He was very modest about his own body. I never got to see his penis. He fucked the babysitter again, wiped himself on her skirt, did his jeans up.

He went downstairs and got Dad's whisky, gave me $5 and left. I never got to Dare him which was lucky, really, because I couldn't think of anything.

Well, I would have liked to ask him to adopt me, but I would never ask that. In my later fantasies, I thought of plenty of things. I had many fantasies about Rick, although I never saw him again.

I didn't bother lying about what had occurred to my parents. I kept my own part of it fairly quiet, though, didn't mention the $5, bottles of lemonade, or my first foray into the adult game of Dare.

My parents took great pity on Nadine. It was apparent I was unharmed, so she did not deserve to die. She had to clean up the mess before she went home, and her mother was told. I was asked to describe the boyfriend, like he was a criminal, and I did it so badly no one would ever recognise him.

Nadine continued to mind me for a few years, bringing quiet, intelligent boyfriends over, who were kind to me and to her, but they did not excite me. Those three days were too much for her. She must have realised that sort of life was too fast. She was a babysitter, and would become a private nurse later on. She didn't live in nurse's quarters, didn't join the parties, the friendship, the support. She didn't like that stuff. She liked talking quietly, not drinking.

"I saw Gramps dropped in a hole in the ground,"

Peter muttered in my ear. "I had hamburgers, and fish and chips, and Chinese. I got to stay in a hotel and watch TV all night. I got cups of tea with three sugars. I got to go in Uncle Mike's car and he told me jokes. I got to have a sip of Daddy's beer. I got to get some new clothes and I still haven't eaten all the lollies I got given."

"Lucky you," I said. I would never tell him what I had done over the three days, no matter how he begged me.

That night we had one of our nice evenings, where everyone wanted to cheer everyone else up.

I did my doggy impersonation, woofing, growling, pretending to eat dog food. I didn't mention how I had seen Nadine in this position not forty-eight hours earlier.

Peter told jokes; he was always very good at that.

He loved to act the part if the words were there for him, and he made us all laugh with his clever mimicry.

Mum and Dad told the funny family stories.

When Peter was five and he wanted to be a fireman, so he built a fire and even lit it and when everyone came to look he put it out by hosing it with wee. And when I was only six months old and loved the nurse who came to help Mum. I loved her giant nose. I kept grabbing hold and not letting go.

"And it was such a huge nose," Mum said, "that no one ever dared mention it."

"It was huge!" said Dad.

And the time Mum and Dad had gone to the policeman's party and both got silly and on the way home they were singing to each other and they got arrested! They got taken to the police station Dad worked at!

"And the reason silly old McCarthy didn't recognise me, apart from the fact that he was too blind to be on the street anyway, only there because everyone else was at the party, was cos I was dressed as Jack the Ripper," Dad said.

I loved that night. And they told the story of my name. It was a good story.

"Little Stevie," Mum said. "Never had another name, have you?"

"No, Mum."

"Because your Mum believed all the superstitious fools that you were going to be a boy. No doubt about it," said Dad.

"No doubt about it," said Mum.

"But you're not a boy."

"No, you're not."

"But the whole time you were in your Mummy's tummy we wanted to talk to you."

"We did it for Peter, too. Little Pete."

"We talked to both of you. Morning, little Stevie," we'd say. And we asked your opinion on things—you chose the wallpaper in the lounge room, by the way—when you were still in Mummy's tummy."

"And by the time you were born..."

"And you were a girl, not a boy..."

"You were already Steve to us."

"Why didn't you just call me Stephen?" I said.

"People didn't do that then," Mum said.

That was the end of the story about me.

At Twenty-One

Dougie Page told me his findings two months before my 21st birth-day. He said, "You're going to be pleased with this news."

"What's that?" It'd been so long, I barely remembered asking him to find out who the house had originally belonged to. The bone pile was building up. "Well, ownership doesn't leave the Searle Family. The place is a hundred years old. Your great-great grandfather built it as a testament to family and God's love."

"Precisely those words?" I didn't like his mocking tone.

"Ooh, yeah. Made the news and all. Seems he used a bit of ground not up for grabs. Somewhere no one else considered building."

"Some sort of burial ground?"

He laughed. "You could say that. Nothing quite so romantic, though." He paused, wanting me to beg him.

"I'm not paying you by the hour, you know," I said.

"You're not paying me at all. It was a dumping ground. A tip. White settlers found it that way, all shellfish and bones, and used it until Old Daddy Searle thought he'd cover it with dirt and build on top of it. Sorry to disappoint you. I know it's not the answer you were looking for. You were looking for some kind of romance, some kind of message."

He stayed for a while, and we drank beer. He asked me about Dad, was curious about what sort of father he'd been.

"He was the best father anyone ever had," I said. "The only thing that makes me angry is that he left without saying goodbye. He went off and died, and I don't know why. I don't even know what happened. There's a great mystery about it, and you'd think I'd be able to figure it out, but I can't."

He said, "You haven't got the resources, Steve. That's all it is. Do you want me to look into it for you? I can do that. Expenses only, what d'ya say?"

What could I say? I took his offer.

I wrote Fuck you in invisible ink on the thank you note I sent him. What makes him think he knew what I was hoping for?

What the news meant about my backyard bones, I wasn't sure. There could have been visitors, couldn't there? People sleeping over and leaving bones behind?

Knowing this ground had always been ours made me more determined to uncover the secrets of the back yard, so when Samantha appeared at my door wanting to move in, it seemed like very bad timing. I couldn't dig if she was there, and I'd have to keep my finds hidden in the shed. Samantha came to our school in Year 9, the only new girl that year. Everyone liked her. She had messy hair when everyone else was fly-free. Her skirt was centimetres shorter than everyone else's, sparking a craze which froze our bums all winter.

Of everyone, she picked me. At first because I was the one who had a spare seat next to me, then because she liked all the things I said in class. We started a comic book together; she was an excellent drawer, and I wrote the jokes.

Peter was in Year 11, then, one of the big guys.

Samantha thought he was pretty cool; I had to tell her otherwise. Peter started hanging around with us, and his mates, too, and suddenly I was popular, because I hung out with Year 11 guys. Next year they would be Year 12 guys. Samantha and I made good jokes together, and she helped me put makeup on, though it brought me out in blotches, and she laughed when I was funny so the guys did too.

In class we always sat together unless we were separated, and even then we made jokes across the room. Other people wanted to sit next to me and I always turned them down.

I felt part of the world for the first time. And when we had our first fight, that clinched it. Girls came up to me wanting to know what she'd done and I told them, but I didn't go all out. I'd seen it a hundred times; you fight, you bitch, you get back together. If you bitched a lot, your friendship was damaged. If you only bitched about the fight, nothing was hurt.

I think she might have told a few of my secrets.

People had forgotten how my dad died; while most of them had been at primary school with me, it was a kids' memory. High school memory said I only had a Mum, but they didn't know why.

Samantha told them what had happened. I don't know why they thought they could be cruel about it; it had nothing to do with me. They called me "bullet-catcher", then "BC", for the rest of high school.

Samantha and I made up after every fight. I don't remember what a single one was about; they seemed to occur like a cyclone, a whirling mass which sucked me in and threw me out naked and bruised. I was not good at fighting like this; a good hard punch-up did it for me. Grudges and slights seemed foolish and dull. She was a good friend to have, though; always had great parties, I heard. Her mother threw her a surprise party once, invited everyone from school. I was very sick so I couldn't go, and that's what did happen. I couldn't stop shaking, vomiting. Mum tucked me into her bed and we read comics until the party was over.

Things were always fun. Science class was so dull Samantha and I talked all the way through. Ian Pope, who ended up a science teacher himself, tutt-tutted like an engine running down.

Things changed when I left school to work and she went on to finish close to the top. I didn't see her much; I was learning about the real world and she stuck to gossip about school and the assign-ments she had.

When she came knocking at my door a month before my twenty-first birthday, I hadn't seen her in three years. Not since Mum died.

She wanted to stay for a while, because her boyfriend Murray kicked her out and she couldn't stand to live with her mum. Her brother Perry was there, the loser. Her sister Meredith was respectable, like Peter. Meredith was a lawyer, lived on her own and, so Samantha and I said, paid men to fuck her.

We had a great few weeks living together. She didn't care about the mess and the place got worse.

The first weekend after Samantha moved in, I had plans. We'd get up early and go shopping together, buy household things, because she knew about that sort of stuff. We'd buy sandwiches and beers and have lunch on the front porch where everyone could see us. Then we'd do something else. The pile of shit out the front; we'd ignore it.

But the fucking bitch wouldn't get up till after one. I had to eat leftover pizza.

"Time to get up, Samantha," I said one Saturday.

It was 8.30 in the morning, a good sleep in. I was sick of waiting for her.

"Fuck off, Steve," she said, so I left her a bit longer. Ten o'clock I tried again, and eleven. At twelve I said *Fuck it*, and went out by myself. She was up when I got home at 1.30.

"Let's get one thing straight. I don't get woken up unless there's an important phone call, and it better be life or death," she said.

"Well, I won't be keeping quiet in my own house just because your sleep patterns are fucked."

"Yeah, well, just see if you can keep it down a bit, all right? Save the shouting for the afternoon."

"Morning's the best time for shouting," I said.

Fucked if I was going to change my habits for her.

Peter came round to visit three times while she was there, without Maria. He even ignored the fact that he hates this house. We sat around the kitchen table and laughed at old times. Sometimes it was things I hadn't been involved with; things I didn't remember hearing about.

So we had a good time, though she could have been more discriminating with her friends. I have never seen a more appalling bunch. She had them over for dinner, eight plus Samantha and me, then another showed up and took my place! I was left in the kitchen eating leftovers. I did some cooking as well; added spice to this and salt to that. Quite an imaginative cook.

"She lives here," I heard Samantha say. I can always rely on her to stick up for me.

Sometimes Samantha and I didn't flush after a shit. We farted all the time. We ate takeaway. We only had the two of us.

Then, after a month, right in the middle of a great midnight horror movie (I don't remember which) she said, "Look, Steve, I can't stay here any more. It's been great, but I really have to get back to some kind of normal life. I'm twenty-one years old."

So was I, as of midnight.

"You probably want to get back to normal too," she said.

I shrugged. "Yeah," I said. "Where are you going to live?"

"Murray said he forgave me for fucking that guy. Isn't that great?"

"Yeah, great," I said. I didn't know what to do.

We had been living the most normal life I'd ever lived over the last month.

I cleaned out Samantha's stinky room and found an empty diary of hers, no message for me.

I stashed it with my other precious things.

I stood by the house. I looked around me. What was it about this place that Dad had loved so much?

Why did he care if we left?

I called Lee. He hadn't been over while Samantha was there. I think she scared him. We went out dancing, and we drank a lot as well. He always liked me to keep him supplied with a bit of dope; said it benefited both of us.

I got a bit carried away on the dance floor; span him round and round and round then let go. He went flying into the wall, I crashed into a table full of drinks.

In the process I gashed the back of my hand, a most impressive blood bath. Lee panicked when he saw it splattered on his own clothes. "It's not your blood," I said. "You're not even hurt." He shrugged. He was hoping for an injury to justify his terror. He looked at me as if I was crazy, and he said, "I'll find my own way home."

Pathetic.

My Mum would never have forgotten my twenty-first birthday. Every year she'd have a huge cake, even when it was just the two of us. We'd play music loud and I'd run about, and it always felt like there were plenty of people there. That's what should have happened.

With Samantha gone, and Lee mad at me, and Mum dead, and Peter too busy to see me, this is what did happen:

Pills. Peter found me. It's so crazy, the way a floppy body can kill you. Take the pills, slip into a coma, your head drops. Your air is cut off. If you vomit you die on that, or you die because you can't get any air.

Or you fall down the stairs and break your leg.

———◆———

I awoke in the room, my limbs heavy. The clicking was louder this time. Crickets in summer, the hoardings at a home game.

Peter's was the first face I saw; he smoked, blowing the smoke into the air, never taking his eyes off me.

"Help me, Peter. Find me." Clinging to him was Darren, still there. It was very smoky. Everyone smoked, all the faces I knew and didn't know. I was being smoked, mummified while I was still alive.

Some guy with a pipe, *puff puff*, keeping it alight while I got drunk with my detective.

I couldn't breathe, his smoke was noxious.

And a woman with her hair in a bun so tight she… the woman from the theatre. How did she even remember me?

The room was crushed with people, click click and the smell of them. I looked for Samantha in the dark room, but she wasn't there. I meant nothing to her, then; I had no effect on her life.

My mouth was covered. I could taste dirty wool, the playground, it was the black jumper I'd taken for a gift when I was eleven. The boy twisted the arms around my neck.

Mr Meyerfeldt was there, glaring, but not his dog. Home eating my rubbish, I said, and I laughed, just a low chuckle, but they shrank with a hiss like vampires in the sunlight. I laughed again but it had to be real, not fearful.

The Krouskas were there, too, and that made me snarl, because I could not watch them fuck any more. Take it down, I snarled, the towel, so I can see, because he had a big dick and she loved it, give it to me baby. Next to them was Mrs Di Matteo, cheeks rouged like a corpse.

I had not yet tried to move. The smoke was so thick I thought perhaps they couldn't see me; though I could see them perfectly well, talking amongst themselves like old school friends.

I wriggled a finger and my whole arm lifted; I was as light as the smoke. I was smoking, but I wasn't. My body was still whole. I sat up and they came close.

A woman with a red scarf, and old woman with white hair, a girl in a green uniform, a guy with neat shoes, all paraded for me, twisting, turning, pretzels of blood and sinew then back to normal.

Mrs Adder, from when I was in the supermarket, a real snake's head, tongue, she sank her fangs into my ankle and I screamed, the pain. A bread knife sawing off my foot.

She slowly turned black. My blood was poison to her.

They danced around me, loyal subjects, a guy with a straggly ponytail, faces I didn't know, the newsagent guy, my boss, others from work whose existence I despised.

They danced and spun, the music was Ode to Joy, *Da da da da Da Da da da*, leaping and spinning, bowing to me. Samantha's friends were there, part of the worship, kissing me, dancing, spinning, loving.

Spitting.

Slicing.

Little holes in my legs. In my breasts. Maria was there leaping, naked, her pubic hair a neat triangle, dancing with Ray's girlfriend, the wonderful man who fixed my car, Ray, he wasn't there, but his girl-friend—sorry, fiancée—was, and she had no pubic hair at all, her flaps poking out like a cow's tongue.

There were people who walked like they had golden syrup on their soles but they came forward, and Mark was there, laughing at my scars, and Jason behind him. They all had rocks, and I curled to protect myself as the first one was launched, curled to give in but Peter found me.

Just like I asked him to.

I was brought back to life. They told me I had been in danger; that I had visitors and things to do. They told me about the events in the hospital, trying to make life interesting. But I had been in the room, mildew, shit and naphthalene, cold, and those faces peering over me. I had remembered the attention, forgotten the intention. I would not have gone back.

"Silly mistake," Peter told me in hospital. "Silly mistake."

Melissa was there, my old next-door neighbour.

"It's so lucky I was visiting Mum and Dad," she said. "Can you imagine if I wasn't? I wanted to see Steve. Mum said she was home, she was always home. But she didn't answer."

"It's all right," Peter said. "It's lucky you found her."

"I wasn't spying or anything. I was just worried. I worry about her, Peter."

"She's all right. It was just a silly mistake."

She found me. Not Peter.

I was not at my strongest. I quite liked being weak for a while; looked after, fed. But I didn't like to lie in bed with myself for too long. I resolved not to dig in the garden again. I didn't want to know any more what was in there.

I broke my resolution as soon as I could get a grip around the handle of a spade.

I also resolved not to slight anyone, ever. Unless I go back to the room I won't know how successful that resolution was.

Crutches leant against the foot of my bed for three days. They loomed over me. I could smell the wood of them, sweat, wood, dirt. It smelt like the floor of the gymnasium at school. It was a comforting smell. I recalled those moments of absolute solitude amongst the crowd, when for whatever reason—a dance step, a moment to wait while someone else performed, stretching exercises—I bent my head to the floor and let my forehead rest.

My nose touching as well. My arms around my head to create a small, dark room all my own, and that smell, that wood smell which never faded.

I reached out and drew the crutches to me. I had imagined the smell; it didn't exist. I struggled down the corridor, looking for a bit of sun to sit in. From behind, a squeal, and my knees were belted forward so I collapsed to the floor. For a moment, the small dark room, the floor, the smell of pine and plastic, then I raised my head. The child was away; its mother helped me up.

"I'm so sorry," she said. "Such energy. We're visiting my husband…

his father…just a minor accident but such a worry. We just can't keep an eye on them every second."

"You should," I said, but I smiled, because I did not want to be in this woman's dark room. She was a bruised thing; eyes black, arms yellow and purple.

Bandages here and there. I saw the scene clearly: a child goes wild in an angry household, a wife had enough of the beatings and whack with a…

"What did you hit him with?" I said.

"Pardon?" she said.

"Your husband. What did you whack him with?"

"Oh, no, he fell over," she said. I was not slighted; I had a feeling she would be going to her dark room very soon.

It came as a shock. I realised I had not considered being slighted by the child. It was the parents. So my parents; how many of mine did they have? How many of Peter's? How had we made them suffer?

What sort of dark room does my mother inhabit?

———————◆———————

It was nice for people to be concerned about me. I went back to my job and everyone smiled at me but no one spoke. I accused Peter of telling them my secrets and he said, "I don't talk about it." Neither did anyone else. It was like it never happened. I got a card from the Grannies: *Get well soon*, as if I'd been sick but all that would be fixed.

I slowly got my breath back. It took days, days. I couldn't move or eat; people fussed about me, keeping me away from the room.

I heard them saying, "Oh, the poor thing. The poor dear." But I didn't feel sorry for myself at all. I had learnt something; I had knowledge which made life worthwhile. I had never believed in the soul. I thought you died, then you rotted, the end. But I had seen my soul, I saw it in another place, and I knew I had a future. It made me shudder.

All I had to do was ensure my future was a better place than the one I had seen.

My counsellor said I need time to sort out my issues. Useless, really. But Peter gave me sick leave, plenty of it, and I dealt with my issues by digging in my backyard. I found more bones, a tarnished gold chain, a tie bar, a wooden spoon handle and a small glass ball, with inclusions.

Auntie Jessie was the only person who believed what I had done. Auntie Jessie paid for us to go away together, soon after I got out of the hospital. Just for a week. Sometimes the look in her eye was that of Granny Searle's when she squeezed me too tight: We *love* you, Stevie.

We took a house on the beach and we walked, talked. Auntie Jessie cooked wonderful food: lobster mornay, paella, seafood soups we ate from giant bowls.

"Your dad had such plain tastes," Auntie Jessie said, but I knew that was only with her. With us he was adventurous.

"We're pretending we're in Spain," I said. I'd walked to the shops and collected some foreign beers.

"There's nothing wrong with pretending," Auntie Jessie said. "I pretend all the time. I'm hardly ever settled in reality."

"Does that make you feel better?"

"Not when I'm settled in reality," she said. We played a game of Chinese Chequers and she cheated to let me win; pretended a vagueness she would never have. She told me stories about how Mum and Dad met, details I hadn't learned before.

She told me stories Dad had told her, strange stories, as if he lived in a fantasy world, too.

I told her about Eve, and about the dark room.

She held my hand and didn't let go until we got in the car to drive home.

She loved to drive. "I could never understand my sisters, not wanting to drive. At least your Mum learnt, drove when she had to. Poor old Mike; the times he was summoned from work to take Ruth to the hairdresser."

"She wants me to do it. Can't remember I still don't have my license. Hates me when I tell her to call a cab."

"What about Peter? Can't he help?"

"He lives too far away. And she thinks he's a bore, anyway. She says I make her laugh."

Auntie Jessie laid her hands around my face, drew me in, stared into my eyes as if she was trying to hypnotise me.

"See? See what you bring people? You are a delight, Stevie, don't forget it. What would your father say about all of this?"

I tried to picture Dad, but it was Mum's face I saw. Smiling at me, loving me. "What would Mum say?"

Auntie Jessie got some cigarettes. We liked to smoke together. It bridged the generation gap.

"One of the saddest things is loneliness," she said. "I should know. And it's not your fault; I'm not lonely when you're here. But it's just something missing. People are lonely for good reason, usually, even if they don't know what it is. There's something about people like me nobody likes."

"You're crazy," I said. If people didn't like Auntie Jessie, what did they think of me?

I don't think anyone at the office even knew I'd been gone. They were all distracted, and every client who booked in for a course, it seemed, had heard the news. Peter and Maria were getting married. It was like two perfect worlds meeting and creating a great veil of glory which rested on everybody.

I couldn't believe how excited they all were.

They kept saying, "So sad his mother isn't here to see it," never mentioning our father. And there were Maria's parents, of course. Much as I don't mind them, the few times I've met them, could they be a bit less obsessed by the whole thing?

Maria came to me and said, "Stevie, I know you had in your mind you might be a bridesmaid.

But I've got my sisters and the three girlfriends and they'd all be devastated if I didn't ask them."

Her three brothers had picked girlfriends who might as well be triplets. Honestly. Pretty little idiots who giggled and loved wearing pink. Her sisters were big lumpy things who'd look foul no matter what they wore.

"To be honest, if I had to stand next to those women I'd be dry retching the whole time, then no one would hear your wonderful vows," I said.

Maria blinked at me. Still struggling with what I consider a joke.

So on their wedding day, I showed up late and no one noticed. That was good. I sat on the groom's side, along with Peter's mates, Auntie Ruth, Auntie Jessie and even Uncle Dom, sitting up the back in baggy trousers, plucking at his pants as if… I don't know as if what.

I took a book to read and kept my head down the whole time. I hope people thought I was praying, but I doubt it. Afterwards, I didn't bother pushing through the throng to congratulate them. Who cared? Peter gave me a wink, but I thought, that's it? A wink? That's my part of your wedding?

The reception was fun, though. I drank the red wine; it was good stuff. One of Peter's more successful clients shouted it for them and it was very good. Easy to drink, didn't stain my teeth. Excellent. I danced around with the brothers, particularly Adrian, who, if he steps away from his family, can be shockingly rude and nasty. I like him.

When no one was looking, he pulled me outside for a smoke. We stood close, hiding around a corner, pressed up against the wall behind a bush. I could smell his aftershave, and his hair. I could smell his skin, warm and sexy, and I could see the little pulse in his neck.

I gently put my finger on it. He turned to me, bent his neck, and kissed me.

I usually hate being kissed. Hate the feeling of the tongue in my mouth. But this was different.

"Dump her," I said. "Get rid of her."

He screwed up his face. Fiddled with his fingers.

It came to me then that his girlfriend had an engagement ring on.

"You're fuckin' kidding," I said. "Dump her!"

"I can't. Her parents are going to give us a house."

I pushed him away. "I've got a house already."

I didn't get invited to his wedding.

At Twenty-Two

In my backyard, I found a cheap pig-skin wallet, a tie pin, a squash ball, a ball of foil and a rotted black ribbon.

The sort of people who attend Peter's courses…I bet they answer a personal ad or two. Losers. If they can't see through Peter, they'd never see through a fake personal ad.

Peter used his childhood experience with our see-saw as an analogy, a motivational tool for stirring people to action. He honed it over the years, though he never mentioned me. I don't know who people pictured on the other side of the see-saw. A best friend, uncle, cousin, a different kind of sibling perhaps. I think his analogy failed there; he should have talked about balance, how good comes with bad, work comes with rest, and these things occur because there is another person on the other side of the see-saw.

He said, on the rostrum, "I like to go up, not so much to go down. But even going down is good, because it is the push which helps us reach the top."

I'd do things so differently. I'd tell people they need to deal with history; make it real, or change it. He didn't agree. In his courses, The Searle Talks, he called them, he told people to let go of the past.

His clients disgusted me. They were weak, cowardly people running away from the things which made them the way they are.

Peter liked to have locked room sessions. They added an air of mystery and made the people feel brave: We are not afraid. The doors were never actually locked because of fire-safety regulations, and who was Peter to break those sorts of rules? He told me once that no one ever tried the doors. They all believed and trusted him absolutely.

Maria had asked me not to attend the courses any more. She thought

I was a distraction, that I upset people unnecessarily, but I said, "Maria, have you seen these people? They get upset if the bus comes three minutes late."

Anyway, my counsellor said I should go to the courses. To see the fruits of my labour, even though Maria can't accept I had anything to do with it.

I was locked (not locked) in amongst people who were scared of their past. I laughed at them then. I was fearless. Now I dream of having just one of them as a friend.

This is what should have happened:

The person sitting next to me and I became firm friends.

This is what did happen:

Peter started out by saying quietly, "Is there anyone here who has painful memories of a past they can do little about?"

One hand, then two, five, ten, then all of the fucking losers waved their arms.

"Yeah!" they said. Solidarity. That's what they thought they had. That's what Peter had given them.

He laughed. He was always good at faking a laugh.

He said, "Perhaps I should rephrase the question.

Who does *not* have painful memories of a past they can do little about?"

Silence. No hands. The whole audience laughed, smiled at each other. I had been tempted to confess to only happy memories, but Peter knew the things of my life.

He waited until they were quiet. He didn't shush them, raise his arms, anything.

"The operative part of my question is, 'can do little about'. I think you know why."

I was thinking, I didn't pay $500 to tell you your job.

He said, "Because you can't do anything about the things you can't do anything about."

There were a few laughs, but then a slide appeared with those very words.

They chanted, led by Peter: *"You can't do anything about the things you can't do anything about!"*

Their shoulders twitched; it was clear they wanted to dance.

Peter's face reddened and sweat dripped from his forehead.

They loved it, loved his passion. He raised his arms and the chanting faded.

He said, "You can't change it, let's scream it out, LET IT GO!"

They all screamed, howled, shouted. The thunder of it shook my bones.

I screamed the loudest, and Peter finally noticed me. He looked shocked, as if he was expecting me to ruin something. He leaned over and muttered to Maria, who looked up from her book. She found his seminars boring; she had heard them a hundred times.

She rose from her chair; I sat down to avoid her look.

They shouted out their shit, terrible stories. From behind me, a blackboard screech.

"I was eight. I was fat. My mother said I was too fat. She said I was too fat to go to school. She made me stay home. She fed me dry toast for one week. I didn't get thin. She tried to cut some fat off but I only bled. I bled until I was sick."

I tried to see the man talking. I guessed it was a man; it was hard to tell from the voice. They all had their mouths open, though. From the other side of the room, an orator's shout: "Can't say can't say can't say. Dark very dark bad smell can't say can't say don't tell broken nose no smell."

Peter raised his hands. They stopped screaming.

They all sat down so quickly I was left standing, I was seen. I sat down.

"Look at the ceiling," he said. They looked. "Does it look darker to you? Dirty?"

None of them had noticed it before, but still the voices said, "It is darker!"

Peter said gently, "I think we've sent a lot of bad history away today."

Then the doors were opened (and no one noticed they didn't need to be unlocked, I'm sure. They were too busy hyperventilating). I got out early and took a seat near the door to watch them come out.

It was the satisfaction I couldn't understand. They came out, unselfconsciously beaming, unembarrassed about their shouting behaviour inside. And there I was, no longer incognito, caught by surprise.

There were always people hanging around till the last minute, asking questions, wanting just a bit more for their money.

These people who worship Peter think he's got some divine knowledge. They don't know the secrets I know. When he talks about "The Importance of Difference," he's not talking about race, colour, size, sex, though it works that way as well. He's talking about his odd feet. All those times a fuss was made, all that teasing.

No one knows about his feet, apart from those of us close to him.

He has shoes specially made, so his feet look perfect, just large enough so people think he's got a big dick. But take a look at his nose. Like a pretty little button.

We had a special man to make his shoes. Sandy Boyle, the shoe man, who'd shown up at Mum's funeral, who cried at the mention of my name.

I was eleven or twelve when we went with Mum shopping to buy school shoes and it must have been January. Hot, and I was bored, once I had my shoes. Peter always took longer because of having one foot bigger than the other.

We ended up at a specialty shoe shop, where there were no interesting shoes but they swore to fit all sorts of feet.

The shop was dark, its window filled with old shoes no one dusted and no one would buy. We had driven a long way to this shop, and Mum was determined Peter would not leave unshod.

Sandy Boyle loved a challenge, and he and Mum talked non-stop and I was ignored, as he brought out shoe after shoe. I was already wearing my new ones; we found them at the discount shoe place.

Every year was the same; my shoes, cheap, we found in the first shop, then Peter's shoes we'd find at about the hundredth shop. This was our first year at this special shop. An assistant in the department store we went to said she used to work there, that the shoes were good but the boss terrible.

"I had to leave," she said, leaning close to Mum, "because he used to try things. He had ideas."

On the way there I asked Mum what ideas were, thinking they sounded interesting. She wouldn't tell me, and it wasn't until I was an adult I realised what that shop assistant had meant. Because I could remember her, very clearly. I thought she was the most sophisticated, mature woman I'd met, and I'd practise saying, "He had ideas," in the mirror for the day I could use it myself. Years later, flicking through a gossip mag I found in a box under an ex-housemate's bed (sometimes they leave so quickly I inherit booty) I saw her face. She had married a lawyer, someone I'd heard of. I saw her face and stared for minutes, some internal scanner flicking, flicking. There she was; the girl who sent us to the place where Mum would meet the second man of her dreams.

Sandy Boyle sold Mum some shoes, too. He was one of those ones who touch your feet when they put your shoes on. I thought he looked silly. His shoulders were stooped and he was very pale. I thought he must stay in the shop the whole time, never leave.

Peter fell asleep, sitting up with his shoes on, while Mum and the shoe man began to talk about food or something. Both of them kept saying, "Oh, really, so do I."

I touched everything in the shop. There were not many shoes on display; it was part of the speciality that they had to go behind and get your shoes.

I took off my new school shoes, which Mum let me wear only inside the shops, and replaced them with a pair which looked like clown shoes, they were so big. I shuffled about the room.

There was a small table with some grey sandals and a sign saying "SALE". The ink on the sign was pale, like invisible writing. I wrote "Poo," in the dust on the sign. There were shoelaces, long and short, brown and black. I swapped them all around so that the lines were all in a pattern. One long brown, one long black, one short brown, one short black. I opened some packs and tied lots of little bows in clumps of hair, to make myself look like a porcupine.

It took ages, but Mum and the shoe man were still talking. She didn't like being at home as much as Dad used to.

I had a look at all the different colours of the polish. I liked tan the best, because it made me feel like an American Indian when I striped it on my face.

"Oh, well, we've taken up enough of your time," Mum said

"Oh, no, not at all. Part of the service." They laughed even though there was no joke.

"Hardeharhar," I said. It was something I'd heard the older kids say and I knew it was very rude.

Mum and the shoe man stared at me. His mouth was open; I stuck my tongue out at him. Mum said, "Right, let's go. Someone isn't mature enough to behave herself when she's out." She said to him, "I think she's having a problem becoming an adult. I'm hoping high school will snap her out of it." I started snapping my fingers in their faces. It angered me she couldn't tell I was acting, but that spoke good reviews about my ability.

Peter was roused and he said, "What're you supposed to be? A fancy dress party?"

"If I'm a fancy dress party, you must be little lunch," I said. The shoe man held the door open.

"Out," Mum said. I slid along in my shoe boats, made it all the way to the car when the shoe man came running after.

"I believe these are yours," he said, and Mum and he laughed again. He took away my big shoes and held my feet to put on my school shoes. Peter and I were strapped in and had to wait while Mum and Sandy Boyle talked even more.

I knew just what to say to get out of trouble as Mum drove home.

"He was a nice man, wasn't he, Mum?" I said.

Peter snorted. Mum looked at me in the rear view mirror.

"Yes, he was rather, wasn't he? Did you really like him?"

"Oh, yes," I said. "He was lovely," and we stopped to buy pizza for tea.

On Auntie Ruth's birthday, which is in June, the shoe man showed up at the restaurant.

"This is Sandy Boyle, the one I've been telling you about," Mum said to Auntie Ruth. We had been staying at Auntie Ruth's more, lately. We didn't know about Sandy Boyle. I said, "That's the man who gets ideas." Peter snorted. "You're an idiot, Steve."

"No, it's the man from the spastic shoe shop where you have to get your shoes." He thumped my thigh under the table, I thumped back, he pinched me and I said, "Mum, he pinched me."

"Stop it, Peter," Mum said.

"You own a shoe shop, I hear," said Auntie Ruth.

"Oh, no, I just work there," he said. He turned to me, then. "You've got a good memory for faces, Steve."

I said, "I always remember a face which looks like a bum." Only Peter heard, and he couldn't stop snorting the rest of the night. But it was a phrase I never forgot. A good memory for faces. If I saw someone standing at a street light, I could recognise them later at the supermarket. I saw lots of familiar faces and I could often pin them down: a kid from a younger class, someone at the pictures, a mother who picked her kid up, someone who nearly tripped. If I saw them again I knew where I'd seen them first.

My feet have never been as comfortable as they were the year Sandy Boyle was with us. He bought shoes from the shop for me as well as Peter, so we missed that dreadful shopping experience. If I were Mum, I would have been very bored with him.

As the months closed, he began to think he was required to discipline us; he was a foolish man.

I was making quicksand at the back step one afternoon. It was warm. I had taken my dress off, because it constricted my movement and because I knew Mum would be pleased if I didn't get it dirty.

I squatted in my undies and singlet, digging, filling the hole with water and dirt, massaging the lot to make it dangerous. I thought the sun had gone behind a cloud, though the day was hot and cloud-less. I tutted at the shadow, ignored it, then glanced at the sky when it didn't pass over.

"Don't you think you're a little old for playing in the mud?" It was Sandy Boyle, standing behind me, blocking my sun.

He was very hard to upset. I'd scuff my shoes, kick them off without undoing the laces; he'd just tell me I was hurting a piece of art.

"Don't you think you should shut up?" I said.

He sat down on the back step to talk. He gave me a little compass as a bribe. I threw it up the back.

"Stevie, you have to accept the fact that you're growing up. Your body will be changing in the next year or so. You shouldn't be parading around the yard in your underwear."

I had mud up to my elbows; my legs were covered with it. My singlet was loose and my underpants had nearly lost their elastic.

"You shouldn't be staring at me, then," I said. He reddened. He continually made the same mistake; because I acted like a child, he assumed I was childish. He forgot how adult my brain was. And he didn't know about Eve, my garden lady. No one really knew about her.

"Trying to see if I've got boozies yet? Well, I haven't, see?" I lifted up my singlet, showed him my chest. When I lowered my arms he was gone.

Mum and he had sex that night. I went into Peter's room and we got the giggles, listening to his grunting, his whimpering. Peter told me a terrible story he'd heard at school, about a man who had sex and got dirty, and had to have a spiky umbrella inflated in his penis and dragged out, and it dragged out all the stuff inside so there was only skin left.

"Mum isn't dirty, though," he said, and we nodded.

I fell asleep in Peter's bed, and that's where Sandy Boyle found us in the morning, when he came to perform his little task, wake the kids for school.

He threw the covers back, waking us with a jolt.

I had been dreaming about swimming in a nice warm pool and suddenly the water turned cold.

"Get lost," Peter said, and reached for the covers.

"This is a disgrace. A disgrace!"

We giggled at him; he couldn't shout without his voice shaking and spittle flying.

"Get out. *Get out*," he spat.

Peter squeezed my elbow. "It's time for school anyway."

At breakfast, Sandy Boyle said to Mum, "Heather, they'll have to stop sleeping in the same bed. It's disgusting."

Mum said, "Oh, really?" which he stupidly took for interest.

"They're of an age, now. It's an established fact that children of their age are giving birth in some countries, so don't talk to me about innocence.

There's nothing innocent about either of them, I don't think anyone would argue with that. And I don't think you should be sending Steve out with torn underpants. What if someone should see?"

Mum made our lunches, drove us to school, kissed us goodbye, all without speaking. She made good lunches, lunches the other kids envied. Always three layers; a boiled egg or piece of kid's cheese, then a fat sandwich, ham, or chicken loaf, or something else which didn't go soggy. Then a treat, chocolate slice or cream cake. Never fruit. We never had to eat fruit. Dad didn't eat it and Mum told us it just wasn't worth the fight. She always packed a throw-away toothbrush, with the tooth-paste all ready to go. Peter used his every day; I kept mine in my desk and used them for swaps. He got clean teeth; I got Superman pencils, lollies, answers and, once, a kiss.

On the way to school I said, "How come Sandy doesn't wear any pants when you're not home, Mum? Why does he show us his willy like that?"

"Peter?" Mum said. "Is that true?"

Her voice was very quiet. I had to lean forward against my seat belt to hear. This was a test for Peter; how much did he really want to get rid of the shoe man? Or did he just say that?

"Yeah, he gets his pants off and follows us around the house. He won't let us have a bath with the door shut. Once he hit me because Steve was late, he tells me off all the time, he doesn't like anything I say."

It was more than I had hoped for.

That night the shoe man was gone.

"We'll get our shoes from somewhere else from now on," Mum said. Peter and I cheered, we had lemonade and fried chicken and pretended to be the shoe man all night.

It was the best night of my life.

Mum said one day, years later, as we drove past the special shoe shop, "I wonder whatever happened to that sick bastard."

It was one of the few times she surprised me. I had imagined she had killed him and knew exactly where he was.

W e sold these little puzzles in the foyer, along with his tapes, books, photos (none of me, or Mum, or Dad. I could never figure out why he would be ashamed of us).

This puzzle was made of graphite, carved, polished, and linked. If you pulled and twisted, the perfect sphere would fall into a still-connected, impossible mess. Push and twist to click it back to its seam-less, round state.

They really were beautiful puzzles, and you could fiddle at night, in the dark, when you couldn't sleep, because you would never lose a piece and it warmed so gently in the palms of your hands. I don't need one; I can never stay awake more than a few minutes once I reach bed.

Maria and Peter came out of the lecture hall with their hangers-on. I had been seen, so there was no point running away. I wanted to see what she'd do.

If she'd snip me off and get rid of me, or if she wasn't clever enough to do that in front of everyone without looking bad. Oddly, it became the one time Maria and I fell into a sense that we would be friends. I should have known it would be erroneous.

One of those dinners evolved which appear to be spontaneous but which have been planned meticulously by one person. Where you all just pile into cars and end up somewhere, but that person had it all in mind. This was the only one I ever went to, but I know enough about them. Maria wanted to eat out; she's in her element in a restaurant. She somehow manages to take credit for the food and the wine, she lords it over the waiters and helps everyone order. She glows in the candlelight.

Peter could barely control his tongue. The table was full of hang-alongs.

"I can't describe the exhilaration of helping people who need help. Just this evening, did you see that poor lonely fella, shuffled in early, sat on his own in the middle of the room and waited for it to fill around him, you know, already fulfilled because there were people around him. And all I had to do was talk to him, mention him, say, 'That man there,' and point to him, did you see him? He lifted.

He lightened. My God, I could see it. I could actually see the black cloud rising above his head."

Peter had a chopstick in either hand; he played the air like it was a set of drums. The hang-alongs had not eaten a bite; Maria and I got most of the prawns and fished out the best bits of chicken, the bits without grey worms of gut. We reached for the same bit of tofu, clicked chopsticks. I could feel the waiter hovering behind me, wanting to ask me for my dessert request. I kept talking, blah blah, because I knew he was hanging about, that he wouldn't leave until I acknowledged him, and I hate being hassled.

"Waiter," I said, "come here and do what you're paid to do."

The shrimp tasted rubbery, gritty, like the ones you get at all you can eat chain restaurants. Maria thought they were wonderful; I began to realise she has no taste.

"I hate restaurants," I said.

"This isn't really a restaurant," Maria said. But it was.

"So, when are you going to launch your backyard?" she said.

I had a sudden vision of how it should be: pagoda, soft grass, tiny flowers, jasmine, shade, laughter, glasses clinking, white dresses. But you can't make that happen with bones and graves.

"I went off the idea," I said.

Peter said, "His face, the cloud, before us all."

Maria rolled her eyes. I said, "His wallet, his money, dinner for us all." Maria cracked up. It broke Peter's spell, and everyone began to scrape at the bowls. Maria and I laughed, laughed. I was nearly sick, I'd eaten so much, and I'd been throwing down the beers so felt pissy, and Maria's lips were swollen from sucking too hard on her wine glass.

I thought then we may even get along. If she could laugh at Peter with me, I thought we'd be friends.

One of the guys at dinner was cuter than the others, and actually laughed when I made jokes. He asked me out.

It was a disaster.

I was having sex at his place, and he got up to get us a beer and I wriggled about to get comfy and somehow smashed his bedside lamp. I didn't say anything, he didn't hear anything, he walked all over the cut glass in the dark and had no idea.

"Something sharp," he said. We were numb with drink; the sex was a failure.

"Wonder what it is," I said. I left before he woke up. It was a hot night; we'd only had a sheet covering us. The sheet near his feet was stained with blood; he'd notice that when he woke up. I was thankful I hadn't told him my real name or given him my home phone number.

Later, I was reading the personals, as I do, because I put odd messages in the personal columns.

"Pookie, please call Nookie"—that sort of thing. I get responses sometimes, but they're all crazy. I was reading see if any of my stuff was there and I saw,

"Miss Cut Glass, please contact Blood Foot for mutual satisfaction."

I didn't call, of course. He had nothing I wanted. I had left my jumper behind but I didn't care. It was only one my Grannies knitted for Peter. I've always got at least a couple of messages in the paper. It amazes me how many people respond, just in case they are Pookie. There are some bloody mad people out there. Desperate. The personals are like an astrology column; you can make everything fit if you want it to.

When they asked for a photo, I'd send them one of me clearly in disguise. A terrible blond wig, glasses, I don't know. The ones who wrote back always told me how pretty I was.

I went back to my digging. I got the yard cleaned up. I found half a child's handkerchief, a scratched gold locket, a smooth pebble and the stub of a grey lead pencil. It looked like the sort Auntie Jessie used.

I found a shoe marked with red crosses, a brass lighter, a book spine and a club badge.

* * *

Dougie Page called me. He'd found out some things. I loved Dougie. He was the one Dad saved, the one Dad died for, and it was like he thought he had to take over Dad's spot. Mum didn't seem to mind. He always told me gruesome stories when Mum wasn't listening and brought presents, like old bullet casings.

He was the one who got rid of unwanted visitors for us. Well, for Mum, anyway.

I had a guy over to stay when I was seventeen. I didn't tell him Mum would be at home. I took his hand and squeezed it about my breast, squeezed hard, so his fingers sank into my flesh.

"Come home and look at my veggie garden, Nick," I said. "I've got all sorts of goodies out there."

I didn't tell him it was a junk-yard, full of stories.

I took him straight to my room and didn't keep him quiet. He shouted my name—he said "Steve" at first, but I think it embarrassed him to be calling a man's name. He called me Steph. He tickled my ear with sibilants. We fell asleep entwined. He woke me with kisses and a morning glory and we made love quietly. It was a beautiful morning, and my room is very sunny.

Nick climbed out of bed, stretched, leaned on the windowsill.

"You never did show me your garden," he said.

"I don't actually have one."

"You're kidding," he said, but so was he.

Mum heard us in the night (heard him, anyway; I was as quiet as a sock) and she showed her displeasure by throwing her weight around in the kitchen, singing at shouting level, calling my name.

"Who's that?" Nick said. "I thought you lived alone."

"That's just Mum," I said, and a change came over his face. He stopped smiling, but he wasn't angry. He was on his best behaviour; he was determined to win my mother over.

He was first into the kitchen. "Let me do that, Mrs Searle," though all she was doing was shoving food down the insinkerator.

Mum continuously improved the kitchen. It was the most modern room in the house; everything else was left to suffer.

She made magnificent food in there, mousses, cakes, soufflés, pies, then we had nowhere to eat it but at the kitchen table.

Nick was twenty-four, five years younger than Dad when he died. I thought, wouldn't it be funny if he was my brother, and they adopted him out when he was born. They say, now, that plenty of adoptive children who find their natural parents as adults enter into a sexual relationship with them. I don't know if it's true. They don't know why it is; perhaps the natural closeness is mistaken for physical attraction. Often their ages are close, because the mother was young when the child was born.

And the father. Sometimes I wonder if I was adopted. That would explain why I don't share Peter's weaknesses and frailties.

Nick said, "Mmm, that smells great." He was piling our dirty dishes into the dishwasher.

Mum always liked to have technology first; she was bored with things by the time everybody else had them.

She had not spoken a word; he didn't seem to notice. She hadn't stabbed him with the bread knife, so she must have liked him.

"She's making bread," I said. "The secret is, she kneads it with her feet."

"Sounds tasty," he said. He rinsed and stacked, rinsed and stacked. He looked outside at the view he'd seen from my room.

"Y'know, that garden's got a lot of potential. I've had a bit of experience with that sort of thing—I'll have a go if you like. Fix up the mess a bit."

Mum stood behind him. A hissy breath and she said, "Don't touch it. There's no need to touch it. We like it as is, don't we, Stevie?" She held her hand out without looking, summoning me to support her.

"We like it looking like a tip," I said.

"It reminds us of Dad, doesn't it?" she said.

"Yep."

"Oh, well, whatever," he said. He sniffed the air again. Mum fed him thick slices of brown bread, with butter and honey. He swallowed them as he swallowed me the night before; the same grunts of satisfaction.

We sat in the kitchen and talked. He told me about himself, blah blah, and I discovered he was nothing like Dad, or Rick, my babysitter's boyfriend. He didn't really have anything to say.

That was when Dougie arrived. Mum ushered him into the kitchen and pointed at Nick; she later confessed she had called for help, unable to handle him alone.

"I don't like interferers," she said.

Dougie stood and stared at my boyfriend. Nick said, "G'day, mate."

"Do you know how old she is?"

"Old enough, isn't she?"

"Old enough for high school."

"I'm old enough," I said. I wasn't a child; I was seventeen. I wasn't sure what the problem was; if Mum was bothered, she should have stopped it while it was happening last night.

"Do you know who her father was?"

"Does it matter?"

"It does when you figure out who his mates are."

My boyfriend plucked and played with the etchings scratched into our table.

"I don't want any trouble."

"Nick!" I said. "I told you trouble was my middle name and you said you loved getting on top of trouble."

"Ssshhhh," he said. "Leave it alone. It doesn't matter," and he gathered his things and left. I didn't see him again.

To cheer me up, Dougie told me a revolting story. "You've got to have a strong stomach for my job…" We were sitting in the lounge room. He had a bottle of beer and he gave me sips.

"I have. I was the one who put the ginger cat in a bag after it was squashed flat. You should have seen it. It was like some floor rug, orange, red, grey, all splattered on the road. The person didn't even stop." I pictured a car-load, one nervous driver, only invited because he drove, all of them pretending it had been a bump in the road.

I hoped no one could hear me lying. I hoped my invention was believable.

"That's good. Good. You'll need that. Some of the things you'll see if you do make it as a cop…"

"Like what?"

"I don't want to give you nightmares."

"Nightmares are only horror movies in my brain and I love horror movies."

"Well, one time, we were called out to a scene, in the country. Isolated. I was working as a country cop, then, one of my first postings. Ya gotta go where they send ya."

"Yep," I said.

"So we get called out there. Seems one of the dogs was found miles away, limping, whimpering, mad with fear. He had been badly beaten. People tried to call the farm but no answer. There was only a small family living out there, husband, wife, teenage boy. People wondered about the boy; he'd been to school for no more than a year, and done so badly family and teacher had conspired to keep him home. You find out these things when you're a cop. People get nervous, talkative, and they didn't know me. I was the new kid, and they all wanted to be the first to tell me."

"Like what?"

"Like why the postmaster never talked to anyone, why there were so many in the McLaclan brood, why the town didn't have a local paper. All the little details they thought I needed to know.

"The family on the farm, they were the Thieles.

Been there a long time, and only a couple of smart ones amongst them. This little fella, honestly, they'd say, you could have taught a pig more. Pigs were considered pretty dumb around there. They ate a lot of pig meat. I still can't stand the smell of bacon cooking."

"Why? Cos you ate so much of it?"

"Partly that. And partly because of what we found at the farm. The first thing we saw as we were heading up the driveway was the tractor out in the field. Now that was odd, to start, because he was a neat fella, the locals said. Wouldn't leave his shoelaces undone. I was out with the captain, who didn't mind a bit of hands on, and he said, 'How are you feeling?' I've never forgotten that, how he knew so soon something was wrong. We reached the farmhouse. It smelt terrible; the only movement was from the flies, buzzing around like a black cloud. The pigs were skinny and dead in the sty, the mud cracked and dry around them. One had died on her feet; her ankles trapped into the now-solid mud. Three dogs lay huddled in a pile by the front door. The captain kicked them over with his toe. They had bled from the belly, each of them, the dog on the top black, the others a dark, rust red.

How are you doing?" Dougie Page said.

"Fine," I said.

"That's good, because I was sick to my stomach by now. It was the smell, and the flies. I still hate flies. And we hadn't even seen what was inside, yet. We picked up a shovel to move the dogs away, and we had to jump over the sludge they left behind.

"'Ted?' the captain shouted. 'Cathy? Rob?' There was no answer, but we hadn't expected there would be.

"I thought it was bad, the animals. Then we found Cathy. The wife. She was hanging by a rafter in the kitchen. It was a big old farmhouse, sturdy, you could swing on the rafters. Like those pipes in your kitchen, but wood. She was in her underwear, and all swollen up like a dressed balloon. Things stuck out of bloodless holes; forks, knives, like someone had thrown things at her after she was dead. Like a porcupine."

"Or an echidna."

"That too. Even the captain felt sick. He went to the sink to splash his face. And found a hand there.

"She wasn't missing a hand.

"There were ants all over the floor but I hadn't noticed. We stood there staring into the sink, and the ants started crawling over our shoes, up onto our shins and they nipped us until we were stirred into movement. We searched the rest of the house. On the lounge room table were spread textbooks and papers, Rob's lessons. Papers were screwed up, books torn, the table deeply scored, ink dried in a puddle around a crushed pen on the floor. I didn't know if we were supposed to speak. I hoped not, because I couldn't think of a thing. It was a long, low house, and we looked in every room. We found Ted, the father, in the yard, flat on his stomach. He'd been shot in the back. His hand was cut off."

"And what about the son?"

"Well, we figured it this way. He was angry at his lessons, couldn't do them. Threw a fit, whatever. We don't know what came first; did he shoot his father as he ran away, or did he knock his mother silly and string her up? When did he cut his father's hand off and why? It was too late to tell. We figured he just went about his business, then. We never figured why he cut his father's hand off, but beside it in the sink were plates, three or four dinners for one, from the leftovers. So he fed himself, he slept, he did a little work on the farm."

"Where was he?"

"Remember the tractor? His Dad never let him use it; everyone knew that. He went out and used it, though, and he got it stuck, and he didn't put the brake on. The thing rolled over him and didn't kill him. They could tell that much. He was trapped and there was no one to discover him. No one to miss him. Both legs caught under. We don't know how long it took him to die, but the maggots were covering most of his legs when we found him. Course, that could have saved him, from infection, anyway. But he was too far gone for that. He must have swiped the things off, while he still could. I know I would have. Really, I've never been keen on meat since."

"I love meat," I said. "And maggots. I like 'em all white and wriggly. We've got a maggot farm in the backyard."

"No such thing, sweetie," he said, but I'd seen them out there.

He stayed for dinner, and I wanted to hear the story again. Especially the bit about the mother.

"Tell me again," I said. "Cos Peter's really stupid, and I want to know if he's going to go mad like that kid in your story."

"That's enough, Steve." Dougie Page was the one man who could have stopped me from what I did, but he never did. He stopped coming around when I was seventeen, and things went off the rails a bit.

I wasn't at school anymore, and I didn't have a job, either. I quit working at the corner shop, and I got my courier job when I got my licence. That was a good time. I could get a lot of customers, cruising around like that. Mum paid for most things; other money I got from selling drugs at my old school.

I blame peer group pressure for starting me on selling drugs. I didn't want to take them and that made me a loser. Mum never even noticed, and I used to do it right under her nose. I started by selling kids the pills Mum kept; she got a new sort every couple of weeks. She told the doctors, "I don't have any energy any more. I used to be on the go all day, running about."

This was true. My memory of her is a fast-moving blur. She was always talking, singing, she drove us places, drove herself, she did night school and day school but never seemed stressed.

The doctors looked at her dark eyes, swollen from lack of sleep. They all thought it was because she missed Dad so much.

I only needed to sell kids a pill each, and I made up what the pills did. They all believed. I refused to sell more than one each; I didn't want trouble. Any collapses, unexplained vomiting, and it would all be over.

That's where it began. The work found me, really; the simplicity of it, the need. People checked me out and offered me deals; and soon I was selling other stuff, leaving Mum's pills alone.

She had a lot of pills. They kept her even. A bit blasé, meaning she left us alone a lot. Peter had girlfriends staying the night from the age of fourteen and Mum just smiled at them in the morning. She thought discipline was a father's role. She wasn't interested in it.

It was a gap in my life; I never got to rebel against parental discipline. I think it makes you strong, standing against people who stood stronger than you all their lives.

Selling drugs wasn't only an easy way to make a living; it was a way to rebel against Dad, even though he was dead. As I grew older, the kids who came to me were older and older. Every time I sent them away with a taste of oblivion, I wondered if Dad could see me from his cold room. I wondered if he noticed me. When I went up to the high school, I felt like I was back in the room, without the pain or the stink. I arrived at my spot down the back without announcement, but the kids knew I was there and they slowly came to surround me. I was relaxed and impressive. These kids looked up to me; all kids do. I like kids.

They're ever-fascinated, envious, of my scars. I'm scary. Scars are as good as tattoos. They show me theirs, and I ask for the story, listen for the slight, and I say, "Not bad." I am always scarring myself.

Knives and scissors. Every time I die, I leave a mark on myself. Those I didn't do were inflicted in the room and carried with me.

I was popular for a while. Starting getting invited to people's eighteenths. Never happened when I was that age. For my eighteenth, I wanted to clean up the backyard and hire a marquee, have a garden party, invite everyone I'd ever met. But Mum and Peter thought that was a terrible idea. Now, the garden is a reminder of my humble roots, that someone had once told me what to do. Nothing was done to celebrate my eighteenth; not one thing. Peter gave me some perfume and Mum cooked me dinner.

Peter held his eighteenth birthday in a pub, so I couldn't go cos I was only sixteen. I'm sure he did it on purpose. People raved about it for years, reckoned it was the best party ever. Dougie Page helped pay for it, organised the bus to take everyone home, everything. I found out later that half the people there were under eighteen, so I could have got in anyway.

Dougie banged on my door with a six-pack and a bottle of whisky. We sat on the back steps for a while. He fumbled in his pocket and pulled out Dad's special little camera. Dad would never let us look into it. I've seen others since; you hold the palm-sized thing up to your eye, aim at the light, press the button. There are images presented for you.

The one I saw had clever little pictures of New York. Dad would never let me see into his one. I tried to steal it out of his pocket once and I was in trouble for being a thief. Others, I know, display nudity and sex.

"He let it in the squad car," Doug said.

"But it was always in his pocket."

"No, no, he took it out at work. Didn't like it going with him where he went." He handed it to me. I held it up to the light, pressed it against my eye and saw Mum, top half, nude, smiling, holding baby Peter, who was smiling, and the photograph was happy and perfect and who ever needed a fucking daughter, ay?

I threw the thing into the yard. Dad had always loved mementoes; let this one join the sick pile in the back. Dad loved things from places we'd been: a napkin with curried egg from Peter's lips, a bit of glass from the window I smashed, everything kept about the place like it meant something. Once he died, Mum swept it all into a garbage bag, where it tumbled and broke in a jumble. That's what should have happened. What did happen; she kept it forever. Now I've got it all.

"I'm sorry I took so long to give it to you," Doug said, His eyes on the spot the camera landed.

"Not to worry, it's only been twelve years. Just as relevant now, don't you think?"

He nodded, but he was distracted, staring at the curious bumps and mounds in the backyard.

"Fixing it up back here," I said, and I showed him my muscles.

"Your Dad used to tell us you always were good for a laugh, Steve," he said, but he didn't laugh. I gestured and we went inside.

"I've always felt bad about you kids."

"We've always felt bad too," I said, then grinned as if it was a joke. "Why? Wasn't your fault, was it?"

"No, no. But I've felt responsible. Like I should have done something for you."

"No good worrying now. Peter and I did just fine. And you were around a fair bit, Dougie. You were there."

"I always knew you'd be all right, way your Dad talked about you kids."

"Yeah, well, he would've been proud."

"Oh, yeah. Yeah. Look at you, nice home, good job. That's what he wanted to see. He wanted you to be normal."

"Why wouldn't I be?"

"I don't know. Alex just struck me as the kinda guy who should never have responsibilities. He couldn't cope."

"Of course he could, you fuckin' idiot. What are you talking about? He was the best father ever. Ever. I always felt so lucky, having him as a Dad. He was such a patient, calm man."

Dougie stared at me in surprise.

"Hang on—you are Alex Searle's kid, aren't you?"

I laughed. "Of course."

"He must have been a different fellow at home, then, love. I don't wanna upset you, but he was a funny man, your Dad. Put the fear of God into anyone who crossed his path. Violent and angry, love. Without speaking ill of the dead. He was a violent, angry man."

"Get the fuck out of here," I said. "What the fuck do you want, anyway? Dad saved your life, right? And that's how you remember him. There's nothing here for you." I kicked him hard in the shins and he was suddenly afraid. "Why come here and tell lies? What's the point?"

"I could tell you stories," he said. "If you'd listen."

"I'm sure you're a lovely storyteller. Go tell it to someone who gives a fuck." I picked up his bottle of scotch and threw it onto the front path. It smashed satisfyingly. He shuffled through the broken glass, turned once at the gate.

"Fuck off before I call the cops," I said.

"We were the cops," he said. Like some fucking clever movie. Peter's voice, talking, talking, telling lies.

"How about I go get some fixings for lunch, Stevie? Can I do that? I need to tell you what I'm finding out."

I shrugged. I didn't want to hear what he had to say, but I couldn't help it.

"Do whatever you want," I said.

Dougie made some sandwiches with bread he went out and bought and we swapped sandwiches, half and half.

"So, have you thought about what you're going to do? Are you still keen to be a detective?"

That was the only time I felt guilty about selling drugs. I decided I'd stop; Peter gave me enough money to live on.

"I sort of lost interest," I said. "It seemed to have no purpose to it, because you didn't catch the guy who killed Dad, so what's the point?"

He scratched his ear. It was a habit I had tried to form myself; I thought it looked very sophisticated.

"Didn't your Mother ever tell you?" he said.

"Tell me what? She didn't ever tell me anything."

"Can we go for a drink? You still drink, don't you?"

"Aren't you on duty?"

"I'm not working at all," he said.

I felt strange, drinking in the pub with this man.

Saddened. If Dad was alive, we might be doing this; sitting about, talking, friends.

I never got to be friends with my father.

He drank whisky. I drank beer. He smiled at that.

"You never were into pretences," he said.

"You're a bit old fashioned. Everyone drinks beer, now. It doesn't mean we fuck like rabbits any more." I threw back the beer and ordered another.

He laughed, a man's laugh, unselfconscious, hearty.

"So, what have you found out?" I said.

He bought another drink before he answered.

"I know you were always interested in what we were working on, even as a kid."

"I loved it."

"Well, I don't think we told you about this one.

It was pretty gruesome, and your Mum would have killed us for giving you nightmares."

"Mum was always squeamish," I said. I swallowed too much beer; my eyes watered.

"I'm so sorry that your Mum died," he said.

"I'm not crying." I ordered us another beer, and got some nuts and chips. I suddenly felt very hungry.

"It's okay to."

"I never cry."

"Yes, I remember that. Your Dad used to tell us stories about you, your stoic little face, determined.

He always said you were tougher than him."

"He was pretty tough."

"He acted that way. He loved your mum, though, and you two."

I thought he said "You, too."

"What about Peter?"

"Yeah, you two, you both." And there I was, thinking I was the favourite.

"Everyone loved Mum," I said.

"Yes. I know I did. Did you know that?"

"I guessed."

We drank our drinks in silence. I thought about the people in the pub and what I'd eat for tea; he sighed repeatedly. Was he thinking about Mum?

"So what have you found out?" I said again.

"It's a bit of a long story. The gruesome murder I was talking about—your Dad and I were investigating it when he died. Two bodies were found on the roof of an office building. They'd been there for months; people hardly ever went up there. They were impossible to identify; the birds had been at it. A man and a teenage boy. Handcuffed together. It was one of those sad cases; you see a young body and you think, someone misses that child. Someone's looking for him. But nobody was. Alex and I hadn't gotten very far. We kept hitting walls, not finding any answers. And then we got that break you wait for. Someone remembered seeing the man and the boy in the building. We had a witness."

"So did the man kill the boy?"

He shook his head. "From what forensics told us, the boy was long dead. That creep had walked around with a dead kid handcuffed to him. Then someone had strangled the creep. I gotta tell you, we didn't look so hard for the killer once we figured that out. Best clue we had was one glass cufflink."

Slightly chipped, I thought. Like the one I have at home in my pile of garden treasures.

"Did you figure out who they were?" I said.

"The man's name was Joel Bennet, we knew that much. He was a bloody banker, plenty of money, everybody loved him, one of those kinda guys. The witness remembered another man, under hypnosis, and we were going to be drawing up a picture of him. But then…well, this is when it gets really weird. The witness died in the shoot-out where your Dad saved my life. They died together."

I said, "You don't need to be delicate with me. I'm not like Peter, big wimp. But I was too young at the time to be told anything. All I heard were whispers."

He shuddered. It was dark in the pub, silver furniture giving only a dull reflection of the low light.

Office workers appeared, strained, alone, nervous, or loud, in groups. I watched them, their simple lives, clear pasts. I was nervous about my next sentence; I had thought it a hundred times, even practised saying it, but it still scared me.

"What is it, Stevie? Your lips are moving but nothing's coming out."

"It's just I always wondered why he died like that. Why he took the bullet. Cos from what I can tell, you were fine, covered. I don't know. Maybe I'm confused."

He smiled, shook his head. "You're good. I'll give you that. Is it only laziness holding you back?" He pinched my hand to let me know he was joking.

We watched a small crowd, one pretty woman, five men. It was so easy for her; all she had to do was laugh. Whenever I try that I'm so boring, people can't keep their eyes open.

He bought us more drinks. I sipped my beer; its bitterness didn't refresh me. I wanted his answer.

I stared at him. He wouldn't look at me; concentrated on tearing a coaster into snow.

"Come on," I said.

"I wondered, too," he said.

"Come on," I said.

"Because he wouldn't have done that. He was a good cop, good at seeing into the future, seeing what would happen. It was like he wanted that bullet."

"Did you tell Mum this?" I said. My ears were buzzing; shock or rage, I wasn't sure.

"That's when she said, fuck off, don't come back."

"My mum said fuck off?"

We both laughed, hysterical little giggles which drew stares.

"I wish I'd known that before she died. I would have liked to know she was capable of saying fuck."

We laughed again, stupid laughter without mirth.

Then he shook his head. "I can't tell you how much I regretted speaking. You know? I lost your mother. And you, too, Stevie. I've missed you."

I looked at him and it struck me he wasn't that much older than me. He would've been twenty when Dad died. I glanced around the bar and wondered if people thought we were together.

"Did anyone else say anything about it? How weird it was?"

He shook his head. "No one else went beyond the hero thing. They couldn't get past that."

Now I had a new, bad question. I couldn't ask it, though, wouldn't. Didn't want to know the answer. Didn't want to know why my Dad had hated me so much he wanted to die to get away from me.

Dougie Page cleared his throat; he was about to ask me the difficult question.

I gabbled before he could speak, oooh, work, ooh, the garden, ooh, my car, no, not my car, ooh, the wealthy, ooh, the state of the police.

"Hmmm," he said." You're right. Spot on, love," he said, until I thought I'd lulled him.

"So, can you tell me about it, Stevie? About your mum's accident.

We never heard. Never got the details."

"Why would you want the details of something like that?" I drank another beer.

"You know, not the details. I mean what happened. How did it happen?"

"There was an accident. That's what happened," I said, and he sucked his head back like a turtle avoiding a hailstorm. Ducking, weaving.

"Fair enough. Don't blame you. Don't blame you."

Who believes anything which has to be said twice?

I tried to tell him about the digging and the bones. I wanted his help.

"That's your business, Stephanie. Keep yourself to yourself. Don't unbury the past," blah blah blah, hours of it, cliché after shut up cliché.

When we finally left, I was empty. Finished. I didn't want to think about what he'd told me about my father. The implications of it. I didn't want to be alone with the thinking and the memories, I didn't want to dig, I wanted to be gone before the smell of the night blooming jasmine took me and made me feel as if life was worth living.

I'm always well stocked. Always. I went to the toilet and had a shower. I wanted to be clean. Then I got my stack of pills, all different colours, and I lay on the bed. Mum's bed, it used to be. Mum's and Dad's. Mine now.

For a while I didn't think I would make it to the dark room. My body resisted. It was like I had a hook through my back, and someone kept tugging, tugging, pulling me backwards away from my destination. Finally chemicals took over, and as I sank away from consciousness, into the smell of mothballs and the sound of clicking, I could hear them murmuring, waiting for me, and my stomach filled with shit, I could feel it like a ball in there, but Dougie found me; pushed open the front door then sought me out in my bedroom.

He confessed he thought I was waiting for him; my knees had fallen apart, my mouth was open, my arms flung wide. Then he realised I wasn't breathing normally. He saw the empty bottle of pills. He panicked. He saved me, when I didn't need it.

The counsellor came to see me in hospital, so I knew things were pretty dicey. She never got off her arse, didn't even open the door for you when you came in for a session. She said, "Steve, maybe it's time you thought about others. I think you need to do something unselfish, something that will make a difference in the lives of others."

The nurse checking my chart looked up. "She should try being a nurse. That'd stop her feeling sorry for herself. The things you see make you feel lucky to be alive."

"What sort of things?" I said.

The nurse shook her head. "I couldn't begin to tell you. Little kiddies dying, terrible injuries. You soon realise you're damn lucky to be on this earth in one piece."

The counsellor agreed. "We'll look into it for you. Okay? Some study will do you good."

"How much study?"

"An enrolled nurse needs a year," the nurse said. "You could start with that."

It was an interesting thought.

Access to the dying. The chance to look into their eyes.

It was worth thinking about.

Peter looked at me distrustfully when I told him the plan.

"I'm hurt," I said. "You want to do good but you won't let me do good."

"You're right. You should give it a go," he said.

Auntie Jessie surprised me by telling me it was a terrible idea. "For someone like you," she said.

"What do you mean, someone like me? A woman?"

"Someone with your interest in death," she said. "These people need help, not your curiosity."

I was offended, truly offended. "I'm not doing it for me, Jessie. It's a sacrifice. It's less money than anywhere else, and it stinks, and you're dealing with sad people the whole time. How can that be for my benefit?"

I knew what she meant, though. I remembered looking into the faces of the dying, when I was in hospital. I remembered the feeling it gave me, the sense of fulfilment.

"I'm doing it anyway," I said.

Sometimes, Auntie Jessie would talk to me about the most gruesome, exciting crimes, or tell me about her latest favourite book, and I couldn't understand her lack of animation.

Auntie Jessie had more books than anyone I've ever seen. She kept most of them in boxes and wouldn't let anyone read them. She said people didn't treat books with respect. It seemed odd she would keep so many books when she had a whole library to play with. I stayed with her quite often as a child, to give Mum a night off and me a treat. Mum never seemed to need a break from Peter.

Jessie had wonderful books about forensics, detectives, murder. When I visited, I curled up in her huge armchair, a pile of books waist high on the floor beside me; I worked my way through.

The books inspired me. I found the sections Auntie Jessie found inspiring, read them, under-lined them again, in pen this time, red or purple, whatever I had. She had a quote by Agathon in one of the books, and I wondered if Stalin had read it too.

Aristotle, Nicomachean Ethics. Book V1, 2

"It is to be noted that nothing that is past is an object of choice; for e.g. no one chooses to have sacked Troy; for no one *deliberates* about the past, but about what is future and capable of being otherwise, while what is past is not capable of not having taken place; hence Agathon is right in saying:
'For this alone is lacking even to God, To make undone things that have once been done...'"

Agathon quote, 1 Fr. 5, Nauck

It gave me an idea for a story, and I wrote it for History class. The only time I ever got an "A" at school. Mrs Nicholson said, "Refreshing and charming." I loved that. I never got words like that again.

It was called "The Sacking of Troy".

The Sacking of Troy
by S. Searle

There are great things afoot in the workings of mankind. Only one man can save the day and it is always a strong man, a good man, a man who shows up on time to work and does not take sickies. A man who has only one girlfriend at a time and does not keep three women waiting while he performs nebulous duties. This man is always honest. This man does not steal food from his employer.

This man is not Troy.

Troy got his job at Woolworths because his big brother worked there for years and was now head manager of the cigarette booth.

Brad had an attendance record which was being noticed in high circles, and he never blew his nose on his sleeve. He was popular because he was going places and there was always a chance he would give out free cigarettes when the floor manager took her tea break.

Brad looked good in his short red coat. He had a smile which was quite believable and a laugh which didn't shock anybody.

There was no reason to think his little brother Troy would be any different.

Brad knew, but he was under the control of his mother, who insisted Troy be given a chance. She could not see Troy in the light everyone else saw him in, because he was charming and he gave her kisses still, although he was fifteen.

The Starting of Troy caused a stir of anticipation. The customers were no cause for gossip—only the ones who liked to catch the cashiers out in errors. They received slow, painstaking service. The best gossip to be had was about each other.

Troy arrived with sunglasses on, greasy hair, sandshoes. Brad received a word of warning; had he not drilled the dress-code into his brother?

Troy wore scuffed school shoes the next day and declared that his ignorance of the difference between a Naval orange and a Valencia would remain just that.

He began to feel besieged the next day when he did not properly pack a customer's bags, and he lashed out. Brad was called to speak with him.

"Troy, you must be careful. The people here are very unforgiving. They don't like temper or any other emotion. Perhaps if you were in Paris things would be different, because the French are a passionate race. But you are here, where we are dispassionate, and you must abide by the laws, however unfair or invasive you find them."

On his next shift, Troy was discovered having sex with Diana, who had gone out the back for a cigarette and been surprised.

"What can I say? He's built like a horse. I could hardly resist."

With that, Troy was sacked.

THE END

M rs Nicholson wrote, "Although your methodology, logicality and metaphors are not always clear, I enjoyed this. A rare glimpse of imagination and humour such as this can make a teacher's week. Well done."

My other great moment in school was also in English. We were study-ing poetry with Alice Blackburn, which everyone hated. I was so bored I cut stripes in my arm with my penknife; just drew the sharp thing across. I drew a weave of blood. I was completely involved in the design of it, the neatness of the squares. I could hear poetry in the background, knew it was poetry because it went up and down, soft and loud.

I became aware of silence; realised they were watching me. I pulled my sleeve down, tucked the knife under my exercise book. I had things spread all over the desk, taking up room, making it look like I needed a whole desk to myself. Like I chose to sit alone, in a room full of best friends, leaning in to each other, shoulders touching, same sense of humour, same taste. They were all pairs, except the ones who were triplets. Samantha was in another class that year. They split me up from the only friend I had.

Sometimes the triplets would fight, split into twins and a lonely only, an enemy. Then I would clear a space and that one would sit beside me. They would mutter, complain, tell me stories of slights I could barely register. And I never learnt; every time I'd agree, I'd help make terrible plans for revenge, I'd throw in my own nasty stories. Then they'd all be friends again, and my words repeated as if they were truly mine. Enemy number one, for a while, until they found someone else to hate.

Alice Blackburn said, "Did you hear the poem? Would you like me to read it again?"

I nodded; I remember thinking she could choose which question I was answering yes to.

She wanted to read it again; I pictured her, sitting alone at night, memorising the poem. She loved it.

Her cheeks were red. The poem was "Lady Lazarus", by Sylvia Plath.

"Can you tell me what that poem is about?" the teacher said, soft voice, she was ignoring the sleeve of my school shirt, blood soaking neatly through.

I was surprised by the simple question. I expected a real test, I thought she'd make a fool of me.

"It's about suicide. And how suicide can be comforting, something to look forward to. I don't know."

She smiled at me. "Very good," she said. She was sacked soon after; there was such a fuss about the stuff she was reading us. It didn't bother me. I thought it was interesting, that's all, the Sylvia Plath poems, *Go Ask Alice*; people seemed to die in all the books and poems she picked.

Alice Blackburn, call me Alice, never lost sight of me after that. Periodically I'd hear from her, and she'd say, "Uh huh, uh huh." Dying to hear bad news. That's what I thought.

I'd finished three months of my nursing course before Peter bothered to ask me about it. Even then, he didn't want to know anything. He wanted to talk about some things Mum had wanted done, which we didn't do.

Peter said, "You realise, of course, Steve, that under the circumstances we are unanimously obliged to fulfil the requirements of our mother's will?"

I snorted; I heard Maria snort too, but it must have been my own echo. I said, "I didn't realise they taught Fucking Wanker at Uni," and cracked up. I glanced at Maria to make it funnier, but she stared at me blankly, as if nothing had ever happened and I had never made her laugh.

Peter said, "Things like throwing out Dad's things, Steve."

"You leave his stuff alone," I said.

My memories of events are autoscopic. I see them as an observer, an adult observer. There is a value judgement in every memory, from hindsight and education. Children don't have any of that, and I've forgotten the innocence, the freedom, of being without them. I can't remember so much of what I thought of the events of my childhood as they were occurring; but I know what I think of them now.

People who say they have experienced near death witness the scene in a similar way; they are detached, disconnected.

I am disconnected.

People won't let me alone. If they're not trying to sell raffle tickets or chocolate, they're on the phone trying to ask me questions. *Ring ring.*

"What?" I said. Who has time for niceties.

"Don't bother," the person said. Touchy. It crosses my mind that they would have many slighted people in their rooms. People who are annoyed, irritated, all waiting for them.

It strikes me that I could ask one of those door knockers in, and no one would know where they got to.

At Twenty-Three

I finished my nursing course. Simple. I don't know why my teachers at school thought I was dumb. I found a spot at the hospice, where they liked me because I worked hard and I wasn't squeamish about the gross stuff. I had the night shifts, usually, because I don't have any family, is how they put it.

I did my digging after I got home, three in the morning sometimes. Sometimes I did it at dawn.

But I liked what I was finding. I liked the feeling of finding this old stuff, and wondering how it all got there. I wanted to put a sign up out the front saying *"Night-shift nurse sleeping"*, because the noise during the day was awful. The Sanderson kid across the road ran home crying after I said boo. I was only getting the mail; he was staring at me. They need to control their children.

I found an elastic band, a rain hat, a tiny crystal heart, a plastic whistle and two small white buttons.

Only Auntie Jessie was proud of me. She called and asked me to stay, said she missed me. I said yes, I'll come. I was a nobody in the family as far as everyone else was concerned; I had seen Peter and Maria just days earlier, and they had an exciting announcement which overrode any news I might have had.

I put my hand on Maria's belly. I liked the activity. I said, "It's like I can read the creature's feelings. It's trapped in there, in the cold, dark womb, all alone. It must be so very dark, no chink of light."

Maria stepped away from me. "You should have your tubes tied," she hissed. If I told anyone she said that? They'd never believe me. Peter said nothing about me being a nurse.

Auntie Jessie said, "It's a matter of urgency," so I grabbed a taxi to her place, jumping in front of a slow woman with three kids. I must have annoyed Auntie Jessie with my fractious stamping, because she showed me the room where she kept all her boxed books and told me to help myself. She said it was a room of old bones, skeletons, but she didn't keep them in the cupboard. She told me a secret.

"You can't tell people about all these. I bring them home from the library when no one's borrowed them for a while. I brought a lot of them home, the ones I scribbled in. But there's too many. I can't remember them all. Every now and then I'll find another and bring it home."

"I don't know why you're taking them out of circulation. Didn't you write the notes for an audience?" I'd recognised her writing in the margins. She confessed when I asked her.

"I'm getting scared in my old age," she said.

"Old!" I said. "Stop fishing for compliments." There were hundreds of books there. "And no one's ever noticed what you've done?" I said.

"Who would notice?"

"What about Lesley?" Lesley was her assistant, a quiet, crabby young woman.

"I told you about Lesley," she said.

"No, what about her? She's a bitch in the library.

She always blames me for damaged books even if they're really old." I could hear my voice becoming childish, my clothes loose, too big for a child.

"Lesley knows a lot about me most other people don't. I didn't know if I could keep the secret anymore," she said.

"What secret?"

She nodded at me. Smiled. "Clever, like your father. I often wondered if I'd said something earlier, what would have happened."

"Come on, Jessie. Don't talk shit. It's me. Steve. What secret?"

"You know very well. His secret is your secret; thank God the accident stopped you having children." She was mad; old and mad. There had never been anyone more fertile than I was.

"What are you saying?" I said. My voice felt too loud.

Auntie Jessie looked coldly at me. "Don't pretend," she said.

It wasn't a dream. That was no dream. She took me to her bedroom and showed me a box of books.

"I always meant to give this to you. But I didn't have the courage. Read them later. When I'm not around." There was a note on top. It said: "It breaks my heart to say it. Thank God Alex is gone, and Heather. But the children remain, and no one to care for them. Why was I so tempted to write it down? Why that need? This is my reason. There is no excuse." It was a weird note. It made no sense.

I wanted it to make no sense.

"Read them," she said. She started passing me the books.

"What, right now?" I said.

"No, Steve. But some time. These books are very important." She passed me *Rebecca*, by Daphne Du Maurier.

"Terrifying," she said. She passed me a romantic historical thing, knowing I hate them, but she said, "Read it."

She passed me *The Devil's Dictionary* by Ambrose Bierce, *In the Wet* by Nevil Shute and a really old *Guinness Book of World Records*.

"I'll look at the rest later," I said. "Thanks."

"This is the key. I thought this would be enough, but it wasn't," she said, handing me *Vendetta* by MS Murdoch. There were strange sentences, some in the sort of simple code we learned how to crack in Primary School.

She had circled letters in the book, but I was no puzzler. I didn't have the patience to find out her message. There were a few letters per page. And it was no message I could have used to save her. That's what upsets me. Why didn't she let me save her?

PHT
HIR
TYF
IVE
PIP
ECW
TWE
NTY
NIN
EWA
TCH
AMS
EVE
NTY
TWO
LIG
HTE
RCS
THI
RTY
THR
EEC

OIN
RRF
IFT
YEI
GHT
BOT
TLE
TOP
GTF
IFT
YFI
VER
ING
GGS
EVE
NTE
ENC
HAI
NPC
SIX
TYT
HRE
EHE
ELM
RTW
ENT
YSI
XWA
LLE
TCT
TWE
NTY
THR
EEC
OIN
HOL
DER
HSF
ORT
YTH
REE

ELA
STI
CBA
NDS
PTH
IRT
YFI
VET
IEB
ARM
WFO
RTY
TWO
SHO
EPM
SEV
ENL
UNC
HBO
XFF
EIG
HTE
ENS
QUE
AKY
TOY
CLT
HIR
TYS
EVE
NTV
DIA
LBK
THI
RTY
SIX
SQU
ASH
BAL
LTS
FOR

TYT
HRE
EBE
LTD
STW
ENT
YTW
OFI
NGE
RNA
ILJ
BTH
IRT
YON
ECU
FFL
INK
THE
SEA
RET
HEO
NES
IKN
OWA
BOU
T

A untie Jessie. I know all about her. She told me so much, so much I didn't need to know. Jessie, the one who read books and would never be an influence on anybody. Though this was not true, as the future told. Jessie, who gained all her knowledge from books and none from school, who pronounced her words as she read them, because she didn't ever hear them. It was never known, because it was rarely reported (because all library users have a fear of being blamed for damage, even if the book was damaged when they borrowed it) that Jessie marginalised almost every book which fell into her hands.

On page 85, *Of Mice and Men*, that little something from Steinbeck, so well borrowed from the library for the bit about Curly's glove and the Vaseline within it, to which the book always falls open, Auntie Jessie wrote in fine letters down the side: "It is clear the wife is no more than an unintelligent, bad puppy, who would have become a 'dog' had she lived. She visits the men out of loneliness, uses her sexuality as a form of friendship, just wants to be treated with gentleness, kindness, for all Curly's soft hand. There's no doubt the woman 'asked for it', asked for death because she wore sexy clothes, she wasn't content to sit and wait in the kitchen for her insecure, smelly husband to return."

She never tired of marginalia, and would scour her books searching for a reply. Sometimes she found one; perhaps just a question mark, or an exclamation. Once or twice she found abuse, but that, at least, proved her words were read.

This confidence, and a feeling of dissatisfaction, led her to embark on her great work; a novel, written in lead pencil on the blank end papers of the novels she shelved.

It was slow work; she only felt the words coming when she was at work. When she took novels home, all she saw were typed words and blank pages. She rested her coffee mug on these pages, though she weekly destroyed people with her laser stare for just the same thing.

She completed thirty-four chapters by the time she died, and could never see the novel ending. This was thirty years' work; barely a book in the library did not have her neat hand within it.

She never read the novel over; she wrote her piece and filed each book without numbering it. There was no sequence to follow; she always imagined her story could be read in any order. This stood in the face of popular opinion, that each word must lead to the next, each sentence, each paragraph, each chapter.

Auntie Jessie did not write this way.

Only one person read it from start to finish, but she never asked for his opinion. Mr Bell, her old school teacher, was a long-time customer. He loved to watch, sit with a book in his hands and watch.

He saw everything Jessie did. He read her novel in order; he plucked out books after Jessie replaced them. He told me this, though I didn't want to know.

He kept a list of his favourite pieces.

1. *Rebecca*—Daphne du Maurier 2. *Kirkland Revels*—Victoria Holt 3. *The Devil's Dictionary*—Ambrose Bierce 4. *In the Wet*—Nevil Shute 5. *Guinness Book of Records, 1960*—Ross & Norris McWhirter 6. *The Growth of the Central Bank*—LF Giblin 7. *Random Harvest*—James Hilton 8. *Bless this House*—Norah Lofts 9. *The Deer Park*—Norman Mailer 10. *The Day it Rained Forever*—Ray Bradbury Though of course the *Guinness Book of Records* was replaced when the new edition came out, leaving a gap in the middle.

Written inside *In the Wet* by Nevil Shute was this:

In the beginning, there was a woman alone.

Only she knew what passions lay within, what heat-filled dreams. She stitched silk smalls to wear near her skin, because no one could know her true desire.

No one but one. A man who, too, was alone. He came so quietly only the woman noticed. Only she saw the perfection of his skin, the seduction of his scent. Only she contrived to be held in his arms.

She was not experienced in the art of seduction. She had been kissed but once, and lovelessly. She read books by the score, was surrounded by them, and from them she received inspiration.

He opened the note. "Meet your love where the good bell rings." He had been lonely since arriving at the town. The people feared his cleverness. They did not see his kindness, his tenderness. He went to the place.

There she waited, alone. Her gown covered her naked body. As he watched, she unbuttoned herself until the swell of her breasts was visible, then he went to her.

Their kiss showed her how right she had been. She felt her body turn to liquid as he pressed against her. His hands were not still.

They cupped and rolled her breasts, they unbuttoned her gown until she stood wanton, naked. He fell to his knees in worship, and wept for wanting her.

She threw her gown upon the ground and they lay upon it. His clothes concealed a body more delightful than she had dreamed.

She touched him and laughed as he shivered.

———◆———

Inside *Kirkland Revels* by Victoria Holt:
There were problems. There were always problems. She had secrets she did not wish him to know. Her life had not always been so quiet and horribly predictable.

When she was younger, she had travelled into the city on a weekly basis to visit an elderly, ailing aunt. This aunt had sharp wit and, of all her relatives, could tolerate only the young woman. The young woman was intelligent, too intelligent for many of the inhabitants of the small country town.

The young woman began to spend longer in the city after each visit. The elderly aunt slept earlier and earlier and gave the young woman money to spend on herself. The young woman bought new clothes, sharp, smart, expensive items, which accentuated her slim figure. She lingered in bookshops, breathing in the fresh paper smell.

There was a certain kind of man who was also in bookshops. They were respectable, intelligent men who admired her. They smiled, then they made comments on the book she held in her hand. She always smiled and if the man was handsome, or exciting in some way, she would go with him for a meal. If the man was very forward, and very insistent, the meal was passed over and entrance gained to a hotel room, where the young woman learnt how to make love.

In *The Devil's Dictionary*, Ambrose Bierce:

See page 81: Love; n: *a temporary insanity curable by marriage or by removal of the patient from the influences under which he incurred the disorder.*

She spent many nights home, alone. Her sisters were married and very happy, although their lives were filled with nappies and other people's events.

She discovered the taste of Whisky. Her brother-in-law drank it in moderation and she joined him sometimes, the two of them talking like men while his wife, her sister, cooked dinner for them.

More often she drank alone, out of a tall glass. She turned her comfortable chair to the wall and tuned the radio to a male voice who talked just to her. He told her about the world and how it worked. He played music, beautiful to match her soul. As the night grew colder and older, the man's voice changed, but each man loved her as much as the first.

The ice melted in her drink but she no longer required it. Shadows from the trees and the clouds enacted a moon play for her and she laughed aloud at the antics.

Sometimes she warmed over and when her cat awakened her at dawn for his morning milk she found she had been bathing naked in the moonlight.

She would wash and dress in her disguise, her maidenly, woollen, drab clothes, brush her hair down so it sat like a cap and go out to her fake life. She would live that life then go home to her comfortable chair again.

From *Rebecca*, Daphne du Maurier:

All the clamour cannot distract them from their rapt examination of one another.

Chimes, klaxons, the holiday summoned with all the music the town could muster.

Under cover of that hysteria he slipped to her side. His charges were happy to be let run wild. Soon their parents would find them and he would remind them he had asked for extra help that day and no one had volunteered.

She had refused the family invitations, the chance to sit as an outsider and watch the family. She waited instead, with strong drink and good food. She again wore her gown. It was a magical cloak.

And so he came to her. He carried the flowers and wine, so he cared somewhat.

They were shy at first. Each remembered their first encounter as a dream.

But as she bent to stir the unlit fire, the circle of her bottom was too perfect, and he walked to her, fell to his knees, sank his nose into her flesh. She gasped. He dragged away her gown and she was naked beneath. She had no pretences as to why he was there. She faced him, leaned against the wall, bent her knees to frame his face. She knew her curls were springy, fresh, sweet. She had washed, powdered, perfumed. He kissed her thighs, the skin above the hair. He kissed the hair.

Then, to her horror, to her delight, he steered his tongue between those lips, and he lapped with its roughness against her tender skin. His tongue sank further inside her and she gave herself completely to it.

Written inside the *Guinness Book of Records*, McWhirter:

Such things you can learn if only you listen.

His voice was gentle, yet so clear she could hear each word from across the park. She was there walking her dog and hoping to see him. He was there as a stranger, to forget he ever knew her. She was wearing a soft, thin, woollen dress, its slightly scratchy material rubbing against her naked breasts. She felt her nipples harden against the wool, and she wished he would look up and see how sweet and ready she was. He was wearing many layers—as many as he could bear on this Autumn day. He felt the sweat at the base of his neck and he wondered how to free himself from the torment of loving her. He too walked his dog—he spoke to it, words she could hear in her heart. "Who needs 'em?" he said. "Women, they're all alike. But her voice, don't you think? You miss her voice, don't you, fella? And the smell of her, so sweet, so exciting. And her hair, like silk, and the way it looked, all messed and free in the morning, after, after..." The dogs were pups of the same litter. They had taken one each. Her cat was still getting used to another pet. She heard every word, steering her dog closer, closer. She spoke to her dog. "Oh, but we can live without him. Who needs those strong, tender hands, those gentle lips, who needs such fulfilment as we've never known, such filling, such swelling." He heard, too, and loosened his tie, then removed it and tucked it into his coat pocket. Then he removed his coat. Their dogs, from afar, spotted soul mates, dragged owners (slaves) inexorably, fatefully, lovingly, sensuously, eternally, towards the face of love.

Inside *The Growth of the Central Bank*, Giblin:

He would wait in queues for the rest of his life, if a glimpse of her each day would be his reward. He became adept at dropping coins, if she wasn't the free teller when he reached the head of the line. "Please, go ahead," to an angry businessman, "I don't mind waiting," to a young woman glancing often at her watch. He earned smiles (a bonus), and he reached the desk of his love. He touched her hand when she passed him his money, slid his thumbs over her fingers, an intimate action. He touched her flesh like that. Both thumbs sliding over her, holding her apart. She asked him every day not to visit her in the bank, but his heart ached after a whole day without her. She waited for him every night, on the steps of his office, because she finished earlier and didn't mind waiting. If she didn't have a book to read she spent the time imagining lascivious things to say to him, words to make him shiver, because she could not quite believe it was she he found exciting, the sound of her voice a thrill.

She had no interest in marriage, though it was expected of her. She wanted his love forever, and enjoyed the feeling of escape she experienced when they left the city limits and travelled to some unknown place.

They didn't have to worry about pregnancy because she was infertile. This discovered during an early, ugly marriage. He was both pleased and repelled. It meant that all love was for pleasure, but that the choice of producing offspring had been taken from him.

In *Random Harvest*, James Hilton:

They went orange picking, two anonymous workers there for the sun, the money, the change. And for each other. No one asked questions. No one cared. There were plenty of huts to sleep in and plenty of food. Like a pack of feral cats, when there was no dearth of comfort, they were generous with one another, kind, and they didn't judge. They arrived together, a bus load of chattering people, getting to know you, making the most of it. She sat next to him, her shoulder, arm, thigh all glued through their clothes in anticipation of what would come. It was a long drive, and that night was feast night, a party. They placed their bags in the smallest hut, the furthest away, hoping to avoid sharing with anyone else, but they need not have worried. They had never spent the whole night together before, but they were not nervous. They left the campfire early, while the voices were still loud, and they laughed.

He held the door open for her but did not offer to carry her over the threshold. They laughed at that. There were no candles, but the electric light was dim. Their mouths tasted of cheap port. He reached out his hand and, with lust rather than tenderness, squeezed her breast like he was testing it for ripeness. His other hand grasped her neck and drew her to him. They kissed. She cupped her hands around his buttocks and drew him closer, closer, and he groaned at her attack. Their bed was low to the floor and thrown about. It had not been made since the last inhabitant. She noticed this but didn't care. "I'm dirty," she said. He smiled.

"Let me wash you clean," he said.

Written inside *The Deer Park*, Norman Mailer:

She had a week off and knew that he did too. She plotted to have him for all that time.

She drove into the city to shop, and purchased goods to last them, men's toiletries as well, though she blushed to do so. She purchased cool new bed linen to welcome him, a nightgown for seduction, she planned they would not step out for a week.

He arrived, expecting dinner. She locked the door after him, should he want to escape. "Come in, Rafe," she said. She wore her nightgown. It clung and revealed, made her desire him because she felt so desirable.

"My God," he said. "You are magnificent."

She was brazen. She took his jacket from him, his shirt, she put her hands on his chest, tucked her fingers into the hairs, she kissed his throat. She kissed his chest, then knelt and kissed his belly. He sucked in his breath. "Not daring to hope," she thought. It spurred her on. "Not daring to hope." She unbuckled his belt, he kicked off his shoes.

She lowered his trousers over his hips, let them drop to his ankles. He kicked them aside. She kissed his shins, his knees, his thighs.

"No," he said. He kissed her, kissed her hair, sank his face between her breasts.

"My love," she said, but softly, so he could not hear, because she did not want him to stop for a single moment for the rest of eternity.

In *Bless This House*, Norah Lofts:

She lived at home with her parents, then her mother died, then her father. He no longer lived in the town, he said it was because there was no work, but she knew he was tired of hiding. "There's no need to hide," she said. She didn't care what people said, people were cruel no matter what you did. It mattered to him—he couldn't stand the talk.

He said he wanted more of a challenge and she thought that meant her as well. She visited him on weekends, when the library was closed, leaving her country proper self in a cupboard where her mother's clothes hung and letting her city pretty self take over. He had the smallest place to live she had ever seen, but it was private, anonymous, and he had it set up nicely. On her first visit, he opened the door. She saw flowers fill the room and small gifts in nooks and crannies.

After they made love he sent her off on a treasure hunt, and she came back with one after another. A fluffy red heart, a book of poetry, a miniature painting, a ticket to the theatre, potted mint, chocolate. The prizes still came, and she loved him for his generosity, but feared him as well.

She could see the "but" in his eyes. The city was full of women, new people, experiences she only knew about through her books. He didn't say "but". She gave him a tiny crystal heart. They made love for many months, many more gifts to the child in her heart, and she began to suffer his sideways glances, his tiny yawns of boredom, his forgetful heart. She began to die inside.

In *The Day It Rained Forever*, by Ray Bradbury:

Oh God oh God oh God he's gone where why why oh it why you know knew it was you always it was but he was there too life a friend when he hurt me it wasn't deliberate it was a mistake it was too much and I loved him too much like a lover does to lovers love oh A A A A it was all right why did you do this I would have lived he didn't live but he could have oh God oh God oh God how can I go to your home your sweet wife and those little faces oh God oh God oh God why tell me I didn't want to know I didn't need to know what you really are oh God what can I do.

The box Jessie gave me was labelled "Alex's Books," and it intrigued me, because my father had never been a reader. He despised the concept of fiction. Newspapers, he read, but anything with a cover wasn't of interest. I had read pages, here and there.

She said to me, "I can't do it anymore." I know she said that. But this is what I heard: "I'm going on a cruise to New Zealand."

That's what I heard her say.

This is what happened. I imagine this is really what happened:

Auntie Jessie saved pills like a squirrel with a tree full of nuts. She sat in her favourite chair, sun pouring in, book on her lap. It was *Great Expectations*. I don't know if she was being symbolic or she just wanted to die with a smile on her face. She made herself a cup of tea. She read, sipped, swallowed, until she fell asleep. Her gentleman friend found her.

Mr Bell, her old teacher. They truly were friends; the two of them were as sexual as a glass of water. The only sparks which flew were the ones from the open fire they loved to sit in front of at his place.

He had been away; his first holiday in years, and he cursed himself for going.

"I could have saved her. We saw each other every day," he said.

If he couldn't see that was the whole point, that she didn't want to be found, she wanted to go to the dark room and meet her people, I wasn't willing to tell him.

I talked to him, to see what family secrets he was privy to, and it seems: none. Auntie Jessie told him nothing. I left him shaking and weeping, a large lavender hanky blotting tears, alone, and I never saw him again. Did he even know why she did it?

That terrible fear of discovery? My only wish was that she had honoured *me* with the secret. That I had been told.

In *Puffball* by Fay Weldon she wrote, *"I must take steps. I cannot bear the knowledge."* Once I realised what she'd done, the idea of suicide took on a certain magic. An attractiveness. Though perhaps she got the idea from me; she copied me.

But she was successful.

No one found her.

I couldn't speak. I wouldn't cry; felt no tears, but there was thick sludge in my throat; I couldn't breathe. I had missed Dad's funeral. I was left behind, minded by one of our hateful neighbours.

Mum's funeral I was still in hospital, waiting for my guts to collapse.

So Auntie Jessie's was my first funeral, for all the deaths there's been. But it wasn't just that. I realised I had known Auntie Jessie for longer than I knew my parents. I realised there was no one left who forgave like she did.

God, how could I live without that forgiveness?

The funeral was a lot bigger than it should have been. People there for Peter, comforting Peter, as if it was his favourite relative who was dead. His mother or something. I hadn't realised until then just how loved he was. It seemed so unlikely.

I dug for a while, my comfort, and I found ten paper clips together, a margarine tub, some bones and the bluebird ring Auntie Jessie gave me when I was eight. My counsellor said I needed to move on, but how can I? I hate to leave the house. The garden is looking good, and the jasmine is flowering. At night I can smell it, sickly and sweet.

I read Auntie Jessie's books, and nothing made sense. I decided to visit the library, speak with Leslie, her assistant, to see if she could tell me anything more.

Lesley was happy to speak to me. She knew about me. "The board hired me when they finally got the funds for a library assistant. They promoted Jessie and hired me to help her." Lesley's face was blotchy. "I feel like it's my fault. They don't. They feel no responsibility for her death. Four months she lasted, now she's killed herself. They say it's a terrible thing, but not caused by any decision made by them.

"You should have seen the back-covering at the meeting. 'We would never have been so cruel as to promote someone over her. She was always so capable,' the chairman said. I could hardly hear him. They would never hold an official meeting regarding Jessie's demise; they were all so busy. The little minute-taker said something about how Jessie couldn't cope and that I, well, they call me little Lesley, was the perfect assistant. Little creep.

"They would never know. I'll stay on alone, as Acting Chief Librarian. Because I've discovered these hidden works of Jessie. It must be her. The writing style, the sharpness of the pencil used, the penmanship, in all the flyleaves and margins are identical to those notes I noticed a month before Jessie's death. And there was only one person who could have written those.

"I was updating the library card system, checking long overdue books, removing the cards on the 'deceased' list Jessie had given me, placing those cards to be re-used in the new members file.

"There had been one new member since I started, but Jessie was sure there'd be more when the school holidays began.

"I plucked out a pale green card, coded that way by Jessie to mean 'requires help to choose books'. I erased the name and address in preparation. I said, 'What was this old fella like?' I tried to read the name. I was trying to find something to talk about. I was bored. Jessie only livened up when she talked about the past.

"Jessie held out her hand to see the card. As I passed it, she saw a word printed at the bottom.

Two words. She said to me, 'He was a dear man.'

She sucked on her pearls, a childish habit which took years off her age. She tore up the card. 'Loved a bit of a saucy romance but was embarrassed. Used to pretend they were for his wife, but she's been dead for twenty years, now. Some kind of infection.

Nothing suspicious, though. No one ever thought he was involved.' Jessie tossed the card in the waste paper bin. Later, when I took the rubbish out, she rescued the card. 'Help me,' the words said.

"When Jessie wasn't there, I flicked through and found other parts of the message.

"Step on ants.

"Help me, a few times.

"Stop him.

"I can't.

"Break me.

"I love you.

"Come to me.

"Smell the flowers.

"Such a lovely garden, four times.

"I wrote down each one she found, then I showed them to her. She didn't seem bothered. I said, but someone's been defacing the cards, and she said, said, 'I'm afraid that's human nature. People can't help being destructive. It's inevitable.'"

Lesley and I sat in silence for a while. She said at last, "I'd better get back to work."

"Lesley," I said. "You realise if you talk about this people will think you're crazy? I wouldn't mention it, if I were you."

She nodded. Weak bitch.

When Auntie Jessie died I was left with Uncle Dom and Ruth as my only family members of the previous generation. Ruth didn't change her behaviour; she didn't suddenly become kind and responsible.

I just got more of her wisdom.

"Never trust a man with a voice higher than your own," was one classic. And she also advised me to keep my shower filth under control.

As Uncle Mike got older and sicker and unable to defend himself, Ruth set about changing the sort of man he was. She changed his history, told stories no one had heard before.

She said he chased her half-way around the world because he loved her so desperately and she was so popular it was hard work. Witnesses were dead, and no one listened to Uncle Mike.

Auntie Jessie had told me that she and Uncle Mike had enjoyed a mild flirtation which he had taken very seriously. Thinking back with adult experience, I can remember Uncle Mike being livelier around Auntie Jessie.

Poor old Auntie Ruth. She's not very good at re-inventing her past. People don't believe her. You need to be subtle, change things gradually. People think, "Why is she lying about that?"

Ruth somehow made me feel guilty the way no one else ever has. Pity, perhaps, is part of it; she squandered her talents, her looks, and all she was left with was bitterness and jealousy. She wanted me to denigrate my own mother, in order to make herself feel better. She thought of Mum's life as perfect. She muttered under her breath short imprecations whenever anything went wrong, "Heather didn't get this. Heather was safe. Heather was never robbed. Heather got Alex, not an idiot." I felt horribly responsible for no good reason, and I fantasised about Ruth dying, leaving me in peace. She was the last of them, though. Her and Dom. We didn't see much of Auntie Ruth when Dad was around. I had a learned dislike for her; Dad had taught me. Peter had his greatest moment of cheekiness, one which stunned us all, the day Dad was talking to us about caring for each other because we were siblings.

"But you hate Uncle Dom and Auntie Ruth, and they're siblings of you and Mum," Peter said. It was great.

"Sometimes things change as you get older.

There's no reason for the two of you to hate each other."

At Auntie Jessie's funeral, Ruth said, "It's about time that old bitch died," she said. Jessie was older by just two years. "She's been nothing but a drain on this family. Spinsters always are." She was making a knife-cut point against my marital status, as if I cared. As if I wanted her life.

Ruth could never understand why Peter and I liked Jessie so much. Spittle flew when Ruth said,

"She's just a silly ditz. How hard is it to work in a library? She couldn't even cope with running it."

"Maybe she didn't want to run it," I said. I had heard this many times; whenever Jessie's name was mentioned, the vitriol would bubble over.

"What is it you like about the woman?" Ruth said. "She's nothing. I've never seen her laugh.

She's never done anything for anybody."

"Dad liked her," I said. Ruth's face tightened; perhaps that was it. Dad liked her.

"Much as I liked your father, I have to say he liked the ladies. I don't like to say, Stevie, but it can't hurt your Mum now. He didn't mind being over-friendly, if you see what I mean. With me.

Auntie Jessie liked to think he liked her. But he despised her mousiness. He couldn't stand the sight of her. Drinking alcohol will make you drunk, you know, Stevie, a lesson your Jessie never learned."

The picture in my mind was of Mum, Dad and Auntie Jessie, sitting at our kitchen table, laughing, wet faces, Peter and I sitting up at the table too, laughing at them laughing. This is what I remember most; the table, laughter, tears. I knew that Ruth had never been part of that.

People went quiet when she walked into a room; you talked about different things when Ruth was present. You talked about her and her family, because that was the subject of greatest interest and because it could be dangerous to talk about anything else. She had opinions. Perhaps Jessie might talk about a library patron who spent his days watching other people reading, and we might be discussing him with interest, wondering.

Ruth's comment may be, "That man should be arrested before he hurts somebody," changing the picture. She might attack the man, come up with terrible theories. Anything to give her the final word, make her feel superior.

I was affected the least by Ruth. She said such strange things I would often just stare at her; I did so until she caught my stare and was quiet. Mum and Dad used to love it. They reminded me it was rude to stare, but smiled at each other. "I've never seen Ruth speechless," Dad said.

"Only before she learned to talk," Mum said.

"And even then she was a good grunter." They laughed, unconcerned that perhaps they were confusing me with conflicting signals.

I was the one selected to receive Ruth's worldly knowledge, and I received it in a continuous monotone over twenty years. "Napi-san is the best thing for whites," I was told, not that I'd asked. Another one was, "Always drive with both hands on the wheel."

Ruth said, "Who would have thought your mum would die so close to middle-age? And Jessie would only just fill the half-century. And me, the wild one, who everyone expected to die young, left behind."

"Mum wasn't middle-aged. She was only thirty-seven."

Ruth tutted. "You really are an ignorant child, Stephanie," she said. "Forty is middle-aged. Don't you realise that? We're not expected to live past 80, you know." It was just another one of her little bits of vital information. She told me this piece of Walker family history.

One time when Heather was sick, they came up with a great lark. Ruth would go to school and pretend to be Heather. They were in hysterics, as Ruth tried on outfit after outfit, because Ruth was taller and slimmer. Ruth looked so funny in clothes Heather looked lovely in. Jumpers went up to her elbows. Skirts hung loosely above her knees.

Ruth headed off, leaving Heather to submerge back into her illness. Ruth imagined they looked quite similar, and came home telling Heather,

"They called me Heather all day, and the teacher said what a good day I was having. I got you an A in a maths test. And that guy Freddie, he's really cute. You never told me he liked you."

Heather laughed at the story, but didn't really understand it. No one called her Heather at school; they called her Hester, as a joke. And Freddie liked all girls; had never shown any particular interest in Heather. Ruth went back to her own class the next day.

I had heard this story from Mum, too. The other side of it. The stuff Ruth didn't know.

Mum never told Ruth that, when she was better and back at school, everyone said her sister was a lunatic. She French-kissed Freddie, giving him the shock of his life, then disappeared.

"She was a witch, I reckon," said Freddie.

Mum told Dad the story, hoping to make him laugh. He shook his head, though.

"I don't trust her," he said.

Ruth said, "Your Dad wasn't quite the innocent," and winked at me. As if I wanted to know her dirty little fantasy.

As if she had any idea what Dad *really* did.

"Anyway, when do you get your licence back? I need someone to drive me to appointments."

"Twenty-three days," I said.

Twenty-three days.

At Twenty-Four

The scar across my forehead I got when I was eighteen. I also got the ones all over my arms. And one across my foot, where my spade had slipped, I got that at nineteen.

Some people like them, though. I don't know what it is. A man came to dig up the dead tree in my front yard and he was neat, good clothes, but there was something in his eyes. He was polite but he didn't mean it. He arrived at seven, both mornings, and I was up and ready to go.

"Early riser, ay?" he said when I brought him a cup of coffee.

"Best time of the day," I said. I knew the pass-words, the responses. I could use them any time I liked. He finished late on Saturday afternoon. He worked then because he gets paid double, and I was there, he said. He could check me out. He couldn't stop staring at my arms, my neck, all the damage.

He knocked on my door. "All finished," he said.

"Balloona!" I said.

"Balloona," he said. His fists clenched.

"Come in, I'll give you a beer," I said.

"Fuckin' flat," he said. Threw the glass into the sink, oh, and the smash.

"Fuck you," I said. I didn't want violence; just the words. I like my ears assaulted. They can't always figure when to stop, but he was smart. Gentle, gentle touch, kisses, sweetness, but this into my ear:

"You are so fuckin' ugly. Someone paid me, you know, big bucks, to fuck you. I said no way, not for a million. You stink, you bore me shitless. You're worthless, no one likes you. You could marry a prince and no one would call you a princess. You make me sick."

He stayed till Sunday night. His name was Scott.

I never hold a grudge. Peter ignored my twenty-fourth birthday, but I still rang him to wish him a happy twenty-sixth. The answering machine was on. I left a message.

"Hello, Mrs Searle, this is Mr Fucky Fuck of the Fucky Fuck laundry. You requested the Fucky Fuck special for your Fucky Fuck jacket which had vomit and blood all over it. The Fucky Fuck jacket is now ready. Please collect it from me or Mrs Fucky Fuck."

He rang me back days later. He didn't say anything about forgetting my birthday. He didn't ask how the hospice was going, he didn't care that the patients loved me and the staff thought I was a gem.

He said, "You're a bloody shocker, Stevie. You're going to have to come visit soon." He had a whinge about being lonely, not having anyone around to laugh at his jokes. I didn't ask how his courses were going, and he didn't tell me. He was in the news sometimes, these days, getting famous.

"Maria's out, I take it," I said.

"Yeah, yeah, out at some women's meeting. Hey, how's the nursing going, anyway? Killed any patients lately?" We laughed at that, and I felt so good I asked him to come for dinner. "I'll even clean up. Cook," I said. "You're all welcome."

He said, "Actually, there were some things I wanted to clear up down there. Since when were you a cook?"

"Since I didn't want to starve," I said.

He laughed as if I were joking. Already Mum's death was in the past; to him, I had always lived alone in that dark house. We never had a mother or a father.

Peter and Maria pulled up and sat in their car for ten minutes. The kids, Kelly and Carrie, fought each other and tried to get out; Maria kept turning around and whacking them. Peter clenched both hands on the wheel as if trying to stop himself whacking her.

When they got out, their faces were a laugh. The manure on my front lawn was dry and cracked, and a fly colony had started a new life. That shit stank. The kids shouted, leaped about, all that energy. They were both filthy, those girls.

The first thing Kelly said was, "You've got a pile of poo, Auntie Stevie."

"Auntie Stephanie," said Maria. "Steve's a boy's name."

"And Maria is the name of a saint. So I guess we're both living a lie," I said. I smiled. "Come on in," I said. "I use the back door."

The smell wasn't so bad once the door was shut.

"Something smells good in here," Peter said. He pulled down the blinds in the kitchen, as usual. He hates looking into the backyard. I had worked really hard to make a nice dinner, harder than I would admit to them. I had even asked the opinion of the lady at the butcher's, who is a shocking gossip once she gets your ear. She suggested I cook something simple for the kids, a treat like meat pies, something easy. So I bought frozen for them.

For us, I made, on the suggestion of the butcher woman, Prawn Cocktails, Beef Wellington and Chocolate Mousse. A menu straight from the RSL.

Kelly ran around trying to find presents. She couldn't understand why she wasn't being spoiled.

Kids of five are like that, I guess. She was like a puppy and I hate dogs; I ignored her. Carrie stared up at her big sister, wondering what was going on.

They both waited and waited and then started crying.

I sat them in front of the TV and brought their pies out.

"Thanks, Auntie Stevie," they said. They kept looking at each other, like, "I can't believe it."

Peter and Maria were in Mum's room, looking at her things. They wanted to take some mementoes.

"Just a couple of special items," Maria said. They took something every time they came to visit.

I knew that all these years (it had been six since Mum died) Maria has resented the fact that I got the house and Peter got nothing. He only mentioned it once; since then he hasn't asked me for anything.

Maria was up there fingering our parents' things.

Mum never threw out Dad's belongings. I'll never throw out any of them, even though Peter says she wanted us to. If she wanted them thrown out, she would have thrown them out herself.

I guessed what Maria would steal; the silver picture frames, saying she wanted the photos. I'd say, "Why not just take the photos, then? I've always liked those frames," just to watch her squirm.

"Dinner's ready," I shouted up the stairs. The kids were shovelling down the hot meat as quickly as they could.

Maria entered the TV room, looked over their shoulders, screamed. "Oh, my God, that's *meat!*" She knocked both plates over and sent the small food remaining flying.

The kids looked stricken. They knew it was meat but had forgotten how evil it was.

"It was nice," Kelly said. There were bits of meat and pastry all over the floor. I don't know if Peter or Maria cleaned it up; I certainly didn't, and I never thought of it again.

"You *know* we're vegetarians," said Peter. It was his Course voice, the one he used for people who didn't quite get it.

"Since when?"

"Since we were married," Maria said. "Since we realised the damage a carnivorous diet can do to the human body."

"Well, you're going to be fuckin' hungry tonight," I said.

I set out the Prawn Cocktails and sat down. They sat down. I ate my Prawn Cocktail. Then I ate Peter's Prawn Cocktail. Then I ate Maria's Prawn Cocktail. No one said a word. When I brought out the Beef Wellington, Peter rose and opened the two bottles of wine on the bench. Dad had quite a collection and I was making a good dent in it.

I suppose Peter thought I should give the wine to him; bad luck. I like to have it for guests.

Peter and Maria drank those two bottles while I ate my Beef Wellington. It was delicious. Peter got two more bottles. They watched me eat, malevolence brimming up.

The kids were quiet. I knew there was a horror movie on, and they were keeping silent in case their Mum noticed and made them turn it off.

Kelly already loved that sort of thing. Carrie, only two, was asleep. Meat poisoning.

I brought out the Chocolate Mousse. The kids had already eaten theirs.

"Is there gelatine in that?" Maria said. She could hardly talk.

"Yep," I said. "Horse's hooves." It looked like they'd have to stay the night; there was no way either of them could drive.

There was no way I was going to go out in the cold to drive them miles home when they should have stayed at my place anyway.

"You'll have to stay here. You can't drive," I said.

"I can't drive? *I can't drive?* You're the one who can't. You're the one who smashed Mum up. You're the one who killed our mother." Peter began to weep, two bottles of red wine coming out as tears. He began to sob. Maria placed a hand on the back of his neck.

"How can you live with yourself?" she said. She sounded almost sober but her eyes could hardly focus.

"You don't know how I live," I said. "You have no idea."

I left them to the house and went to stay with Scott, the new man in my life.

———————◆———————

As I turned into my street the next day, part of me worried they'd take over, that I'd find my stuff on the front lawn, snails crawling all over it, the neighbourhood kids picking through it. But Peter and his family were gone when I got back.

I didn't see them again for a while; Peter forgave me, though. Maria made him suffer for my behaviour. He rang me every day to whinge about her, and I could only agree with everything he said.

Maria found errors in his every movement. If he was home early, she wondered what was happening at work. If he was home late he had to account for every moment. I know there was no sex, but he was used to that. He told me about it: "I can tell you." I wished he wouldn't. And she spoke through the kids, made jokes about him to them.

"And you know how easy it is to make kids laugh. She says, 'Look at Daddy's nose,' and they crack up."

"Her point?"

"She thinks I've got a strange nose. She says it looks like a blobby sausage."

"Imagine what she thinks of mine, then. Just tell her that her stretch marks look like an aerial view of the moon. That'll shut her up. In fact, let me talk to her. I'll tell her."

"I wish. She wants to talk to you, anyway. That's a warning. She's got this thing about the house, she thinks it should be part ours or something. I'm not bothered by it but you know what she's like."

I couldn't imagine him having too many arguments about it.

I'm not a mild-mannered, mysterious type. I like noise and plenty of people. I love a good big fight, the kind where you can whack your fists around and feel that flesh, hear that bone.

Maria showed up at my door without phoning a month or so later. She was dressed all in black with enormous shoulder pads. She was there for a verbal; I wasn't interested.

"Fuck off, Maria." I slammed the door in her face and went back to the kitchen. I was making freezer spaghetti bolognaise; everything out of my freezer went into it.

"We need to talk." She'd let herself in.

"Give me the key." I poked her with my metal spoon, held out my hand.

"This is Peter's key. He's entitled to a key to his own mother's house."

"Look, Maria, you'll have to speak to Mum about that. She's not keen on having too many keys about these days; you never know who's walking up and down the street."

"What?"

I handed her a spoonful of mixture. "What do you think" She grimaced, turning her head away.

"Just a drop more Kit-e-Kat, don't you think?" I said.

"I can't believe you don't even know how to cook. It's pathetic."

"Ssh," I said. I pointed to the ceiling. "Mum's been trying to teach me for years. I've taken to buying takeaway, pretending I cooked it, like in the ads.

She loves it. She's a pretty smart old bird; she probably knows. But anything to keep her happy."

"But Steve. Your mother…"

I looked at her, wide-eyed. She sat down.

"Your mother's dead, Steve. I was there at the funeral."

"You were there for Dad's funeral," I said.

"Your Dad died when you were kids."

I shook my head. Reached out my hand.

"Come up and say hello. She misses you. She thinks you don't like her."

"I liked her," Maria said. She was pale; her eyebrows tilted, turning her smooth expression into a frown.

"Well, come on, then. Come and say hello," I said.

She rose and walked ahead of me up the stairs.

"Where is she?" Maria said.

"She's in her room," I said. Her voice had lost all its aggression. She feared—what? That Mum sat, stuffed, in her old four poster bed? That I would plunge a knife between her shoulder blades and bury her in the backyard? That she was insane; that Mum was indeed alive and her life in the past six years had been a dream?

"Still trying for kids?" I said. She stopped on the stairs but didn't turn around to look at me.

"Kelly and Carrie," she said.

"Nice names. Is that what you'll call them?"

She pushed open the door. The air inside was fresh; I kept it well open, in case visitors dropped in.

"There's no one here," she said. She turned to face me.

I smiled and held out my hand. "The key," I said.

She placed it in my hand, but hooked her fingers; drew her long nails across my flesh. I grabbed her wrist and she slapped me with her other hand.

"Stop it," she said. "I came to talk, not fight."

"We have nothing to talk about," I said. We were at the top of the stairs. "Go home," I said, like I would to a dog. My arms ached with the desire to push her. Her fingers dug into my arms; it didn't hurt. She was a weak, helpless woman. I twisted my neck, drew her left arm towards me and gently sank my teeth into her wrist. Not to cause damage; a cat giving warning of pain to come.

Why should she have children, anyway? Why should those two horrid beasts be alive when there are tiny souls queuing up waiting for my womb to be real? Peter makes a lovely father. I could have been a good mother. I would let my daughter drive, too. Then it would be her own fault if the accident hurt her and I'll never know my grandchildren.

Dougie Page called to say he had some new information for me. That's what he called it.

Information.

I said, "What, no news? Just information?"

He said, "This is serious, Steve. You've started something rolling and I can't stop it now."

Cops love to talk in clichés.

So I invited him over Saturday night, told him to bring some fish and chips, and I'd pay for the beer, because enrolled nurses get paid. Not much, but enough for beer.

It's a good place to work. I'd do it for free, if I was independently wealthy. I love it. The staff are friendly to me, and they haven't figured out yet why I'm there. They like to make the dying feel good about death. I just want to watch the dying.

Ced, who's the registered nurse above me, says I'm a natural with them. He says, "It's like you understand them at a very deep level, Steve."

Nice guy.

I got the beer in on Friday night, drank most of it, planned to get more the next day. But Scott came knocking on my door in the morning. Really morning; at dawn.

"Going down the coast. Wanna come?" he said.

I was in a robe, naked beneath.

"OK," I said. "I'll just grab a few things."

"Bring some booze. And ya got any dope?" he said, and went to wait in the car.

I hadn't asked if we would be camping or staying in a house. I didn't know who else was going. Or how long we would be going for. I was supposed to meet Dougie that night, but he'd understand. He wouldn't mind. I can't really explain what it was with Scott. I could leave the house for longer times when I was with him. It was like the elastic tying me to my house snapped, and I didn't get tugged back. He could have helped me leave the house for good if I ever decided I wanted to.

I didn't call Dougie. I didn't think of it. I called Ced, told him I was sick, got a day off work. That was sorted, then.

It was a house. There were three bedrooms, ten people, which meant I had sex with another couple listening. I kind of liked that. I wish you could get hetero bars like those gay bars you hear about.

(Though I never met anyone who went to one. Do they exist? Or did someone make it up, a rumour about the lives they lead? I hope it's true. I really do.) If I had a dick, I'd like to go to a bar, have a drink or whatever, then go to a room and just stick it through a hole for someone to suck on.

There was one other girl. We were left alone a lot, as the boys went surfing, fishing, drinking. I made myself sick, staying there. She didn't speak a word to me after she realised I couldn't cook and was not interested in cleaning.

"I'd love to be able to," I said. "I just haven't got the knack." She tried to show me simple things, like omelettes, but the smell made me sick. I just didn't feel like eating when he was around.

I didn't ask when we were going back; I didn't want him to think I wanted it to be over.

He dropped me off Tuesday morning without a word. Just a rough tongue in my mouth. He had been up all night drinking and smoking.

I had a lot of time to think about Scott. I didn't see much of him, so I had time to think, and when I was with him he ignored me so I had time to think then as well. Mostly I tried to figure out why, why, when I didn't even really enjoy sex with him. I think it was mostly because I felt safe from him. He was so completely unaffected by me. Nothing I did upset him or pleased him. He would never be in my dark room.

He would never be slighted by me. He was my chance to escape. To change my future and the past.

Peter met him once by mistake, when he stayed the night at my place and Peter came by to pick up some things the kids left behind. It was an excuse; he wanted to see me to bitch about Maria.

And there was my boyfriend Scott, asleep on the couch in front of the TV. His shirt was hitched up over his belly, he snored, his hair stuck up. I woke him up to meet Peter.

"This is my brother,Peter, 'member I told you about him?"

He stared, scratched. "Nah," he said.

Peter snorted. "Good one, Steve." He didn't see how different the guy was to Dad, not that that's why I picked him. But they were different.

Dad was always neat and polite. Scott hardly ever showered, he farted while people were eating, he told everyone to fuck off.

Dad was smart, committed, career-minded. Scott quit school early, gave up as soon as he had an excuse to, and never had a job. I wouldn't like to think about it too much. I just carried on, niggling on him, trying to get a reaction. I cut his jeans up once and he just left in his undies. I fucked his best mate and made sure he found out. None of it even made him blink.

I cringe to think of how I behaved. When I think about it, I should have killed him, because his room must have been as big as a mansion. Instead, I tried to be what he wanted. He likes them feminine, so I acted like a girly. I looked ridiculous in my delicate clothes, all white lace and high heel shoes. No one who knew me ever saw me like that. I felt peculiar, silly; I couldn't hold a conversation with anyone.

Samantha rang once when I was dressed that way, and I couldn't string two words together. I agreed to everything she said.

But he liked me that way, clean and sweet like a lady. He wouldn't touch me if I was wearing jeans.

At work, Ced told me he had to move out of his place because his housemate's girlfriend was moving in. "And she hates my guts," he said. "I can't live that way. And they take advantage of me, use up all my food and never buy more."

"Sounds like you'd be hard to live with, Ced," I said.

"Me?" He looked shocked. He wasn't used to criticism. Everybody loved him.

"I'm kidding. You can come stay with me for a while, if you like." I didn't mind Ced. He thought I was smart and funny. If he hadn't been around at the same time as Scott, I might have paid him more attention. He seemed pathetic in comparison to Scott. Too weak, too nice, too dull. He was one of those people who make a personality out of a name. He hated Scott.

Poor Ced. The patients love him, cos he's funny with them, you know, calling them "young lady" and that stuff that idiot old women like. He calls the dying men "chum" and for some reason they like that. He moved in one weekend. Good stuff, too. A big TV, heaps of music.

The last time I saw Scott, he came around at five AM to tell me that he was getting married. I thought it must be the girl who went down the coast with us, but he said, "No, mine's a teacher."

He had been on his buck's night and his mates dropped him off at my place. Like I've got a red light on my door. Like I'm one last dirty fling. I never knew anyone who made me feel so bad.

I went to the church to watch him be married. I didn't want to slight anyone; I was very careful. I smiled at them all, was very quiet. I wore one of Mum's old dresses, mauve, and a pair of her pantyhose. My clothes are office or slut.

It was fucking boring. I read the prayer book, crossed my eyes, counted the candlesticks and was first out the door when it was over.

Standing outside, I realised I was the only one without a sprig of baby's breath on my person.

"And how do you know the happy couple?" the photographer asked. He was the only one who spoke to me.

"I used to root the groom." I even smiled at the groom's friends, to let them know I didn't want trouble. They didn't smile back. I left before the happy couple emerged, climbed into the welcome of my car and drove home. Sometimes I forget how repellent people are; I think it will be okay.

Then I'm reminded.

Scott was my chance. My chance to save myself.

I returned from the wedding to find a message from Dougie Page: "We need to talk about your father."

No, we didn't. We wouldn't. I wouldn't talk about that.

Ced was supposed to be away for the weekend, but he came back early. I didn't care, though; I had made my preparations and was not willing to hide them from him. I was dressed in my cat suit, a number Ced always admired. A scalpel on the table.

A fresh bottle of rum too. Just to put him off the scent.

"I never know what you're drinking," Ced said, smiling at my unpredictability.

"Whatever sings out in the shop," I said. I poured him a drink. I didn't feel like talking, or being talked out of what I was about to do, so I asked him how his things were going.

"Oh, you know," he said. I laughed. This was a man who bit his tongue sometimes, he talked so much.

"No, tell me," I said. I felt a terrible tenderness for him; he didn't need to be forgiving, because he was never angry with me. He never judged me or blamed me.

Sometimes I felt like I was two people, twins living in one body.

"Come to terms with your sexuality yet?" I said.

He recoiled. His ambivalent sexuality was his loudest, proudest feature. Some long-clawed beast burst out of my heart.

"It's just that it's a bit hard to take a man seriously who masturbates to the afternoon soapies, Ced."

I'd caught him once and never told him, and he was never sure.

"Nothing wrong with that."

"Oooh, no. Whatever. You know, sickness is only in the eye of the beholder."

"Come on, Steve, knock it off." He sounded flippant but he was pleading with me.

"You know what everyone calls you, don't you?"

"What everyone?"

"Everyone who comes here, everyone I speak to. They all laugh about it when you're not here."

"What?"

"The Faker. They reckon you fake the lot, orgasm, desire, personality. They reckon you're a joke, that if someone greeted you dressed as a tomato, before long you'd be holding your breath so you can look like a tomato too."

I had thought fast to come up with that one. No one ever said a bad thing about Ced.

"And what about you? What do you think?"

"I think you only want to be liked," I said.

He smiled. "That's right," he said.

"And I think that's fucked."

I asked him to move out because his hound dog face was depressing me. I said it would be best if he left straight away.

I waited a week, to make sure he was gone, then I sat in the bath and cut my wrists.

He came back, though; said he had a feeling. He has feelings at work, but he doesn't tell everyone about it. Sometimes he'll be heading to a patient in the east wing, and have a feeling, and he'll make it to the west wing just in time to say goodbye to someone. *Farewell forever, mon cherie.* He had one about me, and he came back, and he found me. It might have been the letter I sent him; I don't know.

He just had a feeling to come back. I'm glad it was him, though the sight of me still wasn't enough to make him hate me. I knew what it felt like on the inside; I hated myself.

I hadn't eaten in a week. No one had fed me, no one brought me a casserole to tide me over. I drank vodka, bottle-style, and I smoked until I could no longer breathe.

I sat naked in the armchair with the television on, and I shat, I pissed, I vomited, I spat, until there was a moat of my fluids protecting me.

But Ced had a feeling. A wishful feeling. He wanted me to need him. He wanted to arrive and I'd say, "Thank God! You are the only one who can help me." I think he's as clever as me with his what-should-have-happeneds.

He has no need to lie about his life. His father didn't die a hero. He didn't kill his mother in a car accident. He has many friends and admirers. People love him; I could care less. Perhaps he finds that intriguing. He rang me to say he was coming. I said fuck off. Then I let the blood run and sent myself to the room. Mmmm, sweet smells, sleep, a sea, the dead sea. Red, dead sea, and my blood pumps, pumps, balls together. I can smell shit. Shit and mothballs.

I learnt some lessons in the dark room. I heard snip snip and there was a hairdresser. It took me a while, but she was the one who red-headed me years ago just before mum died, and I knew then why she was so thin, almost transparent.

I knew why the people were in the room and who they were; each and every one had been slighted by me, and each slight, by me or anybody else, snapped up a bit of their soul and sent it to the dark room of some unknowing person. Or to my dark room.

I went back to the room to look at those faces, try to identify who they were, where these people had come from. Why did they wait for me to wake up with such anticipation?

I feel no warmth from the bodies which stand around me where I lie on a hard bed. And bodies there are; leaning over me anxiously, waiting for my eyes to open. I can smell them. That mixture of shit and mothballs you smell sometimes on old people. Decay and the fear of decay.

They surround my bed, more of them each time.

There seem to be hundreds of them now, on my fifth visit.

The smell of them stays with me each time I return from the dead. The smell was the indication that I had gone too far. There was love in the hatred. Because they only existed for me. You love your creator.

And Mrs Beattie waited in the cold, dark room, with the others, waited with her fingernails growing, growing, and Darren was there, the stink of milk about him.

One small cry: Kelly, little Kelly. What could have slighted her? Sensitive little shit. Perhaps the fact I do not have lollies on tap. Orphaned, here, because I could see neither Peter nor Maria. Confused. Why was she there? She loved me. Her hand shook as she came towards me. A pin, long as her forearm, and she pierced my ear drum, a buzz, a scream, but the whisky numbed me, I could feel its magic.

Strangers, strangers, a loser with a side-parting, I needed that job, and two waiters in white coats, Asian, I'd only been to one restaurant since last time.

Then I saw Scott, at the back of the room, taking time out to be there for me. I had got to him, then.

I meant something. It must have been the time I pretended I was pregnant to him. I really did think I was, for a minute or two.

But he did not approach. He did not care I was dead. He was there against his will. My elation was gone, and the local librarian, not Auntie Jessie or Leslie, a bitch, slithered up to my feet. She climbed onto the table, between my legs. I tried to close them but strangers held them open, faces I didn't know, Pookies looking for their Nookies, perhaps.

The librarian grew, she was huge, and she hawked up a lump of mucus which must have come from her rotting lungs.

She opened up my chest like it was a book and spat into it.

Pookies pinched me, pinched tiny bits of my flesh like piranhas. I saw a woman with three children, nodding, yes, yes, yes.

Workmates, biscuit hogs, shoving biscuits into my mouth, holding my nose with their bony ice fingers and I couldn't breathe, I can never breathe.

They began to circle, and there were hundreds of them, like children making a tidal wave in a back-yard swimming pool. Around, around, and I did not move to touch my bleeding because they had forgotten I was there.

Around, around the room began to whistle, and then they were gone and I was lifted by the wind they'd made, tossed, smashed, my eye pierced by my own long fingernail, my wrist bent backwards, slashes all over me, and I screamed and they snickered from somewhere and I couldn't laugh and they wanted to watch for eternity.

But Ced had his feeling, and he found me, and I felt as if my feet were covered with magnets, and I couldn't lift my feet far from the steel road. I took heavy steps in a direction I had not chosen. My life was nothing. All my choices were irrelevant, dust in the balance.

Nothing I did was of my own choosing.

I awoke from being rescued with another resolution; concentrate on my career, make it big. I also resolved, again, not to slight anyone.

I spent money on good clothes, walked carefully in the mall on the hunt. I put things properly on the hanger. I looked people in the eye when I gave them money. I got talking to one nice girl who sold me heaps of things.

"Ooh, it suits you, love your hair," she said, but I'm not influenced by that sort of thing.

"I need something to get me ahead," I said, and she understood. We talked and talked while I tried things on. I was quite bereft when she was called to the phone.

Another girl took over; she whispered in my ear,

"Don't worry about her, she's an absolute bitch. Everyone hates her."

"At least she has taste," I said. "I'm not going to buy anything suggested by someone who's dressed like you."

She left me alone; my friend came back with the perfect outfit.

"Balloona!" I said.

"Balloona? I love it," she said.

I felt great, bags of clothes, a perfume girl tried to spray me but I turned my head away. "Don't ruin the day," I said. I hate perfume.

I smiled at people at the hospice. I invited myself to meetings and made suggestions.

Ced didn't tell them what had happened. And he didn't move out after all. He got two friends of his in to share with us. I don't know if he thought that would make me feel normal, but it didn't. I called them Mo and Ho.

They seemed to be okay, and as Peter took Maria and the kids overseas for Christmas, I thought I would have lunch at home, with my housemates and their friends. But they all had things to do, though, important things, with family. They had presents under their beds; I stole one from each to open on Christmas Day. I wandered up to the shop and bought some turkey roll; I would have it sitting on the front step and I'd watch the street. Ced went to his parent's place somewhere in the country. No way would you catch me there with no way to escape.

He left me a sketch pad and some pencils for a present. Like I'm an artist with inner needs.

From one housemate I got a tie. From the other I got a book about skateboarding. I wore the tie and left the book on the coffee table. I thought that was thanks enough. They never mentioned the presents I gave them: deodorant to the smelly one (in the card I said *"Use it!"*), because a present should be useful. And a vibrator to the girl who never had boyfriends. It's hard to judge these things sometimes.

I was on my own for New Year's Eve, too.

Samantha was out somewhere and didn't get back to me in time. I had a tummy upset and spent a lot of time on the toilet, so I must have missed her calls. Ced was still in the country. Our two housemates moved out; they said it was the best time to move because the market was asleep. They told me to keep the bond to pay for bills, which put me in front, because they had just handed over money two weeks previously. I would have kept the bond money, anyway; I'd need to get his room fumigated, and she smashed three plates and two cups, having a shocking case of the shakes.

I found out later they hadn't found a place at all; they went to stay in a hostel. Fuck them. It gave me more time to dig.

I found a squeaky toy which shocked me when I stood on it, a broken doll, a Chinese food container lid and a beautiful pearl.

At Twenty-Five

Ced says I'm a natural at what I do, but he doesn't really know what I do at all. We had a patient, Mr 42, who was diagnosed with liver cancer six months ago and spent five months pretending it wasn't happening. This is a fairly common occurrence, especially amongst lonely types without anyone to say, "You need to see a doctor", or to pay attention to them in any way. I spent a lot of time with him, talking about the things he'd done. People he'd hurt, those he'd made cry, those he didn't even know existed.

Ced looked in and saw us talking, and later in the tea room he said, "You seem to know the right things to say to make them feel better."

I sipped my lukewarm tea and nodded. He didn't have to know what I told them. That their smiles were desperate smiles: look at me dying on the outside and the inside, I'll be brave, I'll take my punishment.

Good stuff.

I did some more digging. I found a dial for a television, a mug handle, sharp to touch, a spent light globe and a thin leather belt, now green with mould in places, such good quality it could still be worn.

Dougie Page came to the hospice to give me a list.

He hated the place, but I was on double shifts and hard to catch. He didn't like the smell; breathed through his mouth and talked funny.

"It's a list of missing people. We're not sure if there's a connection, but it's some names which have come up in conjunction with each other. And some of the things missing along with them. I don't know if any of them mean anything to you."

I took a look at the list. Four names. Paul Harris, Chew Wang, Albert Mitchell, Chris Stepanos. The names meant nothing. But the descriptions of their items were familiar: a pipe, a cheap watch, a lighter, and an old coin.

"Nothing," I said. I didn't want him to know of the things I found in the backyard. That was my information; knowledge to keep safe.

I got home from work at 3am, unable to sleep. I thought I should sort through some papers, destroy things, destroy stuff I didn't want people to see. But I didn't really know the difference.

One thing I did find was the card my old English teacher had sent me for Mum's memorial. I hadn't thought of her, although she called me periodically and tried to make me talk about stuff I didn't want to talk about. She wanted the details of things she didn't need to know.

I called her, anyway, and she said, "Come to visit, Steve." I arrived there, thinking I'd stay for a day, thinking that would be plenty. She admired my car. It was a good day; she read poetry, some she'd written herself. One was about me, she said, but I didn't recognise myself.

She was mad, but fit, and she lived in a log cabin, built by numbers, out in one of the new plastic suburbs. She was surrounded by strangers who thought she took up room, but they left her alone. She liked that; left her time to write. She was working on her autobiography. I wondered how much her obsession with suicide and death would feature. I thought I'd call her, see her, but I hadn't gotten around to it.

We ate and drank.

She had bought a meat pie, home-made tomato sauce, shortbread.

"I haven't found another student like you, Stevie. It broke my heart when you left school. We could have got you to Uni. I know it."

"I didn't want to go. I didn't want to go," I said. "I wanted the bucks. Studying is for the birds. Anyway, I love nursing. It suits me."

She laughed. "For the birds," she said.

I told her about the jasmine in my backyard.

"Sounds lovely," she said. "I must come for a visit." This was too much; I didn't want her in my home. I was cold and she didn't move to turn the lights on.

"Look, I'd better get going," I said.

"Oh," she said, waking from a dream. "I thought you'd stay. I thought you'd stay the night. I've got a spare room. I thought we could go for a drive tomorrow, see some sights, you know."

"You know. You know. I thought cultured people didn't say you know."

"I know." We giggled. "I've got so much to tell you," she said. "And you me. We can talk about whatever it is that's bothering you."

That was my big cue to fuck off. Analysis by amateurs; everyone wanted to do it to you if you were an orphan.

"Not much to talk about," I said. It was like some magnetic force drawing words out.

"Why don't we get a nice plate or two of Indian food, sit around, talk into the night. We have a certain affinity, Steve. I don't know if you feel it. I certainly haven't felt it for another student, but then you were not like any other student I ever had." I worried for a moment she was being sexual; that was not my desire. But she just liked me. She liked me as I was.

"I'll go up the road and get some," I said. It would be nice to sit on her front lawn, sniff the jasmine.

I thought it was simple, an offer to buy Indian food. I didn't know what would happen. I would have let her go, if I'd known. Let the teacher get picked up in my place.

I wandered out, her money jiggling in my pocket. Let her pay It was the least she can do.

I was walking, walking, because the restaurant was close and the parking bad, and a car slowed behind me. I thought it was her; I stupidly thought it was her. So I turned with a smile on my face, my thumb out, ha ha hitch-hiking.

It wasn't her. It was a guy, and he stopped. He had a baseball cap on. He said, "Get in, I'll drive you." Pauly, I thought and all the others. All the missing children, condemned to life in a room eating dog shit. I picked up a rock and threw it at his window.

"Fuck off," I screamed. I ran back towards Alice's house, but I couldn't find it, I was lost. I didn't want to know if he was following, I knew he was; I knew I was going to be raped and locked in a cold dark room, cold and dark with people who hate me. All the streets and houses looked the same. I found my car, climbed in, drove home. Money in my wallet.

My car is a special family car. We got it when I was eight. Sandwiched between my appendix and Dad's death, eight was a good year.

I loved the new car smell. A smell without history. Peter and I would hang our heads out the windows, letting our mouths dry out so much we could hardly breathe.

Gradually our smells took over. Dad drove it for a year, then Mum, though she hated driving at all, Peter when he got his licence, then me. I insisted Mum give it to me; I needed it. I was a courier. Peter said to me once, "If you hadn't pinched the car off me, Mum might be alive right now." What would he want with an old car like that? Doesn't fit his image.

Peter and I both learned to drive in it. Dougie Page taught us on

Sundays. Mum didn't want the responsibility. I could lean my head back and feel the dent where Dad used to rest his head. If I closed my eyes I felt like him.

My dad loved looking after me, getting me things no other little girl got. We were at the pictures once, a very special event because Dad hated the movies. Mum said, "But our second date was at the movies. Didn't you like it then?"

"And what movie was on?" Dad said, and Mum laughed, and they started kissing and wouldn't stop. I hugged their four knees to my chest so hard they tripped over.

"Do you want to go to the pictures?" Dad asked me. Oh, yes, I did, I wanted to sit between Mum and Dad, and Peter has to sit way up the front because he's half-blind.

The movie was wonderful. I still have the poster on my wall, a girl in army gear, mud on her cheeks. I'm the only one who got one. Dad talked the woman behind the counter into pulling down the advertising one behind her. For me. Mum slapped him all the way home. "Big *charmer!* What a *charmer!*" Peter snuck in one night and drew a moustache on the girl; I snuck in the night after that and drew a moustache on him.

Didn't ring Alice. She rang me. Where are you? Fuck off. Fucking hate you. Fuck off.

At work, Ced said, "How was your visit to the old teacher? What's she like? Does she still think you're a genius?" He said this while we were washing a woman covered with pustules. We were used to it. She listened to us, distracted, enjoying a glimpse of real life.

"She's turned into a lesbian. She tried to have a go at me," I said.

The patient gasped. I took her mind off her suffering just for a minute or two.

At Twenty-Six

I'm thinking surprise party. I'm wondering, how dumb do they think I am? No one mentions my twenty-sixth birthday, no one wants to know where the party is?

I thought I'd let them play their little games.

Every one of them should have known I'd rather be amongst it, planning, anticipating, deciding who wasn't going to be fucking invited.

This is what should have happened:

My friends were so good at keeping secrets I had barely an inkling They called me through the day with birthday wishes, to put me off the scent, and asked what I was doing to celebrate.

"Oh, not much, you know, just a quiet drink at home with Peter, I think. After all, he's the one who's known me the longest."

This is what should have happened:

Peter picked me up from work in his Mercedes and it was nice and cool inside because it's always hot in February, my birthday, too hot for people to care.

The car is cool and he has champagne. Maria isn't there because both children are sick.

Peter starts talking about all the great birthdays, how it's important the two of us are always together.

He says, "We don't need third parties," meaning Maria.

"Or fourth or fifth," I say, meaning the kids, and he laughs. He agrees.

We have a drink in the beer garden of the one real pub in town, then another. Peter leaves me alone for a few minutes and I shut my eyes to the sun, because it sets late here in summer and is at its most benign now.

"I ordered take away from Alla Bussola," he said.

"I thought we'd go home and eat it."

Neither of us like to eat-in at restaurants. It's the one true thing we have in common. It's much harder for Peter, in his job, because he has to do it often. I never do it.

We both love food, love to eat it quickly, chew loudly, slurp, not talk, taste everything, lick the plate. When we have our happy moments we talk about being rich enough to own a restaurant just for us, where we choose off the menu and behave as badly as we like. I still think about it sometimes.

We pick up the takeaway and I can't resist eating the garlic bread. I wipe my greasy fingers on the seat and Peter says, "Oh, Steve," but nicely, as if he's glad I'm like that.

The owner of the restaurant hates us taking his food away. He doesn't let anybody else, but we talked him into it. We lied to him about being agoraphobic and he's a lovely, trusting man, and a wonderful cook. He does the cooking himself, and he serves.

We take away the garlic bread, and this fried cheese which makes my tongue melt. There are garlic prawns on the thinnest, *strongest* garlic pasta.

There is pasta with salmon and vodka, chicken with the greenest asparagus, there's tortellini so tender you don't have to chew. And there's zuppa inglese, a potent, marsala-drenched cream-whipped heaven.

We eat it all in the car up the road from his place.

"Come in for coffee," he says, or should have said, and I do.

If I'd been suspicious, all the cars parked by his house would have confirmed it.

But I say, "Looks like someone's having a party and didn't invite you."

"Bastards," he says.

I still don't get it, even at the front door where someone has strung some streamers.

Peter unlocks the door and pushes it open. He nods for me to go first. I step inside.

"Surprise!" How can I name the hundreds of people who were there, when they only exist in my fantasy? Certainly a good time was had by all. And there, how frustrating my lack of experience in these things is. My imagination fails me. I cannot get beyond, "Surprise!" then all is a blank until I am at the front door, my throat sore from speaking so many farewells. Peter is in the back toilet, helping Maria be sick.

This is what should have happened when I got home:

"Happy Birthday!" The cheer is off-key; it makes me laugh.

"No singers here, I take it?" I said. "No out-of-work performers getting in some practice?"

They ignore me and continue with their blessings. I can see they carry presents; some held in mock secret behind backs, others waved tantalisingly.

"Very nice," I say, "what a surprise!" They look at each other, clap, shake hands. Oh, they are proud of themselves. Such pathetic plans: "Oh, Steve," says Auntie Ruth, "will you drive me to the chemist? I've forgotten to fill my prescription, and I'll be in terrible trouble by the morning if I don't have it?"

Of course I agree—do I have a choice? I have no desire to hear her detail the physical result of my refusal. If I say no, my brother Peter would do it, and suddenly he's the hero again. It is his normal place in life. Somehow he received all the nice genes in our family. I am the lucky one, though. I am the lucky one. People like me in spite of myself. Look at the turn out for my party.

This is what did happen:

I cruised slowly past the chemist looking for a parking spot, then snagged the last spot, sneaking in front of a red-faced arsehole.

Auntie Ruth, of course, took an age at the chemist. I am rarely in these shops—I can't stand the smell. That chemical smell, cough medicine, soap, cheap perfume. I would have realised Auntie Ruth was up to something sooner, with her foolish delays, her questions, dropped coins and sampling of hand creams. But a woman stood at the perfume shelf and fascinated me.

Her hair was an unlikely blonde. She wore a bum-length spotted fur which looked like it had been sucked by her cat. Fishnet stockings, not laddered. And sneakers with purple laces.

She was selective. Out of the twenty types of perfume there, she made a neat stack at her feet, never looking down, but stepping carefully over as she discovered another shelf of perfume. She picked six bottles of perfume for a total cost of $12.

I walked her aisle twice, both times knocking her pile of cheap scent over.

"Sorry," I said. She tutted. I wondered how someone so much on the outreaches of society could be bothered by such a small thing.

It astonished me that anyone could look so bad and care so little. She fascinated me, the way she didn't know I existed, didn't know who I was.

"Can you wait in the car a minute? I have to get something," I said to Auntie Ruth. She was in no hurry. She knew we had nowhere to go, no party, no cake, not a present or a surprise.

"Go on," I said. I gave a push in the small of her back, because she was an irritating woman who would not get moving. She wanted to try a sports bandage on to see if it itched, because Uncle Mike, her useless husband, had a bad knee and couldn't get out to mow the lawn anymore.

"If you come to visit, you'd see the forest I live in," Auntie Ruth said.

"Jungle. People usually say jungle."

"I've never seen a tiger yet." She stretched the bandage around my arm, squeezing my veins till I felt them popping. I glimpsed her spy at her watch and realised she had something planned for my birthday.

"You know I don't want any fuss today," I said.

She said, "Okay," and meant it. She was one of the many who forgot my birthday.

I watched until she settled heavily into the car, then turned to the perfume woman. She had finished with her selection and had balanced each box gracefully along one arm which she held out as if she were shaking hands.

She bent to stare closely at a table of men's underwear. She realised what she was looking at and jerked her head up, embarrassed. She was short-sighted, vain, and she cared more about what people thought than I originally imagined.

She's not what I want, I thought, then I saw her elbow a woman aside to reach the counter.

The woman tutted. The perfume girl didn't notice, just plunked her things on the counter.

"Are you a stranger?" I said to her. She noticed me then; someone potentially less stable than she was. "My mum told me not to talk to strangers," I said.

I felt coy. My face was puckered like a child's.

She said, "Everyone I know is a stranger."

The cashier held out her change and stared at us, wanting us both to leave.

"My husband is not a stranger," I said. I held my left hand tucked under my jumper. "My husband is an intimate friend."

She walked to the door.

"I need to talk to a stranger," I said. It was a gamble. People are either repulsed or attracted to need.

"Go pay a counsellor, stupid bitch," she said, and I knew she was perfect, that she would see what I saw when she died, and if I brought her back she'd tell me about the people in the dark room, waiting to take little bites of her skinny arse.

"Come on, Steve," said Auntie Ruth through my car window. "Never give money to a beggar. They might find your address and rob you."

"Is this your car?" said the perfume girl.

"Car, house, money. I've got two houses and three cars. I've got a wall of stereo and five thousand CDs. Do you like music?"

She knew I was engaging her in conversation and she smiled at me. She pitied me now and was superior; although I had the clothes, the face, and I didn't have ugly fishnet stockings, she was the stronger, now. She was better than me. I offered her a lift. She didn't trust me enough to ask me to drive her home; she said she was going into town to meet a friend. I didn't believe there was a friend. Ruth sat there in the passenger seat, waiting to be delivered home. Ruth did not drive; driving was beneath her. Beyond her, I would say.

"It's Stevie's birthday," Auntie Ruth said. "She's twenty-six."

The girl laughed. "How'd you get a name like Steve? I thought you were a girl." She laughed, and I almost felt slighted.

"What's your name, then?" I could hear my childhood playground voice coming through, my *so what if I'm a girl, I can still beat you* voice.

"Lacey," she said. She was staring at Auntie Ruth, sitting there all over lace and frills.

"And my husband's name is George Glass," I said.

I guessed she hadn't seen that episode of *The Brady Bunch*, where Jan invented the name of a boyfriend by looking around the room.

"Steve Glass, ay?" she said. She laughed. She picked at her nose with the finger stall I had not noticed her wearing on her index finger. She placed the tip of it in one nostril, and I imagined the leather warming there.

"I don't usually take lifts with strangers," she said. I nodded. "But guess I can trust you," she said.

I nodded again, and fate began its fat roll again.

"Are you an actress, Lacey?"

She laughed. "If you were a guy I'd think you were trying to pick me up."

"No, it's just that you've got a really expressive face. I'm a casting agent, so I see a lot of people who think they can act. Some of them can. And then I see some who I think *should* be acting."

"Really?" she said. She would never have enough dedication or motivation to do it. But it didn't hurt to tease. I changed lanes, horns blaring behind me.

Auntie Ruth muttered and chuckled. "Husband!" she said. "George Glass!" She liked a good story.

"Looking forward to your party, dear? Lots of George's friends expected? Lots of yours, too, I imagine. Hundreds of them. No room for a maiden aunt." She chuckled away, well-pleased at her joke.

"You're no maiden," I said. "She's no maiden," I said to Lacey. I turned to face her to talk to her.

"Watch the road!" Ruth said. The traffic was thick and needed my attention.

"She had a lover, didn't you, when you were young?"

"A lovely man. Clever, you know, always a quick word," Ruth said. Ruth was changing history as she became senile. She had no lover; it was common knowledge she was a virgin when she married Uncle Mike. Mum used to talk about what a fuss she'd made about it. It was Auntie Jessie who was the wild one. She never died a virgin.

We reached home and I idled the car.

"I'll see you later, Ruth. I'm taking Lacey into town."

"But what about your party?" she said. Her crest-fallen face, her sad face, made me believe for a moment that she had conjured up some people for me. I wondered if there were people inside, a husband even, waiting for me to come home, "Surprise" and presents and I'll drink a little too much and tire of their foolish faces and stand on the stairs. "Fuck off! Get the fuck out of my house."

Auntie Ruth laughed. "I'll save you some cake."

Lacey climbed into the front seat.

"What about your party?" she said.

"There's no party. Ruth thinks it's funny to make me think there is."

She nestled her perfumes in her lap. I drove us to town.

"Which one's your favourite?" I said.

"They're all nice," she said. I looked for sarcasm but found none. She scrabbled in the sack she carried. "Thank God the old bitch's gone. Wanna fag?"

I don't really smoke but can do if I need to, thanks to Lee and his careful lessons.

As I parked the car, I said to Lacey, "Where are you meeting your friend?" She stared at me blankly, had completely forgotten her lie. "Feel like drinks and dinner?" I said. "I'll pay."

She nodded.

I paid for Lacey's dinner, to see if she could give me an indication of who would be in her room. She thought I was such a sweet listener, asking her about the slights, letting her talk over dinner so her food went cold and she fell in love with me.

"So tell me about yourself," I said. "I'm a stranger—perhaps we'll never see each other again. You can tell me about that little scar on your cheek; who disfigured you, sweetheart? Who would do such a thing to such a sweet face?"

You'll tell me, I thought, and later I'll remember the name, the face, and there they'll be, waiting with knives, fists, to hurt you again to all eternity. I won't need to kill you slowly; they are waiting, ready in an instant. You'll die for me. I'll watch your face in those final moments; see it wrinkle and age, no matter how many years you have left in you. I'll watch and you'll see me. You'll think, "Give me privacy, leave me alone." But the whole point of killing you is so I can see your face.

You'll show me nothing.

Lacey, Lacey, blah blah blah. She said she had dreamt about the sort of life I had. This, knowing nothing about me. Parents, siblings, a family home, school. She would have been angered to hear that I wanted to die; had tried to die three times before.

Lacey had feared for her life at times, but had never considered hurrying fate along.

There had always been violence in her life; and fear. I ordered another bottle of wine, some cake, it was a lively restaurant and people showed no sign of leaving.

"I've got an addictive personality," Lacey said.

"That's what people say. I get addicted to things and can't give 'em up. They reckon I started wrong cos Mum was an addict when I was born so what hope did I have? I don't know if Mum was an addictive personality but when she had me, she couldn't stop taking drugs long enough to love me. What do you think about that? I don't hate her, but. Even though she didn't keep me, she had me, she didn't kill me like she could of. Some women do, kill their babies before they're born. At least I got a chance to grow up.

"She didn't leave me in a basket. She tried to keep us, me and my brother, but one day she went to work and couldn't leave us at home so she left us in the car. Mum said I cried a lot when I was a baby and pissed the neighbours off. And her sister would look after us sometimes too but that pissed her off as well. She would only do it if she had to. I was only a few months old but my brother remembers. He says he was hot and couldn't breathe right. He still hates being locked up. Only reason he works instead of pinching things, if ya wanna know.

"We were in the car all day. My brother says he thinks I died for a while and that he finally figured out how to open the window. He was only five and Mum said she'd kill him if he moved. He said he forgot about that; that he wanted to play outside.

"So he wound the window down. He thought he'd push me out first then follow himself. He didn't think about my landing, flat on the concrete. He was only little. But I had my only one single bit of good luck in my life. Never had any since. Oh, but meeting you was good luck, wasn't it?" She smiled at me. Her lips were stained burgundy. A drunk man from across the room thought she was smiling at him and came to talk to us. "Fuck off, loser," she said.

"This is my second bit. My first bit was, some guy came along and grabbed me as my brother was pushing. Then he opened the door for my brother to get out. Turns out, the guy was wearing blue.

"Turns out he was a cop."

"What was his name?" I said.

"Who knows? He was a nice guy, though."

I don't know, I thought. It could be. It could have been my father who saved Lacey's life.

"So the cop wondered how long we'd been there, but my brother was too shy to talk. The cop looked in the car to find stuff out, stuff which got my mum into trouble. She got put in jail and we got looked after by different families. She hated my brother for that. Said he got her in trouble. You might say sure, sure, heard it all, but we were treated like shit in those places. I'd go on the telly to say it. We came out of it okay, though. Mostly because my brother's so smart, and he's really good to me. Cos I'm not all that smart. Not at school and not in the world.

"I'm supposed to trust too much, but it's mostly because people offer me stuff and I want it, so I forget what sort of person offered it. I'm not very good at looking after myself. I can't even pick my own clothes without looking silly. I have to pretend I do it on purpose, to look trendy. Half the time people believe me. Hey, no, third bit of luck. I found a brooch once, a really nice one, and the person who owned it was too gutless to get it back. I still got it at home. But I try not to have too much to do with people except for my brother. They expect too much. If I cut off from them they won't expect anything at all, then I won't feel bad when I don't give it to them."

On the way back to the car we saw the old lady with her table full of free food.

"Come on," Lacey said. "I always get something here."

"But we just ate."

"It's free."

We jumped in the queue; people grunted around us. They were pretty smelly. These were the regulars, the people who came every night for a feed. I couldn't see why; the soup was only lukewarm and a bit too healthy for me. I took one sip and threw it out.

I took Lacey back home to my place. She was very insecure. She acted careless and tough, but she was always ready for someone to hurt her. She caught her fingers in the car door and merely shook them, looking away, her eyes glazed.

"It's nothing," she said. I hadn't planned to hurt her, but I knew there would be people waiting in her dark room. I could see her dark room so clearly, see the faces of the people she'd slighted. Neighbours kept awake by her crying. An auntie forced to babysit. Jealous fellow students, because she was pretty and would have been a lovely child. A bereft true owner of a cheap brooch. People she had elbowed aside. The sleazebag she had just slighted at the bar. And all those other faces she would not recognise.

It was very different to watching a person die when I was in control. The hospice was a wonderful place to work, but this. This.

I hadn't planned to hurt her. I don't think she felt any pain. I crushed up the multi-coloured pills I have about, and I gave her wine.

"I'm not a wine person," she said. Her voice was soft, now, almost pleasant.

"This is nice wine. My father had it. It's really old."

"You're supposed to drink wine when it's old. I know that much," she said. Softer still, like a small breeze carrying words from far away. I liked that. I liked watching her leave.

"I feel ill," she said. I knelt on the floor and rested my elbows on her knees. She felt no pain. I held her chin up with my hands and watched her eyes.

Propped her eyelids open with my fingers, so I could see.

"Where are you?" I whispered. "What can you see?"

"I feel sick," she said. Her eyes rolled back.

"Is it dark or light?"

"Light. Too bright. My eyes hurt. It's like a knife, like a stabbing. Who's there? Who's there?"

She slumped. I was good at revival; one of my many talents. I cleared the vomit from her throat and breathed life back into her.

"What did you see?" I said. I felt like a terrorist interrogator.

"Bright lights. People. Mean people. Let me up now. Let me go."

No. A small pressure on her temple and it was done with.

She drooled, a kind of greenish drool she hadn't vomited up. I turned to get a washer and I heard her death-rattle spasm. Woof. A dog dying.

It was one way to celebrate my birthday.

I buried her in the yard. I had to dig up a patch of my beautiful night blooming jasmine to do it, but I had to put her somewhere. I thought of my father as I was doing it, and the thought gave me strength.

He did this, I thought. He did this again and again, and it made him a better person.

I didn't feel any better. I felt weak. Sickened. My limbs ached and I couldn't dig any more. I knew I had to get her into the dirt, get her covered. It's what dad would have done.

I had a long, long, hot shower afterwards.

I sat on the back step, surveying my work. Mostly I dig at night. It's cooler, and I feel less under scrutiny. And I feel like I am treading in my father's footsteps, because he was out here at midnight, too.

Dancing beneath the stars.

The front yard was too galling to me; the symbol of sanity in this street.

I had been digging out intermittently for eight years and I had made discoveries about myself and my past, as well as muscles. I had turned over the soil, over and over, and I found little treasures, and then I found bones.

Muffy's bones, my little puss-puss. But there were more; Muffy was small. These bones were big.

We had always thrown our bones up the yard but these weren't chop bones. There were no teeth marks.

I dug and I found what I had to admit were people's bones. There were too many bones. I dug holes and put them back in the earth. That's where I found them. I covered them with dirt, but I felt like I could still see their outlines.

I felt like I could see them all creeping towards one another, to make the skeleton of a giant, with the dirt for flesh and all the chains, belts, wallets, earrings, shoelaces in a tangled ball for the head.

The giant would rise and pick me up in a pinch at the scruff of the neck, and he'd drop me straight down his graveyard throat, and I'll live in his cold, dark belly forever.

I found a cheap watch, the arm of a pair of glasses, a decaled knob from a chest of drawers, and three false fingernails. I knew they were fake when I saw the manufacturer's name, in miniature, etched on the underside.

Lacey broke a barrier for me. I knew I could do it. I knew I was capable of sending people to the dark room. I didn't want to do it again, not even Maria, but then, as I was sorting things, deciding what I needed to burn or throw out, I found the silver bangle Eve had given me when I was eleven.

I knocked on Eve's door a week or so after my no-surprise twenty-sixth birthday.

There was a boy doing her lawn and he was no older than the boys had been when, as a child, I was a regular visitor to the garden woman.

I could never quite forget Eve and that house. It would come back to me in shocks of memory; I could see her pale body, her hands out, begging, pleading, "Come on Stevie, come to Eve."

And I did go to her. I needed to talk, to tell someone what I'd seen, to tell her about Lacey. And I knew she'd listen. Her husband Harry had died in an accident when I was nineteen; apparently he was drunk and tripped over the rake, landing his temple on the corner of the front step. She didn't find him till she opened the front door to let the morning sun in. She said she never expected him home if he wasn't home by ten at night, so she had slept soundly.

But I knew her garden pretty well. There was never a tool left about to rust. Peter went to Harry's funeral and handed out business cards. Did he think he would hurt her that way? She didn't speak when she opened the door. Just wept; tears pouring, goose honks, an unattractive performance. I had not seen her since I was thirteen.

"Oh, Steve, Steviesteviestevie." She couldn't leave my name alone. She always got it right. On the kitchen bench was a beer glass, and she caressed the beer bottle with stroking fingers.

"I hear Harry had an accident a while back," I said.

"Yes, terrible," she said. She smiled at me, false white teeth too big for her mouth. She smelt of stale perfume.

"Did you tell them how he used to hurt you?"

"Oh, no need to drag his name down."

"What name? He wasn't famous."

"Oh, no, but his family, you know. They don't need to know."

"But he was cruel. He deserved to die."

She took my hand and kissed it. "Oh, my darling daughter." She opened a bottle of wine—the beer was just for men. She poured two glasses; I took one and nursed it. I was an adult now. I could share her wine.

"You lost your mother, didn't you? Another terrible accident."

"That really was an accident," I said. I put down my wine. "Which of your boys was careless enough to leave the rake out? How long was it out for? What time did Harry come home?"

She said, "There's something I've always wanted you to have," and fetched a large, Chinese black lacquer jewellery box. She scrabbled through it; she clearly had no particular piece in mind and had never done so.

She plucked out a brooch which glittered white and blue.

"This is for you. It was my mother's," she said. I realised at that moment she had no one to leave things to. I took the brooch, smiled. I knelt on the floor and put my head on her lap.

"It's beautiful," I said. "I wish I really was your daughter."

"Oh, my darling," she said. "Steve and Eve," she said. She was good with sympathy; she had seduced Peter and I with it, a year after our father died.

I visited her a lot, after that. I wore the brooch often, until she said, "That's a little precious to wear about the house."

"But I love it so much. It's safer to wear it here, anyway. If I lose it, at least I'll know where to look."

Eve took my hand and led me to the bedroom.

She fetched down the jewellery box again. I hoped it wasn't obvious how many times I had rummaged through.

She pulled out a long necklace of green glass beads.

"How about you have this for every day, and save that for special?" she said. I agreed. In my mind I wore it all, every last bit. I was laden down with the weight of it. I wondered if she remembered the jewellery she'd given me years before, or if she imagined it was stolen.

Birthdays were important in our house when I was a child. Eve started my jewellery collection on my eleventh birthday and she gave me a little something for my twelfth then my thirteenth birthdays. Peter had long since stopped visiting Eve. He said I was sick for going there; that there was something wrong with me. I never told him about my jewellery collection, in an old shoe box pushed way under my bed. Where it sits to this day.

In later days, I was there when her husband Harry got home, and he would always make sure I was all right and offer me a lift home. I always said no, because I was terrified of lifts with strangers. Always had been.

I can't remember if it was a friend of mine, or someone else, but somebody, somebody got in a car near the school and they were never seen again.

Was it Pauly? Pauly was never seen again but I thought it was because he didn't like me.

There was a rumour around town that he was still alive; all the others forgot about it, but I never did. Alive? In a coffin? Or in a room, tied up, made to eat dog shit, beaten with a dog chain, naked all the time and nothing to do, no books or TV, no one to talk to. Or drugged and dressed like a girl, hair grown long and curly, at an all girl's school, the only one without breasts. Or used as a sex thing, rented out, a rent boy who moans for love. Or do they amputate his limbs one by one to see how people cope? Does he remember me? Would I recognise him if he passed me, his face scratched and dirty from digging his way out of a grave?

Would I recognize his bones if I found them buried?

I think of that limbo often. There's been others, it's not just kids, and you don't have to accept a lift, sometimes you get dragged in, clothes torn, out of your control. I hate it if I'm walking and a car slows down behind me. I would allow myself to die before being dragged in there. They could threaten to stab me and I'd say, "Do it. I'd rather die quickly here." I would. Fuck taking a chance on escape.

What if they had you, kept you there, and you were in their control, you couldn't piss or shit unless they said so? What if they made your dying last a month?

That's why I prefer to drive everywhere, even just up the local shops. Or get a bus, if the bus stop is close by.

This is not just a childish fear; I have had adult experience.

Why did I keep visiting Eve as a child? Refuge.

We became famous at school, after our father had been killed in such a great way. I would never talk about it; I was only nine, a baby, when it happened, but I was affected by it in an adult way.

I vividly remembered the event, but I didn't want to share it with the other children. Neither did Peter; for a while we played together, because there were no questions that way. Pammy Johnson's father had also died, but that was years before and of a disease, nothing interesting. Still, she joined our exclusive group until Peter and I lost our news value and slowly moved back into society. I dumped her then, and not too soon. She stank, was the problem, because her mother was depressed and didn't wash them anymore. Her hair was filthy, greasy. I felt no guilt dumping her. She didn't deserve me.

Mum had known Dad for a long time, longer than my years, and she cried in bed after he died.

When she cried in bed, I visited Eve. But Eve became more demanding when I turned thirteen. She wanted more physicality, she wanted me to go out in public with her, and so I severed all ties. I just stopped visiting when I was thirteen. She never knew where I lived, who my mother was. She didn't want to admit I had another life. Whenever I arrived for a visit, weekends and holidays included, she said, "How was school?" Even if I hadn't visited her for a week.

So I decided not to see her again, and thirteen years passed. These adult visits were different; I was in control. She begged me to stay with her, she was lonely, she said, but no. No.

Uncle Dom showed up, out of the blue. He brought a gift for my twenty-sixth birthday. He said, "I thought I'd wander past, have a look at the old place. I have so many happy memories of it."

He really was a pitiful fellow. His times with us had been few, and, I believe, always stressful for the adults involved. It was okay for Peter and I. We got gifts and attention, and we climbed all over his big belly, played with his beard.

"I was never as happy as I was here," he said. He had always been in love with Mum, he said, and had kept away because he knew she felt the same way. I looked at my huge, grey old uncle and wondered if he had always been self-deluded, or if it had come to him with senility. My mum had worshipped my dad, never said a bad word to or about him, and she hardly ever mentioned Dom. I was angry; I said all this to Dom.

"Did you never realise how scared she was of him?" he said "And perhaps she never mentioned my name because it hurt to do so." Then the horrible man started to cry. I had no idea what I was supposed to do, so I called Peter. They talked for half the night. I went to bed, because I couldn't stand it anymore. They were talking about Dad, and I missed him so much. Dom told stories of Dad.

Stories I hadn't heard before.

Dom had always thought badly of Alex, blaming him for family unrest. Dominic didn't want anyone to discuss anything nasty; he liked things to be nice.

He was always the one to clear the table when they were young. He was a favourite amongst the adults because he sat quietly and listened. He had a soft voice which pleased them as well, but it meant he was never heard amongst the children.

He had a terrible fear of heights and did not like stairs. He loved dogs with more passion than any other thing. This love of dogs and fear of heights came from the one small place; an event only Dominic remembered.

To an adult, there always seems to be twice as many children in a group than there really are.

Each child knows who's there, though; each child knows where they stand in that small community.

In the group of ten that day, Alex was the leader.

They stopped when he bent to pick up a perfect leaf; searched the ground themselves for one to match. They asked him questions and jostled to walk beside him.

Dominic received no special treatment because he was the brother.

They reached a large, muddy hole.

"This wasn't here last week," said Mary, who would not marry and never tell her parents the true nature of her relationship with her female housemate.

"That's because it hadn't rained for months before yesterday," said Alex. He bent and measured the depth of the mud with his forefinger. It sucked and farted as he pulled it from the mud, and the gang laughed.

"Dominic, come here," Alex said. Dominic was really only there because their mother had insisted. He was not dressed for adventure. Even the girls had long pants and boots on, but he had a thin shirt, shorts, and his school shoes without socks on. Their other brother Seb spent all his time doing homework.

Children stood aside to let him through.

"Bend over and look at the puddle," Alex told him.

Dominic always did as Alex said. Alex was older, cleverer, and popular.

Alex wiped his muddy finger on the shorts right over Dominic's buttocks.

"Dom's shit his pants!" Alex screamed, and each child squealed and laughed, squealed and squealed.

Dominic had felt the caress; it made him uncomfortable so he ignored it. Now he had no idea why they laughed.

He didn't ask. He only saw the joke when his mother gave him a belt for getting mud all over his shorts.

Alex said, "I bet the river is way down low as well. I'm going to the bridge to look over." He ran ahead.

Dominic had no fear of heights at this stage. He was happy to join the others crossing the old wooden bridge which stretched between the rocks banking the river.

High above the river now, with the water so low.

The children hung over the railing, staring into the trickle a long way below.

It made Dominic dizzy, but he couldn't look away. The distance drew him down, and he felt that if he let go of the rail he would be sucked into the river bed.

The terrier that loved to run wild with the children and usually ignored Dominic, barked.

"What is it, boy?" he said. He stood up from the rail and saw that, apart from the terrier, he was alone.

"Where are they, boy?" Dominic said.

He wished he had learnt the dog's name, because he could not call to him.

He stood six planks away, waiting for Dominic to move.

"All right, boy," said Dominic, "let's go."

But he could not move his foot. His school shoe was wedged between one plank and the next. He could not move.

In the next two hours, the terrier came close and sat with him. He did not look down again, and as he sat and waited for someone to realise that he was missing, he began to believe the river had put him to sleep for one hundred years (and the terrier too; how else to explain its presence?) and now there was no one left in the world. He didn't look, but he could hear the river so far below; he knew how far it was just by the noise.

When Alex finally came to get him, Dominic did not cry.

"Why didn't you just undo your shoe?" Alex said, viciously doing so. He pulled Dominic's foot out and dragged him home, over stones, bones, all the bumps and sharpies on the way home. The terrier followed; until his peaceful death after a good meal fifteen years later he did not leave Dominic's side. His owner was never identified; his original name was never known. Dominic called him Boyd, because Boy had been his name for those hours.

Dominic received a beating for losing his school shoe, even though he paid another boy to retrieve it the next day. He also received a beating for the muddy pants.

This was the reason he had not even thought of taking it off. It was why he didn't think of many things later in life; he was so scared of consequences he often didn't think of options. He became a postman; how he loved that flat-earth plodding each day, that quiet nod at the dwellers, that pat for the friendly dogs, even the quick step away from the nasty ones.

Dominic never married; another option he never considered. He retained a delight in children throughout his life.

If he had ever been close enough to discuss it with a lover or a friend, this kindness, this love for children, the answer may have been clearer.

"You are looking for the acceptance you didn't receive as a child," the loved one could say, and perhaps Dominic would feel better knowing.

No one ever said it, and he never thought it. He just visited Alex's family every now and then, bearing wonderful presents and willing to play as rough as the children liked. He would watch them jump on the trampoline for hours without wanting a turn. He could make each "Good!" sound different.

Dominic told Peter things I don't think we needed to know. He didn't need to get it off his chest.

Alex learnt some unfortunate information; something he didn't need or want to know.

It wasn't one of his cases, and the police officer who told him didn't connect the surname. He didn't imagine that Dominic Searle, the snowdropper, could be connected to Alexander Searle, the excellent, dependable cop. The station men were disgusted by the details, but they loved to hear them.

And realisation came to Alex, that this was his brother who had committed those crimes. He was freed soon after because the evidence could not be found.

Peter left a note on the floor by my bedroom door.

"Uncle Dom will be staying with me for a while."

That was fine; Peter and Maria could have him.

It was galling to hear that not only did he love their children, meaning that I suddenly became a generation older but also that Maria thought he was wonderful, and he doted on her. I didn't care if he lived or died. I hate Dom now, but he always loved us. I can't understand it. He wasn't very welcome in our house but he still came, because he loved us.

I wouldn't be seen dead in Peter's place, unless both of them begged me. Kelly and Carrie certainly wouldn't be reason for me to humble myself. Irritating, dull creatures. They listen to everything their mum says, with hardly a glimmer of rebellion and no sense of humour. I did my dress-up trick, where I just get anything and put it on weird, and they didn't even smile. Peter loved it; he was in tears. He won't ever dress up himself, but he's happy for me to do it. I think he remembers those times with Eve the garden lady, when we had to dress up. I hated it more than he did; hated being controlled. It hasn't affected me, though. I'm not going to stop dressing up because of it. Peter thinks I'm humiliating myself when I dress up. That's why he loves it so much.

He thinks I've forgotten, I've forgiven. But that's not possible.

I found an old coin, a tin lid, an egg cup and a pipe.

Dougie Page called. "Look, that list of names? Have you thought about it?"

"It means nothing to me. What does it mean to you?"

"Disappearances, some of them. A couple of murders, bodies found with souvenirs missing."

"And why on a list together?"

"Just that your Dad was part of the investigation for each of them. That's all."

"Weren't you?"

He laughed. "Yes, I was too, Steve. I told you, you should have been a detective. Look, I gotta go. I'll talk to you when you get back from… where are you going?"

I forgot what lie I told him, so hung up in his ear.

Satisfying.

I regretted it, though. I needed to know what he was doing. What he discovered. I needed to be warned in the future.

At Twenty-Seven

My counsellor told me I needed to sell my car.

"It has associations you don't need to continue," she said. "At the very least, you should try another form of transport occasionally."

"Is that an order?"

She closed her eyes at me. A habit of hers to block me out. "I think you should try catching the bus. To see there are other ways, other people who travel in different ways."

It was bullshit, of course, but the car needed a good service, and I wanted the dents beaten out. I could afford it, with the regular pay cheque. And one thing I didn't know before I started at the hospice; patients die and leave you stuff. Some of them are there all alone, and a single voice of kindness can make them feel loved. We shared out the bonuses amongst us all, but we all knew who wasn't pulling their weight. Ced was good. He pulled in the most.

Catching a bus reminded me of when I'd lost my licence. Sitting next to strangers, breathing the same air. The seats were in the same place and the same ads were on the walls. Once the drivers got to know you it's like having a private chauffeur. I had an iPod which didn't always work, and I played it loud loud loud.

The old lady on the bus was stout in a cuddly way, with a turkey-gobble neck, white, permed-curly hair, big pink glasses and a pink tracksuit. She always wore a tracksuit. Thought it made her young. She muttered observations to everyone; I am the only one who ever responded. She was always late on the bus and no one liked to give up their seat. Often she swayed and muttered the whole trip. Once, she got the seat opposite to mine by poking the other passenger with her umbrella.

The old woman loved to talk about the tragedies of her life.

She was the age Mum might have lived to.

Though Mum might have died a thousand times by now, anyway. Heart attack, run over by a bus, cancer, pneumonia, measles, stabbed, strangled, burnt, drowned. She could have been dead a thousand times over, rising from the grave to meet her next fate.

"So much death," the old lady said one day, after we'd sat opposite each other three days running.

"You'd think I'd be used to it. Some people just have lives like that. Full of death. I'm Bess, anyway. Bess Colby," she said, as if it was an afterthought. I shivered.

She didn't know anything about me. But we were twins. My life is full of death, too. Right from childhood, when Dad used to show me pictures of his cases, it felt like something I knew. It felt like a brother, someone to look after me. That's stupid.

But I can't help what I think. Bess had never heard of Peter. That helped. She didn't look at me differently, saying, "Oh, you're his sister." I got that a lot.

He was famous, with his damn courses.

Bess was a pathetic creature; wounded and whimpering. She was slow to take offence; I didn't imagine her easily slighted. That relaxed me; I felt safe around her. She gave me the sweetest smile on the bus, as though, every time I got on, that meant her life was worth living. The first time I sat next to her she could hardly speak. No one ever sat next to her; she had that "talker" label—she wanted to tell you about her operation, about the bus schedule, about the weather.

About all the people who died that week. The kind of hypnotic drone which can be so relaxing; so revealing. She leaned close when she spoke; loved touching me. The bus trip was twenty-eight minutes long, unless we missed the lights, in which case thirty minutes of solid talk without distractions. She scrabbled in her bag for a lolly, sucked noisily. Her handbag gaped openly at me; I could see tissues, wrappers, money. The bus stopped suddenly; her handbag dropped to the floor, its contents spilled.

"My dear," she said.

"Sorry?" I said. Was she blaming me?

"Ooh, not you dear." Later she stubbed her toe.

"My dear," she said. "My dear." Bess fascinated me.

The story of her life had so many deaths, she was comfortable with the idea. Of other people's deaths, anyway. This was fascinating. Someone not scared of death; fascinating. She questioned me, just enough to be polite, but I didn't want my life to become part of her repertoire. So I concentrated on complaining about Auntie Ruth; her treatment of me, the way she fell down as a relative. I never discussed my grandparents.

The fifth time we caught the bus together, she said, "You must come over for dinner one night. You're too skinny to be eating well." She squeezed my arm gently, and did not release me from her grip.

"That'd be nice," I said, but the idea was abhor-rent to me. I wasn't happy in other people's homes; Peter's was okay, when Maria wasn't there, and Ruth's was bearable because it was familiar; I knew what was around every corner. Instead I invited her to my place.

"I'm having a party," I said. I had already brought home the alcohol, a bag full on each trip. Wine for Peter and Maria, beer for my friends.

"There'll be plenty to drink, but no food," I said.

"I could make some scones."

She started to bring in samples, little somethings she'd cooked for herself. "Plenty leftover. No point cooking for one." The more I liked it, the more she brought in, until she was providing my lunch every day. The idea of her being in my home was appalling. I liked the person she thought I was; the daughter or granddaughter she thought I was. To her, I was a kind, thoughtful person with a regular job and a full life. Thinking of her in my home, I realised how I had misled her.

"I'd love to meet your parents and tell them what a wonderful job they've done with you."

"I'm afraid they're overseas. They left money behind for my birthday, though. They're always thinking ahead."

"How sweet of them. And how are you managing on your own? Or is your brother there?"

"No, he's at his place, but he'll be coming for the party. He wouldn't miss it." I wondered how old she thought I was. I said, "Actually, the place is in a bit of a mess, so I hope no one minds. First time without Mum and Dad and all that."

She looked shocked. "We can't have your party in a mess. I'll come early and help you get stuck in."

So that is how it was that she came to my home at eight AM on Satur-day morning. She could see immediately it was not just a couple of week's grime built up. She wandered through the rooms, barely suppressing a "Tut tut" till she coughed with the strain of it. I poured her a taste of brandy which she swallowed first and thanked me for after. She sat on the edge of the couch, eyes closed, as if wishing she was in another place.

"It's a big job, I know," I said.

"Exactly how long have your parents been gone?" she said. That was a question I wasn't willing to answer. I sat opposite her, taking the comfortable position we shared on the bus.

"Do you ever feel like we are family?" I said. That made her happy.

"Oh, my dear, yes. I have no one, you know. It's so nice to think somebody would notice if I wasn't around for a few days." Though I wouldn't, of course.

"Of course I'd notice," I said. "Sometimes it feels like you are the only family I have, and I'd hate to lose you." She patted my hand, all supportive and forgiveness. "Come on, then; let's get to work on this place."

We stopped for lunch. The poor old thing was pale and had the shakes, so I poured her a taste of brandy.

"Looking good," I said. She'd done a marvellous job of the lounge room. I had washed the dishes, which made the kitchen appear far cleaner. Larger, even. There was no food apart from the ingredients for party fare she'd brought with her so I walked to the corner shop for fresh sandwiches.

It was a pleasant day, though I talked too much, she saw too much, and I knew my image was tarnished. I bought ice and more beer, I turned the music on, I tipped chips into a bowl and ate them.

She cooked baby quiches and chicken wings, spicy rolls and chocolate biscuits. We were set up and ready by six o'clock.

"What time are you expecting guests?"

"Who knows? 8, 9, 10…you never know with young people."

She had a chuckle at that. I think she liked being with me, preparing for a young person's party.

"I remember my twenty-first birthday," she said.

"Has that got *anything* to do with me turning twenty-seven?" I said.

Time passed. We watched a movie on TV, neither commenting on the movie nor jumping up during the ads. The doorbell rang. The fucking Williams kid. They hate me; I never buy raffle tickets, but they keep trying.

"No, I'd rather suck a dog's cock," I said, but quietly, so my friend couldn't hear. *Tick. Tick. Tick.* It became clear that no one would be coming to my party. Not even Peter. I ate the baby quiches, one by one, quickly; pop it in, three chews, swallow.

She watched me, I know; I could see the whiteness of her face in the corner of my eye. When I looked at her I felt like Mum was still alive. She fell asleep for a while. I drank a lot of the beer. It got cold and dark in the house but I was pretending not to be home. I took some chocolate biscuits and went to sit in my car. It surrounded me, the smell of it, the crush of it. The passenger seat was still faintly stained with Mum's blood, just a fake tan colour on the upholstery. I closed my eyes and went to sleep.

She found me. I was dreaming nothing, black, and I heard my name, "Stevie, Stevie," and for a moment I thought I'd done it again but this time gone somewhere else, a place where my mother called me, waited with open arms.

"Stevie." It was Bess. She was shaking. I got out, led her to the passenger side, helped her settle, walked back to my side, climbed in. Each action I performed carefully. I had done this for my mother, too. Helped her in.

"I was cold. I didn't know where you were. I didn't know where I was," she said. Her voice was weak and gentle. She looked at me; I was supposed to say something. I realised she was a dependent; that suddenly, without choice, I had someone relying on me.

"You know, my mother died in that seat," I said.

She stopped her puppy-whimper. "What do you mean?"

"Died. Car accident," I said.

"Oh, my dear," she said, and that little show of understanding, sympathy, plus the beer I'd drunk and the empty house set me off.

I went through my poem of death:

> "My grandpa died when I was five
> My mother, then, was still alive
> My father was a famous cop
> Famous cop gets famous shot
> My mother died when I was grown
> She died from seed that he had sown
> Muffy was a little cat
> She died too and that was that
> Auntie Jessie died in Pain
> Died in pain and died in vain
> Little Pauly, when I was seven
> Disappeared and went to heaven.
> Then there's Lacey
> Nice young thing
> Found out later she
> Loved to sing
> And I have gone myself
> Four times
> Close to death and
> Then revived

I'll go again
Again it seems
I'll see you in
Your nightmare dreams."

She did not speak; tears began to fall from her eyes, but she didn't cry.

"Don't be sorry for me," I said. "I hate to be pitied." And I lay my hand across her arm. Her neck snapped about so she faced me. I closed my eyes, felt tears forming, a puddle of sting.

"So you see why I hold the value of human life with such contempt," I said. She was a very brave woman, near the end. She had listened to me without daring to speak. I imagined her limbs were stiff and painful, her heart a hammer.

"I think I should go home, now," she said. I had to reward such courage, and the fact she said goodbye.

"Are you right to drive?" I said. "Haven't had too much to drink?"

"I'm fine," she said. She climbed slowly out of the car and stood by the roll-a-door, waiting for me to release her. I consider this to be one of my greatest moments. I released her. I gave up her secrets and slights. I let her go. No car started up; she stumbled up the road, an old woman's run, because of course she didn't have a car, she caught the bus. I didn't catch the bus again.

To make up for not coming to my party, Peter invited me over. This was a rare occurrence; Maria thought I was too ugly to be in their home. It was a rich person's home; Maria had been brought up rich. The house was enormous, the lawn neat. Inside it was perfect; even the kid's rumpus room (there was no rumpus in there) was neat, with colour-coded boxes and toys so nothing ever got mixed up.

Maria came from an intellectual family. They were allowed no modern novels, no slang. They sat at the table and had discussions during and after every meal. Both her parents were still alive; they saw a lot of Peter, Maria, Kelly and Carrie. They weren't thrilled with Peter as a son-in-law, because he couldn't hold his own at the table. I was fine; I just talked shit.

Peter met me as I pulled in, jumped in the car and we had a good bitch about Maria's parents.

"Then they just ignore them, sit around and crap on," Peter said. "Carrie was sitting there crying for five minutes and none of them did a thing. I'm there on the phone, waiting for one of them to pick her up. No, it's gabble gabble gabble, so I have to get off the phone and make her better. Don't worry, Peter'll do it," he said.

"Well, he will," I said. "The fucken idiot."

He rolled his eyes at me. "Don't say I said anything." He was already scared.

It was a pointless deception, but I bought a cake and put it into one of Mum's old cake tins. As I unpacked, the kids hung around to see what I had. I pulled out the tin, revealed the cake, said, "Who wants a piece?"

"Me, me, me." They both wanted cake.

"Go get a knife, then, Kelly," I said. It was Maria who came back with the knife.

"I'm wondering why you're sending over-excited children running around the house with knives."

I shuddered. "Singular for both, Maria," I said. I took the knife and cut into the cake, a cheesy, chocolaty, unhealthy thing.

"Bake it yourself?" Maria said.

"Of course," I said.

"You must let me have the recipe," she said, and stood, arms akimbo, waiting for my answer.

I assessed. Did she want me to confess the cake was shop-bought, or did she believe I made it and considered me capable of poisoning her children?

"Actually, I didn't make it. It was the lady next door. She thinks we're such a lovely family."

"After dinner, then," and she lifted the tin out of reach. I left without the tin, never thought of it again, although it had contained some of the tastiest treats of my childhood. I had a fantasy, sitting with the two girls. They are taken from their parents when Maria turns into an alcoholic and I am given custody. They become fat and healthy. This is probably what would happen: Maria would send her children to boarding school. Anything but me, the evil aunt. It'd do the kids good to get away from that mother. Little brats. Climb all over you in the car, though they do like my jokes.

"Motherhood would have been good for you," Maria says to me quite often. As if it was too late. "It makes you responsible."

Maria and Peter had a huge backyard, concrete, tiles and swimming pool, no spot to dig. The girls were hanging all over me, wanting to hear me swear again. Earlier, I'd told Maria to fuck off, and I thought the foundations were going to crash into the centre of the earth.

"Do you know what that word means?" Carrie said. "You should only use words that you know what they mean."

"I know what it means. Do you?"

"It's bad," said Carrie.

"No, it's not. It's a beautiful thing. Your parents have done it at least twice."

They were horrified, ran to their rooms (because they had one each, of course, full of every girly delight produced in the world) to escape the horrible truth. Ten minutes later they were back again, poking their heads through the child-proof fence, watching me sun-bake topless.

"You're not supposed to show your bosoms," Carrie said.

"You are if you want a fuck," I said. I got up to let them into the pool area.

"Don't listen to what your mother says about any of this. She's frigid."

They giggled. I know Kelly called Maria *frigid* a few weeks later, because Peter told me on the phone. He could hardly stop himself from laughing, so I must have guessed right, but he tried to be stern.

"Now, where would they learn a word like that?" he said.

It was one of those days which is hot enough for kids to swim, far too cold for adults to do so. I watched the kids by the pool, laughing when they splashed me. Carrie scratched Kelly with a toenail, and they began to fight, vicious, adult words. I watched that, too, feeling sleepy and lazy in the autumn sun.

"Stop that, you kids." Maria came out of the house, wringing her hands on some piteous rag.

"Where's your auntie? I thought she was supposed to be keeping an eye on you."

The kids giggled. I waggled my hand in the air.

"Present, miss," I said.

"You're supposed to be watching them."

"I am. I'm watching them fight."

She sighed, went inside. She didn't care that much that she would look after them herself.

I saw Carrie stamping from one foot to the next.

"What's the matter? Need to go wee? Just hop back in the pool."

The kids giggled again.

"I hate it when Mum yells," Carrie said. "I get all upset."

I scratched my index finger on my knee, summoning them. I'd seen Peter do it, but he'd never be half the father Dad was.

Kelly and Carrie came to sit by me.

"I know a fantastic way to feel better. Do you want me to show you?"

They nodded.

"OK, but you can't get frightened. It might seem scary, but it's good fun. Ready?" They nodded. I stood up, stood with legs apart, hands cupping my face. I tickled my chin with my thumbs. Then I screamed, the most blood-curdling terrible scream I had the strength for. The girls started to cry. Peter and Maria came running out. I was pleased with my scream.

Maria glanced at me, and I was smiling; I could feel it in my cheeks. Peter gave the two girls a smack.

"Peter," Maria said. "Don't smack them."

"They're my girls," he said. She gathered up her crying children and gave Peter a look.

"Talk to her," she said.

"What's wrong?" he said. Nice of him to ask.

"Nothing. I just screamed."

"What sort of a scream was that?" I thought it was a stupid question, and would have said so, but the scream echoed in my head and I knew where I'd heard it before.

I said, "It's the scream of a mother dying."

He started crying too, like his children, just tears leaking down, no sound. I wondered what it felt like, tears on your face. I wondered what tears tasted like.

I stepped over to him, braced my hands on his shoulders and took a lick. He pushed my face away, then with both hands pushed me away.

"You'd know about that, wouldn't you. You'd know what it sounds like."

"Well, I was there, Peter. Unlike you."

"Oh, no. If I'd been there, she wouldn't have died. I would have died first before I let her die. But then, I'm not you. Thank God. Sometimes I think you must have been adopted, devil's baby he shat out and didn't want. Sometimes I'm falling asleep and you die, someone kills you and you get buried next to Mum and Dad."

I couldn't breathe or swallow. He wouldn't look at me, muttered his poison to the sky.

"But I'm your sister. I haven't got anyone else."

"Of course not. No one wants you. No one cares about you. Why don't you fuck off?"

"All right," I said. I was too shocked to argue or defend myself. As I walked away he said, "I thought she died instantly. Painlessly."

"That's just what they said," I said.

But she screamed with such pain; like, I imagine, she screamed giving birth to me. Or, Peter, he being the first born. One long, breathless scream.

Did she see the room? Glimpse it as the pain subsided, and death calmly took over? I couldn't see her eyes. She had them squeezed shut.

Maria called up the stairs, "We're just off to my family's. No need for you to come if you don't want to, Steve. It'll be a bore for you. You can just hang out here, watch TV, have a swim, whatever." That was what she wanted me to do.

Peter said, "You're not coming. Don't think you're coming. You don't deserve it." But the kids came scratching at me, begging me to come.

"Can't let the kids down," I said. "I need to pick some things on the way."

I felt too shaken to drive, so sat on the outside toilet, staring at walls, until my knees were still.

Then I went up the pub. A girl with really big tits kept staring at me. I stared back. She came over.

"My boyfriend says he fucked you once."

"Is that my fault?" I said. Pathetic, these women.

She pointed him out.

"If he says that, it's because he wants to dump you. I reckon he wants to pass you on to that other guy there. He seems pretty keen."

A fight started over all that bullshit, and she got a tooth knocked out. Hardly my fault, any of it, and I was back under control by the time I started the long drive to Maria's parents' place. I like to drive myself, so I have the option of getting away. I shot through a red light to get there, and beeped my horn to get people to move. I had to park around the corner because all the suck-arse family was there, taking up car space. It was a big family do that night, but Peter and I were the only ones from our side. Maria has five siblings, all loud, all arrogant, all parents of at least three children. Her mother huffed about the kitchen in a cloud of flour, rolling, stuffing, frying.

Daughters helped, sons and sons-in-law discussed the way the house was looking structurally.

Daughters-in-law sat in the lounge room and talked in whispers. I listened.

"Honestly, you'd think it was Jesus and Mary, not Peter and Maria. Way they bullshit on."

"I know, can you believe it? If I hear one more time how many devotees they've got to their fucking cause, I'll scream."

Just a few years younger and I would have set up a video to catch them at it. It was good to hear, though. My brother wasn't adored by everyone.

"No offence," someone said every now and then, when they were particularly cruel.

"All just idle talk," I said.

"You're not part of this family, you know," someone said to me, and they nodded. The bitches nodded. None of their husbands were like Peter.

Their men were strong, dependable, didn't like women as friends. Their men left them to it, didn't mess about in the kitchen, whatever. Their men had big cocks and liked to use them. I realised as I heard them talk that all three were jealous. They had married brothers who had grown into triplets; Maria, having known those brothers all her life, found someone different. It made them sick.

It made me sick, too, once I realised.

They wanted Peter for themselves. Does that mean I have to marry the opposite of Peter? Someone like one of Maria's brothers? I went outside to play with the kids.

I brought along a magic ball. If you dropped it it would squash flat for a moment, then bounce back into your hands. If you threw it into someone's hands, it would squish between their fingers and they would squeeze their fingers closed. It always felt cool and never looked grubby. The kids loved it. Maria's parents had a large front yard, rarely used by the adults because it was too far from the back door and the front door had been blocked by boxes many years earlier.

Inside the boxes were some astonishing things and some very dull ones. All of them a story, a memory, an excuse or a crime. I visited once when Peter first met Maria, because he took me along on a lot of trips then. While they were in the kitchen being nice, telling lies, I discovered the boxes, and I pulled them out and emptied them.

"You are a child," Maria's mother said. I shrugged.

Sticking my tongue out is what I should have done, what I did do is ask her about the things. Or is it the other way round? I seem to remember the taste of dust on my outstretched tongue and none of the stories.

There was a plastic mask and a penis candle, an orange bikini top, a cookbook which featured "Eggs, Nature's greatest gift." There were fifteen pens which didn't work; each had a tiny blue knob of ink. There were three small plastic bowls, pink, blue and green, each stained yellow at their base.

A wooden stick, the remains of a flag, a flat china plate with a cow painted on it, a green belt. Books with the titles worn off, yellowed, smelly. A pink apron. Various medals, some for school sport. A packet of tobacco papers. Each thing important to somebody; each thing somebody's life.

There seemed to be a hundred kids playing with a ball as I watched. The garden was a wonderful place. Daphne everywhere, and early daffodils and jonquils, and the most astonishing violets. Magical flowers; you suck in their scent until you can't smell them anymore, then you rest, and the smell attacks you again. I'd love to wear a violet perfume, but all commercial scent turns to cat's piss on my skin. Some people find the smell of violets makes them sick. Weaklings.

There were winter roses, too, pale blue ones looking nothing like a rose. Maria's sister Elise came out for a while to watch the kids.

"Isn't the garden lovely?" she said.

"It takes a lot of work," I said. I didn't mind her; she always made an effort to speak to me. I bent to sniff a winter rose.

"I think this one's my favourite." She sniffed too.

"I can't smell anything. I don't think these ones have a scent."

"Of course they do." I sniffed again, smelling nothing. "Beautiful. Heady. Smell it."

She sniffed again. "God, you're right. When you know it's there, it's like a blast in the face." She stayed and watched me play with the kids for a while, then she went inside. The smell was so sweet out there the kids became delirious. They squealed as the ball came to them, they rolled for it, fought for it. When I didn't tell them to calm down, they squealed louder, and I threw myself into a cart-wheel between them, yip yip yip. I landed on my arse with the ball enclosed in my hands. I held the ball under my chin and opened my fingers. I knew it would glow; I didn't know the sun would go behind a cloud at that perfect moment. The kids were quiet, watching me. They could sense magic.

"Did I ever tell you about the worst man who ever lived?" I said. I looked to each one, a dare straight in the face. Stop me. "The worst man who ever lived called himself Dominic. He also called himself my uncle."

Kelly gasped. "It's true," she told the others. She had met Dom.

"Once upon a time he wasn't evil. He was a nice little boy, like you, or you. But there was something inside him which made him frown instead of smile, shout instead of whisper. That made the other kids hate him.

"'Why don't you just smile?' they said. 'We hate him,' they told the teacher, and because she hated him too she told him he had nothing more to learn.

He had to leave the school *immediately*." I pointed my finger to some distant place and the kids focussed there; Dom, stumbling away from school.

"No school. Cool," said one of the cousins.

"Shut up," the others told him.

"When he got home he snuck up to his room, because he didn't want his mother to know what had happened. He did not want her or his father to find out, and he knew it wouldn't be long before the teacher told them. So, that night after dinner, Dom said he would make coffee for his mother and father. In it he stirred some terrible poison, which couldn't be tasted because coffee is so bitter. He collected the suitcase he had already packed and he stood in the doorway and watched his own parents die a terrible, painful death."

One of the younger ones began to cry; his sister put her arm around him. The tiny sobs helped my story.

"For the next ten years Dom wandered. He was only a child and people took pity on him. You can only pity those people. Each of them died a terrible death. And so did their children. And then he decided he wanted to be part of my family. We knew nothing of his past. He was only a lonely man who needed a family. So we took him in."

The kids sucked their breath in. How could we have not known he was a monster?

"Things were okay for quite a while. Then my Dad started to think maybe it was time for Dom to find a place of his own. It was very crowded at our house. Dad told him at the dinner table.

"Dom said, 'Fair enough,' and your Uncle Peter and I kicked each other under the table. You see, we were starting to suspect there might be something wrong with Dom, because kids always know first. We heard him creeping around at night, digging up the backyard, and we *knew* he wasn't planting flowers."

The kids weren't breathing. Neither was I. For the moment this story was true, it had happened.

"That night, we heard a terrible sound coming from the tool shed. Do you know what it was?"

No one had a guess.

"It was an axe being sharpened. Peter and I ran into Mum and Dad's room to warn them, but they told us it was a bad dream.

"'But we *both* heard it,' we said.

"'Off to sleep,' they said. We knew we had to get help. We crept downstairs and out the front door, and we ran as fast as we could from house to house, looking for somewhere with a light on. We knew that if we woke someone up we'd have trouble making them believe us.

"We ran so far we reached the police station. So we ran inside.

"'Uncle Dom is sharpening his axe and we think he's going to kill

Mum and Dad!' I shouted to the policeman at the desk. We thought he was going to laugh his head off. But he didn't. He said, 'What's Uncle Dom's whole name?' and Peter told him. He said, 'Oh, my God,' just like that, and he started pressing buttons and talking into a microphone.

"'Now, kids, I want you to be calm, and very carefully tell me your address.' He sent cars around there, one of them picked us up on the way.

"'Stay in the car, kids,' they said, but as if we would. We wanted to see Mum and Dad, we wanted them to tell us how clever we'd been.

"But it was too late. Far, far too late. There was blood on the footpath. In the hallway. On the stairs. And in the bedroom were Mum and Dad. IN FIFTEEN BITS EACH!"

The kids screamed. They stared, they cried.

"And what happened to Uncle Dom? I don't know. He disappeared that night and had never been seen since. People say if you talk about him, or even dream about him, he will appear."

I looked over the kids' shoulders. I widened my eyes until tears formed. I opened my mouth.

"Uncle Dom," I whispered, and the kids screamed and ran away.

Maria insisted I answer all the calls that night, and every one of her relatives rang to abuse me.

"The kids can't sleep. They keep waking up with nightmares." This went on till three in the morning.

All the kids were having nightmares. I had a different answer for them all.

"At least that proves your kids have got a brain," I said. "Get them to write it down. You might be able to make a movie out of it." I looked forward to the phone ringing again. It rang for a week.

Maria's oldest brother was furious because his son kept tipping coffee down the sink.

"'It's bitter, Daddy,' he says. What sort of shit is that? He never even knew coffee existed until you told him the story. Now, every time we make a cup he tips it down the sink. I thought Sharon was going mad at first.

"'Your coffee's on the bench,' she says, and it's not there. So she makes me another, and I go for the paper and it's gone. I had seen it sitting there.

"So I make it this time and hide around the corner, and here's the bloody kid tipping it down the bloody sink!"

"Kid's smarter than you, then," I said, and hung up. Adrian, the youngest brother, rang me too. We talked for an hour. I realised later he didn't even have a kid old enough to be scared by me.

I still visited Maria's parents after that, but usually when the others weren't there.

Lucky for me Peter's a victim of guilt and a practitioner of denial. He called me a week or so later to talk, as if nothing had happened at all.

I practised my scream in the backyard. It always made me feel better and eventually the Rat Trap neighbours stopped investigating.

The nightmare-giving eclipsed the fact I taught the girls to scream. No mention was made of the day of the screams. Peter didn't want to hear more, or for me to apologise for killing our mother. He wanted to pretend it had never happened, that I was just a naughty aunty who taught his children naughty words. Nothing more. I didn't exist apart from that.

Eve gave me a pair of drop pearl earrings for my birthday. I was beginning to tire of her attentions; she wanted to talk about life when I was a child, foolish woman, as if I would remember that time fondly. I had taken to collecting her sleeping pill scripts from the chemist, and had decided it would be better for her not to take them for a month or so. "You'll feel better," I told her, and she believed me. I went to visit her; she was bounding about the place, dusting things left dirty for years.

"Stevie Stevie Stevie!" she said. "Never felt better, never felt better, ooh, my old bones feel new again. I remembered I hadn't given you your pressie."

I said, "You go get the pressie, I'll make us a cocktail."

She gave me the jewellery box. "You choose, dear."

"I will later. Let's have a drink, first. To celebrate your new lease on life."

Her eyes were bright and clear. We drank. Her nose wrinkled. "It's a bit nasty, darling."

I turned down the corners of my mouth, said nothing.

"Oh, but very nice, too," she said. She swallowed the lot, pills and all.

I stared into her eyes, wanting to see the movie there. Nothing.

"Eve?" I couldn't revive her, and I cursed myself for carelessness. I felt a great chill, an iciness in my bones.

I sat her comfortably in an armchair, put a book on her lap, surrounded her with her pictures and knick knacks. I took my birthday present and went home. The press reported LOCAL WOMAN SUICIDE. I never heard about my inheritance.

"And Lady Eve
Has passed away
Straight to Hell, or
So I pray."

Stalin said: "The main thing is to have the courage to admit one's errors and to have the strength to correct them in the shortest possible time."

That's the thing. Fixing the past without ignoring it. The Granny card arrived. *"Come see us and tell us all the news!"* it said. And:

"We know a girl
Her name is Stevie
And we think
She's really greevie!"

I have no idea when their birthdays are.

Ced came to me and said he had some friends who were keen to move in. He has so many friends.

The noises of the house have been disturbing me lately. Even when Ced's not around, I hear footsteps and bangs. Door slams. Whimpers. It would be good to fill the house, have real movement. Ced's sister Pauline and her boyfriend Barry moved into one room. She looked exactly like Ced, and talked like him, too. If I was in bed and heard people talking downstairs, I could barely tell who was who. Another friend of Ced's, Russell, took the last room. I could never figure out how the two of them were friends. Russell was a root rat, nothing but. He had women in every night, or he spent the night out.

It was a really pleasant time. I didn't think of dying while they were there. I didn't hear so many noises, and they included me in things, because Ced knew me. Thought he knew me. Sometimes I'd look out my bedroom window onto the sea of jasmine and think about Lacey underneath. I wondered how her room was going.

We had good times, hardly any fights. Pauline made pretty good golden syrup dumplings. One night Ced and I brought Chinese for us all, cos they couldn't afford food all the time. Russell brought out a bottle of whisky he found in the cupboard and we drank heaps. Pauline kept tripping over and I said, "Watch out for the ghost."

"What ghost?"

"Haven't you guys heard it? It's really noisy." As long as I can remember I've heard noises in the night, things being dragged and dropped, voices.

None of them had. Barry said, "Let's have a séance, see what it has to say."

I had wanted to do something like it but must confess to a certain fear. Not of the ghosts, but of who they might be. Mum, or Dad, watching me, seeing what I was doing. Lacey. Some of Dad's people.

"Why not?" I said.

We cleared away the kitchen table and Russell found another bottle. They were all laughing, joking, pretending they weren't scared. Russell lost some of his smoothness, began to slur his words and I wondered if he wanted to back out.

Pauline wrote the alphabet on bits of card and laid them neatly in a circle. She wrote "YES" and "NO". Barry brought in a glass, and I didn't realise, until it smashed on the floor beneath my feet, that it was my father's special glass, the one none of us were allowed to touch. I kept it in a box, in my bedroom cupboard, and it worried me that Barry had found it there.

We sat and rested our fingers on the glass. We kept giggling; do people ever lose that desire to giggle when they're supposed to be quiet? We had no music; we wanted silence. Ced wouldn't speak, but he sat with the rest of us, waiting. Then Russell's root from the night before appeared. She was dressed in white; we stared.

"I... came in the back door. It was open," she said.

"It's always open," I said, "But there's an invisible sign there. It says, 'Intelligence line. Do not cross.'"

Russell laughed. "See ya, anyway," and she left.

It became very cold and our throats were dry. We got a mess of letters, senseless, until Pauline, said, "Are you trying to tell us something?"

The glass moved to *YES*.

Then, *EVE*.

"Steve?"

Nothing.

"Who are you?"

VICTIM.

"Whose victim?"

Nothing.

"Whose victim?"

Nothing.

"Victim of what?"

MURDER.

Pauline sucked in her breath, threw the glass at me. "I hate this," she said. Then she gasped, touched her stomach. "I've got a pain," and she touched her arm, her head, her back. She began to cry.

"It hurts," she said. She stood up and curled to the floor, began to jerk as if she was being kicked.

"Pauline. What is it?" Barry said. He leant to comfort her, then began to choke, cough.

"I can't breathe," he said.

Ced began to cry. I couldn't draw breath either. I felt strong fingers around my throat; my hands rose there and tried to pull away things which didn't exist. Russell clutched his head. He thought he'd been shot.

Ced walked backwards out of the room, tripping and crying. He said, "This is what you've lived with all your life? Like this?"

"It was different when Mum and Dad were alive," I whispered. I didn't like the way they were looking at me. As if, why are you here. What are you doing in this house?

I turned on the TV to drown them out.

Ced called Peter. As if he would care. He hates this house. He's never been into pain; he's a master at avoiding it. We never discussed that night, the bruises they all suffered. Peter didn't come to visit while they lived there. He said, "They aren't the sort of people who suit my image," but that was bullshit.

It was a week or so later that Paula and Barry moved out. Thanks, they said, but we can't live here any longer. Not in a haunted house.

Russell moved out, too. That disappointed me. I didn't think he'd be affected.

Ced stayed. Out of pity, mostly. Also out of guilt avoidance; he knew that if I died, he'd be to blame.

He would never forgive himself.

It was just Ced and me after the ghost people moved out. I can't think of everyone at the séance in any other way; they're ghost people.

They brought ghosts with them, kept the ghosts hidden in their bedrooms, then revealed them to me, to scare me out of my own house. My house.

We scared them off, though. I smashed their dishes, mimicked their orgasms, stole their toilet paper, invited Samantha and her friends over to stay and walked around naked. It was that last, I think, which finally scared them away; all my scars.

I wear long sleeves at work. My hair is cut in a fringe, to cover most of the scarring. I don't want the patients to think of me that way. Ced used to tell me I needed to own the scars, and I told him he sounded like my counsellor. "That's not a good thing," I said.

I called Dougie Page when they moved out. I said, "My housemates think the house is haunted and they've moved out."

He laughed. He laughed a lot, Dougie. He said,

"Who'd be haunting your house?" but he said it jovially, like he was keeping a secret from a kid by making a joke.

"You tell me," I said.

I thought, "You stupid man. You think I don't know? You think you're protecting me?"

At Twenty-Eight

I had not intended to have another housemate. The temptation was too great to turn them into lovers and that always led to trouble. But when Ced moved out at last, thinking I was safe, my house creaked and groaned around me. An ant's footsteps echoed in the place.

So I went back to my old habit of playing with the classifieds, something I hadn't done seriously for years, but I still liked to read them. It felt like news, gossip; opening the back pages was like telephoning a friend who prefaced every conversation with, "Have you heard?"

I didn't want anyone living with me, but this intrigued me.

I can cook and give toe massages and I'm not looking for a friend. Is there room for me?

So I answered the ad, and Robert moved in two days later. Dougie Page did a check on him and said Robert was clean.

I liked him immediately because he didn't do a double-take when he saw I wasn't a guy. Was he expecting a guy? Did guys like toe massages and no friendship? He didn't say, "If your name's Steve, mine's Gloria." He said, "Show me to the best room in the house." I bowed my head.

"Of course," I said in my quietest voice. I led him up the stairs. Opened a door; gave him a shove and pulled the door shut.

"Welcome to your new home," I said through the keyhole, and I would have run away but I couldn't for laughing.

"Ha ha," he said. He meant it; he really was laughing. "I assume I'm not really to be in the bathroom."

"Only if you find it suits you," I said. "No, this one's my room; that one's a good one, you get a good view of the bedroom next door, when they forget to cover the window, and this one has always been the master bedroom but I never got around to moving into it. So please yourself."

"How about this one, then?" he said, and dumped his garbage bag in my room. I stared at it; listened to it rustle.

"All right then?" he said. "Promise I won't hog the blankets or snore too loud. And you'll be able to discover what sort of a massage I give with my toe."

So he didn't intend to pay rent or buy food, presumably. But his voice filled the room and didn't bounce back.

"If you can make golden syrup dumplings, you're in," I said, but I was going to let him stay no matter what his cooking was like.

After a while he asked if a friend of his could move in. It was another guy, Ben, who was a great cook and gave me lectures about Jewish history. He was a bit of a pain in the arse; no sense of humour.

There was such a great movie on TV I called Ben to watch. He huffed and tutted halfway through, till I said, "If you want to do some heavy breathing, go phone one of your girlfriends. I'm trying to watch this movie."

"And you had no idea how offensive this movie would be to me?"

"Why would you be offended? It's just a movie."

It was about Nazis, told from their point of view. Very sympathetic. Ben was such a sensitive thing. I came out of the bathroom a couple of days later, my towel around my waist. I caught him skulking around at the top of the stairs. He gawked at me, he shuddered. I said, "What's the matter, Nazis goose-stepping on your grave?" It's long been a favourite of mine. He hid in his room without a word.

I was glad he was there when the police arrived, though, banging at the door and shouting, "We've got a warrant to search these premises."

I opened the door. I had fluffy slippers on, my hair in pigtails. "This place? What for? Do I need to tidy up first? God, sorry, it's such a mess. Does anyone want a cup of coffee first? Before you get started?" I herded them down the hallway as I spoke. They began pawing my things while the boss cop followed me to the kitchen. On top of the fridge is a picture of Dad. In uniform. With me on his knee, wearing his hat. I slammed the fridge door when I replaced the milk; the photo wobbled, toppled. The cop jerked to catch it, missed, braced himself for the smash.

"No glass," I said. "Happens all the time. I like to keep it up there, though."

He replaced it. "Your Dad?"

"Yep."

"Does he work with us?"

"Did. He died quite a while ago, on a job."

"I'm sorry."

"Yeah, I know. Mum's dead, too, before you mention her and feel awful."

"That's no good. I would have thought people would be more sympathetic. Leave you alone."

"Not around here. I think I remind them of their own mortality."

He shook his head, swallowed coffee in gulps.

"Look, I'm sorry about this," he said.

"What's it about, anyway? Neighbourhood gossip come up with something, has it? They don't like me, anyway, and even more because, I don't know, I just act like any other young, healthy woman. I don't think I should be in mourning all my life, do you?" My voice cracked.

"Commendable. Commendable," he said. "The thing is, scuttlebutt says you're involved with the supply of drugs to the high school. I know we're not going to find anything, but we need to be seen to be doing something."

I let my mouth drop in horror. I had never managed the art of summoning tears on call, though.

"Well, anything to stop that going on. I work in a hospice and I've seen what happens to people. Vegetables, some of them. It's a terrible thing."

They didn't find anything.

They didn't look in the backyard.

Robert and Ben were pretty pissed off about the raid. Robert paid me back by taking my car the next day, while I was asleep.

"I need to impress someone," the note said. He left me the keys to his bomb, like I had no one to impress. Just a bloody job to get to. People relying on me to get them through the day. Look into their eyes and say, "Tell me what you see. What do you smell?" Take an interest in their dying that nobody else takes.

I jumped in his car and the bloody thing wouldn't start. I revved and revved, feeling the minutes pass by, I was late for work now and I hated to be late. I hate that. They think I'm reliable, there. They ask me to do things they wouldn't trust others to do, because I'm reliable. Finally the engine kicked in. As I drove away, I saw Mrs Pleat rocking her screaming baby and glaring at me.

"Fuck you, too," I said, my smile wide enough to break my face.

I didn't figure out who dobbed me in until the next time I returned from the dark room.

I waited a long time for my twenty-eighth birthday to be celebrated. The only thing in the mail was the Granny card. No plane ticket. I rang them to say hi but they were out. The card said:

"Happy happy happy day

We hope your blues just go away."

How did they know? And why didn't they do something about it? I heard Ben and Robert muttering and I thought, great, they're planning a surprise dinner. But it wasn't that. "She's never out of the fucken place," Robert said. "We'll have to do it while she's upstairs." They were going to wait till I was asleep, then they were doing a runner.

Dougie Page called me, told me things he shouldn't know. Things I didn't want to hear spoken. My teeth ached, my stomach filled with acid. At midnight I lay in my backyard and beneath the smell of jasmine was a deeper smell.

My history.

The slighted don't have to die to appear in your room. I ran over a kid's dog, on purpose, and told him the dog was not worthy of life. That was too much. It was beyond a slight.

I didn't shower for a week, went to a concert, farted, lifted my arms. I stank. Everyone around me hated it. I memorised their faces; they were there, all right, when I went to the dark room, and unless thirteen strangers died within a few weeks of each other, they were still alive. The word suicide seems to jump out at me. I see it everywhere. I have a list somewhere, which I scrabble out and add to whenever I hear of a new way, a new reason. The lists for both are pages long.

There's one thing I've noticed, a similarity. Not in every case, but in a lot. The person left behind says, "We were just about to...." Go to Europe, celebrate someone's twenty-first birthday, get married, buy a house. Always something special.

It's never after, always before, and that's where they're different from me. I would never ruin a good night like that. A woman at work once had her hair done, hours of work, missed half a day, and she popped in to show us. She was going to a ball, some huge ball, and she thought she would meet someone nice there, she'd heard about him and he sounded nice, their friends were matching them up.

We didn't see her for a week and we assumed she'd return with honeymooner's cystitis. She slumped at her desk and didn't speak.

"So, how was the ball?" someone finally asked.

"I didn't go," she said. We laughed; it was a joke.

"No. When I got home that day Liam had killed himself. So I didn't go." Liam was her brother.

"How did he do it?" I said. I got shushed, kicked.

"What?" I said. People are so picky.

She didn't say; she never said. It was a subject of great frustration to me.

Then it was almost midnight and I knew the only friends I could trust. They waited for me, clicking their teeth, waiting. They all waited, not with beer and a plate of fresh prawns, but with tiny mouths, which pucker and suck, little nails sharp as knives to paper-cut you to death. I remembered the caresses now, why they sickened me. I remembered that, as I was drawn out of their clutches, on my last visit, their fingernails had dug in, sunk in like claws.

I started Robert's car and waited for him to come home. Fuck him. Let him get the smell out. Let him remember me forever.

I locked myself in the garage and visited the dark room for the fifth time. Sixth. I went there for the sixth time.

Robert's car became my special womb, exhaust fumes smelling like perfume, and a brown bottle of brandy I bought for my birthday. I played Swan Lake; my toes twitched, my fingertips felt light as feathers. If I could have stayed right there, at that point, I wouldn't have needed the dark room. I wouldn't need to know about the dark rooms waiting for other people.

There were many more this time, and my eyelids felt heavy; I could barely keep them open to take in the faces around me.

The driver of the other car was there again, the one who shouldn't have been on that road, at that time, and said to me, "If it wasn't for you I'd have been home free."

And there were many others. I breathed in the car's exhaust. I curled up like a baby, because I was safe here. The room was a long way away and I wanted to see it again. I wanted to be noticed.

Old, reliable Darren was there to greet me, not a day older than when I threw the milk at him. And Peter was there. I stretched my hand out to him but he stared coldly at me. Why? What had I done to slight him? Darren had a yo-yo and Peter had a stanley knife. He was so kind outside the room; here I was seeing into his soul.

"Peter," I said. Miaow. I couldn't speak. I reached my hand to him, but he sneered.

Mr Williams took it. He pressed something there; a raffle ticket, how subtle. He's slighted because I don't buy fucking raffle tickets from his crappy little cunts of children. I laughed and he cringed. The other neighbours surrounded him and drew him back; the Oakes, all five, and Jody Morris, poor resentful bitch.

I felt stronger, somehow. I felt they were scared of me. I sat up, took my first step on the floor. It was soft, foam mattresses, and I walked carefully.

They stood, cringing, while I stared into their faces.

Lacey; because I knocked her perfume bottles over. She didn't have time to resent her death. I could smell her cheap perfume; the fumes of it made my eyes water.

The room smelt worse, this time. Shit, naphthalene, cheap perfume, and a pauper's stench, unwashed, old clothes, cheap food coming out of the pores, free soup dripping like snot. The filth under their fingernails would rest in the cuts they made and little mushrooms would grow like maggots.

I felt rats nibble my toes, but it wasn't rats, it was Mrs Pleat and Mrs Sanderson, loving thy neighbour, chewing my toenails to the quick but I couldn't get my legs away and when they tore the nails out with their teeth I screamed, and I heard all the people in the room snicker.

Auntie Ruth was there, her jaw flapping and snapping, wanting to capture jewels. And all those concert faces; what did they think of the stench here? If they couldn't bear my sweet smell? They breathed through their mouths; I could see ants crawling over their teeth.

I saw a girl with big tits, and she smothered me with them. They smelt of beer and semen, and I felt her hand on my own tits, squeezing like they were play-doh, and I could feel my flesh changing shape between her awful fingers.

Then I saw old Bess. My old friend Bess, oh, Bess, how is your life? Would you like a seat? Oh, please.

She watched me, licked her lips, an excited observer. I stared into her eyes; she looked away. She was guilty. They were all guilty. Shallow, empty people with nothing to complain about.

I passed the ghost people, those housemates I'd called friends, and I laughed at their fear. "All in the mind," I said. Weow, weow. Their hands covered their eyes, they fell to my feet, they cut me, tiny lines across my shins, criss-cross like a charm to ward off evil. One of Russell's roots stood beside him; together forever ha ha. I skipped around the room, bumping, bumping, shoving. They grabbed me, wanted bits of me. Scott's wedding guests were there; I recognised the baby's breath. They muttered, whispered: Did you see the dress she's wearing her very presence sickens me can you believe that fake smile snob who is she didn't bring a present not wanted here sat up the front doesn't mind turning her back she's scared the children how could she come to a wedding with a ladder in her pantyhose?

There were other voices, people with shopping bags and name tags, mall dwellers: She's so rude how could she ignore me I thought I was the only one with that coat she nearly knocked my kid over trod on a dropped magazine she's better-looking than me piss me off.

I put my hands over my eyes, shut my eyes, that made them stronger, too strong. Robert and Ben picked me up and threw me back on the table, Ben would peel me for a lampshade and Robert stuck his toe in my cunt, his foot, his whole leg was inside me and I was ashamed because Maria's family were there, not her parents, but sisters, brothers, not Adrian, in-laws. Why is she here she doesn't belong.

And the drivers are back, waving their keys, red light abuse, pulling out change lanes, strangers, strangers from the library, the street, the pub, all know me and I don't know them. Faces I can't put a tongue to.

The housemates who moved out at Christmas, Mo and Ho, they hurt me, I was the one, they are here to cut and spit, slice me up and bleed me, suck my guts out and stop me from breathing.

Those faces around me. I am the great I am.

Robert came home, he came home thinking I was asleep, came home to get his things, just a bag full. Get his things and leave me. But he found me, and he stopped me from staying in the dark room. I hated him for that. I imagined it was some other woman he went to, someone not scarred, on wrists and about my head. Sometimes I lie about what caused the scars. More often I'll say casually, "Oh, that was when I cut my wrists," and leave it at that.

An air of mystery about me. I thought Robert really loved me. Ignored my damaged body. He left me, though. He had been with me for two months. I think he was scared of my desperation. Thought I might take him with me one time. He found me after midnight and they took me, still warm, to hospital. I was told these events. Robert came to the hospital once, to see his handiwork.

He said nothing, just sat there discomfited. I didn't feel like helping him; he had brought me back from the place where everybody loved me.

"You're looking pale," he said.

"That's nice."

"Cos I didn't know, at first, when I found you.

The stink was awful, but you were pink-cheeked, healthier than you ever looked before. I thought you must have taken a massive dose of vitamins or something."

"That would've been typical behaviour, wouldn't it?"

"And suicide is?" he said. He was a self-centred, unobservant idiot.

I remembered one face, Mrs Beattie, from that visit to the dark room clearly, could hear her breathing, her presence was so strong. The next time I saw her, I looked for signs of illness, thinking that for her to be so strong in the room, she must be close to death. I walked into her corner shop without a care.

"How are you feeling, Mrs Beattie? I'd be careful if I were you. You never know what's around the corner."

"Are you threatening us?" her husband said. He rarely spoke a word; she must be sick.

"Why would I do that?" I said, but suddenly it hit me; they were the ones who called the police on me, precipitating the raid. It was only lucky I'd had a sell-out and there was nothing in the place; not a pill or a puff.

Now Mrs Beattie thought I was after revenge for her dobbing me in.

"I'm just saying," I said. "She doesn't look well.

You should get away to the sunshine."

They did, too; left the shop in the care of their daughter and went up north. The only person that move helped was me; I couldn't be blamed for a death so far away.

Mrs Beattie was massive in the room when I went back.

I think I'm shrinking. Every time I get smaller, as they take pieces away from me. My legs ache because they cut pieces away. My arms are the same.

I was forced to go back to counselling. An habitual attempted suicide. Habitual. Like it was something beyond me, out of my control. Like the room ruled me. I was capable of making my own decisions. My resolution then was never to slight anyone, be *careful* about it, just beware. And be good to the relatives.

Blood and marriage ones. Be polite and interested.

Too fucking hard. Relatives are such a bore.

Friends are a bore. Lovers are a bore when they're not actually doing their job. It takes too much effort to be nice. No one trusted me, anyway.

"What are you after?" Maria said when I rang up just to chat.

"I haven't got time," Peter said when I offered to help him with his courses, though he had time to drop me off at the new counsellor. Another unfulfilled resolution.

It was a small room, stuffy, and the counsellor wouldn't open the window.

"It lets fumes and noise in," he said.

"So you like to pretend you're living in the country?" I said. He smiled, and I thought, "Here we go."

It took about three sessions before he got stuck into me. Every visit I made myself uglier; massaged peanut oil into my hair and skin for greasiness, wore bad clothes, sprayed on the vilest perfume I could find. I didn't want him becoming attracted to me, touching me. But he said, "Steve, I get the impression you're putting up a barrier. Are you protecting yourself from something?"

"You're a fucken sleazebag," I said. He smiled. He said, "Perhaps you're trying to cover up some of the scars on your body. You don't want to discuss how they got there."

I realised I had dog shit on my shoe—I thought it was his bad aftershave—and I wiped it on some papers I peeled from his desk. His smile took a downward turn.

"Steve," he said, "have you ever considered the notion that suicide is one of the most selfish acts?

That some people will attempt suicide just before an event in their family's lives, thus damaging that event irreparably?"

I shrugged. He said, "And that sometimes an act which appears heroic is in fact careless, and this carelessness could be considered suicidal?" His smile was back. He was trying to hurt me. He wanted me to think Dad killed himself. I would never believe that.

I called Peter to say I wasn't going to go to the counsellor anymore. I wanted him to fix it for me.

Make it so I didn't have to go. I had to leave a message on the machine. I put on a real deep, sleazy voice. "Maria, darling, I know you said never to call you there, but I just got to thinking about your big tits. Come over, darling. Oh, it's Johnny, in case you've got more than one of us."

Peter called me back. He still pretended my attempt was an accident. That I didn't need counselling anyway. "Accident-inclined," he said to me, and it could have been Dad talking. He didn't want the responsibility of my life. If he'd asked I would have told him the truth, that I was doing it for research.

I said, "Did you know that human blood has a richness unmatched in other species?" I had Auntie Jessie to thank for that one. On page 77 of *West with the Night*, Beryl Markham's autobiography, she wrote a recipe for Steak and Kidney Pudding near a description of the Masai drink, blood and milk.

She says, "Human blood has a richness unmatched in other species."

I made it into the newspaper; they reported on me.

I was that aggrieved I wrote a letter to the paper, and didn't *that* piss people off. In it I said, "It's the fault of the other people, not the suicide person."

Funny how you think less about your childhood the older you get. It becomes distant. Long gone.

At Twenty-Nine

Maria and I had a screamer over the phone, just before my twenty-ninth birthday.

I had two housemates at the time; really fun guys who smoked heaps and made me laugh. They hated cleaning up, too, and loved it that I didn't hassle them. We had a great time. The only thing was, I always made them pay for the dope. No free rides here. When they moved in I asked them if they could make golden syrup dumplings and they said, "We can learn." But they didn't.

We watched TV, ate, hung out. I put on weight while they were there. I couldn't absorb the crap the way they did.

I rang to ask Peter to come to my place for a birthday barbie in the backyard, just us and the guys.

He said, "I don't think that's a very good idea.

Why don't we have it here?"

"Why don't you fuck off?" I said. "Get over this thing about our house."

Then Maria came on the phone.

"Look, Steph, the story is that we have a lovely home here, very nice, very large. Why don't we have just the family, a nice, comfortable day?"

"What's it got to do with you? I wasn't even going to ask you, you dull bitch. Or your fucken kids." I loved this stuff. I just said whatever came into my head.

"All that aside, the story is that we don't like the kids at your place. Your housemates aren't very pleasant and you can't seem to do even the basic cleaning. What's wrong with you? Last time we were there the kids got food poisoning and had nightmares for days."

I laughed. "Tell you what, Martyr. You tell Peter I hate you so much I'd rather spend my birthday on my own. Tell him I'll mix myself up a nice cocktail." I hung up.

I'd never threatened suicide before, or used it as leverage. But she was so manipulative. I had to get her somehow. I didn't hear a word from them. My birthday passed unnoticed, apart from the Granny card. It said:

"HELLO STEVIE HELLO DEAR
COME UP HERE AND
HAVE A BEER"

I'm seriously thinking about it. I mentioned my birthday to my housemates but they forgot and then they moved out. The timing was bad, because I was going to ask them to help me pay for the fence the Krowskas are insisting on. Who needs a new fence, anyway? The old one is fine.

I spent hours shuffling through the books Auntie Jessie'd given me over the years, and the ones she'd left me, hundreds of them, dusty, dirty, yellowing, musty. They were already smelling mouldy; when they became mine, after Auntie Jessie's death, most had a fine green dust which sank into my pores and my lungs when I sorted the books. She left me her pearls, too. Three strings, and a padded box with loose ones. She never got around to having them re-strung.

Much later, I began to flick through those books, read them, sometimes, or read again favourites like *Of Mice and Men*. Some were different than I remembered. Some had messages; some had pages of pale pencil words. It was hard to read; too old. It tired me.

I read some of these books as a child, then again as an adult, and it's amazing how much more sense things make when you're an adult. You know what things mean, how to change them. You understand words and jokes, and hardly ever need things explained to you. This is a comfort to me. And I hate it when that sense of bewilderment periodically returns. Age has nothing to do with it, nor the comfort of confidence.

Auntie Jessie's books are both a comfort and a distress to me. They gave me knowledge I didn't want to have. My Dad was a good man. The only chance I have is that my Dad was a good man. But when I read through the books, the comfort comes because I feel like she's there, alive, and she loves me. In the book *Magnetism* by EC Stoner, published 1946 but unborrowed in her entire time as a librarian, on page 39 — "In the ethane group each carbon atom may be regarded as forming the centre of an electronic distribution of the 'closed configuration' type, while in ethylene and acetylene the two carbon atoms approximate to a single centre for the outer part of the electronic charge" — she wrote: *"He has killed again."*

I made a song up, "He Has Killed Again", and I felt lonely. Auntie Jessie wasn't there to talk to, Dad was gone, Mum. I went to a night club to pick up someone. Not a habit. It was too hard to see people's eyes; I couldn't tell what they were thinking.

I danced with a man in a singlet top; his nipples were pink, like they say a virgin's are. He kept apologising to people he bumped and smiled too kindly at me.

I left him without explanation, knowing he was too cowardly to follow. I stood beside a group in their business clothes; women flawless with ironed shirts, men more wrinkled, expensive suits now beer-stained, jackets discarded. They groped and leaned on each other, ordered drinks rapidly, watched the dance floor without joining it. One man was central to the group; so central as to be almost separate. He watched, returned kisses, accepted drinks. His eyes were empty, staring, blue.

I saw a gap and slipped in.

"You're a very magnetic man," I said. He smiled at me.

"And you're interrupting my night," he said.

"From where I'm sitting, you seem to be bored out of your brain."

"Never," he said, but he winked and put his arm around my waist. He leaned over, collected someone's lighter, lit a cigarette, pocketed the lighter. All without words; almost without movement. I kept the lighter, later, when I found it in his pocket.

"Tell me about your enemies," I said. "Who hates you?"

He laughed. "That guy whose lighter I just stole, for one," he said. If he was joking, he was in for a shock, when the guy showed up in his dark room.

I said, "And there's a dick over there who thought he could magnetise me. He's thinking, 'If that arsehole wasn't there I'd be in.'"

"And that girl with red hair? I just ignore anything she says. She probably hates me."

He didn't ask me the same question, or any questions. His self-absorption made me think there would be lots more in his dark room. I said, "Do you have to be home by a certain time? Is there some patient, trusting female, cup of tea ready, legs shaved just in case?"

He gave me his full attention now, looking at my face. "Do you want to take me home?" he said.

I took his hand and led him to where I wanted him to go. I am very good at measuring the timing of these things; I can push them over or bring them back, depending. This man, his name was Dennis, Den, he fought me, he had been there before and didn't want to go back.

"Interesting home you have," he said, and I raised my head and it was my Dad standing there, talking, talking, honey voice all full of caring.

And I was my mum or some stranger woman; my skin tightened into a smile as his words seduced me. His words made me do something I didn't want to do.

Although he was like my father, I couldn't love him. It was his shoes. Who could love a man who wore black and white shoes? He dumped his keys on the coffee table. They had a little key ring; #1, it said.

Smooth talkers are the most attractive types, but they always disappoint. After we became intimate he told me about the time he nearly died, but he lied. He must have been quite healthy and just dreaming. A fantasy about some fucken tunnel, fucken light, fucken voices calling him back. It really made me angry, that he lied. Because no one had ever called me back. Not a whisper or a shout.

I went into the bathroom to make with the diaphragm but I had him use a condom as well. Can't be too careful. Don't want any babies, babies, running around, crying, cooing, clinging, growing, trouble. Who wants them, anyway? Who needs them?

He told me it had been an accident, that his father hadn't meant to hurt him so badly, it was a slip of the fist. And of the knee. It was the slip of a son in hospital. It made me so angry I couldn't look at him any longer. We drank whisky; I found glasses without greasy lip stains and poured it in. He seemed bewildered by the mess of the place and my lack of apology.

"Not much of a housekeeper, are you?" he said.

He shoved newspaper out of the way to sit on the floor and uncovered some CDs I thought I'd lost.

The covers were cracked.

"I'm dirty," I said. "I'm so dirty dogs won't lick me. All my clothes are filthy and my body stinks."

He knew that wasn't true; his nose had been nestled under my arms, in my belly button, behind my knees. He sipped whisky. I drank from the bottle; straddled him, standing. Seduction never sat comfortably with me; I always feel ridiculous.

"Show me," he said, and I unbuttoned my short silk top, let it drop, I stood up and unzipped my short skirt, let it fall. I had matching underwear; I had bought it that morning.

"Magnetising," he said. I filled his glass again, gave him ice from the kitchen, gave him a little something to make him sleepy.

"Let me tell you about magnetism," I said, and I read to him from my special yellow book:

"To ensure that values characteristic of free molecules are obtained, it would be necessary to make measurements on gases. The volume susceptibility of gases is proportional to the pressure, the molecular susceptibility being constant.

Some experimental results, which were taken to indicate that at low pressures the volume from a linear relation, have not been shown to have been due to secondary experimental effects. It has been shown by Vaidyanathan (1927) that generally, though not invariably, measurements of the susceptibility of a substance in the liquid and vapour state lead to approximately the same value for molecular susceptibility."

I flicked through the yellowing pages of the strange little book, the science nonsense of it comforting me. These things were said a long time ago; history can be changed.

I led Den to the bath. He sat on the toilet while I filled the bath with hot water and sandalwood scent.

He didn't know the lid was down and forgot I was there; he pissed, the whole lot spilling and spurting onto my dirty white floor. It was good when there were no housemates. I was tired of housemates.

"Filthy," I said. I don't think that's what decided me to let him die; it was more that I couldn't be bothered with the small talk later, making him coffee and toast, going through the "I'll call you" lie.

He had stripped his clothes off clumsily as we walked up the hallway, imagining he was still capable of sex. He would have fallen asleep immediately and been too embarrassed the next morning, too keen to escape me as soon as possible, to ask what had happened.

"Into the bath, then," I said. I made sure he was sitting up safely. I wouldn't be able to see his eyes underwater if he drowned, and he wouldn't talk. I needed to see if he reached his own dark room, would hold his eyelids open with my fingers to look into his eyes.

I took one wrist, then the other, and sliced them long ways. It made me think of a joke I saw in *Punch* magazine. A man with cuts on his face says, "These scars? I cut myself attempting suicide."

"What do you see? Talk to me!" I held his eyes open; my knees pressed into the bathroom tiles and they were damp. I couldn't tell if it was from his piss or overflow from the bath. His arms flapped; I gently placed them back in the water. I stared into his eyes, hoping for a movie there.

The thing is I can defend this. I don't do it because I want to kill them. I do it because I want to talk to them afterwards. But it's so hard to time. I get caught up—I don't want to bring them back too soon. I want them to spend time in the room so they can tell me.

Den began to pant, and the blood flow seemed weaker. His lips moved. I considered bandaging his arms, stopping the flow, but he hadn't been there yet. He hadn't seen it. Just a few more moments, he needed to be closer.

I could see the dark room approaching in his eyes. I stared harder, stared until my eyes stung.

I allowed myself to be slighted by him, to see what happens when the person dies. There was a momentary shiver, was all, as that snippet ends up in the cold room with the dead person. So those shivers we all get, and we say someone's walking over my grave, but the truth is someone we were slighted by has died. It felt an itch, like a lost limb. A small piece shaved away. I shivered, goose-step on grave.

He shook his head from my grasp, widened his eyes and said, clearly, "Dark." I was elated. He had seen the room, then, the dark, the razor teeth, smelt the shit. I smelt it too, but it was him, the bath a mess of blood, oil, shit.

Then he sank away from me. His pupils were wide and black. I could see my own staring monkey face. Slowly, a thin cloud filmed over his eyes, and his eyeballs seemed to flatten. His face was grey, flat, toneless. He seemed to shrink; he was half the man he had been when we set out.

"Talk to me," I said. "Is it golden? Is there someone there? *What do you see?* "

When I was cleaning the bathroom later I saw, at the end of the bath, staring with glass eyes, my rubber ducky. Duck. Not dark. Duck.

I buried him in the backyard.

The phone rang as I was finishing in the garden.

Peter said, "God, took you long enough."

"I was digging in the garden."

"Hmph. I thought you'd finished with all that.

Look, I just wanted to tell you about Kelly's birthday. She's ten, you know. We're just having a party at home."

I said, "I thought you hated those. We always went somewhere for your birthdays."

Silence.

Peter said, "Yes, but we had to."

I said, "What do you mean? Mum and Dad loved kids."

Peter said, "Come on, Steve. You know what I'm talking about."

I said, "You tell me, Peter."

Peter said, "I don't want to discuss it."

I said, "Peter, if you say the words it'll be okay.

My counsellor said so."

Peter said, "It was Dad, Steve. I was ashamed of him. I thought he might lose it."

I said, "You're kidding. What are you on about?

Just because he liked me better than you doesn't mean you should lie about him. I wouldn't be seen dead at your ugly child's fucken party." I hung up.

It was amazing they kept asking me back to these things. Just weeks later it was Maria's birthday; her parents threw her a party like she was a child. I didn't want to go; she never comes to any of mine. I told Auntie Ruth and she harrumphed as I knew she would. "Who does that family think they are? Do they think they're *your* family? You've got family of your own, Steve. You just come right over here if you want company. I've made some special soup and we'll watch TV together. I've made a lovely banana cake…always use bananas which are almost black, Stevie, and you won't go wrong."

That night was medical drama night; three of them in a row, and Auntie Ruth imagining she belonged in a hospital. I could never be sure if she preferred the idea of being a patient or a doctor. She told anyone who'd listen the commercial stations were best because you had time to go to the toilet during the ads.

I could taste the soup just hearing about it. Auntie Ruth was a frugal person. If things were going off in her fridge she turned them into soup, anything. Yoghurt, mashed potato, tomatoes, meat, chicken, sausages, pumpkin, Brussels sprouts, anything went in, all vitamised to a texture and served with a sprig of wilting parsley. She called them her "vitamin soups". I called them vitamin goo.

So I went to Maria's birthday. Half of them weren't there; sick politics in that family. We were served oysters and everyone nudged Peter, rude bastards, as if they knew something.

I said, "I wouldn't eat it, Peter. Maria prefers them limp and in the other bed, doesn't she?" Peter was the only one who laughed. I looked into the faces of each of them, smiling.

"What are you doing, Steve?" her sister Elise asked me.

"Just being careful," I said. These people were my family, and Peter's, and I didn't want to slight them.

It's so hard to be aware. You have to listen and respond to everything, watch where you walk, and when you get to the room they're waiting, anyway.

I have never felt more of a pariah than I did that day. I felt like opening up my wounds and bleeding right there in front of them, just to make them pay attention. Say something. Not one mentioned the fact that I wanted to die. No one even asked me how I was. They might start, saying, "How…." But they don't want to know the answer. So they'd say,

"How famous is Peter, now?" or they'd ask me if I'd tried the Mexican dip. Fuck that dip.

Do they think suicide is catching?

At Thirty

Peter rang out of the blue. "I want to let you know of a decision we've made. It's about my future."

I didn't speak. His life was boring.

"It's just that I don't feel like the courses are going anywhere. We've reached the end with them."

"Thank fuck for that!" I said. "So what're you gonna do?"

"We were thinking of politics."

"Maria thinks it's a good idea, does she?"

"She thinks I could make a go of it."

"So long as you promise to legalise homicide," I said.

"Whatever you say, Steve."

They had a Peter launch and I was invited. They wanted me to hand around the plates of food. I don't think so. There were men there with dark eyes, mirrors, and I was all prepared. I'd been back to family planning, to make things safe. They give you what you want there. Every doctor I've been to has refused to give me a hysterectomy. They say I don't need one, that the accident caused problems with reproduction, but those eggs make me bleed every month. I know they're waiting.

Some sycophant said, "So, Peter, why join the world of governance? Seems to me you were doing well where you were."

"Yes, but I had the call to politics."

He worried about my stories; that I'd spill the family history. He knew the stories as well as I did; Mum liked to talk. But he chose to forget them.

Whenever I spoke he'd laugh loudly, to cover up my words and send the message that I was a clown.

That nothing I said was to be taken seriously.

I don't even know why he invited me to his launch. Dougie Page was there, standing in the corner looking uncomfortable. He avoided me. I wanted him to lay off Dad, leave it alone. I knew that Dad's stuff would lead to me, and I wanted Dougie off me so I ignored him. Easy.

A lot of people came to talk to me after Peter made his decision to get into politics. Journalists from the local paper, investigators who didn't say where they were from, all wanting to find out if Peter was who he seemed to be: perfect, unblemished, with no terrible secrets. As far as the world was concerned, Peter's adult life was without guilt or error. I would have hated the results if they had been about me. They needed to go back as far as his early teenage years to find trouble, and that kind of trouble was something to be proud of.

He rang me the day after the launch. "Thanks for not telling tales, Steve," he said. "I owe you a trip to the zoo."

"Oh, yeah. Saturday OK?" I said. It was a joke between us; we both hated the zoo, thought it was the dullest place to visit. "What did I ever do for you?" I said.

"True," he said. "Apart from saying nice things to anyone who asked over the last few months. I really appreciate it. I relied on you cos you're my only sensible relative."

"Apart from Auntie Ruth and the Grannies. And Uncle Dom."

"Yeah, miles apart." We chuckled.

"No," he said. "It was good of you. Not that I've got any secrets, but I know what you're like."

I laughed. "Thanks and insults and a trip to the zoo all in one breath."

He did very well from the start. A lot of the sort of person who votes for a person because their name is familiar said they'd vote for him and he was soon experiencing the power Maria had dreamed of. No one saw the irony of a sales-man becoming a politician.

My Granny card hasn't arrived. I called them and there was no answer. I rang Peter to see if he had heard anything from them. Rang Ruth too.

"Don't talk to me about your grandmother She sent me a photo. She's going to be dead of skin cancer before too long."

I rang the Grannies again, and this time they answered. They were fine. Grampa had been in a chess tournament and they had let things slip.

"Thanks for calling, Diana," Granny Walker said.

Bitch. I went outside to work on the car. People ask me about it in the street, sometimes, because it's so old and flash. They're impressed when I say I look after it myself.

I didn't realise how much other kids loved their grannies until we were adults, when I saw the delight Peter's girls had in seeing Maria's Mum.

They squealed, wriggled, chattered. Peter often shrugged at me, I don't know where they get it from. It struck me that this was how our Grannies dreamt we would be. Mum told me how much the Grannies had dreamt of grandkids, and then they get us, two kids more interested in the world outside. They got Ruth's sucky little losers, Diana and Cary, though, and Dad's brother Seb had Nate, the most pathetic thing, who never looked alive. The poor little mutant would cry if you stared at it; we lost all contact once we hit our teens. Nate was there in my dark room a couple of times; why, I don't know. The time I shaved a bald spot on his head: the time I farted in his face? I think he took Peter's course once, but we didn't talk to him.

Ruth's two geniuses are both business heads living overseas. They never have time for her. They send her money and she spends it.

Dougie Page called to tell me there were developments. He wanted to take me to dinner, discuss the news.

I said I didn't need to eat that day.

At Thirty-One

On the night of the local election, I ordered pizza, chilled two bottles of champagne in case Peter dropped by to celebrate, and filled a bucket with ice to hold my beers so I wouldn't have to move except to piss. My housemate Isaac sat up in his room and barely bothered me. He was only staying at my place because he was the son of one of the women dying at the hospice, and she'd asked me to look after him. He sat up in his room. He's a very depressed person. I've never seen him smile. He makes me feel light and fluffy. He thought I was a guy. He thought I was a gay guy. I loved it. He told me all sorts of guy stuff I bet he regrets

There was some big party at Peter's place, but he said they were all wankers and would stand around talking instead of watching the election on TV. Peter was running as an independent, figuring it was his best way; people often make protest votes at local level, putting independents in to make a point to the government, without actually causing the government to lose power. He had broadened his appeal, building on his popularity as a self-help guru. His line was, "I believe in the little picture. If you're happy, society is happy." I wrote his victory speech for him.

That's what should have happened. This is what did happen:

I rang his house as the night progressed and Peter's numbers rose. Each time an excited stranger answered; in the background I could clearly hear the TV and people being shushed. I rang at regular intervals, just to piss them off. Each stranger said Peter was engaged.

"What is he, a fucken toilet?" I said.

Peter won his seat; I rang to congratulate him but the phone was engaged. It was engaged for the rest of the night. He's such a weak man, but people seem to find weakness charming. The more charming they find him, the more confident he becomes, and the more charismatic he appears. He never has trouble. He smiles, talks, and people give him what he needs. Maria arranged for the kids to stay with friends. (And haven't their friends changed, now?

Maria got them into some fancy school, and all the parents are lawyers, politicians, crap like that.) In the morning after the election Maria answered the phone, "Maria Searle." All efficient, suddenly.

Hoping it was the Prime Minister, ringing his congratulations. She had aspirations; that was obvious.

She only wore designer clothes, always looked impeccable. But what's *peccable*, anyway? Would I be considered peccable?

She was so ecstatic she forgot to be mean to me.

"Stevie, sweetie, you must rush over, it's all on here." She remembered herself. "Though I know how much you hate scenes."

"Don't worry, Maria, I wouldn't spoil your celebration by showing up. I'm happy whooping it up here in my own home."

"It really is Peter's home, but of course he wouldn't dream of putting you out. Not at a time like this."

It was actually my home; Mum left it to me. She said in her will, "Because she is so like her father, and will follow in his footsteps." Then they upped the entrance level in the cop force and that blew that idea off.

"You must be very pleased with yourself," I said.

"Well, as I do like to say, I remember clearly the moment Peter finally agreed with me that politics was the next logical step for him. He had conquered his own small world and it was time to travel over the ocean."

The idea of Peter as conqueror was very funny; he was such a whingeing sook.

"So I said, Peter, it's time."

"How original," I said.

"And look at him now! Who knows where the next step will carry us."

"To the Lodge, perhaps?" I said, sarcasm clear.

"Oh, no, that's not for us," she said, but even a fat deaf dog wouldn't believe that one. I called her First Lady for months after that and she loved it until Peter overheard and said, "There's no need for sarcasm," and she realised I was joking.

He was very busy, but not too busy to send me a patronage in the mail. A video camera for my birthday. He had recorded a message for me, had the sense not to let Maria show her face.

"Hi, Sis. Sorry we can't be there for your birthday but you know how it is."

I knew. I'd known for years, now, that my birthday was no longer important to anyone but me. It was one of the things that made me a grown-up. I rewound the tape and recorded over it immediately. I took a movie of the backyard and how nice it was. I rang Peter to thank him for the video, but no one was home. "I'm sorry, Mrs Searle, but the test results came back positive. You are a man," I said to the machine.

Got my cousin Nate's Granny card by mistake.

"NATE, NATE, YOU ARE GREAT," it said.

It surprised me that no one tried to commit me.

They thought counselling was enough. As if anyone can read anyone else's mind. Because those tries I made, so many tries, some people would think that was mad. At the hospital, I seemed to get put under a different name every time, depending on who brought me in. Stephanie, Steph, Steve. Steven.

Isaac put me in as Steven.

He was gone by the time I came home from hospital.

I fixed the video camera so it was close up on my face. I planned to keep my eyes open for as long as possible, because I wanted to see the movie there.

I read a couple of chapters of one of Auntie Jessie's.

On page 157 of *Erewhon*, the imaginative piece by Samuel Butler, Auntie Jessie wrote: *Egalnuula sekat dna mih rof sgnileef ym swonk eh. Wonk ot eno eht em ekam eh seod yhw? Llet I nac ohw. Em truh ylno nac ti. Egdelwonk siht tnaw t'nod I? Semirc sih fo llet eh tsum yhw.*

I sliced my wrists this time with a smooth, sharp knife. I wanted to see if the room was real; if it was true that those people waited for me. I wanted to see my kingdom again.

I sat in the bath, locked the door so Isaac couldn't get in and he didn't realise I was in there, which is why I went to the room again, began to identify some of the faces. I saw a friend I had not seen since high school.

I said, "Hey, mate," hoping he could tell me where I was, but he shrank from my voice. I did not have time to ask again. Housemates were there; every single last fucken one of them. It was a real shock to find they all disliked me and felt slighted by me; I thought they were my friends. I didn't see any of them after they moved out, but people have busy lives. *I* have a busy life.

I heard a noise. The smell was there, the faces, waiting. I sat up and could see them leaning against the walls of the room. I glimpsed faces I had seen, angry faces in other cars, waving fists, impatient, frightened, all so very slighted they are here, sliced away, to eat me up.

"Fuck you," I said. It was all strangers here; my loved ones had gone. Friends of Peter's from his election party, oh yes. Did they even know what I looked like? I hadn't been presented to Peter's society. There's something about it, whether it's my life or someone else's but I feel more in control than anything else. I feel like I'm tricking fate, taking it by surprise, and that it is my choice.

I never quite expected it would be allowed to work. It was never supposed to work. People would come in time, they'd find me and love me for my helplessness. I have made six attempts to end my life. More truly, on six occasions I placed myself in positions from which I needed to be rescued.

I had already killed people. But Lacey wasn't in the room this time. Neither was Den. Perhaps because they didn't have time to think of revenge, whereas the slighted remember clearly, and they stew. I didn't see Eve. Mrs Beattie was there, but I didn't kill her.

They crowded around the bed, their faces hanging over me. Fingernails appeared and they began to caress me. The stroking became stronger, and I heard the noise, the strange clicking noise. I heard a sound like dice clicking, or knuckle bones. I could not tell what it was as they began to fade.

Strangers, strangers, then Peter, and Danny, still there, still a child. As they shifted towards me I glimpsed a door. Truly, a door. I had not imagined there was a way out.

I moved my legs, swung them, sat up. People helped me, Mr Stefanovic, a kindly hand, Isaac, who thought I was a guy but now knew otherwise, a gentle shove.

My dope-smoking housemates gave me a joint; I thought, it's nearly over. I will walk out that door and there will be a golden path, and a voice,

"Come, Stevie." My love. I sucked smoke back and choked. The room snickered. I tried to snicker with them but the growl I produced was drowned in their hysteria. The guy who tried to kidnap me was there, his baseball cap in his hands full of rocks. He tossed them around the room; people caught them and came towards me, spinning rocks, raising them,

"Oh, very funny. Amusing. Laughing at another's distress, how mature." Nothing but a mumble. Laughing. I walked towards the door. I would not need to trick these fools. They left a path, fell silent, and I was strong again. I heard a voice on the other side, "Stevie," it said. It sounded like Peter, but he was here, giving me a neat push in the small of my back. People thumped me, best wishes, see ya, Stevie, and I grasped the door handle. It was warm, as if someone had been keeping it ready for me.

"Surprise!" A chorus. A lecture hall full of faces, strangers, lovers, friends.

All of them *click click*, waiting for me to finish dying.

I watched myself die. I could see the moment when it happened; I slumped, my tongue fell out. I had focussed on my face; I wanted to see my eyes.

I had seen surprise in some eyes, relief in others.

Never horror.

In mine, I saw horror.

This is what did happen; this really did happen: I was found by Isaac, who thought I was a guy. The greatest shock to him was possibly seeing me with tits and a cunt. I imagine this is what he thought.

"Who is that girl? Steve's girlfriend? Not a bad score for a guy I thought was gay. Where is Steve? Why is his girlfriend in the bath? Why is the bath red?"

This is what he did think. He was disgusted beyond words at the sight of me videoing my own death. My nudity. He was sickened by my fleshiness. But he still saved my life.

They thought I was done. They thought I wasn't coming back this time. And Peter found the time and sat by my bed and confessed every secret, every piece of knowledge, using me like a whispering wall, like a wishing well, a mirror.

I came back from the dark room to Peter's voice.

He wasn't there to rescue me, though, call me back to life. He was saying goodbye by telling me things I already knew but didn't want to face. He had a list in his head and ticked it off, neatly, in black pen.

His head was full of black pen.

He was talking, but I could see the words. Like I was reading them, a book in my mind. I can close my eyes and read them now. But I can't open the cover. Someone has locked the book.

He said, "I never said it before. I don't want scandal. And what good does it do? Who will it help? Not the girls. Not you. But you weren't so good without knowing. Would you have been better off knowing? I wish I could have told you. I wish you knew. I wish you knew things that weren't about yourself. You didn't even know what pain was as a child. We protected you from it. I hate pain. It scares me. It means something is out of control."

I'm thinking, now. Seeing his words and thinking. Mum was good with other people's panic, though she was a mess with her own. I remember one particularly late home-coming. Eve cooked sweet biscuits and let me eat them straight out of the oven, so hot they burned my air tunnel. They tasted almost liquid, like I had caught them in some magical transformation stage, between fantasy and reality.

It was past ten when I got home, pitch dark in the back streets between infrequent streetlights.

Houses were dark, too, because it was a school night, except for the rare place where they sat up watching television. These were the gaunt people Mum pointed out to me wherever we went; sick-looking people with hold-alls under their eyes, a lazy slump. These were the people who sat up all night watching television.

I walked very slowly home because I felt quite sick and didn't want to jiggle my stomach much.

Even so, I must have been home before ten-thirty—nowhere near the witching hour.

There were police cars out the front. Three. This was exciting; some of Dad's old friends come to visit and bring presents. I ran towards the house, sure that Peter had taken all the attention and the goodies, angry at Eve for keeping me so long.

"Stevie!" My mother, pig noises, squeals and grunts, and she rolled on top of me like I was an unwanted runt.

"Get off, Mum," I said.

"Where have you been? Look who's here, we're all worried sick."

There were six policemen (no women, though I didn't wonder about that at the time) sitting around with cups of tea, talking, surreptitiously watching the late night comedy hour playing silently on our TV in the corner. A present from Uncle Dom, Mum always kept the volume way down, as if by being uncomfortable when we used it, we weren't being disloyal to Dad.

Mum's arms were bruised; Peter told me later she had been throwing herself at my cupboard, thinking I was in there somewhere, and the police had held her down.

"She's been at it since I got home from school," he said. "Screaming, punching." He showed me his own bruise. "And all because of you." He gave me a bruise of my own.

The police stayed twenty minutes, thirty. Peter found some whisky and gave Mum a glass after the cops left, and she slept for twenty-four hours, woke up thinking I was still missing, then she hugged me for too long.

But when Peter was scared—when some big kids teased him, or if a stranger tried to get him in the car, or if he got lost, and he was shaking with fear and unable to speak—it was, "There, there," and perfect calm.

He burnt himself once, very badly, when I told him to pick up the wood from a fire by the red bit because that was colder. He knew it wasn't true but he did it because I told him to in such a positive way. The pain was so great his finger was sucked onto the wood; he couldn't let go. He whimpered.

Mum looked up, dropped her whatever, laid hands on Peter.

"Just let go, darling, that's the boy. Drop it down," and he did. Almost burnt the palm off his hand; he went around with a thick bandage for weeks, so my trick backfired. He got all the attention and care.

When I was younger, I took great pleasure in showing him all my cuts and bruises, describing carefully where they came from. Even other people's pain made him wince.

He said to my body he thought was dying, "He never hit Mum. Never hurt her. I was the big man.

I was the one who copped it. I never told her the whole story, either. I don't know, Stevie. It scares me, sometimes. Do I have the potential to commit violence like that? Am I the one he passed it on to?"

I didn't tell him he needn't fear. That I was the one.

Peter said, "I only ever wanted the world to be a better place. But I couldn't always do the right thing. God, Stevie. It should have been me. I'm the one who should have stayed trapped in the house.

I should have found what you found in the backyard."

I thought, "Why didn't you ever say you knew what I was finding? Weak bastard. Why didn't you share it with me? But I never felt trapped. I felt free, released. I felt I could do anything, that there was no law for me, no punishment. He told me so many things. Some things I knew; some I didn't. I knew that they never locked the doors at his lectures, and that no one ever tried them. That made him feel good about himself; people trusted him.

He said, "I never had parties at our place cos of Dad. I was scared of him, Stevie. You weren't; you loved him. You didn't see. You saw what I had, though. You saw my future. You said one day, "You can tell a lot about people. You listen to people. I just remember their faces." It was one of the only nice things you ever said to me. It got me thinking.

Sometimes, if I was feeling like a failure, I'd remember what you said, your face, and that you believed in me. Maria would die if she knew it was you, the most, who inspired me. Not her. Fuck her.

He never hit Mum. But it hurt her when he hit me, especially when I was whacked for her, or for you. He never hit women."

Peter was dreaming. He had a fantasy world, this is what should have happened, where he had an excuse for being bitter. It didn't happen.

"Women are special glass creatures, handle with care, fragile," he said. His words a balloon.

"God, Stevie. Why were you such a smart kid, but so dumb at the same time? That time you were angry at Mum and me, cos you thought we were laughing? We were crying, Stevie. God, bawling. You never had to cry like that. And another thing. About your eighteenth. We didn't want the garden dug up, because we knew what he had buried there. And we were scared for you, also, Stevie. Because you didn't have many friends. Not enough to fill the laundry, let alone the back yard. And neither of us could stand to see you there waiting for your friends to show. Then you started digging, after Mum died, and maybe I hoped you'd find out and ask me some questions. Ask questions of somebody, do something. But you never did. I thought you'd deal with it, but nothing happened. Did I dream it all? Did I make it up? Or don't you care what our father was?"

Words, words, words. He said, "My throat is sore. I've worn it sore from talking. I know Dougie tried to talk to you, tell you about how Dad died.

But he said you didn't want to hear that Dad was deliberately careless that day. Dad feared discovery. I don't know what Dougie knows. That's why he hung around Mum so much. He wanted to comfort her. Tell her it wasn't her fault. She knew that. It wasn't her fault. I didn't think suicide ran in the family. At least you don't pretend to die a hero. You're true. But you couldn't see what he was like. You don't know what it was like, Steve,"

Peter said. "I know you felt unloved, because he didn't hit you. But who needs that sort of love? I know you thought you had to suffer to be loved. I know that; it's why I've forgiven you so many times."

He was talking about me in the past tense. He wanted me gone.

I flicked open my eyes. My timing was perfect.

"Peter?" I said.

He nearly fell off his chair, and the nurses surrounded me before we could speak.

I wouldn't hurt anyone through violence or slight.

That was my promise. But as time went on, I forgot the circumstances of my promise. As people do.

Some women forget the pain of childbirth and have another, someone's husband doesn't die and they forget they said they'd give up their lover. Everyone does it. Not just me.

I didn't die.

I got my Granny card this year. Handwriting not too bad: *Hello darling, hope all is well*—but no plane ticket. If they want me alive that much, why don't they get me up there to look after them?

Then Gary showed up back in the street. Gary, who used to offer me his hard pink pencil when I was just a kid, eighteen. Who thought he'd be my father or my lover and was neither. He and his wife had split up, and she'd got the house. But I'd heard she'd died, and now he was back. Uglier than ever.

He had bad teeth, yellow, with the front top two tilting in, as some do. When I went out to get my mail, he recognised me immediately.

"Well, who would have thought? Little Stevie.

All grown up, ay?"

I looked at him with different eyes, now. He was a hated person. Much hated. I wondered what would happen when he died?

At Thirty-Two

"Truth or Dare?" I said. "Truth or dare, truth or dare, truth or dare?" I loved that game. It always gave me the thrill of the illicit, even as an adult.

Gary stared at me. His eyes were bulging with over-indulgence. I had fed him a creamy, fatty, gassy meal; he licked the plate and asked for more.

I poured wine into his glass, watched as he drank it down, down, down, down.

"More?" I said.

"What else have you got?" he said. He winked at me. He couldn't believe his luck. He was trying to pretend things like this happened all the time.

He still couldn't believe I'd let him in; he'd been trying since I was eighteen. Since my mother died.

"Tell me about your day," I said. I wanted detail; I wanted to know who he had slighted. It's a difficult question—most people don't notice those they've slighted.

He loved to talk, this man, and he thought he had the storyteller's knack. I taped it; I like to tape their last story.

"In detail," I said. He was surprised; very rarely did people want to listen to that sort of personal material.

"I woke up, farted," he said. He looked at me, wanting me to laugh, but I just nodded. Nodded again to get him started.

"Had a shower."

"Did you go to the toilet first?"

"Nah, pissed in the shower. Blew my nose, farted, came out, house-mate says, 'Couldn't you let me go first if you're going to be that disgusting?' He says it every morning; I always set my alarm to make it up before him."

"What happened to your wife?"

"She left me. Couldn't keep up with my demands." He winked at me, the arsehole.

"So what else did you do today?"

"Got my car going—always takes a while."

"What do the neighbours think of that?"

"What do you think of it?"

I pinched him.

"They hate me, mate. So I leave it running for a while, just to piss them off."

"What about breakfast?" I shivered.

"Stopped off at Macca's. Couldn't make my mind up in the queue but, hey, it's a free country. The food was shit, but it's fast and cheap, so that's okay. I got to work early, like to be on board before the others, gives me time to settle before all the shit starts to come down. Had a coffee, read the paper, then I get my first call of the day." His voice changed, became harsher, took on a whining twang I guessed was his work voice.

"This fucking wanker from upstairs thinks we're all here to serve him. Like there's no one else in the building. He says, 'Gary, I need you to get an envelope to blah blah', right, way over the other side of town, right, and he wants it there now! Fuck! What am I, a magician? So I go, 'Look, mate, we're talking peak hour, we're talking double rates. Traffic. I can't promise you a thing.' So he goes, 'Look, mate, I'll take it myself,' and he fuckin' did. Hops in his fuckin' beemer and drives it there himself. It was a fuckin' laugh."

I moved closer to him, as if his words were interesting. They were only interesting because I could see the slights; his room was going to have to be the size of a football stadium. He filled a ninety-minute tape with this vomit, pausing only to drink the wine and eat the sweets I brought out for him.

"And then I came here," he said. He had arrived late, with no wine, from the pub. He had not showered. I was slighted by his behaviour; there's no doubt. I couldn't stop it; at least I would know what that shiver meant, when he died. I'd be in his dark room.

I said, "Do you want to play Truth or Dare?"

"That sounds good," he said. His imagination was so poor he could not guess what might happen. He was a strange little man; thought he was eccentric because he wore a silver earring, a leaf of a pot plant.

"Me first," I said. "Truth or dare?"

"Truth."

"Okay. Do you want to have sex with me?"

"Yes. My turn. Do you want to have sex with me?"

"No. Have you ever masturbated?"

He didn't answer. It had been a double whammy.

"You have to answer."

"No."

"The game is called Truth or Dare. If you lose, you have to pay a forfeit."

"Like what?"

"Like losing a finger." I sliced down with the bread knife. I missed deliberately.

"All right, yes. Have you."

"Of course. Have you ever had sex with a man?"

"No fuckin' way. Have you?"

"Of course."

"Had sex with women?"

"That wasn't the question. Truth or dare?" I knew he wasn't enjoying truth. He didn't answer me. I lost patience.

"Truth or dare?" I said. "Truth or dare? Truth or dare?" I shouted it in his face.

"Dare."

"I dare you to strip naked." He did that, so arrogant he forgot how vile his body was.

"I dare *you* to strip naked." I did that, and he forgot my earlier truth. He grabbed me.

"I dare you to let me put handcuffs on you," I said, and didn't he love that.

I handcuffed him, led him to the kitchen. I had tied the noose before he arrived, and it hung from the old gas pipes running across the ceiling. I knew these pipes were strong; Peter and I used them as monkey bars when we were kids, and I'd done it since, racing lovers across the ceiling for favours.

I thought the pipes would hold.

"Stand on the chair," I said. His short, fat penis quivered, lifted. He climbed onto the chair. I tied his feet without asking.

"Steph, what're you doing?"

"Steve. It's Steve," I said. I climbed another chair behind him, stroked his white dimpled thighs on the way up.

"Oh, yeah," he said. "Go, Steph."

I placed the noose around his neck and tightened it. He tried to look up but was dizzy; he stumbled and could not steady himself.

"Falling," he said. I moved my chair away and sat watching as he tried to stand steady; the noose tightened, the chair tipped back and fell away.

"I want you to remember what you see, because we're going to do this again and again until you do," I said.

His eyes bulged; he couldn't talk, his tongue was thick. His body shook and wriggled like a fat fish which had never seen daylight.

I watched his eyes, looking for something, listened for the bowel movement. Once he'd released all his shit and piss, it'd be too late to bring him back.

He morse-coded me with his batting eyelids.

"All right," I said. "You don't like it so much."

I pushed the chair back under his feet. He scrabbled with his toes. He coughed, breath rasping in his throat. He sucked in the air like it was water.

I gave him a glass of vodka. He swallowed it slowly, not closing his lips between sips.

"Thanks," he said. He watched every move, his limbs shivering and twitching. He nodded at me.

"Where've you been?" I said.

"When?" he said.

"Just then. Were you here? Was it black?"

He closed his eyes, remembering. "I was very cold. And I didn't know how I got away from you."

He flicked his eyes open, scared I was offended.

"You didn't," I said. "It was cold."

"And it was dark. I was walking and I felt really light, my feet weren't flat, I was young again." He looked down at his fat, white body. A tear spilled from one eye. "I was young. And I walked, I knew where to go. I don't know why. I just walked and it slowly got lighter and lighter. I could smell a familiar smell."

He began to cry.

"Shit? Was it shit and mothballs?" I spoke too quickly; I felt my heartbeat in my throat. I couldn't breathe.

He looked at me in astonishment. He couldn't believe I knew it; he looked at me with worship.

"Tell me what you know. Tell me everything," he said.

That made me feel good; it made me feel as if I was powerful, very powerful. I was a monarch. I was the queen of knowledge. The room made me feel that way; the feeling is addictive.

That's what should have happened. This is what did happen:

He looked at me like I was weird. It was okay for me to strip him naked, almost kill him, and he likes it. Mention something which comes out of everyone's asshole, and he thinks I'm sick.

He said, "I only smelt nice things. I smelt Dad's special soap. He kept it in a leather box in his drawer. It was very expensive and no one else was allowed to touch it. He had sensitive skin. He was a delicate man."

"I don't care."

"I could smell his soap, and it was getting lighter.

I was on a conveyor belt, moving somewhere. It was like I'd polished off a bottle of vodka. I couldn't feel the pain in my wrist or my neck. Then a face came into my mind. My grandson."

"You've got a grandson?"

"Yeah. Oliver. He's only one. I'm not that old," he said. He was still thinking about sex with me, gross old man.

"So your grandson called to you?"

"No, no, he doesn't talk yet. He's only one. I just thought of him. I thought about him heading off to school, in his uniform. I didn't see any of my own kids going. My wife held it over me. She said it made her the best parent, because she had shared all the details of their lives. Fucking bitch."

I said, "You didn't see what I saw? Smell it? You open your eyes and you are in a cold, dark room. You can see figures, people and they smell like shit. You smell mothballs as well. You hear clicking noises, click click." I clicked my teeth near his cheek. "And their fingernails are long and sharp. You know them, but only just, and they bend over you, parting your legs, fingers cold as marble probing, squeezing, scratching. Someone bites out your clitoris. Spits it down. Rats would chew it if there were rats. And you see your brother but he doesn't help you. Then someone brings you back to life."

He shook his head. "God, I didn't see that! I didn't see what you see. I swear!"

He made me so angry I sent him back to the room forever.

"Are you going to let me hang you again?" I said.

He laughed. "Forget it."

"I'll suck you off while you're hanging." He smiled then. I wondered how long he'd been dreaming of having his cock sucked. "I'll only tie it loosely," I said. I strung him up and kicked the chair away. He stretched his fingers towards me, dreaming now of killing me. I took a packet of chips into the lounge room and turned the TV on loud. It was an action movie, so-called, lots of screaming noise, drum music. When it was over I cut him down and buried him in the backyard. I was glad of my medical training, if only to know how to control the death when I needed it controlled.

I felt a bit sorry for making the people suffer, but I remembered a lesson Dad taught me; he told a story about two little boys playing in the sandpit, and one was happy because the sand was wet and he could make perfect castles with his new bucket and spade, and the other one was sad because he didn't have a bucket and his pants were getting wet.

Dad said that feelings rarely match because people never do, even when they are doing the same thing.

So even if I tried to make these people happy they wouldn't be so.

Human life is so dreadful. To fear death more than to crave knowledge is weak. We are stopped still because people are not willing to die to learn.

I find that need to know, to see, is like a tight shirt, a childhood favourite worn seeking comfort.

But I cannot face my own dark room again. I want to see those of others.

People gossiped when Gary disappeared and they thought I was weird for not joining in.

I could have told them a couple of intimate details which would turn their tongues blue. I nearly did, once. Mentioned his job, some dull detail.

"I didn't know where he worked. How well did you know him, Stevie?"

"He used to tell everyone about it."

"No, he didn't," and the fucking idiot went squealing up the street. Did *you* know where he worked? Did you?

I saw my future, while I was waiting to see Gary's room. I knew things other people didn't know. I was in control. I became a grief counsellor at work, talking to them about things beneath. I'm sure it helped. The chief nurse didn't like me because the patients asked for me, not her.

"You're an enrolled nurse. You're not qualified.

She had no idea how qualified I was.

"Assisted Deaths" dropped as people became fearful of death.

Ced admired me, the things I said. He didn't mind sharing the limelight; they all loved him. Kind, funny, philosophical, everything people want in a near-death carer.

I spoke to them, told them the truth.

I said, "The last time I died, I did not see my father in the room. I saw the old lady I had failed to give a seat to and the sandwich maker I had not thanked. I did not think these people were dead. I did not see how that was logical. I thought they must wait for me to die without dying themselves. When you dream, you are not in control. This is what the room is like." Ms 16, there with an inherited blood disease, sitting up with lipstick on to try to look pretty.

"I think often about that place. Their caresses, their worship. I remember the way they touch me.

It gives me a slightly sickened feeling, just a cold hole in the pit of my stomach. They touch me with such desperation, such need. I feel great power over them, these people who mean nothing to me. What happens when you die? The world ends. There was some face I didn't remember, then realised I had seen him at a job interview, I had beaten him for a job. Not my fault his life was over, but I lied about my experience. Who doesn't? It was almost a thrill, to be in the room, to be queen. The smell seems worse, though, on each visit. More powerful; there are more of them. And that clicking, and I can't talk, even when I recognise people, see the shopper whose place I took in the queue, see the librarian who opened the book I sneezed into. Your husband beats you? That is not a slight. You can hate him for that. You will not be in his room."

Mrs 48, mother of four, more concerned about leaving them behind than leaving herself.

I told them what I saw and they went away, a little more fearful of death. What faces would they see? I could see them adding up the slights, remembering faces of hurt people. Why would the giving up of a train seat matter more than the anniversary of my father's death? I imagined people were more careful with their lives after I spoke to them. I taught them not to be petty, not to remember the slights. Because it is them who wait for me. Them who suffer.

"I see the same look on every face," I told people, "but I couldn't identify it until I caught a train one morning. As we pulled into the station, I saw a platform full of people with the look. Boredom, anticipation, and desperation, desperation for the boredom to end. Until I realised what was waiting for me after death, I despised life. Even then, I found death enticing, because there I am queen. The centre of attention. Even after I realised what the people were waiting for, I couldn't stop their numbers from growing."

I became popular; in demand. I spoke to the people who came to see me at the hospital, some who had returned from death and wanted to know the truth in what they saw. Some saw the dark room. I told the others they had not seen the truth; that they blocked the truth out.

I said, "The people waiting in the room suffer. They are alive, but part of them is snapped away at each slight. The snapped bit attaches itself to the offender, and this is what he sees after death. So the more you believe you are slighted, the lesser person you become. The horror of it is that if someone hurts you, you are in their power, because you remember them forever, whereas they will soon forget. The one who does the hurting usually doesn't care what happens to the other, or will certainly forget that particular hurt. It is foolish to be wounded by such small things; the paper cuts of life, the slights, when the world is so terrible around us." The other staff members listened. They loved this stuff. It made sense of what they did.

I met a lot of people who'd seen death after life.

They came to hear what I had to say; they wanted me to hear their tales. Every one of them felt special, singled out.

"So, what did you see?"

"It was terrifying," Mrs 51 said. I was thrilled. I'd found a soul mate. She said, "It was very dark. I walked and walked, because I didn't want to stand still. There was a flash of something up ahead, and a voice said, 'Come to the light.' But I didn't know what the light was, and I turned and ran the other way. Into darkness. But everywhere I turned, light appeared. 'Come into the light.' It was so terrifying I had to climb the air to get away, and that was how I clawed my way back to life."

She closed her eyes, remembering.

"What about you?" she said.

"The horror is the unimagined, unavoidable, forgotten slights; the man you snubbed, the woman you bumped, the teacher you teased. Nobodies, nothing events, and yet they guide your fate. In all my trips to the afterlife, I have never been guided by a light. There is no journey; there is only awakening. And from the looks of horror which come over the faces of those who have died in my arms, my mother's screams, they see what I see. I can only think that those who talk of light, tunnels, loving faces, were not really dead. Or they are lying."

I felt in a better place than I had for a long time, so when Peter called me, I didn't hang up in his ear.

"So, want to come to a thing at Maria's parents? Should be okay. Her parents ask about you, believe it or not."

"Hey, I believe it. You're the one who hates me."

"Ha ha ha. So, ya coming?" I could hear a difference in Peter's voice when he spoke to me. He was eleven, I was nine. We had not progressed much past there.

"Free food?"

"You have to bring some wine or something."

"I'll bring a surprise."

I brought a case of beer.

The youngest daughter-in-law, the one married to Adrian, got very drunk on the homemade wine they had provided. She dozed, the others went to check the children, and I was left, ignored.

Adrian came in. He bent, looked into her face, straightened, smiled at me.

"She's asleep," I whispered, feigning concern.

"So I see."

"She doesn't know how to hold her liquor. I don't seem to have that problem." I licked a non-existent, wayward drop of beer from my fingers.

"Luckily."

He smiled. I had heard reports his wife had gone off sex since the six month-old was born, and that he and his brothers were known for their appetites.

Adrian was broad and brown. He had a smile which creased his face, a flicking tongue which mesmerised me. And I was full of magic; I was teaching people how to live their lives. And people were listening.

"Let's go for a drive," I said.

"Sure. I'll just tell the others."

"Let's just *go*."

I didn't wink, though I was greatly tempted to.

We walked to my car, not talking. That's when it always fails, when I'm supposed to talk, because I can't invent words like that. I find it a terrifying challenge.

Adrian and I flirted from our first meeting, years ago at Peter's wedding. Adrian's wife was his fiancée then, but she was preoccupied with sucking up to his parents, so we flirted and cheeked each other. I thought maybe he liked me enough not to marry her. We reached my car. He looked in the passenger side. Others who'd done that went silent, or said,

"Is that where…?" I don't think he had any idea.

"I'll take you for a drive," I said. He was leaning against the door. "Get away for a few minutes." I reached my arms around him, laid my head on his chest. He had a very broad chest. He wore a jumper his wife had knitted. Unwittingly, she had made him something sexy.

The stuff she wore herself was terrible: cardigans, jumpers too short, scarves garish, little pert hats in grey. This jumper was dark brown, thick, soft, my head against his teddy bear chest and I unlocked the door behind his back.

"Where will we go?" he said. He took the keys from me; he wanted to drive. He wanted to drive me, too, turn my wheels, and I would be an instrument. I would not speak, I'd hum and purr. I'd need some petrol which he'd give me, a nice whisky or a beer, and I would take him from A to B.

"I'll drive," I said. Let him be the car; let me steer fate. I drove to the local park. Missed it once and chucked a U-ie, roared past a slow coach in my desire to get there. There was no one about in there; it was a very dull place. The playground equipment was a sticky slide and an old railway carriage, off its wheels. Kids were scared to go in there: beer bottles, broken glass, evidence of adults hidden inside.

Some kids hate the smell of an adult.

We kissed at Peter's wedding when everyone was drunk. He pretended it never happened; I had the bitten lip to prove it did.

"I want a swing," I said, and I squeezed my bum onto the child-size seat.

"Steve," he said, rolling his shoulders, embarrassed. "Come on, Stevie."

I swung my legs to get started. "Give us a push."

"I push my kids all the time." He had two others, apart from the sex-stealing baby.

So swings weren't a sexual thing for him. They reminded him he had a family.

Maturity was what he liked.

"I've never done this before," he said, thank God, saved me from saying it because it sounded pathetic.

"Done what?" I said. I leaned over and kissed him. "That?" and I bit him on the palm. "Or this?" I said. He closed his eyes; his conscience needed to be seduced.

He shivered as I played him, shivered, his eyes shut like he was dreaming. When I stopped he squinted at me. I leant and breathed in his ear,

"Come on, Adrian," and he growled, he kissed me, the back of my throat, and now I meant it, I shuffled my jeans off and he touched me, his hands gentle, his body shaking with the effort, and I rolled his jeans down for him. I pushed him back into his place and a knee on either side of his thighs.

"You're gorgeous, Stevie," he said. "Gorgeous gorgeous gorgeous." He said it faster and faster. I didn't want to escape; I wanted him as my own.

He winked at me afterwards, casually, thinking it had meant the same to us. I wondered how he would clean up but I didn't care; I shoved him out at the end of the street, and sang ad lib to *Ode to Joy* all the way home.

I'd had a shower, I was in my pyjamas, and Peter called.

"I fucking hate you sometimes. Where did you go? And what happened to Adrian?" he said.

"What do you mean? What's wrong with him?"

He whispered, "He's pissed off. Someone asked him if he wanted some cheese and biscuits and he just started shouting."

"Don't tell me you're still there. I thought you would have left hours ago."

"Kidding. The girls are acting up and Maria's in her element, 'But what is it, Adrian? Please, darling, what is it?' Like he's going to tell her."

"Maybe he just doesn't like cheese and he can't hide it anymore."

"Ha ha. What did you *do* to him, Steve? I've never seen anything like it."

"I know you think it's funny. Don't try to pretend you're shocked."

He laughed. "You're terrible, Steve. Tell me what you said to him. In case I can use it myself."

"Think of your own mean things to say," I said.

Actually I didn't want to confess just how awful I had been. When I pushed Adrian out of the car I'd said, "By the way, I bet your daughter an ice cream I could suck your cock before I went home. She said, 'No way, he only likes kids my age.'"

I could hear shouting.

"Oh, fuck," Peter said. I could tell he was smiling.

I hoped he wasn't hysterical; the girls needed one sane parent to keep them steady. "The mother's into it now. I can't quite see, but I think she just chucked a bowl of jelly at the father."

"Where are you?" I said.

"I've got the phone in the hall cupboard. It's too bloody dangerous out there. There's punching in the backyard and the women keep accidentally scratching each other with their nails."

"And Adrian won't stop shouting."

"Waah! Waah! Gotta go," and he hung up.

Peter told me later that Maria was silent all the way back, and went to bed wordlessly. Kelly went out without asking and Maria left it up to Peter to deal with.

"What, it's your fault, is it?" I said when he described the scene to me.

"I'm responsible for you. People blame me for you."

"People? What people?"

And he was fucking silent.

"What people are you talking about?"

"Maria. Just Maria."

I wanted to believe that was true.

At Thirty-Three

Dougie Page said, "Stevie, you need to move away from your house. It's a bad influence on you." I let him take me out for dinner, but I wouldn't spend a night away. What would happen to the place if I wasn't there? Anybody could come in. Anybody could dig, if I wasn't there to stop them.

He told me terrible things, whispered them to me, showed me proof.

He took me home and showed me this wall, that picture, that crack, all of it meaning things about my family I didn't want to know. He said, "You need to get away, Stevie. Don't you know anywhere you could go? Somewhere to make you feel better?"

My old neighbour Melissa had a boyfriend with a place in the country. She'd told me about it often enough, to make me jealous or something, I don't know. The walls were different to me now, the smell of my home, all the memories I thought were happy now sickened me. It was all wrong. Dad's chair, Mum's stove, Peter's bed, all of it different and with a whole new story.

I don't often drive in the country. I like to get somewhere, find things on my journey, not just seeing the lovelies of nature. Melissa's boyfriend's place sounded good, though; secluded, atop a rise so I could stare out over a kingdom I could claim.

My car rattled and farted. It was used to smooth, tax-payer roads and I was asking too much of it. I arrived in the early afternoon and found a large tin shed. It had windows, and the windows had curtains, it had a door. This was it. I carried my food, books, magazines in. The place was warm but dark; someone had built it so the sun didn't come in but that tin heated up. Useless design. It made me sleepy; I sat on the couch, ate a bag of chips and woke freezing. Really freezing, and it was dark, and all I missed was the smell of shit, because I could smell mothballs, all right, fucking mothballs. I had not even noticed where the light switch was. I was too scared to move around in the dark, touch walls, anything *sensible* like that, in case I touched a face, pointed teeth. So I lay on the couch all night and when I slept I dreamt of snow and snowing and very very cold.

Ho, ho, and in the morning everything was lovely. I found all the light switches and the heater, I closed all the curtains and created an artificial world. I found the mothballs; old coats in a cupboard, each pocket holding two of the kool-mint stinkers. I threw the coats onto the back porch. The smell of them upset me.

It was all right, in that place. I made it warm and light and I didn't go outside until it was time to leave.

I hate staying in strange places.

When I handed the keys back to Melissa, she said, "Thanks for that," and asked me for the rent.

I couldn't believe it. I was only a business thing to her. She was no friend at all. I could imagine how many people she had slighted.

I told her she had to come to my place to collect it. She had plenty of people waiting in her dark room. I wanted to see some of them.

This was enjoyable. So many years I waited to hurt that girl. This was the first time I enjoyed the journey, the pain she felt. Why did she stay loyal to me? That deserved punishment in herself.

It took her a while to realise what I was doing. I stalked her around the house, a knife behind my back, and she laughed at first, thinking we were playing a game. She never was my speed. Then I backed her into the bathroom, and she began to feel nervous.

"I don't need to go, Steve," she said.

"Why did you charge me to stay at that place?"

"Because it's a place you pay for! Everyone pays! It's no big deal. If you can't afford it, owe me the money. I don't care."

"I care. You're supposed to be a friend, but you treat me like a business associate."

She looked confused. God, she was annoying. I pulled the knife from behind my back.

"Steve?" she said.

"Have you never had any hint about what I am?" I said. "Never, in all our dealings, have you had the sense to be frightened of me."

I jumped forward at her and she screamed, fell backwards into the bath. So helpful. I bent down and slit her throat before she could even blink.

That's how fast I was. The blood came thick and fast. I held her head to keep her still in the bath, and I watched her eyes as they flickered.

She gurgled at me, and I realised I'd made a terrible mistake. I'd cut her throat so she couldn't talk. How could she tell me what she saw?

In fury, I slapped her. "Useless to the last," I said to her.

As soon as it was over, I realised what I'd done. I was slighted by her, and now she was dead. I would be in her dark room. I shivered. They call for me.

They are terrified at the prospect of dying without a priest there to wave an arm, toss some magic dust, save the soul. There is no time for that. Or for confessions, explanations, last words. I'm not interested in their needs; I have my own to look after.

I think my actions are beyond my control. It is habit. My father had it too and perhaps his father.

So what can I do? It's my birthright.

M y Granny card said:
"Here's a card
For a birthday girl
One who doesn't
Mind a burl"

There was a poor cartoon of someone gambling.
Most unlikely.

D ougie Page wouldn't leave me alone. "Be careful, Steve," he said, like he knew. Be careful of who you talk to. He said he understood my Dad, he said, "It's the ones who are guilty, but who figure they did it for a reason. That it was justified—they only killed those who deserved it, wife-killers, baby-killers. Those who would have escaped justice otherwise."

Anyone who thinks they can justify murder is dishonest. It's a self-serving thing; you do it for yourself. Anything else is a lie.

"You should go away, Steve," he said.

"I did. It didn't work out."

"Try again. Find a lover. Go with someone who loves you," he said, as if that was an easy thing to find.

A drian acted like a man having an affair, and organised a weekend away for us in the mountains. I pretended we were married; he liked the idea we weren't.

We lay in bed with candles burning and he told me how wonderful I was.

"Do you take after your father or your mother?" he said.

"My father," I said. It was true. A moment of realisation and acceptance that I was my father's daughter.

"I wish I'd known him," Adrian said.

"So do I. So do I," I said.

At dinner all he could talk about was his wife. I drank a lot so I couldn't hear him. I fell asleep in a chair in our room. I woke up to find him watching me.

"This isn't going to work, is it, Steve?"

I looked hard at him for a sign of regret. None.

A journalist came sniffing around, looking for Peter's back story. They like him. They're all looking for his story. I told him about my job, and how I dealt with the patients, and that got me the sack, didn't it. Bastard printed it, and everybody saw it, and they sacked me.

Fuckem.

At Thirty-Four

When Samantha, my high-school friend, arrived at my doorstep, I wasn't happy to see her.

"I've been thinking about how much fun we had when I lived here," she said. I could see her knap-sack around the corner. "Thought I'd drop in, say hello."

"I've just had the place fumigated. Won't be able to go in for another week. I was going to stay at the Hyatt, but maybe I could crash at your place instead," I said.

She had no idea what she'd done wrong, why I wasn't all over her. I knew how little she thought of me.

"Well, actually, I've left Murray again."

"For good this time," I said, in her voice.

"Well, I think so."

"So, coming to the Hyatt then?"

"Oh, it's not the money or anything, but I might drop in and see Peter. It's been ages."

"Good idea," I said. Peter and Samantha flirted an awful lot for friends; Maria would hate it. Then I relented. "Actually, it should be okay, if we leave the windows open." And so I had a housemate again. I felt differently about her this time. Hers hadn't been the face near mine, either in the room or when they saved me again.

"God, it's dark in here," she said, throwing open the curtains in the lounge room. "I didn't want to go home to Mum, she's all weepy still about bloody Perry."

Samantha's brother was dead after lying on his bed getting fat for fifteen years, then he drank a bottle of scotch and killed himself. It was totally hushed up. Their mum put it about his heart had always been weak, and that he had lasted as long as he did through pure bravery.

Then one night, after she'd been with me for three weeks, I was all set to watch TV, eat a hamburger, but she came home with a bottle of vodka.

She wasn't paying any rent, because I couldn't ask my oldest friend to pay. She brought home booze, shit to eat, to make up for it.

"What are we celebrating?" I said.

"Just being friends, I suppose. Sticking together.

Old piss-heads sticking together."

The smell of vodka was like a fist to my stomach.

"Come on, girl, let's get pissed," she said.

I had been drinking too much lately. The smell of any booze frightened me; the fist was a reminder. Don't talk, don't say it all. I said it all to my friend, Bess, old pink tracksuit, and I scared her off. She was a good friend even though she was old. I could remember that night very clearly, although it was out of my control. Like those first moments, when I'm leaving my body, it's all so clear but I can do nothing.

I'm not in control.

"Let's go out," Samantha said. "Come on. We'll have fun, like last time."

Last time we went out, this guy comes up and says, "What're you girls drinking?" and I made a joke no one got. Samantha ended up going home and fucking the guy and I was left to get a taxi on my own. They always know, too, if you've been dumped.

She didn't meet anyone this time.

She hitched her tight black dress up around her thighs to piss on the front lawn when we got home, too needy to wait until I regained my night vision and opened the door, and she did not tug it back down again.

We drank Dad's whisky and the vodka and she says, "So are you going to tell me?"

"What?"

"You never told me. You can tell me. What happened with your Mum. What happened with the accident?'

She looked at me like a lady. She was a friend of mine, o'mine, she took me out to celebrate and no one else. Now she stared down at me, she wanted to know.

I lay, my shoulders propped against the couch. I had borrowed Samantha's clothes to wear out, so there was a stranger's body attached to my head. Yellow sandals, with heels, torn brown pantyhose. My legs stretched out before me.

Samantha stood over me. Her hands were on her hips. Her hair fell forward.

I could see the crotch of her black pantyhose, and she had folds around her ankles. Her eye-liner was in drips down her cheeks.

"Tell me. Tell me what happened." I don't know where her need came from. Whether she needed to be better than me, after all these years. Or if she was looking for a reason to hate me.

I told her anyway. Blah blah blah, out it came.

I didn't cry, though. I never cry.

"I wasn't drunk. But she was shitting me, really shitting me, and I couldn't bear to look at her. She was a pain in the arse. I was driving, fantasising I was thirty-five and Mum was dead, only just.

Peter shared the house. People kept thinking we were married and we laughed at them. Mum gasped. Opened my eyes. Kid on road. Not a kid; coloured box off a truck. Swerve. Wall. Not my fault. What if it had been a kid? Mum would rather die than let a kid die. Mum screamed, screamed, going somewhere she didn't want to go. Going away. Take it back, I thought. I still had the smile on my face from pretending to laugh.

Take me instead, I said. But all I got was a scar.

Oh, God. Did Mum go to a dark room? Is that why she was screaming? Has she been there ever since? Please let her be safe. She must have known what was going to happen. It must be what she wanted."

We drank vodka. More vodka. I can't remember how much.

Now I'm writing I'm finished writing the vodka fuckin Samantha on vodka mad she kills me I should kill her she said what she said fuckin cunt she's a fucken cunt.

In the morning, my head was full of pin balls which rolled and crashed each time I moved.

Samantha was in the shower. I stood at the door and said, "I thought vodka didn't give you a headache." No response. I opened the door enough to put my lips through, said it again.

Samantha appeared, towel wrapped loosely, wet, shower still on behind her. "You want the shower? It's yours." She walked, wet feet slapping like a seal's, to her room.

"No, I don't. I just wanted to say about MY HANGOVER." I shouted the last words because she slammed the door in my face. Peter loved doing that, too, when he lived here. I can trace cracks across the door with my finger.

The shout hurt my throat.

"Did we sing last night? My throat is killing me."

"You were talking in your sleep," she said through the door.

"Did I say anything interesting?"

She didn't answer. She was putting things together *smash crash*. A wash of cold came over me.

"What're you doing?"

"Nothing. Go put the kettle on."

"Are you cleaning up?"

"Make some coffee, Stevie."

I did as I was told, because my head hurt, my throat was sore, I was scared she was going to leave me.

She came down with a fat garbage bag.

"Where's my keys?" she said. They were under the couch. She took off one key, laid it beside her coffee cup.

"I made you coffee," I said.

"I don't want it. I'm moving out," and she swept the fat bag over her shoulder and disappeared like magic.

Her car didn't start; it never did.

I watched her through the front window, pulled a chair up, sat and watched the show, drinking my coffee.

First, she threw her stuff in the back, banged her knee on the door, slamming it.

Then she got in, started it, already looking behind to see who was coming, as if she was going to be taking right off. She didn't. The car farted like a bottle of flat lemonade being opened, and she lay her head on the steering wheel. She got the horn, lifted her head. She cried. I could tell it from my front row seat. She got out, looked at the house. I waved. She stared. Lit a cigarette, staring.

I got out of my chair, thinking, I'll go down there and we'll laugh about it.

I opened the front door. "Hey, good one," I said, and she threw her cigarette down, didn't stamp on it, ran next door to the Oakes'. They hate me because my tree overhangs and drops leaves. She banged on the door. They weren't home. I stood on the front step, now. She ran across the road to the Meyerfeldts'. They hate me because their dog eats my rubbish.

"You can call from here, Samantha," I called from the front door. "Or you can stay till tomorrow and I'll see if I can fix it again." Her body was ready for a star jump. I started to walk down the path; she ran to Jody Morris'. We were friends for a while but I ignore her, now.

"Don't go there, Samantha. She's a bitch."

She banged on the front door. It opened. She pushed in, slammed the door. A moment passed, then the curtains parted, and I became the show.

"Yeah, well, FUCK YOU TOO," I said. My throat killed. I went inside. Didn't watch the rest of the show.

Samantha ran straight to Peter to tell all. Her desire from the start. It turned out they worked very well together, and Samantha was so shit-hot with ideas he hired her to work in Public Affairs for him. She called herself PR, but it's like someone who takes ads over the phone for the classifieds saying they work in advertising. Maria was hurt.

She liked to think *she* was the ideas gal. It was unpleasant for her to realise that she couldn't fulfil all of his needs. I didn't think Samantha would be very good for Peter's career; she had such a past.

All her advice would be tempered with the cynicism of over-experience.

I pulled out the diary I'd found a hundred years before, fourteen years before, kept safe all this time. She hadn't gotten any further than writing the date up to March 12, and "Today I" on January 1st. And she'd written in the inside front cover, *Diary Of The Artist Before She Got Famous By Samantha Cord*. There was no year marked. The temptation was too, too much. She wasn't famous; she would never be famous. I would be more famous than her, if anyone ever dug up the back yard.

I found that writing in another hand was a genuine challenge. It made me feel like a different person. It made me feel like I could do anything, pretending to be Samantha as I wrote in her diary.

I picked up Samantha's diary and began to write.

Diary Of The Artist Before She Got Famous
By Samantha Cord

Jan 1. Thursday.

Today I decided to record my thoughts, because I cannot express them all to those around. Although my dear friend Steve is a trustworthy confidante and a worthy friend, she would not like to hear what I have to say. So it falls upon you, dear diary, to be my ears in my time of conflict.

Jan 2. Friday.

It is odd. I feel I need to speak formally to this formal, blank page, as if to speak in any other way would be to denigrate the activity.

I speak so naturally in my day to day, so comfortably, and yet.

He likes my voice. Loves it, he says, but am I to believe that? I am not a compliment-virgin. Tonight, I cleaned out my bedside drawers before I went out.

Jan 3. Saturday.

Last night I ended up going to a party with old friends. I did not take my friend Steve because she finds their company dull. I must confess, their jokes are beginning to bore. Did not see him, but spoke to him on the phone this morning. His voice breaks my heart.

Jan 4. Sunday.

One more day until I see him.

Jan 5. Monday.

Work today. So much history in those two words. So much happiness. Work Today. He was there, he greeted me at the door. He had already put the coffee on. He told me his wife had scratched his face because he burnt the toast. I would cook his toast, butter it, eat it off his wonderful stomach.

Jan 6. Tuesday.

Rang Steve for lunch but she was busy.
She's always off somewhere.

Jan 7. Wednesday.

His wife has her family night every Wednesday. Peter is excluded, because, as he tells me, as we laugh, his family is not good enough for hers. Moreover, he does not wish to go. He finds her family dull, insensitive and sleazy. He tells me he had to extricate Steve from the clutches of one of the MARRIED brothers. Truly disgusting.

Peter has a surprising penis. For such a gentle man. It is all the more galling that he is called upon to be a considerate husband.

Jan 8. Thursday.

Last night was wonderful. I can't tell Steve. I know how she feels about her brother, and about me as well. I'm like a sister. So she thinks Pete's like my brother.

He's not. He was for a while, he's not now.

Maybe she could see how perfect we are for each other. He is the only one who ever came close to understanding me. He is very proud of his sexuality, though I sense he is kinda terrified, as well. Is there some secret in his past, some pain he can't share with me?

Jan 9. Friday.

Went out, drank too much. I'm afraid I find it difficult to keep a civil tongue sometimes. I'm not sure whom I offended last night. Must ask Steve.

Jan 10. Saturday.

I hate Saturdays because he's with his family, playing Daddy, playing Hubby, neither which sit well with him. I do my chores grudgingly.

Jan 11. Sunday.

Slept till 1pm, disgusted with myself for wasting the day.

Jan 12. Monday.

Work today.

Jan 13. Tuesday.

I wish I were sharing with Steve again. We were such good housemates, and I would see Peter whenever he visited her. I could even go on a visit with her to his place, see the evil Maria. See what his kids are like. They love Steve, so they can't be too bad.

Jan 14. Wednesday.

Glorious Wednesday. It has a whole new meaning now. It means love, satisfaction, music. Sometimes I try to remember when I first looked at Peter and loved him.

Jan 15. Thursday.

Peter does this wonderful thing where he acts out Maria's family dinners. He turned into Adrian, unzipped his jeans, pulled out his penis, said, "Ya want it? Ya want it?" and Maria's Dad, weak, saying, "Oh, yes, hello all, hello all, who wants some money?" And he did Maria, did a Gestapo march around the room. Hilarious. He confessed something rather sweet to me. He said that when they shared a home, he and Steve played a game.

She tried to grab glimpses of his cock, he tried to reveal himself in subtle ways. We have begun playing the same game, and for a childish game I must admit it feels rather adult.

Jan 16. Friday.

Hectic at work—campaigning. Was telling Steve about it and she came up with a great idea. Peter knocked it back— sibling rivalry I guess.

Jan 17. Saturday.

I think I need a holiday. I just can't get out of bed. Can Peter do without me? I don't really want to know the answer.

Jan 18. Sunday.

Went to a housewarming, friends of Steve's. She's so good at keeping the mood high, I get quite sick with envy.

Jan 19. Monday.

Work today. Told Peter I needed a week off, next week. He just nodded. "You'll be fine here, then?" I said, because I've got a stack of work. "If you need it, you need it," he said. I felt like I'd failed my own test.

Jan 20. Tuesday.

Long hours—there 7.30, left at 8. Wore me out, but that was a good quantity hit together. No fights and no tears. I think we'd live together easily.

Jan 21. Wednesday.

Peter brought food to my flat, and he made me act like a rag doll. He fed me, mouthful, mouthful, mouthful. I sipped rich wine from a glass held in his strong hand. He wiped away the drops with a soft cloth. "I'll miss you," he said. I almost gave in, but I needed him to miss me. It would be a good idea.

Jan 22. Thursday.

Two more days and I'm away for a week in the sun. My mum called to say happy birthday. I said, "It's not my birthday." She said, "Who's is it, then?" I said, "I don't know, Abraham Lincoln's?" "You don't say," she said. Sometimes I'm a big fan of dying young.

Jan 23. Friday.

Worked till ten, got a pizza, took it round to Stevie's. She was home, thank God. She said she'd collect my mail for the week.

Feb 1. Sunday.

Left my Goddamn diary at home. Had heaps of good thoughts and I can't remember a single one. Genius is so transient. Wanted to call Peter but didn't. I feel good. Men tried to pick me up. I slept, I ate, no one spoke a sensible word all week.

My kind of town.

Feb 2. Monday.

Work today. He was there early to greet me, he had flowers and another present I wasn't to open till I got home. Omigod, underwear. Not quite a proposal of marriage, but it must have cost him.

Feb 3. Tuesday.

It's like I was never gone.

Feb 4. Wednesday.

Wore the underwear. When he hugs me, I nestle into the terrain of his body like lava.

Feb 5. Thursday.

Gave Steve a call. I really missed her company while I was away. Arranged dinner and dancing for Saturday.

Feb 6. Friday.

Stayed home. Really tired. Once a week isn't enough. We had a fight today. I wanted him to come over. He said Maria expected him. I said "Fuck Maria", very quietly, and he didn't ask me to repeat.

Feb 7. Saturday.

Slept in. Out with Steve tonight.

Feb 8. Sunday.

Great night last night, but I'm sick as a dog today. Never laugh as much as I do with Steve. Peter's no comedian. We were at this pub, there's dancing upstairs but we were having a drink downstairs. This guy comes up to us and says, "Hey, girls, what're you drinking?"

"Our own urine," Steve says. I laughed so much I spluttered in the guy's face, and he backed away, terrified.

Feb 9. Monday.

Work today. Peter looked tired around the eyes, so I asked him how he'd slept.

"You came to me in the night, didn't you?" he said. He pushed me into the kitchen and kissed me so deeply I could taste the after-dinner mint he'd eaten last night. He wants me to come to work with my thighs tied together.

Feb 10. Tuesday.

I hate Tuesdays. It's too far from Wednesday but just close

enough. Went shopping, bought a pair of ski pants and a silk shirt.

Feb 11. Wednesday.

When he left I asked him when he could spend a whole night with me. I despise the wrench. He said he couldn't do it. Maria couldn't know. He said he's never deceived me on that. I said that's true but don't you love me. He said of course but love isn't enough. I couldn't sleep after he left. I'm going to be tired tomorrow.

Feb 12. Thursday.

Could barely function. He sent Maria roses. I think she must be a witch, to be so cruel and have such a hold over him.

Feb 13. Friday.

We had lunch together today. I had his full attention, his eyes didn't wander and he listened to every word I had to say. It was an opportunity I managed badly. I waffled and blurted out my feelings about Maria.

"I wish there was something I could do," he said. Sometimes I wonder if perhaps he is weaker than he appears. "She is so terrified of being alone. And of the dark. And the cold. And death."

I'm trying to remember if he placed any emphasis on that last word, or if it was a sick wish within myself.

Feb 14. Saturday.

I can't get out of bed. I just haven't got any friends. I can't even eat. I don't like anyone.

Except Steve. She calls me always at the right time. It's uncanny. She made me get up and we went for a drive. I wanted to take my duvet, but she insisted I sit up straight, breathe in the fresh air.

We sang childish songs and that made me laugh. I stayed at her place. We drank beer and watched horror movies. Not the most romantic Valentine's Day.

Feb 15. Sunday.

Called Peter. Maria answered. Hung up.

Feb 16. Monday.

Work today. Peter had black eyes again.

Maria doesn't want him to spend so much time in the office. She thinks he should be out and about, pressing the flesh.

She seems to imagine that's something simple.

Feb 17. Tuesday.

Couldn't get out of bed till noon. Rang work. They said take the week off. They said there wasn't much on. But of course there is.

Peter wasn't there. "He and Maria are testing the waters," they told me.

Went to the doctor. I feel so tired.

Feb 19. Thursday.

I can't believe it. I missed our Wednesday.

I've slept two days. The doctor put me to sleep. But he also gave me something to make me happy, not bouncy. I'll go see Steve on Saturday. She's always so invigorating.

Feb 21. Saturday.

By the time I arrived at Steve's for her birthday party, the world was wide awake and well into its day. Peter's car was there. The family version. They were having a good family day. I was happy from the doctor. I climbed out of my car and fell over.

Neighbours stared. I walked up Steve's path, slowly, I watched my feet. When I reached the front door they were all there staring at me.

Feb 22. Sunday.

Phone rang last night. Didn't answer.

Steve broke in to see if I was all right. I asked her for more pills to take but she denied. I called her a bad friend, told her to go.

Feb 23. Monday.

Work today. I managed to get a good amount done, considering the in-tray I was presented with. I sat properly all day, worked very well. I didn't go to lunch. Peter did not come to work.

Feb 24. Tuesday.

Peter did not come to work today.

Feb 25. Wednesday.

Today is Wednesday. Peter arrived, as is his habit. I massaged his body, his muscles, his bones, I rubbed his body until he loved me again.

Afterwards he told me Maria was aware of our relationship

and had asked him to call a halt. I was unwilling to call a halt. He said we still worked together very well. I said we should discuss this more. He said he would see me for one more Wednesday, and at work the next day.

Feb 26. Thursday.

Had a great day. A GREAT DAY. My mind seemed to click over. In a few hours. He left, last night, saying it was over, and I knew it was. I could go back to work. It was almost a relief.

Feb 27. Friday.

He wore my favourite blue shirt today. He winked at me. "I'm not playing it cool," I said. "You were right."

"No, you were right," he said. "We're meant for each other," and he kissed me hard in the kitchen.

I went to another doctor.

Feb 28. Saturday.

He came over today. He told her he was going shopping. He said he hated her. I hate her too.

Mar 1. Sunday.

Hate. Hate.

Mar 2. Monday.

Work today. He was cool and calm, as if we had not discussed killing his wife. He says I mustn't tell anyone. I'll keep this diary until the night before, I've already written the days in, then I'll burn this book.

It's been here, when I needed it. That's enough.

Mar 3. Tuesday.

Peter said we must be very professional at work. I was annoyed. I have never been anything but. He has promised me something special for tomorrow night.

Mar 4. Wednesday.
Mar 5. Thursday.
Mar 6. Friday.
Mar 7. Saturday.
Mar 8. Sunday.
Mar 9. Monday.
Mar 10. Tuesday.
Mar 11. Wednesday.
Mar 12. Thursday.
M Day.

I kept boxes full of clippings about Peter in the same place as I stashed the diary. Mum would be disgusted; I get that many newspapers I could set up my own recycling plant. One box was for good stuff, things where Peter was hero. That box was full. The other was for negative articles; just a scattered few. My favourites were those which lampooned Peter for his meticulous footwear, wondered why he spent so much on shoes when people were starving. One cartoon had Peter lying back in a sun lounge, while children dressed in rags licked his shoes. "Yum, beef flavour," one says.

I didn't miss Samantha. I hadn't wanted a housemate anyway. Adrian and I were seeing a lot of each other, and we liked privacy. He managed to spend an hour on my birthday with me. He brought flowers, kissed me, looked sheepish and sad. I shared my Granny card with him:

"Kiss kiss smooch smooch
How'd you like
To be our pooch?"
I rang up and said, "Woof woof."
"Hello?" Grampa said. "Who's there?"
The next time Adrian came over, he said he was there to break up with me, but he could have done that over the phone. Or not done it at all—he could have just not spoken to me. But he wanted one last fuck. He pretended he didn't, but he was in no hurry to leave. I offered him a brandy.

"Just a small one," he said, and he settled himself on the couch. I got the bottle. Straddled him.

"No glasses," I said, and I poured some down his throat. He gulped and swallowed; some spilt on his chin. He wiped it away before I could lick it up. I tipped my head back and filled my mouth with brandy. He leaned into me, his lips at my throat. He groaned. "We can't do this, Steve," he said, like I was begging him for it.

"Okay. Would you like some biscuits? I just bought them. Nice and fresh."

"Can we have them upstairs?" he said.

I laughed. "So long as you don't twist this and remember it as my idea."

"I won't. I swear. Come on," and he led me upstairs, where it was great, because we thought it was the last one.

"I wish things were different," he said afterwards.

He was in post-coital euphoria. He had forgotten how flawed I am. "We could go away somewhere, live together. Imagine being like this every night."

"Why don't you leave her, then?" I said, just to see his reaction. I didn't want him.

"I couldn't," he said, wanting me to talk to him, convince him.

"Yes, you could. Just pack up and leave. She doesn't need you. She's got your family."

But she did need him; I'd seen her looking. It was like the line of sight was a life-line; if it broke she would drift to some terrible place.

"You're meant for so much more," I said. That was Peter talking; he believes in complete unaccountability, that you should only be judged on the actions you are currently performing, not those of the past or the future. Peter found it difficult with me. Every time I did something he said, "Oh, Steve," and it became harder and harder to relegate things to the past.

Adrian liked my body naked. "You're so perfect, everything in place, but you've got these scars and scratches everywhere."

I liked it at first, the way he kissed the markings of my body. But it went on for so long, the kissing, I stopped laughing and wriggling and pointing out others. I lay stiff as concrete and just as smooth. He realised, stopped. "How about a hug?" he said. He sounded like a father.

"I'm too big for hugs," I said. The words made my stomach clench like I'd swallowed lemon juice.

The next time I saw Adrian he'd had his head shaved and he talked loudly. He wanted the family to hate him so they would be glad when he left. I winked at him in the driveway and he grinned.

"I quit my job. I'm going to be an artist," he said.

He had a painting in the back seat which he presented to his parents. It was "Untitled". It was a wonky lamp throwing purple light onto an empty table.

I looked at him and for a moment thought it was all possible. That we could be together, that I could have a lover, a husband, I could be stepmum to his kids and learn how to cook, I could clean the toilet and get a good job, one where people don't die, I could make a clean start of it.

But when I closed my eyes I saw the book, Peter's confession, everything he ever told me. The things he told me last time, when I videoed my death in the bath. And I knew that nothing normal was possible.

Peter wanted to know what I'd done to Adrian, to make him behave like that.

"I'm surprised you've got time to notice, you're always at council meetings. I never see you." I was acting as his chauffeur, taking him the places he wanted to go. It meant he could read his notes or whatever in the back seat, while I did all the driving. I think he liked the image it gave him; man being driven around in a cool old car.

"Maria is upset. She says he's changed."

"It's always my fault, isn't it?" I said. "I suppose Dad was my fault too." I changed lanes too fast. The man behind swerved to miss us.

"So you knew?" he said.

"So you knew?" I said.

"Only a bit," he said.

"How could you 'only a bit' know?" I was flustered, and made a wrong turn. Peter looked at his watch.

"I didn't believe it. There was no proof. It was only what Mum thought. So I thought it too," he said.

"I found proof." I closed my eyes and imagined the backyard. I saw it segmented; there was Dad's bit, taking up most of the room, and my bit over in the corner, my little effort, my visitors to the dark room.

"But why didn't you or Mum tell anyone?"

"She only started thinking it for real once he was dead. And I could never figure it out. Who would I tell? Who would it help? What would it do to us?"

"Fuck all to me," I said.

"Why don't you tell, then?"

"I speak to Dougie Page about it. He's investigating. I'm trying to slow him down," I said. "I don't know why you were so incurious. Didn't you ever want to know what all those midnight noises were? That weird dragging sound spade on dirt sound, doors slamming? Voices, things dropping? Weren't you curious as to what the ghosts were doing?"

"There's no such thing as ghosts."

"Yeah, right, we all just imagined what happened after the séance."

"It was Dad."

"Dad at the séance?"

He shrugged. "Dad who made those noises, Stevie."

"Why are you denying the ghosts? There's no need to be scared of the afterlife." Though even saying this scared me; I caught a glimpse of the slighted people Peter would find after his death. I could smell them.

"Nothing to be scared of." I said, but let him off the hook. I didn't make him discuss the séance again. I pulled into the council hall and let him out.

I felt taller with knowledge. I saw Peter staring at me, thinking, "Do you know? Did you hear what I had to say?" I liked him looking at me.

"I'm thinking of a veggie garden in the backyard at home," I said. "The soil is so rich."

Later on, I took a box of findings to his home, made him go through and guess who the items belonged to.

———————◆———————

I found a shoe heel, a pen, an empty face cream container and a small silver ring.

Dougie watched me clean the things and put them on my special shelves. "You should get rid of that stuff, Stevie. When the police arrive, they're going to be able to use all of it. Every last bit."

"They won't come."

He looked at me.

"They're coming, Steve. I don't know how long, but they're coming. They're the next generation. They didn't know your dad. They don't have the loyalty we did."

"What do you mean? The other cops knew?"

Dougie started to cry. I hadn't seen that before. I wanted to look into his eyes, see what I could see when he cried. "They knew. We all knew. And we knew why. But we couldn't let him go on."

"What did you have to do with it? You didn't arrest him, did you?"

Dougie shook his head. "We couldn't do that. But when those two were found, the man and his victim, and what your Dad did to the man was something… it was an escalation, they call it these days. We knew we had to do something about it."

"I don't want to know any of this. I'm better not knowing. Why are you telling me?"

"Because I'm trying to terrify you, Steve. I want you to run. Go. Get out. Because I don't want to have to help them convict you."

"You killed Dad."

"We let your Dad be killed. But there's no difference. No difference."

I was confused.

"I don't understand why you've been investigating all this when you knew the answers all along."

"I didn't want you getting someone else to do it. Someone who wouldn't know what to do with the answers. I wanted to protect you from prosecution. Persecution. I guess I've failed."

"Well, they've got nothing on me."

"Do you know a woman called Mrs Beattie? She died in Queensland. Police want to talk to you."

I had nothing to do with that. I wish I had.

Apparently no one knows where lolly shop Mrs Beattie is. She didn't even make it to the Gold Coast after all. Silly woman; it would have done her good.

The local paper is curious, and it is formulating a list of other missing local people. Gary, for one. Step by step they are coming to the Searle house.

And then I did a terrible thing. Terrible. But Peter hated me anyway, once he realised I knew all his secrets. So there were no deterrents. Nothing.

His daughter Kelly, at fifteen, knew she was onto a good thing with me. She begged to be allowed to visit when I invited her. Maria and Peter refused, but she begged and begged till their eardrums burst and they said yes. No, that's not true. They would never have said yes, not even at gunpoint. The kids were staying with Maria's parents and I wanted them to stay with me, because I knew Maria would hate it, would never allow it. I had been spending some time at her parents' place when the rest of the family wasn't there. Her mum was teaching me how to cook; we were having a bit of a break-through. I could make marvellous asparagus soup, and my poached chicken was perfect. I sat quietly with the father and we read newspapers without that irritating commentary most people seem to feel is necessary.

Her parents liked me. Best thing about it was imagining my name being mentioned, people jumping at the invasion. Adrian red, Maria angry, Peter concerned. The kids were there for a week while Peter and Maria were away on a "fact finding trip". I called it a "fuck finding trip". I called on Wednesday morning. Twelve rings, then a harried father answered.

"It's Stevie!" I said.

"Stevie, Stevie, hello Stevie!" he said. The kids squealed in the background.

"How are you?" I said.

"Oh, good, good, got the girls here, they're a bit much."

"That *is* a bit much. Really. Do you need a hand? I'd be happy to come over."

"No, love, couldn't ask that of you. Though we are out of ice cream and it's hard to get out. I don't suppose you could pick some up for us? You know what kids are like about ice cream."

"I'll be right there." They hadn't figured out yet that the girls were nearly grown up.

The poor old buggers were exhausted. I made them a cup of tea and packed a few of the girls' things.

"They'll come and stay with me tonight," I said.

The girls squealed. They like me, probably because I can't stand them. Maybe I should get a cat; they work on the same principle. I wondered what Maria's parents would say about me and Adrian. I'm sure they'd like me as a daughter-in-law. This is what should happen. I marry Adrian. I have that life.

Adrian's parents are mine, now, and so is his family.

That's what should have happened.

We stopped at the shops on the way home, slow, slow shop, for bad food. Carrie tried to impress me with shocking facts.

"Did you know that nails and hair keep growing after you die and they dug up one old guy and the whole coffin was full of hair and nails?"

"It's not actually true, sweety. The body shrinks up, so it looks like nails and hair are growing, but they aren't really. Did you know you can survive in the desert by drinking your own wee?"

"Oooo, gross!" she said. I was the master of the revolting. Carrie went to play *TombRaider 6000* or whatever. I had Kelly to myself. I hadn't planned to do the terrible thing, but we were exploring, squatting down under the beds and finding treasures, and she kept doing Silent But Deadlies.

"What have you been eating, Kelly? You're too young to be farting like that," I said after one particularly deadly one. She looked at me innocently. "It's not me," she said, and I was slighted, *slighted*, that she should blame her own fart on me, although it was just something kids did. While I was steaming about it, she found a bottle of pills under Mum's old bed. I really fucking hate cleaning up. I tell people I like to leave Mum's room as it was, because she left it the way it was when Dad died, so it's a shrine to both of them. But it's really because I hate cleaning.

She found one of the bottles of pills left over from my selling days. Kelly found them, shook off the dust and heard the rattle.

"What are they?" she said.

The thing is, in the back of my mind I knew they were many years past their Use By and would be ineffective. I knew this.

"Diet pills," I said. "But they're stale. How about some apple, downstairs?" Thus, I left the decision up to her.

"Oh, well," I said. "You keep exploring. I'm going to get the dinner ready." We all loved barbecued chicken; I had three in the fridge, one for each day.

We stripped off bits when we were hungry, standing with the fridge door open, stuffing white meat in. But I'd promised Maria's Mum to give them salad every day, and I knew questions would be asked, so I opened tins and set the table. When

Kelly didn't respond to my call, I knew I had done a terrible, terrible thing. I called an ambulance and then, I climbed the stairs to look into eyes I would have to hold open. I shivered, shuddered. I ran.

That's what should have happened. Most of it did; but I didn't call an ambulance. I shivered and ran up the stairs, and she was curled up on my bed, wanting to be found.

"Stevie," she said, sweet little voice, and I could see her eyelids flicker, what was she seeing, and I couldn't wait any longer but I did, just a moment.

Then I stuck my finger down her throat—fuck the duvet, I thought, I'll get a new one—as the pills came up. I could see them, pink and gelatinous, the coating barely eaten through. We got up and walked around, around my room, Mum and Dad's room, Peter's room, bathroom.

"I'm tired, Stevie. I want to sleep."

"Tell me a story instead. Tell me where you just went."

She was breathing strangely. "What's wrong?" I said. She sucked air in through her mouth with her tongue sticking out, blew it out through her nose with her face screwed up.

"The air tastes all right on the way in and foul on the way out," she said.

We went to my room where I scrabbled around for a sweet cough lolly. "There, this'll make your mouth taste better," I said.

"Lollies are fattening," she said. We walked. She began to lean less heavily on me.

"Tell me about the place you went," I said.

"There wasn't a place. Ow." I squeezed her arm.

I knew there was a place.

"Why won't you tell me? When you went to sleep and you went to another bedroom where the walls were round like a ball and it was dark as dark and cold as cold and there were people with sharp teeth to eat you up."

She began to cry and didn't stop. Peter came to collect her; he said, "That's it, Steve. The end," but it already had been. It was like he was telling me what to do. I saw her face, still crying, turned to face me as they drove off, and she could not resist a wave. I waved back. The girl had forgiven me already. Maria would have me arrested, crash bang fuck off Steve.

Peter won't answer the phone. I can only get a minute of words on the answering machine, and I'm trying to be concise. Maria called me to say I was to leave her parents alone.

"They're my mum and dad, not yours, and they love me. I am the daughter. Just because your Dad was a bully and your Mum was a slut doesn't mean you can claim somebody else's parents."

"What are you talking about, witchy poo? You never knew my parents. How are you fit to even talk about them?"

"I'm only going off what my husband told me."

"Oh, your husband, is it? Well, he was my brother first, don't forget. I'm the one who gets to bury the body."

"What?"

"Look, I only saw your parents because I felt sorry for them, anyway. None of you kids appreciate them."

"We appreciate them. And we'd appreciate it if you left them alone," she said, and slammed down the phone, effectively cutting off my access to the last word.

That's one reason I was the last to know. Because Peter could hardly bear to talk to me. I don't know if I was the last to know; I certainly wasn't the first. How Peter heard before me when she was my oldest friend, I don't know. Perhaps I was out when they called; I must get an answering machine.

"Steve, I'm afraid I've got some bad news about Samantha." Peter's voice was cracked and weak.

"Murray? What's he done now, the arsehole? If he's hurt her, I'll kill him."

"It wasn't Murray. Well, they don't know who it was. Hit and run, Stevie. It was hit and run."

"Well, did she get the number plate or anything?"

"No, Steve. I've done this terribly. She's not going to make it. Well, she hasn't made it already. I mean, she's dead."

My first thought was—always had to do everything first.

"But why would she do that?" I said.

"She didn't do anything, she was run over." Peter was frustrated; he thought I was being obtuse.

"Thanks for telling me, Peter. I'll spread the word." But when he got off the phone, I realised there was no one to call. I didn't know the phone numbers of any of her friends.

I found out where the funeral was and I showed up in black. I whispered to her friends. I knew her best; I was the one who saved her from loneliness when she was a new girl. I was her housemate.

"Why? Why?" I whispered. "When she had so much to live for? Why did she do it?"

"She didn't do anything. It was a hit and run," they told me one by one, the same words, the same tone.

"But she was on the road," I said. I just wanted them to think. If she had wanted to die, then we should be happy for her success. We don't have to cry or feel sorrow. She got what she wanted.

She got what she deserved.

I looked at photographs of us together: at school, growing up, in fancy dress, drunk. I played her favourite music, a bit of George Michael, and I drank vodka in memory of her.

The last time we drank vodka together was the night before she left my house without speaking.

And didn't speak to me again. That's another reason I didn't go to the funeral; we hadn't spoken.

I heard a knock on the door. I had photos all over me. The vodka spilled, I dropped my cigarette.

There was a man with a parcel when I opened the door. A padded envelope, a note inside: *Stephanie, Samantha wanted you to have this. Mrs Cord.*

Inside was a tape. Written on it was a coincidental date; the night we had last drunk vodka together. The label said *Steve Searle* and the date.

The writing was shaky. Underneath it was the label of a George Michael album. Sticky tape covered the no-record holes. She really liked George Michael; why would she tape over him?

I played the tape the next day. It took me a while to realise she had recorded my dream talk. She had invaded my dreams and stolen the words I spoke in my sleep. That voice sounded different; it was my other voice. My research voice. My voice sounded wonderful, seductive. "Can I help you? Why not talk a little, ease yourself. You know I'm a good listener. Just tell me this and that. Your little things. Nothing else matters, does it? Only those little annoyances. We can be happy if those are settled."

Silence for a moment.

Screams, then, and shouts, then growls.

"Mmmm," my voice said. "Mmmm. Comfy? Can I adjust anything for you? Can I help you, Sam? Tell me *slights*. Tell me tell me tell me what you see ooh dark. Mum. Safe and dark and cold. Not warm. See ya there, old friend to celebrate. Slice slice, very sharp. It's nice. Alive. Makes you feel alive since high school is too short."

Screams again.

"Mum," I said. "Wait for me. Wait for Samantha. We're coming."

I can clearly remember the dream. In it, I died and went to a place which was very crowded, glary.

I saw Mum there, a glimpse of her hair, and I shouted to be heard.

At Thirty-Five

No one will talk to me. No one. The journos have picked up some tension between Peter and I and are edging closer to my front gate. Do they know what the cops know? Dougie Page sent me a plane ticket, he wants me to run, run, run away.

I re-read Samantha's diary and wanted to do something with it. It was a good piece of work, my most creative yet. I thought ahead: I send the diary to a tabloid, it's published, Peter is investigated, Maria leaves him, Samantha's death is investigated and the diary is discovered to be a fake. An investigation into who faked the diary. I am discovered.

Too complicated. I sent the diary to Maria instead, with a note from Samantha. "I thought you'd like to see this." They never twigged, as I did after I sent the thing, that, according to the diary, Samantha thought Maria was going to die. Why would she send the diary? My plans went awry, anyway. I didn't hear from them for two weeks, but I called and left messages as I usually do, all things normal. I called Maria's parents, because I knew they loved me and wouldn't dump me. Always the long rings, then, "Hello?" Her Mum, nervous.

"It's me, Stevie!" I said. I wanted her to weep for joy.

"Oh, Stevie, what did you do? Why did you upset our girl? Why hurt Kelly like that? She has bad dreams all the time."

"I didn't do anything, Andrea. You know what teenagers are like. They get away from you."

"Maria makes us feel so bad for giving the girls to you. She's saying me or her, me or her." She did a good impersonation of Maria's brake-squeal voice, and I laughed "Not funny, Stevie. We can't see you any more. Not even in secret." I never realised they kept my visits secret.

"But that's silly. It was only an accident."

"I'm sorry, Stevie. We liked it when you were here, but you can't come here any more. We can't manage." It looked like I wouldn't be going to their place for Christmas after all. That was the saddest thing. She hung up. I sat there, the phone saying beep beep beep, and I felt far greater loss than I had with the deaths of all my people. My lungs swelled to fill my chest, I sucked in air in tiny wheezes and blew it out in gusts. I had a headache behind my ears, and pressure on my throat. I blinked. Blinking stung my eyes. I rubbed them and they were wet.

The realisation I was crying made me cry. I never realised how painful it was. I always thought it was quite a pleasant, if weak, thing to do. But it hurt, my shoulders, my back, eyes, lungs, throat. It is violence. I've seen people do the same thing, when they're dying, not crying. The fight that goes on between tired body and instinct to live. The death agonies, though they are past suffering, gasps of breath, shouts, shoulders heaving.

I'm crying, not dying.

Then Peter called to say they were coming to visit, not to bother with biscuits, they would bring some. They always brought their own food, and sometimes their own plates, so I wasn't overly concerned. Maria made a cup of tea and we sat at the table, waiting for the fun to start. Peter said, "Steve, I want you to tell Maria that you wrote the diary."

"What diary?"

"The one you sent us, Samantha's diary."

"I found that under the bed."

"And the note?"

"It was in the front cover. That's the only reason I sent it. I didn't want to cause trouble but it was Samantha's wish from the grave. Why, what was in it?"

Maria laughed. "My goodness, you are highly moralled, aren't you? Didn't even read it."

"It wasn't my diary," I said.

Maria laughed again. Her fingers seemed thinner, like claws. Her whole body seemed smaller, like she was drawing herself in to protect herself from contamination.

"Did you write it?" she said slowly.

"No, I did not," I said slowly. I ate a biscuit. Convention is such a comforting thing. My brother and his wife arrive to accuse me of forgery and they bring tea and biscuits which we enjoy.

"I swear I didn't write the diary," I said.

Maria said, "Well, Steve, either way, I think it's best if you don't see the girls for a while."

"Oh lord," I wanted to say, "don't throw me in the briar patch."

I hate those fucking girls. "That seems a little harsh," I said. "You're punishing me for something I just said I didn't do."

"Oh, we know you did it. We just wanted you to admit it," she said. She took a last swallow of milky tea. I picked up the milk carton.

"Oops, sorry folks, three days past Use By."

Maria's mouth turned down. "Goodbye, Steve. Come on, Peter." She left the room, without the remaining biscuits. If I could get Peter to leave without them, I wouldn't have to cook dinner.

"Look, Peter, no matter what you think, I didn't write the diary. You can't dump me for something I didn't do." He looked at me quite tenderly and I forgot he was my brother. I closed my eyes.

"Steve, it'll be okay. Just give her time to see the joke, all right? And no more jokes for a while."

I grinned. "Always I am deadly serious and people laugh into my facial features."

He punched my shoulder, but gently. "We'll see you in a little while," he said, and left, without the biscuits.

But he was lying. I never saw him again. I explained what happened, message after message on his machine, what had happened to me over the years. I said, "If you'd ever taken the time to listen to me you'd know all this. You could have stopped me." I said I wanted to start again, from childhood, and I wouldn't make him cry. I wouldn't be Dad's favourite. I wouldn't go out for lunch with Mum. I wouldn't scare off Samantha, or Bess. I wouldn't go out with Scott or dump Ced. I wouldn't hurt anybody, or myself. I wouldn't stay in the house or the same job or keep the car or hate the shoe man or throw milk at Peter. I wish I could change my past now I know my future. Stalin did it.

Peter never called me back. I sent letters, photos, I got a courier to drop off a big photo of me and Peter as kids, two grinning kids squeezing each other. I remembered later that, just before the photo, I had deliberately wet my pants on Peter's leg to pay him back for telling everyone I wet the bed, so there is a stain for all to see. It was a bad choice of photo.

I sent him a telegram: I'M FINISHED, it said.

IT'S OVER. But he didn't come running. He didn't save me.

I wished I'd kept a copy of the diary. It was probably burnt by now, my greatest literary effort since "The Sacking of Troy".

There is a report on the news: "Police are taking steps to track the killer dubbed as 'The Local.'" Nice of them to let me know.

I needed to take steps of my own.

I bought giant orange garden refuse bags and cleaned out the garden.

I piled every bone in there, even Muffy's, and the ones which looked like lamb shanks. The compost heap had done the best job it could. I took them to a building site where the foundations had been dug but not poured, and I threw the lot in. Some of it wasn't bone; I threw that in as well. The smell was sickening. It had been okay spread out; all together it smelled like slaughter. I can imagine this: they build over the bones I laid. The building is completed, a monument to comfortable living. The people move in, and stay, or move out. It is a noisy building, and not just because the walls are thin. It groans, shrieks sometimes, and suggestible tenants think words are spoken. The stories grow. Ghosts are seen, accidents occur. People feel depressed in certain rooms; in others arguments erupt, in the hallways people are rude to each other, in the lifts they make outrageous jokes others repeat for days. There is an elderly couple whose son lives overseas; his spirit comes to them every couple of weeks. They annoy him by calling him to see if he is still alive.

"No, I didn't send my ghost to see you last night. No, I was here. I didn't leave. Yes, I'm fine."

There is a young woman who has a demon lover, a young man who has one too. A child who finds a playmate, an outsider who finds a friend. The apparitions come and go; the people are always available.

I left the bits and pieces at home. That was Dad's collection. It belonged there. No one would care; it was just a pile of old junk, no matter what Dougie Page said. I gathered the things all together and covered them with dirt, a nice dirt mountain. If anyone pulled down the mountain they would think the things were ours, a family mountain. I now had a collection like Maria's Mum's: lots of lovely little things with personal stories. I shuffled through them, each item precious.

I wondered what people would think of my collected mound of rubbish. Peter would try to stop them; he has a tendency to overestimate people's intelligence. They won't make any connections.

He'll become visibly distressed as the various items are unearthed, and won't offer a reasonable explanation for their presence. He'll say that the backyard had been used as a rubbish dump for as long as he could remember, and each item could have been a family one. He'll try not to look at the mound. They won't bother to ask me.

I sat amongst my treasures, my clues. An earring depicting a marijuana plant, a purple shoelace, a set of keys with #1 on the tag, a beige earplug, a red brick, a mop head, a paint brush and a popped balloon. A cheap plastic watch; a brass lighter; an old coin; a bottle top; a gold chain, tarnished; a shoe heel; a wallet, empty, mass-market pigskin; a coin holder; an elastic band; a tie bar; a shoe marked with red crosses; a child's lunch box; a squeaky toy; a TV dial; a squash ball; a damaged glass cufflink. A pipe, pearls, white buttons, false fingernails, a silver ring, a silver earring, a belt, a tie pin.

I wished I had read all of Auntie Jessie's books when she was alive; she could have explained so much. I finally made it through the box. Three days after my thirty-fifth birthday, I have finished my box of books. I finally found the one that began, "Dear Stevie," and the one that ended, "From your Auntie Jessie," and I realised all the messages in between were for me. That she already knew what I would do; what I would become.

I picked up the book on magnetism and I stared at it in the dim light of the grey afternoon, the old-fashioned writing a scrawl to my untrained eye.

Then I put it back with the other things.

This is what she wrote in the margins of the different books in the box. In *Children and Others* by James Gould Couzens, she wrote:

PH thirty-five pipe:

Alex's family moved to a townhouse when he was twelve, and they stayed till he was seventeen. The Searle townhouse was the fourth of a six-complex block, with a long, shared yard behind, walled courtyards you only needed to stand on tippy-toes to spy into, thin walls.

It was a closed community. They looked out only for the inhabitants of the six townhouses, and many grim fights were held with the other neighbours.

At school, his neighbour Sally from across the road used her breasts for attention. She unbuttoned her blouse as low as she dared and sat on the bottom steps leading up to the home economics building. The boys would quietly push for position on the steps above her. There were four steps, one boy to each step.

The step closest to her afforded the best view and a chance perhaps to brush those breasts with the back of your hand. But you had to talk, though, which made it hard work.

The second step was still good for vision, but the chance of a tactile encounter was gone, unless you could lose your balance as you passed her. You were also required to talk, and to communicate what was being said to the two higher steps. Thus it was a position of power; you could make faces without Sally seeing.

The third step was the least desirable, but never remained unfilled. You could not hear what was said, and the boy on the fourth step muttered constantly, "What'd she say?"

All the boys hoped her next sentence would be one of offer.

The fourth step was good because you were not required to be amusing, and it was high enough that sometimes you could see right down her blouse.

Alex often sat on the first step, because he knew Sally from across the street and he was never stuck for words. The others hated him for it.

Sally sat on the bottom step, without lunch or drink. The boys fought to feed her.

Fat George bought her a roast beef sandwich, but it was on brown bread.

"Is my skin white or brown, Fat George?" she said.

"White," said Fat George.

"So what colour sugar do you think I like?"

"White," said Fat George.

"And what colour bread do you think I like?" said Sally.

Fat George didn't answer. He was close to tears. He would not be given another chance to bring lunch. That night, when his father hit his mother because she had cooked a poor meal, Fat George didn't defend her as he usually did. He said, "Yeah," under his breath and left her to cry. That earned him an hour with the comics at his dad's feet, instead of a punch in the solar plexus, and the difference was so vast, so easily achieved, he never told his father how unfunny he found the comics. Sally tossed the sandwich down and accepted a jammy half from Alex.

"Perhaps you like black bread," he said, a great joke. His best received; certainly it was quoted about the school for many weeks.

Black bread was available in the shops ten or so years later. When he first saw it, Alex could not believe that something he had invented as the most ridiculous-sounding thing was there, at the delicatessen rather than the milk bar, of course, but there. He wondered if anyone remembered his joke, and thought him even cleverer.

"You're so funny, Allie," Sally said. "Sally and Allie."

There was silence on the steps and for miles about. The sun went behind a cloud and Sally shivered, a magnificent, shimmering movement they watched in slow motion.

"Sally and Allie," Alex said.

His left hand shook so he sat on it and reached for her shoulder with his right. She shivered again, and the whole school sighed.

The competition was over. He had won, and now they could relax, leave him to it, live through the stories he would tell if they had to beat it out of him.

The other girls joined the sigh, because they wished for love too, but it all seemed so difficult, so uncomfortable.

Alex became good at pretending he wanted what she wanted, and liked what she liked.

Sally and Allie sat on the steps alone. He couldn't say to her, "Don't call me Allie," because he had a feeling it was the only reason she had picked him. If there had been an older boy called Callum or Malcolm, there would have been a battle.

He wasn't sure what was expected of him physically. He was content to watch her shivers, curl his arm around her waist, but was she getting bored?

The weeks passed, and he began to struggle for things to say. He was tired of flattery, and that made Sally peevish. So he decided to take a drastic step.

Two of the older boys were known sex-addicts. Alex began going out with them at night, to sit with them on another set of steps, the ones leading to the Town Hall.

All they talked about was sex, and Alex remembered everything. He never asked questions; was so quiet he was barely noticed. He learnt about in her pants, which finger to use, what to do if she was wearing waist-hugger underpants. Everything but what to say to her parents when they caught you at it.

After three weeks, Alex realised they were repeating themselves and that he was getting more practice than they were.

He began at a neighbourhood party, a sixteenth. Everybody was there, dancing with the lights off. Sally brought two friends, quiet and fat, to keep her safe, but as she was leaving, he said, "Goodnight, Sally," and pinned her against the wall.

He kissed her then, quickly but deeply, felt those lovely breasts against his chest and pressed harder.

"You're very forceful," she said.

They stopped sitting on the steps at lunch time, stopped eating lunch. They began going out of bounds, to the sloping grounds outside the school oval. To the sounds of soccer and British Bulldog, they kissed. To make it real, she gave him the top two buttons of her shirt. Small and white, he carried them in his pocket.

She would not let him touch her breasts; her mother had told her that much at least.

Alex now knew what was expected of him.

He no longer had to think about it. It was out of his control.

He learnt to whisper in her ear, tell her what sort of grass they lay on, who tended it, when soccer was first played, why West Germany had won the world cup the year before, anything to distract her, take her mind from his soft and gentle, his roving hands.

Alex had in his mind that he would like to make love for the first time in a bed.

That was the way he imagined it, the way he thought was natural. He had a good friend whose parents had a granny flat in the back of the house. This was a place for smoking, drinking, swearing, kissing. Alex asked for the place, just one night, a school night, the others wouldn't mind. The date, the place, the time was set. He spent an evening with Sally's parents, winning them over.

When Alex got home from seeing Sally, the house was full of the smell of burnt food.

"I ate at Sally's, Mum," he said. She shrugged and scraped the food into the bin.

He bought some roses, wrapped them so the thorns couldn't hurt him. He bought some special snacks. A little feast of chocolate and cheese. He didn't really know what to buy, but Sally was just as unsophisticated.

Sally came to the place dressed prettily, like a bride. They nibbled at the food, swallowed the sweet soft drink he had also brought. They kissed, touched, they gently stripped each other's clothing away.

Everything was perfect until he fumbled and struggled with the condom. He knew all about them (wet-checks, frangers, rubbers, raincoats, dingers, prophylactics). It was not so easy in practice, though, and he fumbled, became distracted by feelings of inadequacy.

At least, he thought, she was a virgin too.

Sally laughed as he tried to balance forward on his knees, tipped, landed on his face. She laughed harder.

The moment was ruined forever.

"What's so funny?" He didn't want to scare her off by being too aggressive.

"It's just he always knows what he's doing."

Alex sat beside her, looking, horrified, at her face. Was she lying now, or had she been lying in the past?

"I thought this was your first time."

"First time I've wanted to do it," she said.

The boys on the town hall steps hadn't indicated there was a difference.

Sally shut her eyes, and he could see movement behind them. Alex realised why Sally both wanted and was terrified by sex.

Was it her father, or someone else?

"Don't cry," he said. "We can just hold each other."

Then she did cry.

"That's what he says, and next thing I know it's happening. Don't tell anyone. I don't want them to know I'm a slut."

Alex was angry, an unselfish, adult anger.

"I don't think you are a slut, if you didn't want to do it. Even if you wanted to do it."

"I didn't. I never do."

"How often?"

"Every time Mum and Dad aren't in the house."

"So which one is it?" He tried to imagine one of the Town Hall Boys with her, forcing her—how? With words of seduction he had not yet learned? With strength?

"Mr Harris," she said.

"Which Mr Harris?" Surely not the pipe-smoking, upright, strict man next door?

"How many do you know, Alex? And stop asking questions. I don't want to think about it. He hasn't come around since I started going out with you— oh, just that night of the party. He drove my friends home and wouldn't let me out of the car."

Mr Harris. Alex had thought it had to be someone young, someone their age. Mr Harris lived next door. He had a wife who didn't like to venture outside the house much, two boys younger than Alex. He was a round, red-faced man who was always shiny with sweat.

Sally was crying again. He used his shirt sleeve to wipe her tears, and held her as her shoulders shook. He could feel his pulse banging in his ears. This little girl, little Sally, being hurt by an adult. He could look after himself; Sally could not.

He walked Sally home.

Alex thought with all the wisdom a fifteen-year old owned. He already had an interest in the law, and knew he needed to pass this terrible information on to adult hands.

But he barely had the words for his complaint, let alone the courage to speak them. So he did nothing. Nothing.

Sally and Allie went back to sitting on the step. There was much speculation; people wanted to know what happened. It was better for Sally that way, and Alex thought of her differently now. Like a sister he needed to protect.

He talked to her a lot about Mr Harris. He asked her to call him the next time Mr Harris came over.

There was the night when Sally's parents went to the music show Alex's mother was singing in. Half the adults in the street went.

Alex's father stayed home to keep an eye on things. He had seen the show before, again and again, and it still made him cry. Alex's mother finally said he must stay behind; his sobs disturbed the audience.

So Alex and his father settled for a night at home. They played a game of cards, but Alex was restless. He thought about Sally, alone in the house, and Mrs Harris, who'd made an exception and left the house, and Mr Harris who didn't go to the show because he didn't have an ear for it.

Alex said, "I was reading a book the other day about a married man who started forcing himself on a young girl."

"Where did you find a book like that?" his father said. He had thought the library far more stringent.

"One of the older boys had it. Is it OK, though? Even if the girl doesn't like him?"

Alex realised another secret of the adult world; sometimes things are suspected, but never spoken.

His father said, "We don't see your friend Sally about much, these days."

"So you know, too?"

"Knowing is different to guessing."

"But it's disgusting."

"I'm not sure what we can do. We don't want to shame Sally. After all, she's only fourteen."

"Exactly. How is it her fault? We have to stop him, tell his wife or something."

"You can't interfere in other people's business. It's only a sexual act, Alexander.

You'll realise soon enough how little it means.

This was possibly the worst advice Alex ever received. He became anxious for adulthood, when he would be in a position to help. He would not back away in a cowardly manner.

He performed his first detective task; kept watch on Mr Harris's front door.

It opened at 9pm, one hour after the crowd had departed for the show.

Mr Harris stood on his front step, smoking his pipe. Just casually, as if he was going for a stroll. He looked up the street, saw no one.

Alex was well-hidden. Alex took a photo of his smug face. Mr Harris tapped out his pipe and tucked it into his back pocket. He never went anywhere without his pipe, and told the story of where he'd found it, what it was worth, what he'd got it for, why he couldn't let anyone touch it. He had beaten his son Sam till the boy ran screaming into the street one time, defended himself by saying, "He actually sucked on my pipe, the little shit.

Clenched his teeth around the stem."

Sam was a wonderful mimic; he did a great version of his father, standing tall and purveying the world like he owned it. It was this, perhaps, rather than the sullying of the sanctity of the pipe, which distressed Mr Harris so much.

Mr Harris crossed the road, sauntering to a place he wasn't welcome.

Alex wanted to smash his head in with a stone, shoot him, make him bloody. But he followed, once Sally had allowed the man into her home. She left the front door ajar, as Alex had told her to do and disappeared into the darkness of the hallway.

Alex didn't have the strength or the age to beat Mr Harris.

Alex had been reading a lot of true detective magazines; he knew how these things were done. He crept up the hallway and then he had to wait until the photo he took would be undeniable proof.

"I don't like it," Sally said.

Mr Harris squinted at her. "You just haven't got used to it yet. Just think how happy your boyfriend will be when he finds out how experienced you are," he said.

"Alex isn't like that."

"All men are like that," he said, nodding.

Then silence, for a minute, two minutes.

Alex realised he didn't know what he was listening for. Sally whimpered. He pushed open her bedroom door, camera wound, flash ready, he was armed like a cop.

He lifted the camera to his eye, knowing his chance would be very short.

Through the viewfinder, he saw Sally sitting on the bed, her eyes shut, her mouth open.

He saw Mr Harris, his trousers down, his Y-fronts down, knees against the bed. His eyes were shut, too, and his mouth open, though the differences in their expressions taught Alex something he never forgot; Feelings rarely match because people never do, even when they are doing the same thing.

Alex snapped the picture and ran. He wanted the film safe. He locked himself in his parents' bedroom, which was at the front of the house, and called Sally from the phone by the bed.

"Are you all right?"

"He's gone. He's really angry."

"Scared, more like."

"What are you going to do now?"

"Call the police."

"Can't you just keep the picture in case he does it again?"

"I can't watch him all the time, Sally. And if it's not you, it'll be someone else. He has to be stopped. Men can't take advantage of women that way."

"But everyone'll know I'm not a virgin."

"Sally, everyone will know it wasn't your fault. No one'll hold it against you."

"You'll have to look after me now, Allie.

My family won't want me."

"I can do that," he said. His father was listening to music on headphones, doing a crossword.

Mr Harris crossed the front lawn.

"He's here. I have to get off and phone the police."

Mr Harris banged on the front door.

"Open up, you little shit. Open the fucking door." Alex wondered briefly if his father would intervene, but knew that wouldn't happen.

Alex called the local police to tell them there was an intruder. He thought it was the best way to get them there quickly, and it worked, but it went against him later. They said he'd lied, and that made him untrustworthy. They didn't accept the photo evidence; said he'd probably tricked it up.

"How?" he said, but that was too smart for a fifteen year old boy.

He was not to lose his virginity to Sally.

That happened at a school dance where somebody had smuggled beer in, and he lost it in a two-minute fumble against the science block. He remembered the girl's name only because she followed him around for the rest of the term, wanting to belong to him.

Wanting to make him forget Sally. Because Sally was gone to him. And Alex was no longer considered a worthy neighbour—he had told of things best kept secret, revealed the underfelt of their lives. They feared his childish honesty, were nervous of him revealing back-fence hopping, drunken gropes, those kisses exchanged after cocktails. He was too young to understand human sexuality. He didn't know about need. The Searle family were no longer considered neighbourly.

The street withdrew support for the Searles, as if they, as a whole, had deliberately and cruelly set out to destroy the fantasy of a happy place. Mr Horton, who mowed everybody's nature strip, no longer mowed the Searle's. Alex's father sought a transfer, and they moved.

No one offered to help. The whole street stood on their own front lawns, watching as the family loaded box after box into the hired van. No one waved as they drove away.

Alex and his family did not find a new home straight away. They wanted something perfect, his parents; they didn't learn the lesson of perfection, how dangerous it could be. They went to Mr Searle's family home; his parents were happy to have them. They loved Alex's energy, and his brother Dominic's quiet wit, and Sebastian's obedience.

The Searles thought they would be safe there. But there are no secrets in a small world, and when Mr Harris (and he would never be anything but Mr Harris; he didn't have a Christian name; he didn't have a Christian burial) came for Alex, his mind on violent, bullying revenge, he didn't imagine Alex would have the strength now to stand up to him. He was unprepared; Alex was even less ready. It wasn't blind rage, because in his mind's eye Alex could see each detail; the look on Mr Harris's face as he sauntered towards Alex. Smug, greedy, angry. Alex saw the fists clenched, the heavy boots. He could feel the smile stretched across his face, its foolishness deliberately deceptive. His hands clenched too; his logical brain said, "No, he's an adult, nothing but *trouble, who would believe he provoked you, that's if you do win, which you won't because he's bigger than you." Alex found his hands took their signal from a part of the brain he could not control.*

His grandfather saw it all. Saw Mr Harris—though he didn't know it was Mr Harris, not till later, when the papers had his face on their missing person pages—come up the front path, trip over the cricket set left there by Dom. Heard him bang on the door, shout,

"Come out, you little shit." Grandfather saw and heard all this.

He heard the fight downstairs and ventured to help his sixteen year old grandson, but he saw his grandson fell Mr Harris with a blow.

Alex's grandfather alone saw Alex bury the body in the backyard, because it was night and dark and the others were out. He did not help; he didn't reveal himself. He never told Alex what he'd seen, but he told his wife. They loved their Alex. They knew he was the future of the Searle family; already it was clear that Dominic would not be having children. He never told anyone but his wife. They were the only ones who could protect Alex; they could provide him with sanctuary. Alex's grandfather had killed at war; he knew how shallow human life was. So they decided that the best way to protect Alex was to let him stay when he needed to, and they would leave their home, with its secrets, to him.

Alex wouldn't know that his grandfather knew; that when Alex thought the house was empty, his grandfather was upstairs.

Alex's parents never knew about Mr Harris.

◆———————◆

In the margins of *Middlesex* by Jeffrey Eugenides, Jessie wrote this:

CW twenty-nine watch:

Chew Wang bought the watch from a friend, in exchange for entry into a group of wealthy children-lovers.

Inside *The Cold Six Thousand* by James Ellroy:

AM seventy-two lighter:

Albert Mitchell, an elderly man, but age is no defence. War criminal intentions. I fought for you, he says, as if that excuses the pain he inflicts. I fought for you. The lighter came from a grateful mate's will, ooh, they shared some memories. Good times, girls with rotting cunts, like rock-melon left in the sun, all warm and seedy, but cost a pittance and who ever imagined your dick could fall off, make you a mad man, madman, this is what I think of dirty cunts, and this. This is what you get.

In *A Piece of the Night*, Michelle Roberts:

CS thirty-three coin:

It was lucky, the old coin, very old, very lucky for Chris Stepanos. It was worn thin around the edges from owners rubbing, saying please please please. Please don't let my daughter tell.

In *Immaterial*, Robert Hood:

RR fifty-eight bottletop:

The bottletop was squashed flat and no longer sharp; it was from Rex Robert's first beer. He liked a beer, did Rex, and his women, though women were not so keen on him. That was fine. At least they moved when he fucked them. Moved and screamed.

He was past all that, though. Too old. Just him and the movies, it was now.

In *The Vicar of Morbing Vyle*, Richard Harland:

GT fifty-five ring:

Alex met him in a milk bar where they were both buying cigarettes. He was first in line, and dithering, deciding. He spun a broad silver ring on his middle finger, a nervous man.

Alex wanted to be away from there; he wanted to return to life. He considered time spent shopping, waiting, travelling, as necessary but also a cessation of life. He'd rather be rolling the giant blue plastic ball to his daughter, watching in delight as she grabbed and fell into its soft centre.

"Would you like me to go first while you're gathering your thoughts?" Alex said to the other customer.

"Well, thank you. That would be kind."

Alex snapped up his preferred brand, placed money in the palm of the tobacconist.

The tobacconist winked. "See you tomorrow, Mr Searle."

"Not if these kill me first," Alex winked back.

Alex returned the next day. He changed his visiting times daily, always hoping to enter an empty shop.

"Interesting character, that one," the tobacconist said. Alex raised his eyebrows.

"Mr Slowpoke, from yesterday. Wouldn't know it to look at him, but he's the fella who killed his wife and got away with it.

It didn't take Alex long to discover this allegation was founded. The report called it death by misadventure, but it was clear to Alex that deliberation played a major part.

Gordan Truman wept in court for his wife, but there were strange things the jury didn't hear. This was his third dead wife. The first one had died in a car accident, the second in a farming accident, now this one had fallen off the roof. The jury also didn't know she had gone up there because he sent her. He wanted her to fiddle with the aerial, and if he'd been asked, the little boy next door could have testified the husband said, "Back up. Step to the right. Back further. A bit further," and that the wife had then stepped trustingly off the roof.

It was this evidence the jury of the street heard.

Alex waited in his car across the road from the tobacconist, and eventually Mr Slowpoke, Gordon Truman, appeared. He was a slow smoker as well; the tobacconist said he only came once a week or so.

Alex followed. Truman drove to the other side of town, where he made a purchase from an adult video store. He emerged with his brown paper bag, lit a cigarette, and continued his journey.

He went home.

Alex liked to know people before they knew him, so he studied Truman, followed him, read his file, got to know him.

Alex parked two blocks away and walked. It was dark enough so he would not be noticed.

He knocked on Truman's door, knowing that Truman would be comfortable by now, perhaps naked, and he would be disoriented by any intrusion.

And so it was. Gordon Truman answered the door with a robe on. He said, "What is it? I'm busy."

"I'm afraid you are," Alex said. He showed his badge. "May I come in?"

Truman was terrified. He had bought his tapes legally, but he wondered what he could have done wrong.

"There is an alert on the tapes you purchased," Alex said. "We're interested in the sort of person who would purchase such things."

Truman sucked saliva down the wrong way; choked.

"But these aren't bad ones. Not really. Not compared to some of the other things they have there. They have some terrible things."

"Everything's relative," said Alex.

Truman passed the two covers to Alex. A classroom scene, naked teacher, glaring, legs spread as she perched on the desk. Called School for Punishment. And the second: two women, pink tongues, called The Clit Sisters.

Alex clenched his teeth to keep from vomiting. Who would believe this could lead to the murder of an innocent woman?

Clenched teeth, eyes staring, Alex looked insane.

Now Alex smiled. "Is that what you said to your wife? That these aren't so bad?"

"Sorry? But... my wife's dead."

"Not dead. Murdered."

"No, no. She died."

"That's what the court said."

"It's what I say. It's what she'd say, too. It was terrible."

"What did your wife think of this business?"

"She… liked it."

"Of course she did."

"She didn't mind it, anyway."

"Did she really know about it?"

"Not in detail, no."

"That's not a good excuse."

"What for? What are you on about?"

"Why don't you pop one of those in and I'll point out what we find so offensive about them."

Gordon Truman smiled. He thought he had Alex figured. Just a cop who wanted to get his rocks off.

He bent to the video player, cocky now.

And Alex shot him in the back of the neck.

The removal of the body was always a challenge, though it wasn't necessary in every case. And with the blood there, it was clear something had gone on. Alex knew he was just trying to avoid a nasty and difficult task. His own backyard was the only place he could control the situation.

He always liked to take his people home, where he could look out onto the backyard and think about the lives he'd saved, the futures he rescued. He never left any of his people where they fell.

Truman was not a big man. Alex had entered the home with a large overcoat, three pillows tied beneath. If anyone noticed these extra pillows on Mr Slowpoke's marital bed, they did not say.

He strapped the body into place and left.

The neighbourhood rested, even curious little boys and inquisitive citizens.

And this. Jessie wrote this in *Under the Volcano* by Malcolm Lowry:

GG seventeen chain:

The gold chain belonged to a teenage boy, George Gazel, who beat to death an old woman.

In *The Transit of Venus*, Shirley Hazzard: PC sixty-three heel:

Percy Court had been meaning to get his shoe heel fixed, but it was hard to get out of the office. He didn't ask his secretary to do it because he was scared of her. She had stopped asking him questions about his wife, though she was clearly dissatisfied with his answers. He would sort her out, though.

In *Great Unsolved Mysteries of Science*, Jerry Lucas:

MR twenty-six wallet:

Max Rankine's empty wallet was bought at a local craft-market at a secondhand stall and held photos of loved ones who didn't love one in return. Who didn't deserve to live.

In *The Collected Works of Max Haines*:

CT twenty-three coin holder:

A present from his mother, Colin Thake's coin holder symbolised to him constriction, lawfulness, boredom. He broke the law smash bang, but not the way Alex thought.

Written in Eva Trout by Elizabeth Bowen: HS forty-three elastic band:

Hugh Smith used an elastic band to tie back his hair. He flipped it around his wrist when he let his hair fly. When he lost one he found another. He was seen dragging his girlfriend by the scruff of her neck. Alex didn't always need to know too much about his people. A little was enough, sometimes.

In *Dorian* by Will Self:

SP thirty-five tie bar:

Silver, stylish, Sam Polato's tie bar caused comment. It got him women. He bit women, liked the feeling of his teeth in their warm flesh.

In The Grotesque, Patrick McGrath: MW forty-two shoe:

Martin Webster, a religious man who marked his skin, his clothes, his shoes, with red crosses to protect himself from evil thoughts.

Evil actions were not yet under control.

In *The Third Millennium*, Stableford & Langford:

PM seven lunchbox:

Only Alex knew that Pauly Murray once lay, strangled and buried, in the dirt in the Searle's backyard, his lunch uneaten.

In The Map Approach to Modern History, Brown & Coysh: FF eighteen squeaky toy:

Frank Firenze carried a squeaky toy in his pocket. What was he doing with a child's toy? Little more than a child himself, stumbling, destructive and bitter.

In *Day of the Locust*, Nathaniel West:

CL thirty-seven TV dial:

Claude Loftus had a nervous habit. He carried a TV dial in his pocket like a security blanket, a lucky rabbit's foot. A skinny man, betting type, losing streak, kill for money, kill for it, die for it.

In *The Cherry Orchard*, Checkov:

BK thirty-six squash ball:

Squeeze squeeze, finding affinity with the small black ball so you could smash your opponent, never lose. Bernie Kerr was good for his age. He was good at smashing faces, noses, scarring faces. He was good at causing offence.

And in *Priests on Trial*, Alfred McCoy, this:

TS forty-three belt:

Its long dead owner, Tom Sykes, was once a man of very good quality. He was a doctor, one of those men people talked to, confessed things to. He was trusted and loved and he threw his wife off a cliff after beating her to death. Only Alex knew this; only Alex knew the truth. The community mourned with the man, the doctor, and could pity him at last.

The pieces of his wife were gathered and buried, and only Alex saw Sykes smirk as she was lowered away from harm. Tom Sykes went through the courts and was washed clean of guilt.

Alex went to Tom Sykes, the doctor, soon after, for a check-up, and he told Sykes secrets he knew would be of interest.

"It's my knuckles, doctor," he said. He made a fist, slammed it into his palm, made the air punch. "I keep slamming them into things, and they're starting to hurt."

Sykes' fingers twitched. Alex had been keeping him under surveillance, and he had not hurt a woman for a while.

"Oh, yes?" he said. He prescribed a muscle-relaxant so Alex would have less trouble with jerking limbs. He walked Alex from the surgery, saying, "Please, call me at home if you find the prescription isn't effective."

He scribbled his first name and his number on a five-dollar note.

"I'll do that," Alex said. Sometimes he could smooth-talk with barely a word.

He waited three weeks, because he needed to settle himself, then he called Sykes. Alex was invited to dine; don't bring a thing, Sykes said.

Sykes wore soft, baggy pants, a sky blue jumper, finely knitted. His hair was deliberately mussed. Alex thought he had drawn dark makeup under his eyes.

Alex wore thin, tight clothes, which clung to him but did not constrict movement. They nodded when they met.

"So, how's the medical business?" Alex said.

"Oh, fine, fine. And how's the…what business are you in?"

"I'm a cop. And it's fine."

Alex wanted Sykes to experience terror, because the death Alex had planned would be short and merciful.

Tom Sykes fingered the loose tongue of his leather belt.

"That must be interesting work. Do you get involved with a lot of cases? I mean, are you interested in what the other cops are doing?"

Alex smiled at him. The man didn't see, he was staring at his glass. "Naah," Alex said.

"I'm far too self-obsessed." He didn't want the man wary. "If it's not my case, I'm home with my family."

He pulled out a photo to show the doctor.

It was one Steve never saw. In it, Heather sat up stiffly, a pained expression on her face.

Her eyes seemed dark-rimmed. Peter stood in front of her left knee. Her arms were raised; her hands clutched Peter's forearms from either side. Her fingers visibly sank into his flesh. Peter had his eyes squeezed shut; his mouth was slightly open.

At their feet Steve played with a toy train.

She didn't look at the camera.

"Lovely family," Tom Sykes said. "I only had my wife, I'm afraid, and no photo, no photo at all."

"Some women just don't like having their photo taken," Alex said. He thought, and some have no choice, because the doctor's wife had been photographed many times after her death.

"Sometimes women don't know what's best, and they need helping along." Alex stared into his glass as if remembering.

Tom's eyes glittered, yet he didn't seem to drink much. Alex guessed he enjoyed use of his own medicine cabinet.

"So, here we are," Tom said. They had been on a short tour of the house, had reached the sauna.

"Am I supposed to say, 'You have a lovely home?'" Alex said.

Tom gave one tone of a laugh. "No, no, that's for the ladies. Ladies like trivialities."

They smiled at each other. "I feel like I'm on an outing," Alex said.

"No, no, just two men with similar interests, out to become acquainted."

"And perhaps not just with each other,"

Alex said, and winked. Tom smiled, relaxed; he was not mistaken in Alex's intent.

They ate a meal Tom had brought home with him from town, spent hours talking about war, politics, women and money. Alex refused to take his gloves off.

"Are you cold? I can turn up the heating."

"No, I'm fine," Alex said. Afterwards, he washed up the glasses and plates and put them away.

"Now, you're a pleasant guest to have," Tom said.

It was all very seamless, as it is when two people have the same motives, the same goal, and they are not anxious about achieving this. They talked, they ate, they took Alex's car. Tom settled himself, breathed deeply.

"New car, ay? Nothing like it," he said.

"My kids hate the smell. They insist on having their heads stuck out the windows," Alex said. They drove to the streets and they picked up a prostitute.

Alex drove while Tom was in the back with her. There were giggles and low mutters and squeals of pain.

"Not so rough," she said.

"People say I've got soft, gentle hands," Tom said. "That's what I'm told."

"Yeah, well, where are we going, anyway? I'm not interested in a back-seat job."

"Won't be long," Alex said. He drove to a quiet beach. They pulled the girl out of the car, and they beat her, carefully. Alex could see how much Tom enjoyed it.

"Here's a little something to ease your pain," said the doctor, and he injected her with the contents of a syringe Alex suggested he bring. No one would believe a girl with her blood mix.

They left her stretched on the dry sand, safe from the tide, and she wouldn't be found until she stumbled on to the road.

This major event in her life changed her, because she wasn't an automaton. She gained self-respect, oddly, because she had not wanted to be beaten, neither did she deserve it. She KNEW that. She could honestly say it.

She accepted a job in a safe house, where the men came for sexual release in a safe environment. They didn't want danger.

They wanted their regular, a shallow relationship, they paid well. She became involved with management and found she had a skill for it.

She always bore the scars of her beating.

They drew sympathy and kindness. She was reminded of the Somerset Maugham story, The Verger. Imagine if you hadn't been beaten, she said to herself. You would still be on the streets.

Tom Sykes laughed, hopped in his seat, pulled at his seat belt. He made little popping noises with his mouth, noises which sounded so much like words Alex said,

"Pardon?" twice. Sykes ignored him.

"My place for a drink?" Alex said.

Sykes said, "What about your family?

Midnight visitors okay there?"

Alex said, "They're at her mother's."

Alex rolled the car into the garage. He said, "We'll go in the back door." The doctor climbed out of the car, pop pop and waited, rocking on his heels, staring at the moon.

"Key's under the mat, believe it or not,"

Alex said. He shone the torch to the back door.

"I don't believe it," said Sykes. He aped Alex's whispered tone.

"Take a look."

Sykes bent over, and Alex bent behind him and chopped him, pulling his body backwards in a jabjab movement. The body fell onto the dirt, where it twitched then rested. Alex cut the throat.

There was no hint of a visitor by the time the family returned.

He never killed a woman. There was one woman in his children's future who may have been deserving; he drove past her house every morning and night on his work travels. He noticed the neat garden and despised it for its prissiness, but he would never have guessed his children would be hurt by the woman inside.

Alex would always say that it was the unplanned murders, the crimes of passion, which people get away with. It was the planned crimes, so meticulous, which would fail, because there was too much thought involved. Those killers thought of each possible contingent and had an answer ready for everything, the perfect emotion ready to go. They had answers down pat, always suspicious. The unplanned crime caused panic, and the human mind thinks better under stress.

It was an opinion far from that held by almost everybody else at his police station (and of the world, but his scope of research wasn't broad).

No one ever imagined he held this view because he had killed in passionate rage.

He rarely joined his workmates for drinks and was teased as a Family Man. He always smiled at the nickname, genuinely unhurt by it—he couldn't see how it could possibly be an insult.

He was always there for celebrations, though: the big bust, the retirement, the promotion. He was painstaking about these things.

Some nights he would appear out of the blue, and shout the bar, scream at jokes, act with an hysteria the others found frightening.

And Jessie wrote this in *God's Little Acre* by Taylor Caldwell:

DS twenty-two fingernail:

David Sparrow was a volunteer. He helped fight fires, he delivered meals, he handed out food at the soup kitchen.

He was also, Alex knew, a killer, a deliberate arsonist who caused the death of five children. It was the look on his face during a TV interview; a shiftiness of eye. That's what gave him away to Alex.

That's why Alex hated him.

Jessie wrote this in *Looking for Mr Goodbar*, Judith Rossner:

JB thirty-one cufflink:

Joel Bennet was a dapper man, cufflink wearer, and seductive, people shouted his name in the streets to be seen with him. He liked the feel of a dead body dragging him down, liked to pretend he was a conjoined twin, with a dead twin.

And this. She wrote this in *Confessions of an Advertising Man,* by David Ogilvy:

Jessie was not a violent woman, but she was fascinated by violence. She read all the banned books, loved them in private. And she was fascinated to be so close to it. It sickened her as well, and she couldn't eat.

Jessie didn't read all the books. Sometimes she read the book flap, or looked at the photo of the author, or thought about the title for her inspiration. This great romance writer never married, though she was the subject of gossip for many years, because it was known she had a lover. Was he a married man? Why didn't they marry?

Jessie and the school teacher, Mr Bell, kept up a friendly relationship. She relied on him to keep her from dying of loneliness.

Mr Bell did not read her novel in full. Only the first few chapters. It began on the end papers of "In the Wet" by Nevil Shute, which she gave him to read on a train journey.

I knew I had to burn all of the books. I knew it.

The Grannies didn't forget me:
"Stevie, you're the sweetest one Life with you is so much fun."
It wasn't enough. It didn't come close to being enough.

I still can't picture my father angry. Not furious, anyway, not leap up and down, beat in heads, bury the body. I can't believe I was the only one who saw him as a gentle, kind man, always.

I rang Peter, "Peter, can you come over, please come over, Peter, please let me have a go on your bike. Please come over. I've got something to show you."

There is no one to save me. I stand alone in the kitchen. I string my rope up from the railings. And I let myself go.

This moment is the worst, when I can't breathe.

The discomfort is great. I survey my garden; am pleased by how neat and green it is.

I see my twin in the window and I wave. The prophecy Mum read has not come true. I am only thirty-five. Nowhere near middle age. I have beaten fate; I am dying before fate decided I should.

And then I am in the room. Oh God, take me back. They are all around me. There are straws between my toes, suck, suck, and a cock in my mouth, soaking up my saliva. Snip, snip, bandage scissors, rusty with blood, cut my hair off centimetre by centimetre. Someone grabs my hands and pulls me up. It's Granny Searle. I think she's going to lead me away but she ties my hands high in the air and plucks out my arm pit hairs. I laugh and they shrink away. I'm not supposed to be enjoying it. They have paper cut fingernails. They slice and cut until all the lines of my skin are filled with red.

Someone has an apple peeler and little bits of my skin are taken away. Peter is there again. He was almost always there. For a brother who appeared unbothered by my actions, he was very slighted.

The only time he wasn't in the room was when I was twenty-four, and hadn't seen him for months.

I never saw Maria after I was twenty-one. Her hatred was too intense for her to be in my room.

And then a neighbour cuts me down. I have never been so relieved. This time I will stick to my resolutions. I will change. I don't want to go back to the room, nor send anybody else there. I became a believer, in God, Heaven, Hell. I went to church, I donated all I had, I learnt floral arranging and I made the morning tea. I met someone nice. The cop, Laurie, that young cop from Mum's investigation, he tracked me down, I tracked him down. We set a date to be married, put a deposit on a house.

We always held hands.

Then I started to smell mothballs in strange places. I didn't tell anyone; didn't want them to think I was going mad.

I saw a doctor, told her all. She had a good look at me. She said, "You're the sanest person I've ever seen."

My clothes seemed tight around my neck, choking me. I was always cold. But at least I was alive.

I sold my car and my house. I called Maria and met her in a restaurant, and I cried and told her how much I cared for her, how good she was for Peter.

And then a neighbour cuts me down. I had a new life. A career, a career woman. I had three children, a lovely husband. We are gathered for our twentieth wedding anniversary. I eat a mothball, mistaking it for a kool-mint.

And then a neighbour cuts me down.

And then a neighbour cuts me down.

That's what should have happened.

This is what did happen:

I forgot how much the Rat Trap neighbours hated me. How they ignored me.

And it was Ruth who was dead, not Jessie. I had been dreaming all this time. I hadn't heard Ruth tell me never to ask a man for advice. Or to only wear vertical stripes.

It was Jessie alive.

We went for a picnic together, on a cliff facing the sea. The air smelt of jasmine and dirt but the ground was hard, rasping my skin.

The air was thick. I breathed through the pores of my skin, great soakings of air, and I felt like I had bubbles in my blood.

Jessie looked wonderful. She looked forty-five, hadn't aged in years. We were closer, now. I'd caught up. We ate a mother's feast: boiled eggs with little screws of salt, ham sandwiches cut thick and wrapped in flapping greaseproof paper; a thermos of hot chocolate; a piece of chocolate slice.

Jessie laughed at the way I ate, gobbling like a turkey.

"You haven't eaten like that since you were sixteen," she said. She held my hand and I shivered.

"You know what's going to happen next, Stevie."

"I have no idea. Could be anything."

"Oh, no," she said, "Only this," and she lay down and began to rot.

I thought I wanted to go back. I wasn't sure if they would still be waiting. It had been a long time.

But the memory of all those faces focused on mine, all of them waiting for my whim, was exciting. I was addicted to them. There was the kid I saw every time, the little shit from primary school who I pissed on after showers, the teacher was Mrs Sammett, the one I had laughed at because she was fat, the friend I had stopped talking to when I figured he wouldn't get my jokes any longer. They leant over me, faces I knew. Something really hurt; there were faces there of people I had helped in the hospice. People whose lives I had changed; people who listened to my stories of death. They all believed they had been slighted. I began to cry with the hurt of it. And there was Darren, clutching his jumper, staring and waiting. He was no older in the room, though I was sure he danced in anticipation in hundreds of other rooms, just like mine. My counsellor, no counsel there, no help, just confusion and lust.

He was a tree, a leaf, landing on earth to stab me with his paper knife. Strangers saying *broom broom*.

All there. I heard that clicking noise, and I could raise my head and I saw their mouths flapping, their teeth clicking together, like those wind-up teeth everybody once had. Their hands were raised, their teeth clicking, their fingers beginning to reach for me. I remembered I had kicked the chair away too far; my legs could not reach it. I could see as I raised my head, they waited in circles about me, six or seven circles, I couldn't tell. I lowered my head and closed my eyes to think again.

I could not reach the chair.

I came here to feel the power, to watch their faces. But they are stronger this time. There are so many of them.

I am naked on that bed, and I see they are too.

They look at me as I draw my knees up to make a resting place for my elbows. They count my orifices with their fingers. I feel a moist rasping on my back.

A stranger lolls her tongue out. She is lapping at my back, taking off the first layer of skin.

Then a neighbour cuts me down.

People couldn't believe my transformation. I was positive about life; loved it.

"See?" they said. "All you needed was something to believe in." I told them what I believed in; when I died I would go to a place where everyone with a slight against me could bite, scratch, fuck, flay, keep me for all eternity. The noise and smell of the place sickened me.

I gave up driving a car, smoking, and drinking. I gave up all drugs and meat. I quit my stressful job and took a low paying one which took nothing from me. All these things made me safe. I would not die.

Then I opened my eyes and knew I did not have another chance. I swung from that rafter and would not be found.

Is this what will happen?

I swing in the kitchen for many days. The smell of frangipani, of jasmine, fills the house. The smell edges its way out of the open window, out of the back door always open, and it pleases the noses of neighbours long past caring.

"Have you smelt it?" they begin to say, when the smell is no longer gentle, and they sniff up and down the street until they reach the Searle home.

They enter through the back door, and, although I am beyond rescuing, a neighbour cuts me down.

A neighbour cuts me down.

Nobody hears anything, sees anything. When interviewed, most of the neighbours say, "But there were always screams and strange noises coming from there. We're used to it. No one was very interested. Even when her father was alive, screams and shouts. People said the place was haunted and that there were ghosts crying in there."

Is that what will happen?

I see them shrinking from me. They have been in my power all along, because they have remembered me forever, I forgot them in an instant. Some of the faces here I know; many more are strangers, people I affected who never registered in my brain.

They are nobody to me; and yet they wish me ill.

There are so many of them. So many, hundreds, millions, everyone in the world waited there to gobble me up. Dear old Granny Searle, clicking her teeth like a lunatic. Peter smiling, flicking his teeth with his thumbnail. Forget I said anything.

All the faces, all the people.

All knowing more than me. Because I believed I wanted to live.

I wanted to live.

And they knew they had me at last.

I end alone. One by one, they vanish from the room, leaving me alone in the cold, dark womb.

They are finished, now. All done. Bite and bite and scratch, they took those slices back. And now, I am rising. The bones of my body lie on the table; I leave them to their final survey. And I am on a golden path, the sun warms my back, and I can hear my mother's laugh, my father's voice. My step is light and I am free.

Jessie's Puzzle Solution

PH (Paul Harris)	THIRTY-FIVE	PIPE
CW (Chew Wang)	TWENTY-NINE	WATCH
AM (Albert Mitchell)	SEVENTY-TWO	LIGHTER
CS (Chris Stepanos)	THIRTY-THREE	COIN
RR (Rex Roberts)	FIFTY-EIGHT	BOTTLE TOP
GT (Gordon Truman)	FIFTY-FIVE	RING
GG (George Gazel)	SEVENTEEN	CHAIN
PC (Percy Court)	SIXTY-THREE	HEEL
MR (Max Rankine)	TWENTY-SIX	WALLET
CT (Colin Thake)	TWENTY-THREE	COIN HOLDER
HS (Hugh Smith)	FORTY-THREE	ELASTIC BAND
SP (Sam Polato)	THIRTY-FIVE	TIE BAR
MW (Martin Webster)	FORTY-TWO	SHOE
PM (Pauly Murray)	SEVEN	LUNCH BOX
FF (Frank Firenze)	EIGHTEEN	SQUEAKY TOY
CL (Claude Loftus)	THIRTY-SEVEN	TV DIAL
BK (Bernie Kerr)	THIRTY-SIX	SQUASH BALL
TS (Tom Sykes)	FORTY-THREE	BELT
DS (David Sparrow)	TWENTY-TWO	FINGERNAIL
JB (Joel Bennet)	THIRTY-ONE	CUFFLINK

THESE ARE THE ONES I KNOW ABOUT